### Critical acclaim for Ian Rankin

'As always, Rankin proves himself the master of his own milieu. He brings the dark underside of Edinburgh deliciously to life . . . Rankin's skill lies mainly in the confident way he weaves the disparate threads into a cohesive whole'
*Daily Mail*

'His novels flow as smoothly as the flooded Forth, and come peppered with three-dimensional characters who actually react to and are changed by events around them . . . This is Rankin at his raw-edged, page-turning best . . . With Rankin, you can practically smell the fag-smoke and whisky fumes' *Time Out*

'A first-rate thriller' *Yorkshire Evening Post*

'The internal police politics and corruption in high places are both portrayed with bone-freezing accuracy. This novel should come with a wind-chill factor warning'
*Daily Telegraph*

'Real life and fiction blur in this cynical, bleak tale. You'll love every second of it' *Daily Mirror*

'No other writer in his chosen genre is producing books as rich and comprehensive as this: Dickensian, you might say'
*Literary Review*

'Rebus is a masterful creation . . . Rankin has taken his well-earned place among the top echelon of crimewriters'
*Observer*

'Rankin writes laconic, sophisticated, well-paced thrillers'
*Scotsman*

'First-rate plotting, dialogue and characterisations'
*Literary Review*

# BY IAN RANKIN

All Ian Rankin's titles are available on audio.
Also available: *Jackie Leven Said* by Ian Rankin and Jackie Leven.

Born in the Kingdom of Fife in 1960, Ian Rankin graduated from the University of Edinburgh and has since been employed as grape-picker, swineherd, taxman, alcohol researcher, hi-fi journalist and punk musician. His first Rebus novel, *Knots & Crosses*, was published in 1987 and the Rebus books have now been translated into 26 languages. Ian Rankin has been elected a Hawthornden Fellow, and is a past winner of the prestigious Chandler-Fulbright Award, as well as two CWA short-story 'Daggers' and the 1997 CWA Macallan Gold Dagger for Fiction for *Black & Blue*, which was also shortlisted for the Mystery Writers of America 'Edgar' award for Best Novel. *Black & Blue*, *The Hanging Garden*, *Dead Souls* and *Mortal Causes* have been televised on ITV, starring John Hannah as Inspector Rebus. *The Falls* and *Fleshmarket Close* have also been shown on ITV, starring Ken Stott as Rebus. *Dead Souls*, the tenth novel in the series, was shortlisted for the CWA Gold Dagger Award in 1999. An Alumnus of the Year at Edinburgh University, he has also been awarded four honorary doctorates, from the University of Abertay Dundee in 1999, from the University of St Andrews in 2001, in 2003 from the University of Edinburgh and in 2005 from the Open University. In 2002 Ian Rankin was awarded an OBE for services to literature. In 2004 *Resurrection Men* won the Edgar Award for Best Novel. In 2005 *Fleshmarket Close* won the Crime Thriller of the Year award at the British Book Awards. Ian is the winner of the Crime Writers' Association Diamond Dagger 2005. In 2005 he was also awarded the Grand Prix du Littérature Policier (France), the Deutsche Krimi Prize (Germany) and the Icons of Scotland award. He lives in Edinburgh with his wife and two sons. Visit his website at www.ianrankin.net.

# Ian Rankin

writing as Jack Harvey

# Witch Hunt

An Orion paperback

First published in Great Britain in 1993
by Headline
This paperback edition published in 2000
by Orion Books Ltd,
Orion House, 5 Upper St Martin's Lane,
London WC2H 9EA

Reissued 2006

Printed and bound in Great Britain by
Clays Ltd, St Ives plc

The Orion Publishing Group's policy is to use papers that
are natural, renewable and recyclable products and
made from wood grown in sustainable forests. The logging
and manufacturing processes are expected to conform to
the environmental regulations of the country of origin.

www.orionbooks.co.uk

*For Peter Robinson*

'The female of the species is more deadly than the male'

— Rudyard Kipling, *The Female of the Species*

'If woman had no existence save in the fiction written by men, one would imagine her a person of the utmost importance; very various; heroic and mean; splendid and sordid; infinitely beautiful and hideous in the extreme; as great as a man, some think even greater'

— Virginia Woolf, *A Room of One's Own*

'A woman's desire for revenge outlasts all her other emotions'

— Cyril Connolly

# Contents

# Arrival

# Monday 1 June

It was a pleasure boat.

At least, that's how owner and skipper George Crane would have described it. It had been bought for pleasure back in the late-1980s when business was thriving, money both plentiful and cheap. He'd bought it to indulge himself. His wife had nagged about the waste of money, but then she suffered from chronic sea-sickness and wouldn't set foot on it. *She* wouldn't set foot on it, but there were plenty of women who would. Plenty of women for George Crane and his friends. There was Liza, for example, who liked to stand on deck clad only in her bikini bottom, waving at passing vessels. God, Liza, Siren of the South Coast. Where was she now? And all the others: Gail, Tracy, Debbie, Francesca ... He smiled at the memories: of routes to France, Portugal, Spain; of trips taken around the treacherous British Isles. Trips taken with women aboard, or with women picked up en route. Wine and good food and perhaps a few lines of coke at the end of the evening. Good days, good memories. Memories of the pleasure boat *Cassandra Christa*.

But no pleasure tonight, the boat gliding across a calm British Channel. This was a business trip, the client below decks. Crane hadn't caught much more than a glimpse of her as she'd clambered aboard with her rucksack. Brian had gone to help her, but she hadn't needed any. She was tall, he was certain of that. Dark maybe, as in dark-haired, not dark-skinned. European?

He couldn't say. Brian hadn't been able to add much either.

'Just asked if she could go below. Better down there than up here getting in the way.'

'She said that?'

Brian shook his head. 'All she said was "I'm going below". Not even a question, more like an order.'

'Did she sound English?'

Brian shrugged. He was a good and honest soul, unburdened by intellect. Still, he would keep his mouth shut about tonight's work. And he came cheap, since he was already one of George Crane's employees, one of that dwindling band. The business had overextended itself, that was the problem. Too big a loan to push the business into new areas, areas drying up just as George Crane arrived. More loans to cover the earlier loan . . . It was bad luck. Still, the business would weather it.

*Cassandra Christa*, however, might not. He'd put word out that she was for sale, and an ad had been placed in a couple of newspapers: one quality Sunday, one daily. There had been just the one phone call so far but it was early days, besides which maybe he wouldn't have to sell after all. He glanced at his watch. Five minutes short of three in the morning. Crane stifled a yawn.

'Want me to check the cargo?' Brian asked. Crane smiled.

'You stay where you are, you randy little sod. The cargo can look after itself.'

Crane had been told – had been *ordered* – not to be interested, not to be nosy. No chit-chat, no questions. It was just a delivery, that was all. He didn't know quite what he'd expected. Some chisel-chinned IRA bastard or ex-pat felon. He certainly hadn't expected a young woman. Young? Well, she *moved* like a young woman. He had to admit he was intrigued, despite the warning.

4

The worst part would be coming up soon: the landing on the coast. But she spoke English, so that shouldn't pose any problem even if they were stopped. A midnight cruise, take the boat out, breathe in the ozone, that sort of thing. A nod and a wink to Customs or whoever. They understood these things. The pleasure of making love on the deck of a boat, sky above, water all around. He shivered slightly. It had been a long time. The good days seemed an awful long time ago. But maybe they'd return. A few more runs like this wouldn't go amiss. Money for old rope. And to think he'd worried about it for weeks. Shame really that he was selling the boat. But if he did a good job, a smooth job of work, they might employ his talents again. Another job or two would save the *Cassandra Christa*. Another couple of jobs like this one and he'd be home and dry.

'Shoreline, Skip.'

'I told you I don't like "Skip". Skipper's okay.'

'Sorry, Skipper.'

Crane nodded. Brian's attributes included sharp night vision. Yes, there it was now. The coastline. Hythe and Sandgate probably. Folkestone just a little to the east, their destination. Folkestone was the drop-off, the danger point. Then they'd turn the boat back towards Sandgate where it had its mooring. More instructions: after depositing the cargo, head back out to sea before making for final mooring. Do not hug the coastline as this would make them more likely to be spotted.

A silly order really, but he'd been told at the start: you either follow the orders to the letter or you don't take the job.

'I'll take the job,' he'd said. But the man had shaken his head.

'Don't make up your mind so quickly, Mr Grane.' That was the way he'd said it – Grane. He had trouble with

5

consonants. Danish? Something Scandinavian? Or Dutch maybe? 'Take your time. You need to be sure for yourself. I'll telephone you next week. Meantime, happy sailing.'

Happy sailing? Well, plain sailing anyway. Crane didn't expect trouble. There was no Customs activity to speak of round here these days. Cutbacks. The British coastline was like a net – full of holes through which you could push unseen anything you liked. Crane had been definite about that.

'Not if it's drugs. I won't have anything to do with drugs.'

The foreigner had shaken his head slowly. 'Nothing like that. It's just a body.'

'A body?'

'A *live* body, Mr Grane. Very much alive. Someone who wants to see England but finds themself stranded on the Continent without a passport.'

'Ah.' Crane had nodded at that. He had his ideas: missing peers, runaways, crooks from the Costa Del Sol who'd decided they'd pay anything for the pleasure of an afternoon in a British boozer. 'What about a name then?'

Another shake of the head. 'No names, Mr Grane.'

'So how will I know I've got the right person?'

An indulgent smile. 'How many people do you think will be in the middle of the English Channel at midnight, waiting to meet a boat?'

Crane had laughed. 'Not many, I suppose. Any night in particular?'

'I'll let you know. I must warn you now, you won't get much notice, a few hours at most. So make sure you are home every evening. Make sure you remain available. And Mr Grane . . . ?'

'Yes?'

'Better think up a story to tell your wife.'

His wife! Least of his problems, he'd assured the man. But the man had seemed to know quite a lot about his problems, hadn't he? The way he'd approached Crane that early morning outside the office, telling him he might have some work for him. But he hadn't wanted to discuss it in Crane's office. They'd arranged to meet in a pub instead, that lunchtime.

With nothing to lose, but suspecting some kind of trap, Crane had gone along. What he hadn't told the man was that one of his own men, Mike McKillip, was in the bar too. First sign of trouble, Mike's orders were to wade in. Mike liked a bit of a barney, and Crane had slipped him a twenty as drinking money.

But there'd been no barney, no trap, just a muted conversation, mostly one way. A business proposition . . . believe you own a boat . . . financial difficulties . . . would like to hire your services. That was the way he'd put it: 'I would like to hire your services.' Like George Crane was some tugboat skipper. But then the man had started to talk serious money. He offered £1,000 on acceptance of the contract – he'd called it that too, making it sound like 'gontrag' – £2,000 on delivery, and a further and final £2,000 twelve weeks after delivery.

'Three months? How do I know you won't . . . I mean, I'm not suggesting . . . but all the same.' Crane's head spun with thoughts of money. He gulped a mouthful of whisky.

Cue the smile. 'You are a businessman, Mr Grane. Cautious, prudent, and suspicious. You are quite right. But the time-lag is so we can assure ourselves of your silence. If we don't pay, you could go to the police with your story.'

'Hardly! I'd be an accomplice.'

'Nevertheless, you could tell your story. We would

rather pay for your silence. Two thousand seems to me a small price to pay for the gift of silence.'

George Crane still wasn't sure about that. What story could he possibly tell? Still, he'd have done the job for three grand in any case, and three grand was what he'd have by the end of tonight's little adventure. Three thousand beautiful pounds, a thousand of which had already been lodged in what he called his 'Number Four Account', one of several he'd managed to keep hidden from the Inland Revenue's sniffer-dogs (the same sniffer-dogs he'd suspected of laying a trap for him in the first place). There was fifty quid to pay Brian, of course. It didn't seem much, but anything higher and he might start to get suspicious. Fifty was just right for Brian: enough to buy his fidelity, but not enough to get him excited.

There were lights along the coast, welcoming lights. He turned to Brian now. 'Better tell her we're home.'

'I think she already knows.'

And here she was, coming in a crouch through the small doorway and on to deck, pulling her rucksack behind her. She stood up straight, stretching her back. She was tall, five-ten or thereabouts. Tall and thin. Hard to tell much more through the waterproof she was wearing. She had a package with her which she held out to Crane. He accepted it.

'Brian,' he said, 'take over here for a sec.'

'Right, Skipper.'

Crane made his way to the side of the boat, nearest to the land. There was enough light to see by. He didn't want Brian to see how much money was involved. He tore open the package and flipped through the wad of notes. Fifties. Looked like about forty of them. Well, he wasn't going to stand here counting them out like Shylock. He stuffed them into his inside jacket pocket, creating a comfortable bulge, and returned to the wheel. The woman was looking at him, so he nodded towards her. Only towards her, not *at* her. It was difficult to meet her eyes, difficult to hold their gaze. It wasn't that she was beautiful or anything (though she might be in daylight). But she was . . . intense. And almost scowling, like she was spoiling for a fight.

'Round the coast a little way yet, Brian,' Crane said. 'Just outside the town, that's the drop.'

'How much longer?' she asked. Yes, European, thought Crane. Probably British, but she looked as if she'd been away for a while.

'Five minutes,' he said. He produced a hip flask from his pocket and unscrewed the top. 'A drop of malt,' he explained. 'Care for a tot?'

She shook her head, but as he drank deep she said: 'Good health.'

He exhaled noisily. 'Thank you. And here's to yours.' Then he passed the depleted flask to Brian, who finished it off in a mouthful.

'We've got a dinghy,' Crane announced. It was good policy to look helpful if he wanted future contracts. 'We can row you ashore.'

'I'll swim. Just get me close.'

'The water's freezing,' Brian protested. 'You'll catch your death.'

But she was shaking her head.

'And what about your bag?'

'It's waterproof, and so am I.'

'It'll sink like a—'

She was taking off the waterproof, slipping out of her shoes, undoing her jeans. The two men watched. Underneath, she was wearing a one-piece black bathing costume.

'I must get one of those for the wife,' Crane muttered.

9

She was stuffing her clothes into the rucksack. 'I'll change back when I reach shore.'

Brian, staring at her long white legs, seemed to be picturing this. Truth be told, Crane was picturing it too. She might not be beautiful, but she had a body. Christ, she had a body.

'Thanks for the thought,' she said finally, with a slight twist of her lips. It was as if she'd been reading their minds.

'It's been a pleasure,' said Crane. 'A pleasure.'

They dropped her off and watched for a few moments as she struck for shore. She swam strongly, dragging the rucksack after her. They were no more than a hundred yards from land. It looked like she'd make it with ease. Then Crane remembered his orders.

'Back out to sea with her, Brian. We'll come around to Sandgate. Home before dawn with a bit of luck.'

'She was something, wasn't she, Skip?' Brian was still gazing towards shore.

'Yes, son,' admitted Crane. 'She was something.'

She changed quickly. The rucksack contained quite a lot, including several changes of clothes and shoes. It also contained air pockets to help keep it afloat. She deflated these. The rucksack had been heavier early on in the evening. She smiled at the memory. Wrapped in polythene in an already waterproofed pocket was a diary, and beside it some odds and ends of make-up. The make-up was like a talisman to her. Make-up was the beginning of disguise. What else was in the rucksack? You could tell a lot about a woman from the contents of her bag. If you tried hard, this rucksack would tell you a lot too. Passport, driving licence, money. A few small tools. Some packages of what looked like plasticine. A tarot pack. A handgun. That was about it.

She didn't look out to sea, but she listened to it. The steady clash of waves, the whistling wind. Exhilarating. Her hair, pinned back, was still drying quickly, her scalp chilled by the wind. A sharp salt smell clung to her. Her eyes were closed slightly as she listened. Then, in the distance, she heard a loudish pop, there and then not there. Like the meeting of balloon and pin at a children's party. She knew she had measured the amount of the charge well, and had placed it well too, down in the bowels of the boat. The hole blown in the hull would be a couple of metres in diameter. The vessel would sink in seconds, seconds of shock and horror for its crew. And if the explosion didn't kill the two men outright . . . well, what chance of their reaching land? No chance for the older man, minimal for the younger. Minimal was as much as she liked to leave to chance. But she hung around for a while anyway, just in case anyone did reach shore. There was a certain amount of shelter so she did not freeze. In fact, the breeze was growing almost warm. Or perhaps she was just getting used to being back.

No sign of the two men. She waited seventy-five minutes, then unpinned her long hair, letting it fall forwards over her face. A simple trick, but one which reduced her age by several years, especially when she was not wearing make-up. She thought of the boat a final time. It would be a mere oil slick now. Perhaps banknotes were floating on the tide. Useless things anyway.

She made her way to the main road and began to walk. Hitching along the south coast. Going to visit a friend in Margate. (Or Cliftonville: dare she say Cliftonville?) Didn't get a lift out of Folkestone, so spent the night there, sleeping rough by the roadside . . .

That was the story she would tell to whichever

11

motorist picked her up. Someone *would* pick her up. Some man, most probably. She was a single woman, young. They might lecture her about the dangers of hitching alone. She would listen. She was a good listener. A lorry driver might even go out of his way and take her to Margate or Cliftonville in a single run. Of course, he would expect a favour in return, something more than her good ear. Her good mouth maybe. But that was all right. That wasn't a problem for her. She was someone else after all, wasn't she? And tomorrow she would be someone else again ...

# Cassandra

# Tuesday 2 June

Everyone in the Collator's Office had what might be termed a 'clerical mind'. Which is to say that they were scrupulous in their filing. They were, in fact, a kind of pre-information technology production line, feeding data into the central computer. This was their purpose in the Collator's Office. It was up to the computer to decide whether some news item or other might be important. The computer was capable of taking a petrol station hold-up in Kelso, the abduction of a girl in Doncaster and the finding of a body in rural Wales, and making of them a pattern.

But most of the time it didn't. Most of the time it just sat wherever it sat, a glutton's bottomless stomach, ingesting story after story, item after item, without excreting anything in return. A lot of false roads were taken, a lot of palpable nonsense spewed up by the computer. And occasionally a nugget of truth, but not often. No, not very often.

There were times when Collator's Assistant Jack Constant thought that the only things keeping him sane were the editions of French newspapers which he brought into work with him. Constant thought he'd plumbed the depths of boredom and futility during his year-long stint as Clerical Assistant in the office of Her Majesty's Collector of Taxes. He'd spent the year sending out demands and reminders and final notices, noting payments and passing the non-payers on to his boss. A year of ledgers, producing in him a ledger mentality. But then computerisation had 'saved' him by taking over his most onerous tasks, and a series of shuffles between departments had seen him dropped finally into the Collator's Office. The pit.

'So how goes the Font of All Knowledge?' asked Cynthia Crockett, a fellow CA. Each day, sometimes in the morning, sometimes after the lunch break, she asked this question with the same quizzical smile. Maybe she thought it was funny.

'Foak knows,' replied Constant, FOAK being the Font of All Knowledge, the central computer. Another CA, Jim Wilson, had another name for it. He called it the Fat Controller, or, when in a bad temper, even the Fat Bastard. He'd once come into work wearing a T-shirt printed with the legend WHO'S THAT FAT BASTARD? Mr Grayson, the office head, had summoned him into the inner sanctum for a quiet, disciplined word about dress code.

Afterwards, Wilson had not been mollified. 'Wants us wearing suits and bloody ties. I mean, it's not like we're dealing with the public, is it? We never *see* anyone. Nobody except old Grayskull himself.'

But he hadn't worn the T-shirt again.

Constant suffered his colleagues, even 'old Grayskull' of the shiny head and tweed-knit ties, drifting towards his pension. Mr Grayson's wife packed him exactly two salmon paste sandwiches, one apple, and one small chocolate biscuit for his lunch every day. Yvette would never do that. It would be a fresh baguette and some Camembert, maybe with pickles or a small salad with vinaigrette. The French took their food seriously, and Yvette, Constant's girlfriend, was French. She lived in Le Mans, which meant that they met only for holidays and occasional frantic weekends (trips barely sustainable on a CA's salary, not when his phone bill was so big). Yvette was still studying, but would soon come to England for good. She'd get a job as French assistant in some school. They would be together.

Meantime, he had his newspapers. Usually *Le Monde* but occasionally one of the others. He read them to improve his French, and also because Yvette didn't seem so far away while he was reading. So whenever a break was due, Jack would reach into his desk drawer and bring out his French newspaper, something to digest with the unspeakable coffee.

He read the snippet of news again. It was squeezed onto the front page below a much longer story about forest fires in the Mediterranean. A boat had sunk in the Channel, barely twenty kilometres from its home port of Calais. There were no survivors. Four sailors dead. The story jogged Jack Constant's memory. He'd filed a story earlier in the day, something about a boat sinking off the south coast of England. Coincidence? He wondered if he should mention it to someone. He looked up from the paper and saw that Mr Grayson had appeared from his inner sanctum. He was looking around as though bewildered to find himself there. He saw Constant looking at him and decided to approach for a conversation. Another day, someone else would suffer. Past the computer screens and the brown file-cases and the newspaper cuttings and the print-outs and the fax sheets he came. Past the clack of keyboard and the sizzle of disk-memory. Towards Jack Constant.

'Jack.'

Constant confirmed this with a nod.

'Everything quiet?'

'Quiet as it gets, sir.'

Grayson nodded seriously. 'Good.' His breath smelt of salmon paste. With a sad half-smile, he began to turn away.

Why not? thought Constant. It might pep the old

bugger up a bit. 'Oh, sir?' he said. 'I've got a story here might be of interest.'

Mr Grayson seemed to doubt this. To be honest, Constant was doubting it too.

# Wednesday 3 June

In the service, there was always someone above you. But the information ladder could splinter – a missing rung. The information ladder depended on people like Jack Constant reporting something to someone like Mr Grayson. And it depended on Grayson's instinct or 'nose', his ability to weed out what was interesting from what really was mere coincidence. The information was then passed up the ladder to his superior, who might make further inquiries before either filing the piece or passing it on to someone more senior yet.

These were lofty heights now. Working from his own small office Grayson had never met his superior's superior. He'd once received an inquiry from that person. The inquiry had been dealt with as a priority. Mr Grayson's office had never had to deal with inquiries from yet higher officials.

The item, the bare comparison of two sinkings on a single night, was passed quickly from rung to rung until it reached an office somewhere in central London where a twenty-five-year-old man, only two years older than Jack Constant himself, read it. He was humming an aria and chewing a pencil and had his legs stretched out in front of him, one foot crossed over the other. He had pushed his seat out from his desk to facilitate this, his legs being too long to stretch beneath the desk itself. There was a wall immediately in front of the desk, with memos and postcards and fire instructions pinned to it.

He read the item through three times. Spotted in *Le*

*Monde* of all places. Either somebody was on the ball or this man ... what was the name, Grayson? Yes, this man Grayson ran a tight ship. Poor metaphor under the circumstances. The item had grown unwieldy by now, attached as it was to notes from the various offices through which it had passed. But though unwieldy it was also irritatingly flimsy, constructed from thin sheets of fax paper. It had been faxed (standard practice) by the last office to see it. The real thing would turn up here eventually, but the fax was supposed to save valuable time. Michael Barclay did not like faxes. For a start, no matter how often the Engineering Section explained it to him, he couldn't see how they were safe from a tap. Tap into a fax line with your own fax, and you'd get a copy of anything sent to the original machine. Codes could be decoded, scramblers unscrambled. As he'd told his colleague from Engineering, 'If you can make something, you can unmake it.' To prove his point, he'd rigged up his own interception device. It had worked, just, proving his point if nothing else. After all, GCHQ made a living from information intercepts, as did the listening posts dotted around the UK. If anything there was an intelligence overload these days. Too much information to assimilate.

Assimilate? There was too much to *sift*, never mind taking any of it in. Which was why this little story interested him. It was a fluke that it had come this far. The image that popped into his head was of a particular sperm breaching an egg. A fluke. This fluke called life: those very words were printed on a memo above his desk.

Well, this particular fluke did have its curiosity aspect. It would bear investigation. There was only one thing for it. Barclay would have to show it to his superior.

Michael Barclay did not think of himself as a spy. Nor

20

would he even say he belonged to the secret service or the security service – though he'd agree security was at the root of much of his work. If pressed, he might nod towards the word Intelligence. He liked the word. It meant knowing a lot. And 'Intelligence' meant knowing at least as much as and preferably more than anyone else. This was the problem with the word 'spy'. It belonged to the old days, the Cold War days and before. Breaking and entering, sleeping with the enemy, microfilm and microphones in ties and tunnels under embassies.

These days there was no black and white: everyone spied on everyone else. This was no revelation, it had always been the case, but it was more open now. More open and more closed. Spy satellites were toys only the very rich and the very paranoid could play with. The spying community had grown larger, all-encompassing, but it had also grown smaller, forming itself into an elite. All change.

He'd actually used the word 'paranoid' in one of his selection board interviews. A calculated risk. If the service didn't want to think of itself as paranoid, it would have to recruit those who suspected it of paranoia. Well, he'd passed the exams and the tests and the interviews. He'd passed the initiation and the regular assessments. He'd begun his own slow crawl up the ladder. And he'd seen that the world was changing.

No spies any more. Now there were only the technicians. Take telemetry for example. Who the hell knew what all that garble of information meant? Who knew how to ungarble it? Only the technicians. Machines might talk to machines, but it took a wonderful human mind to listen in and comprehend. Barclay had done his bit. He'd studied electronic engineering. He'd been a dab hand with a few microchips and LEDs ever since his early teens, when he'd constructed his own digital clock. At sixteen he'd been building loudspeakers and amplifiers. And at seventeen he'd bugged the girls' showers at his school.

At university he'd been 'noticed': that was the way they'd phrased it. His work on long-range surveillance had been noticed. His grasp of geostationary satellite technology had been noticed. His special project on miniaturisation had been noticed. Fortunately, nobody *noticed* that he'd cribbed a lot of the project from early R&D done by Japanese hi-fi companies. A career path lay ahead of him, full of interest and variety and opportunities for further learning. A career in Intelligence.

Michael Barclay, Intelligence Technician. Except that he'd ended up here instead.

He didn't need to knock at Joyce Parry's door. It was kept wide open. There was some argument in the office as to why. Was it to keep an eye on them? Or to show solidarity with them? Or to show them how hard she worked? Most of the theories bubbled to the surface on Friday evenings in the Bull by the Horns, the frankly dreadful pub across the road from the office block. The Bull was a 1960s creation which looked no better for its 1980s refitting. In the 80s, refitting had meant a lot of fake wood, eccentric ornaments and books by the yard. The effect was kitsch Edwardian Steptoe and Son, with sad beer and sad graffiti in the gents'. But on the occasional Friday night, they managed somehow to turn the Bull into a cosy local, full of laughter and colour. It was amazing what a few drinks could do.

Joyce Parry's door was closed.

Unexpected refusal at first hurdle. Barclay, who had rolled the fax sheets into a scroll the better to brandish them, now tapped the scroll against his chin. Well, no matter. She was in conference perhaps. Or out of the office. (That was one thing: when Mrs Parry wasn't at home, her office door stayed firmly locked.) Barclay might do a little work meantime, so he could present her with not only the original item but with his notes and additions. Yes, why not show willing?

John Greenleaf had the feeling that somewhere in the world, every second of the day, someone was having a laugh at his expense. It stood to reason, didn't it? He'd seen it happen with jokes. You made up a joke, told it to someone in a pub, and three months later while on holiday in Ecuador some native told the joke back to you. Because all it took was one person to tell two or three people, and for them to tell their friends. Like chain letters, or was it chain mail? All it took was that first person, that someone who might say: 'I know a man called Greenleaf. Guess who he works for? Special Branch! Greenleaf of the Branch!' Three months later they were laughing about it in Ecuador.

Inspector John Greenleaf, ex-Met and now – but for how long? – working for Special Branch. So what? There were plenty of butchers called Lamb. It shouldn't bother him. He knows Greenleaf is a nice name, women keep telling him so. But he can't shift the memory of last weekend out of his mind. Doyle's party. If you could call twenty men, two hundred pints of beer and a stripper, a 'party'. Greenleaf had debated skipping it altogether, then had decided he'd only get a slagging from Doyle if he didn't go. So along he went, along to a gym and boxing school in the East End. That was typical of Hardman Doyle who fancied himself with the fists. Raw animal smell to the place, and the beer piled high on a trestle table. No food: a curry house was booked for afterwards. There had been five or six of them in front of the table, and others spread out across the gym. Some were puffing on the parallel bars or half-vaulting the horse. Two took wild swings at punch-bags. And the five or six of them in front of the table . . . They all muttered their greetings as he arrived, but he'd heard the words that preceded him:

'. . . eenleaf of the Branch, geddit?'

He got it. Nothing was said. Doyle, his smile that of a double glazing salesman, slapped him on the back and handed over a can of beer.

'Glad you could make it, John. Party's been a bit lacklustre without you.' Doyle took another can from the table, shook it mightily, veins bulging above both eyes, then tapped the shoulder of some unsuspecting guest.

'Here you go, Dave.'

'Cheers, Doyle.'

Doyle winked at Greenleaf and waited for Dave to unhook the ringpull . . .

And Greenleaf, Greenleaf of the Branch, he laughed as hard as any of them, and drank as much, and whistled at the stripper, and ate lime chutney with his madras . . . And felt nothing. As he feels nothing now.

New Scotland Yard . . . Special Branch . . . this is supposed to be Big Time for a copper. But Greenleaf has noticed something curious. He has noticed the truth of the saying, 'It takes a thief to catch a thief.' Some of his present colleagues don't seem so different from the villains they pull in. As narrow-minded as terrorists, as devious as smugglers. Doyle was a good example, though effective at his job. He just didn't mind cutting corners. Doyle refused to see the world in black and white, as a sharply defined Us and Them, while Greenleaf did. For him there were the good guys and then there was the enemy. The enemy was out there and was not to be suffered. If it was useful as an informant, then fine, use it.

But don't reward it afterwards. Don't let it slink away. Lock it up.

'John?'

'Sir?'

'My office.'

Oh hell, now what? His last big job had been putting together a report on aspects of security at the forthcoming London summit. It had taken him a fortnight, working weekends and nights. He'd been proud of the finished result, but no one had commented on it – yet. Now here was the Old Man himself, the Chief, the Boss, here was Commander Bill Trilling summoning him into the office which smelt perpetually of peppermint.

'Sit down, John. Mint?'

'No thanks, sir.'

Trilling took out a sweet and slipped it into his mouth. It was seven months since he'd given up smoking and he was up to four packs of mints a day. His teeth were in ruins and he'd gained half a stone – half a stone he could ill afford. Seated in his chair, with its high armrests, it looked as though it would take a crowbar to get him out again. There was a sheet of paper on the notoriously tidy desk in front of him but no sign of Greenleaf's report. He picked up the paper.

'Bit of a job for you, John. May be something or nothing. A sinking off Folkestone. We've been asked to look into it. Happened a couple of days ago. Can't say I saw anything about it.'

It was well known that Trilling only ever looked at two newspapers, the *Financial Times* and the *Sporting Life*. He was a betting man, sometimes putting his money on a sure-fire stock or share, sometimes a horse or dog. Nobody really knew how successful he was since he didn't share information, even when goaded by Doyle.

'I think I read about it in my paper, sir.'

'Did you? Good, well . . .' Trilling handed over the sheet. 'Report back when you've got anything.'

'How far do I take it, sir?'

'As far as a day trip to Folkestone. Better liaise with Doyle.'

'Doyle, sir?'

'I've put him onto the French end.' Greenleaf looked puzzled. 'Didn't I say? Another boat sank the same night off Calais. We're to look for a connection. Doyle speaks passable French apparently.'

A day out in Calais for Doyle, an afternoon in Folkestone for Greenleaf. Typical.

'As I say, liaise with Doyle. You might even consider travelling down together. But see what you can do by telephone first. We don't want expensive outings on office time if we can avoid it, not with *them* counting how many paper-clips we use. Like the man says, John, value for money. Maybe you should write a letter rather than use the phone.'

The Commander was smiling. This was how people knew he'd made a joke.

# Thursday 4 June

His first 'liaison' with Doyle was at eleven the next morning.

'Bring your chair over,' Doyle said, thereby seizing the initiative: the meeting would take place at Doyle's desk, in Doyle's territory. Greenleaf lifted his heavy metal-framed chair with both hands, first resting his notes on the seat of the chair itself. But as he was placing it in front of Doyle's desk, the notes slewed floorwards. Doyle affected not to notice. His own notes, Greenleaf noticed, were neatly word-processed: not because he'd laboured hard, but because he had a 'close friend' in the typing pool. No doubt she'd ignored more important work this morning so she could prepare these sheets for Doyle. It all looked efficient, a single paper-clip holding the whole lot together. Doyle now slid the paper-clip from the corner of the sheets and let it fall to the floor. He spread the sheets in front of him.

'Right,' he said, 'what have you got?'

'A small touring boat,' Greenleaf said from memory. 'Must have sunk about two miles off the coast, just south of Folkestone. There was an automatic alarm system on board which alerted the coastguard. The system only operates in two situations: when set off by a crew member or when it's exposed to water. No sign of the boat itself, just some debris and oil and the two bodies.'

'Post mortems?'

'I'm waiting for the reports.'

'What time did all this happen?'

'The alarm went off at three twenty-seven.'

'The French boat sank around three,' Doyle added. 'So who was on board?'

'Two men, George Crane and Brian Perch.'

'Crane and Perch?' Greenleaf nodded, and Doyle produced a gust of laughter. 'Were they out fishing?'

'Not fishing. If anything, the boat was a pleasure cruiser. You know, a sort of motorised yacht. I don't know much about sailing but that's what they tell me.'

'So what were they doing out at that time of night?'

'Nobody knows.'

'Where had they been?'

Greenleaf shook his head. 'Crane's widow didn't even know he was taking the boat out. He told her he was going for a drive. He suffered from insomnia, she says. All Perch's family know is that he was doing a job for Crane. The boat's mooring is along the coast from Folkestone, a place called Sandgate.'

'But the boat itself was nearer Folkestone when it went down?'

'Other side of Folkestone from Sandgate.'

Doyle tapped his fingers against the edge of the desk. His suit looked crumpled but comfortable. Greenleaf, on the other hand, felt as if he was wearing a restraint of some kind. Time to buy a new jacket or start a diet. 'What did Crane do?' Doyle asked.

'Had his own building firm.'

Doyle stopped tapping and reached into his jacket, scratching slowly. 'Figures with a name like that. Do you know why the boat sank?'

'They're going to try to recover it this afternoon, for what it's worth.'

Doyle brought his hand out of his jacket. 'I can tell you what they'll find.'

'What?'

Doyle smiled and looked down at the sheets spread across the desk in front of him. Eventually he looked up. 'They're a bit quicker off the mark than us across the Channel. They haven't quite got the boat up yet, but the post mortem's been done. I spoke to the *pathologiste* this morning.' He smiled again. Greenleaf hated him for the way he'd dropped the French pronunciation into his speech. '*Docteur* Lagarde had some interesting things to say. Incidentally, they reckon there were four on board the vessel. It was a fishing boat, registered in Calais.'

'So what does the doctor say?'

Doyle smiled at Greenleaf's impatience. 'Well, for a start the bodies suffered some puncture wounds.'

'What sort?'

'Splinters of wood, metal, glass. Lagarde took a nine-incher out of some poor sod. Embedded itself in the stomach and punctured the heart.'

'Meaning there was force behind it?'

'Oh, yes, there was force all right. *Upward* force. And burn marks too. One of the bodies in particular was badly scorched.'

'An explosion,' Greenleaf commented.

'Absolutely.'

'Anything else?'

'Only what they found floating around in the surface oil. Hundred-dollar bills. Fifteen of them, not in very good nick. They got a couple of serial numbers. The Americans are checking.'

'Fifteen hundred dollars. What do you reckon, drugs?'

'Drugs or arms, but probably drugs.'

'You think the two boats met mid-Channel?'

'It's an idea. There's only one way to tell for sure. We need the PM results from Folkestone. Want me to give you a lift?'

'What?'

Doyle leaned down behind his desk and raised a bulging holdall high. 'I'm off to Calais on the evening ferry. Spending the night there, do a bit of sniffing tomorrow, then hit the *hypermarché* before heading back. I got the nod from Trilling an hour ago.'

'The luck of the Irish.'

Doyle's face darkened a little. What had he said? Ah, Doyle was touchy about his name's Irishness, was he? Got you, thought Greenleaf, got you!

When Doyle spoke, he was still subdued. 'I've got to alter my headlights, dip them the right way, but after that I'm ready to leave. So if you're heading for Folkestone . . .'

'I'll take my own car, thanks.'

'Suit yourself,' said Doyle. He seemed to be staring at Greenleaf's straining suit as he said it.


'I wish you'd come to me with this earlier, Michael.'

It wasn't quite the opening line Michael Barclay had expected from his boss. Joyce Parry sat there, invulnerable behind thick-rimmed spectacles, his report held up in front of her. Having glanced at it for effect, she laid it back down and slipped off her glasses. They hung around her neck by a string, and she let them dangle against her chest. From time to time, they grazed the triple-string of Ciro pearls resting just below her throat. Her throat, thought Barclay, was the oldest part of her, permanently lined and stretched. Her good legs, face and hair might say early-40s, but the neck gave the lie to this. Late-40s, the neck said to Barclay.

'Sit down,' Joyce Parry's mouth told him.

Barclay had always believed that he was attractive to women. To women *and* to men actually. He had used his good looks and steady unblinking gaze to good effect both socially and professionally. He felt that he'd always got on well with Joyce Parry, being at his charming best in her office and at meetings where she was present. So much so in fact that someone had sent him an anonymous Valentine addressed: 'To a creeping, slimy, boss-loving toad'. The card was pinned above his desk, its sender still a mystery.

Barclay didn't mind it. He didn't mind envy in the workplace. He didn't mind that others thought he was getting on well with the boss. He'd always imagined that there was something *special* between Mrs Parry and him. He might almost have called it a 'special relationship'.

And now this.

'I really wish you'd shown me this earlier, Michael.' She used his first name softly, the sentence fading away, to show that she was disappointed in him. As he sat in front of her, his legs felt overlong and clumsy. He rested his hands on his knees, hiding them.

'I did try, but you were—'

'You should have tried later. Any news from Commander Trilling?'

'Just that he has two men working on it. One of them's off to France, the other to Folkestone.'

'A bit too early for Special Branch,' she said. 'You should have done some digging of your own first. You should have spoken to *me* first.' Now the endings of her sentences were like stabs at him. 'You jumped the gun.' She nodded slowly towards him, letting this sink in, then wheeled her chair to the corner of her desk where it met with another in an L-shape. Her main desk was all paperwork, but on the side desk stood a computer, the screen angled just enough so that no one sitting where Barclay was could see it. This large desk also hosted printer and modem, while in a far corner of the room sat a fax machine and document shredder. There were three telephones on the main desk. One of them rang just as she was accessing the computer. She pushed her chair back into place and, instead of lifting the receiver, hit one of the buttons.

'Mrs Parry here,' she said, swivelling back to her computer screen.

A small female voice came from the telephone's loudspeaker. 'I checked the computer files—'

'I *told* you not to bother, didn't I?'

'Yes, but I—'

'Mr Elder belongs to the pre-microchip days. He believed in *paper* files.'

Sensible man, thought Barclay. Elder ... the name was familiar. The voice was speaking again.

'Yes, well, I've got those files too.'

'Good,' said Joyce Parry. 'All I need to know is ... no, on second thoughts, bring them in here.'

Once more she wheeled back, this time to cut the connection. Then forwards again, her fingers fast on the keyboard. Barclay knew that his superior had computer clearance far above his own. He knew too that he could beat the computer system, given time and the will. If he wanted to, he could access anything. If he wanted to.

'Ah, here we are,' said Joyce Parry. He studied her profile. Classically English, whatever that meant. The way she raised her chin as she read from the screen. A long straightish nose, thin lips, short well-kept hair, showing just a little grey. Grey eyes too. She was one of those women who grow better looking as they get older. She pressed a few more keys, checked that the printer was on, then pressed two more keys. The laser printer began its quick quiet work. She swivelled back to the main desk and handed the first sheet to him. He had to rise from his chair to take it. The paper was still warm from the machine.

There was a sudden tapping on the wide-open door.

Parry signalled for the secretary to come in. She was carrying two bulging folders, tied securely with what looked like shoelaces.

'Thanks, Angela, leave them on the desk.' Joyce Parry extracted two more sheets from the printer. Barclay tried to concentrate on the piece of paper he was holding but it was difficult not to stare at those two files, the files of someone called Elder. The name definitely stirred a memory, but this wasn't the time for reflection. Joyce Parry began untying the shoelaces while Barclay read from the laser-printed page.

The report was dated six years before, and had been filed originally by the CIA before being passed along 'for information' to the British authorities. What Barclay now held was formed as a precis, as abridged by D. Elder.

'On 16 May,' he read, 'a small fishing boat left the South Korean port of Pusan. Crew of six. Known and well liked in the port. No hint that the crew were involved in any illegal activities prior to this time, though most boatmen in the area regard smuggling as above the law anyway.

'On 17 May, debris and bodies (six) washed up on the island of Mishima, off the Japanese mainland. Earlier reported sighting of the boat near the Japanese coastal town of Susa. No reason why boat should have been in this area. Skipper/owner an experienced sailor. Scale of damage to vessel suggested an explosion rather than collision, grounding, etc. However, no report of anyone seeing or hearing a blast. (Southern-Asian ears and eyes not always fully functional. Remember, to them pirates are still an occupational hazard rather than a 1930s Errol Flynn film.)'

Barclay smiled and started on the second sheet.

'Investigation undertaken by Japanese and South Korean authorities. No further evidence uncovered up to date of this report. However, there was talk in Pusan of a young woman who had been seen talking with the boat's owner in a bar a few days prior to the final voyage. She is described as being tall with short dark hair, probably speaking English.

'From 18–20 May, International Conference for World Peace (ICWP) based at various locations in Hiroshima, Japan. Conference attended by 240 delegates from forty-six countries, supplemented by invited guests (e.g.: from Japanese universities, media) and, to some events, general public. World media invited to attend. Four intelligence agents among those accepting. (See file no. CI/46377/J/DE.) Six keynote speeches given prominence during conference. Other activities included film shows, art exhibition, theatre events, and concert by Music for Peace (the latter with its HQ in London, investigated 1984: see file no. UK/0/223660/L/JP).'

JP: Joyce Parry's initials. Barclay was beginning to sense what this was all about. His hands grew clammy, sticking to the sheet as he read on.

'On closing day, 20 May, final keynote address was to be given by international peace activist Jerome Hassan (CI/38225/USP/DG). However, Mr Hassan was taken ill with suspected food poisoning and his speech (much abbreviated – Hassan was known to work by improvisation) was delivered by a colleague, Dr Danielle Brecht.

'Mr Hassan died in hospital on evening of 20 May, just as live telecast at closing concert was beaming messages by pop and film luminaries into Japan.

'Post mortem was carried out on morning of 21 May, with Mr Hassan's hotel (and over 100 diners from the previous day) keenly awaiting findings. Laboratory analysis showed atropine poisoning. (Atropine is an alkaline found in Deadly Nightshade. From the Greek *atropos*, "the Fate that cuts the thread of life".)

'While still conscious, but thought to be delirious, Hassan spoke of a girl, a student probably. He spoke of her "beauty and generosity". Hotel staff when interviewed acknowledged that on the night of 19 May, a young woman had accompanied Mr Hassan to his room. No one saw her leave, despite a twenty-four-hour reception area. Descriptions given varied. One assessed her height at nearly six foot, another at only five foot six. One said black hair, another brown. Hair was probably cropped short, and woman was fair-skinned though tanned. European perhaps, or Asian. No one heard her speak. She had crossed the lobby with Mr Hassan and entered the lift with him. She was dressed in black denims, light T-shirt, light-coloured jacket. Mr Hassan was carrying a plastic carrier bag, weighted down with books. Reception staff got the impression the bag belonged to the woman.

'Woman has never been traced. Hassan's previous sexual history questioned. (Widow not forthcoming.) As a footnote, woman's entry to the country was clumsy, creating immediate suspicion. And her use of atropine, or at least the dosage used, was also clumsy, since it allowed the victim time to talk before dying. Pity is, he did not say anything useful.

'See: WITCH file.

'Final footnote: Susa is c. fifty miles from Hiroshima.'

Barclay turned to the third and final sheet, expecting more. But all he read were edited newspaper reports of Jerome Hassan's murder, mentioning poison and the mysterious young woman. A jealous lover was hinted at. He looked up and saw that Joyce Parry was immersed in the contents of one of the Elder files. He glanced through his own sheets again, quite liking Elder's tone – the explanation of the word atropine; the mention of the final night's rock concert; that nice late mention that Hassan was a married man.

'You see the coincidence,' Parry said without warning. She was looking at him now. 'An assassin is dropped off on the Japanese mainland and then destroys the boat which landed her. Now, six years later, something similar occurs.'

Barclay considered this. 'Special Branch are thinking more along the lines of drugs or arms.'

'Exactly. And that's why I'd rather you hadn't alerted them this early on. They may be off on half a dozen wild goose chases. Then, if we approach them with new information, they'll wonder why we didn't come up with it sooner. Do you see what I mean?' Her glasses glinted. Barclay was nodding.

'It makes us look bad.'

'It makes *me* look bad.' She wet two fingers with the tip of her tongue and turned a page.

'What's the Witch file?' Barclay asked.

But she was busy reading, too busy to answer. She seemed to be suppressing an occasional smile, as though reminiscing. Eventually she glanced up at him again.

'The Witch file doesn't exist. It was an idea of Mr Elder's.'

'So what *is* Witch?'

She closed the file carefully, and thought for a moment before speaking. 'I think it would be best if you asked Dominic Elder that, don't you?'

Once a year, the fairground came to Cliftonville.

Cliftonville liked to think itself the genteel equivalent to next-door neighbour Margate. It attracted coach tours, retired people. The younger holidaymakers usually made for Margate. So did the weekenders, down from London for a spot of seaside mayhem. But Cliftonville was struggling with a different problem, a crisis of identity. Afternoon bingo and a deckchair in front of the promenade organist just weren't enough. Candy floss and an arcade of one-armed bandits weren't enough. Too much of the town lingered in the 1950s. Few wanted the squeal and glitter of the 90s, yet without them the town would surely die, just as its clientele was dying.

If the town council had wanted to ask about survival, they might have consulted someone at the travelling fairground. It had changed too. The rides had become a little more 'daring' and more expensive. Barnaby's Gun Stall was a good example. The original Barnaby (whose real name had been Eric) had used rifles which fired air-propelled corks at painted tins. But Barnaby had died in 1978. His brother Randolph had replaced the cork-guns with proper pellet-firing rifles, using circular targets attached to silhouette human figures. But then Randolph had succumbed to alcohol and the charms of a woman who hated the fair, so his son Keith – the present Barnaby – had taken over. Nowadays the Gun Stall boasted *serious* entertainment in the form of an auto-matic-firing airgun rigged up to a compression pump. This machine gun could fire one hundred large-bore pellets every minute. You just had to keep your finger on the trigger. The young men paid their money gladly, just to feel the sheer exhilaration of that minute's lethal action. Afterwards, the target would be brought forward. Keith still used cardboard circles marked off from the outer to the small black bullseye, and attached to the heart of a human silhouette. The thing about the automatic was, it couldn't be said to be accurate. If enough pellets hit the target, the cardboard was reduced to tatters. But more often than not the kids missed, dazed by the recoil and the noise and the speed.

The more dazed they were, the more likely they were to come back for more. It was a living. And yet in other ways the fair was very much an old-fashioned place. It had its ghost train and its waltzers, though this evening the ghost train was closed. There were smells of spun sugar and diesel, and the scratchy sounds of the next-to-latest pop records. Onions, the roar of machinery, and three-balls-for-fifty-pee at the kiddie stalls.

Gypsy Rose Pellengro's small caravan was still attached to its Volvo estate car, as though she was thinking of heading off. On a board outside the caravan door were letters of thanks from grateful clients. These letters were looking rather frail, and none of them seemed to include the date on which it had been written. Beside them was a scrawled note announcing 'Gypsy Rose back in an hour'.

The two windows of the caravan were tightly closed, and covered with thick net curtains. Inside, it was much like any holiday caravan. The small sink still held two unwashed plates, and on the table sat not a crystal ball but a portable black and white television, hooked up to the battery of the Volvo estate. The interior was lit by calor gas, the wall-mounted lamps roaring away. A woman was watching TV.

There was a knock at the door.

'Come in, sir, please,' she called, rising to switch off the set. The door was pulled open and a man climbed into the caravan. He was so tall that he had to stoop to avoid the ceiling. He was quite young, very thin, and dark-skinned.

'How did you know it was a man?' he asked, taking in the scene around him.

'I saw you peering in through the window.'

The man smiled at this, and Gypsy Rose Pellengro laughed, showing the four gold teeth in her mouth.

'What can I do for you, sir? Didn't you see the notice outside?'

'Yes. But I really would like my fortune told.' He paused, stroking a thick black moustache, before adding meaningfully: 'I think I have a lucky future ahead of me.'

Gypsy Rose nodded, not that she'd been in any doubt. 'Then you've come to the right place,' she said. 'I'm in the futures market myself. Would you like to sit down?'

'No, thank you. I'll just leave this . . .' He reached inside his jacket and brought out a large brown envelope. As he made to place it on the table in front of the woman, she snatched at his wrist and turned his hand palm upwards.

'Yes,' she said, releasing it after a moment. 'I can see you've been disappointed in love, but don't worry. The right woman isn't so very far away.'

He seemed scandalised that she had dared to touch him. He rubbed at his wrist, standing over her, his black pupils shadowed by his eyebrows. For a moment, violence was very close. But the woman just sat there with her old, stubborn look. Weary, too. There was nothing he could do to her that hadn't already been done. So instead he turned and, muttering foreign sounds, pushed open the caravan door, slamming it shut behind him so hard that it bounced back open again. Now Gypsy Rose could see out onto the slow procession of fairground visitors, some of whom stared back.

Slowly, she rose from the table, closed and locked the door, and returned to her seat, switching on the television. From time to time she fingered the large brown envelope. Eventually, when enough time had passed, she got up and pulled her shawl around her. She left the lamps burning in the caravan, but locked the door behind her when she left. The air was hot, the night sticky. She moved quickly, expertly, through the crowds, occasionally slipping between two stalls and behind the vans and the lorries, picking her way over cables, looking behind her to see if anyone was following. Then back between two more stalls and into the crowd again. Her path seemed to lack coordination, so that at one point she'd almost doubled back to her starting point before striking off in another direction. In all, she walked for nearly fifteen tiring minutes. Fifteen minutes for a journey of less than four hundred yards.

Darkness had fallen, and the atmosphere of the fair had grown darker and more restless, too. The children were home in bed, still excited and not asleep, but safe. Tough-speaking teenagers had taken over the fair now, swilling cheap beer from tins, stopping now and then for passionate kisses or to let off some shots at an unmoving target. Yells broke the night-time air. No longer the sounds of fun but feral sounds, the sounds of trouble. Gypsy Rose remembered one leather-jacketed boy, cradled in a friend's arms.

*Jesus, missus, he's been stabbed.* He didn't die, but it was touch and go.

Less than four hundred yards from her caravan was the ghost train. On the narrow set of tracks between the two double-doors sat the parked carriages. The sign on the kiosk said simply CLOSED. Well, there wouldn't have been many people using it at this time of night anyway. A chain prevented anyone gaining access to the wooden-slatted running boards in front of the ride. She lifted her skirt and stepped over the chain, winning a cheer and a wolf whistle from somewhere behind her. With a final glance over her shoulder, she pushed open one of the double-doors, on which was painted the grinning face of the devil himself, and stepped inside.

She stood for a moment, her eyes adjusting to the newer darkness. The doors muffled much of the sound from outside. Eventually, she felt confident enough to walk on, moving past the spindly mechanisms of ghost and goblin, the wires and pulleys which lowered shreds of raffia onto young heads, the skeleton, at rest now, which would spring to its feet at the approach of a carriage.

It was all so cheap, so obvious. She couldn't recall ever having been scared of the ghost train, even as a tot. Now she was moving further into the cramped construction, off the rails, away from the papier mâché Frankenstein and the strings that were supposed to be cobwebs, until she saw a glimmer of light behind a piece of black cloth. She made for the cloth and pulled it aside, stepping into the soft light of the tiny makeshift room.

The young woman who sat there, sucking her thumb and humming to herself, looked up. She sat crosslegged on the floor, rocking slightly, in her lap a small armless teddy bear, and spread out on the floor a tarot pack.

'He's been,' Gypsy Rose said. She fished the envelope out from under her skirt. It was slightly creased from where she had climbed over the chain. 'I didn't open it,' she said.

The thumb slipped wetly out of the mouth. The young woman nodded, then arched back her neck and twisted it to one side slowly, mouth open wide, until a loud sound like breaking twigs was heard. She ran her fingers through her long black hair. There were two streaks of dyed white above her temples. She wasn't sure about them. She thought they made her look mysterious but old. She didn't want to look old.

'Sit down,' she said. She nodded towards a low stool, the only seat in the room. Gypsy Rose sat down. The young woman gathered the tarot cards together carefully, edging them off the tarpaulin floor with long nails. She was wearing a long black skirt, tasselled at the hem,

41

and a white open-necked blouse beneath a black waistcoat. She *knew* she looked mysterious. That was why she was playing with the tarot. She had rolled her sleeping bag into the shape of a log against the far wall. Having gathered up the cards and slipped them back into their box, she tossed the box over towards the sleeping bag and took the envelope from the older woman, slitting it open with one of her fingernails.

'Work,' she said, spilling the contents out onto the ground. There were sheets of typed paper, black and white five-by-eight photographs with notes written in pencil on their backs, and the money. The banknotes were held together with two paper rings. She slit them open and fanned the money in front of her. 'I've got to go away again,' she said.

Gypsy Rose Pellengro, who had seemed mesmerised by the money, now began to protest.

'But I won't be gone for long this time. A day or two. Will you still be here?'

'We pack up Sunday afternoon.'

'Headed where?'

'Brighton.' A pause. 'You'll take care, won't you?'

'Oh, yes,' said the young woman. 'I'll take care. I *always* take care.' She turned one of the photographs towards the woman. 'What do you think?'

'He's nice-looking,' said Gypsy Rose. 'An Asian gentleman.'

'Asian, yes.'

'The man who made the delivery was Asian, too.'

Witch nodded then read through the notes, taking her time. Gypsy Rose sat quite still, not wanting to disturb her, happy just to be here. She looked at the money again. Eventually, the young woman placed everything back in the envelope. She got up and lifted the tarot from where it lay, tossing it into Gypsy Rose Pellengro's lap.

'Here,' she said, 'take the cards.' There was a scream from outside. A girl's scream. Maybe a fight was starting. It might be the first tonight; it wouldn't be the last. 'Now, Rosa, tell me. Tell me what you see. Tell me about my mother.'

Gypsy Rose stared at the tarot pack, unwilling to lift it. The young woman slipped her thumb into her mouth again and began to hum, rocking backwards and forwards with the teddy bear on her lap. Outside, someone was still screaming. Gypsy Rose touched the box, pushed its flap open with her thumb. Slowly, she eased out the cards.

# Friday 5 June

Greenleaf was in the office early. He'd spent the previous late-afternoon and evening in Folkestone, getting in the way, bothering people, not making any friends, but finally gathering all the information he needed, information he just couldn't get by telephone alone. He'd spoken to George Crane's widow, Brian Perch's parents, Crane's accountants, to people who knew the men, to other boatmen. He'd asked questions of the coastguard, the local police, forensics, and the pathologist. He'd been busy – so busy that he hadn't left Folkestone until ten o'clock, arriving home in Edmonton at close on midnight, thanks to a jam on the M20 and the Blackwall Tunnel being closed. Shirley was pretending to be asleep with the bedside lamp off but still hot to the touch, and her book pushed under her pillow.

'What time is it?' she'd muttered.

'Ten past ten.'

'Bloody liar.'

'Then stop trying to make me feel guilty.'

The hour was too late for an argument, really. The neighbours had complained in the past. So they kept it jokey and low-key. Just.

He'd taken her toast and tea in bed this morning as penance, despite feeling dead on his feet. And the drive into work hadn't helped. A car smash at Finsbury Park and a defunct bus holding everybody up between Oxford Street and Warren Street. There was nothing he could do about it except consult the *A–Z* for useless shortcuts and swear that he'd start travelling to work by tube. Good old public transport: a brisk morning walk to the bus stop, bus straight to Seven Sisters, and hop onto a Victoria Line tube which would rush him to Victoria and the short final walk to his office. Good old public transport.

Only he'd tried the trip a few times and it didn't work like that. From the half dozen crammed buses that glided past his stop without slowing, right to the crushed and sweaty tube compartment and the feeling that he would kill the next person who jammed their elbow into him ... Good old public transport. London transportation. He'd stick to the car. At least in the car you had a *choice*. Stuck in a jam, you could park and wait it out in a café, or try another route. But stuck in a tunnel in a tube train ... well, that was a tiny rehearsal for hell.

He thought of Doyle, dawdling over croissants and coffee at some French bar, making ready to stock up on cheap beer and duty free. Bastard. But Doyle was useful. Or rather, Greenleaf's dislike of Doyle was useful: it goaded him. It made him want his work to be efficient, and that included his reports. Which was why he was here so early. He wanted to get his notes typed up into presentable shape, so he could hand them to Trilling before lunchtime.

Basically Doyle had been right. The pathologist noted burns, scorch marks, on both men. A razor-sharp section of plastic had almost taken off Crane's head. And there were splinters and shards – of wood, glass, metal, perspex – embedded in both bodies. Definite signs of an explosion.

'Somewhere beneath them,' the pathologist added. 'Below decks. The two men were probably on deck at the time. The various angles of penetration are all consistent with a blast from below, sending the shrapnel upwards. For example, one splinter enters above the left knee and makes its way up the leg towards the groin, the exit wound appearing on the inside upper-thigh.'

There were photographs to go with the doctor's various graphic descriptions. What couldn't be shown, and might possibly never be shown, was what had caused the explosion in the first place. That was all down to deduction and supposition. Greenleaf guessed that a bomb wouldn't be too far out. One of those simple IRA jobs with timer attached. Messy though, blowing the whole caboodle up like that. Why not shoot the men and dump the bodies with weights attached? That way the bodies disappeared, and the boat remained: a mystery, but without the certainty that murder had been done. Yes, a loud and messy way to enter the country. In trying to cover their tracks they'd left a calling-card: no forwarding address, but a sure sign they'd been there.

And could now be anywhere, planning or doing anything, with a cache of drugs or of arms. It had to be a sizeable haul to merit killing two men. Six if you included the French . . .

Well, so much for the doctor. The local police were on the ball, too. Inside George Crane's jacket they'd discovered a wad of bank notes, £2,000 or thereabouts. The wad had been pierced by a chunk of metal, but the notes were still recognisable. More important, some of the serial numbers remained intact. Steeped in blood, but intact.

There were ways of checking these things, and Greenleaf knew all of them. He'd faxed details that evening to the Bank of England, and to the Counterfeit Currency Department inside New Scotland Yard, supplying photocopies of several of the cleaner notes. The photocopies weren't great, but the serial numbers were the crucial thing anyway. The notes themselves he was careful not to handle, except with the use of polythene gloves and tweezers. After all, it was unlikely that Crane carried so much money around with him on every boating trip (unless he was planning to bribe some customs officials). It was much more likely that the money had been a payment made to him by whomever he'd transported from mid-Channel to the English coast.

As such, the notes might well boast the odd finger-print. The corpse of George Crane had already been fingerprinted – on Greenleaf's orders – so that the dead man's prints could be eliminated. Somehow, Greenleaf didn't think George Crane would have let Brian Perch near the money, but his body was being fingerprinted too. Best to be rigorous.

Perch was an employee, a no-questions-asked hired-hand who would, as a fellow worker had put it, 'go to the end of the earth' for Crane, so long as there was overtime in it. Why had Crane taken him along? For protection? Because he didn't trust whomever he was carrying? Maybe just for company on the voyage out to mid-Channel? Whatever, Brian Perch didn't really interest Greenleaf, while George Crane did.

The accountant to the building business wasn't about to say that Crane's company was in terminal trouble, but he agreed that times were hard and that the company was 'overstretched financially'. Which meant there were bigger loan repayments than there were cheques from satisfied and solvent customers. For example, a larger than usual contract had gone unfinished and unpaid when the company employing Crane's firm had them-selves gone broke. Crane just managed to hold his head above water. Well, in the financial sense anyway. He still had the big house outside Folkestone with the swimming pool and sauna. He still had a Porsche. He still had his boat. But Greenleaf knew that often the more prosperous a man tried to look, the deeper he was sinking.

He'd considered an insurance scam. Take the boat out at dead of night and blow it up, then claim the money. But it didn't add up. Why not just sell the boat? One reason might be that no one was buying. Okay, so why did *he* have to die too? A miscalculation with the timer or the amount of explosive used? Possible. But Greenleaf still didn't rate it. Why take someone else along? And besides, there was the French sinking to consider. It *had* to be tied in with the British sinking; too much of a coincidence otherwise.

Bringing him back to murder.

Crane's wife didn't know anything about anything. She knew nothing about her husband's movements that night, nothing about his business affairs, nothing about any of his meetings. All she knew was that she should wear black and deserve sympathy. She seemed to find his questions in particularly bad taste. Crane's secretary, when tracked down, had been no more forthcoming. No, no meetings with strangers. No sudden 'appointments' out of the office which couldn't be squared with his diary. No mysterious telephone calls.

So what was Greenleaf left with? A man in debt, needing a few thousand (well, fifteen or so actually) to see him back on dry land. Personal financial affairs which had yet to be disentangled (it seemed Crane had been a bit naughty, stashing his cash in several accounts kept hidden from the prying taxman). A midnight boat trip which ends with him two grand in pocket but not in any position to spend it. It all came back to smuggling, didn't it? Just as Doyle had said. Arms or dope or someone creeping back into the country unannounced. Well, hardly unannounced. Whatever it was, it had cost six lives so far, which was too high a price to pay, whatever the payoff.

Most of these thoughts Greenleaf kept to himself. On

paper, he stuck to the facts and the procedures followed. It still looked like a tidy bit of work, scrupulous and unstinting. He began to feel quite pleased with himself. He'd get it to Trilling before lunchtime. Definite. When would Doyle file *his* findings? Not before tomorrow. He was due back tomorrow morning. Say tomorrow afternoon then. Giving Greenleaf over a day clear, a day during which he'd be ahead of his nemesis. He breathed deeply and decided to pause for another cup of coffee.

When he got back from the machine, his phone was ringing. He almost spilled hot coffee all down his shirt as he lunged for the receiver.

'Yes? Greenleaf here.'

'John? Terry Willard at CC.'

'Morning, Terry.' Good. Terry Willard was one of Counterfeit Currency's best workers. 'What can you do for me?'

'You sound chirpy for a man who must've been in – where was it? – Folkestone? – till all hours last night. We're not used to getting faxes after six.'

Greenleaf laughed and relaxed into his chair. 'Just conscientious, Terry. So you've got some news, have you?'

'The notes aren't counterfeit. I'm pretty sure of that.'

'Oh.' Greenleaf tried not to sound disappointed.

'Better than that, really,' said Willard. 'I've already traced them.'

'What?' Greenleaf sat forward in his chair. 'Terry, you're a genius. Christ, it's not even ten o'clock yet.'

'To be honest, it wasn't the hardest work I've done. The computer picked the numbers out inside a couple of minutes. Those notes are ancient history. You probably wouldn't have noticed that last night, the state most of them must have been in, but take it from me they are *old* banknotes. And they've been out of circulation for some

49

time. We were beginning to doubt we'd ever see them again.'

'What do you mean?'

'I mean they're marked. The serial numbers are on record. They're part of a kidnap pay-off.'

'A *kidnap?*'

'Best part of five years ago. In Italy. A British businessman's daughter was kidnapped by some gang ... It's a bit of a long story. Want me to send you over what I've got?'

'Christ, yes. A *kidnap?*' Greenleaf's head was reeling. 'Yes, send me what you've got. And Terry ... ?'

'Yes?'

'I owe you a beer.'

'No sweat.'


Commander Trilling showed no emotion as Greenleaf told his, or rather Willard's, story. Greenleaf's report was in front of Trilling, as was the file sent over from Willard, and he glanced at them from time to time as the Special Branch officer recapped.

'The father's name is Gibson, sir. At the time he was an executive with the Gironi chemicals company in Turin. The daughter, Christina, was in a private school near Genoa. She disappeared during a visit to an art gallery. She was missing two days before Mr Gibson received a telephone call from the kidnappers.

'By that time the Italian police were already involved. They know that when a rich businessman's daughter goes missing, there's usually a ransom demand somewhere at the back of it. They'd set up telephone taps at the Gibson home and the Gironi headquarters before the first call came.'

Trilling crunched down hard on a mint and nodded.

'The problem was timing,' Greenleaf went on. 'The

gang telephoned on four occasions that first day, but never for more than eight seconds, not long enough for any tracing system to work. The first call merely stated that Christina had been kidnapped, the second identified the terrorist gang responsible, the third stated how much of a ransom was required, and the fourth was a plea from Christina herself.

'Another two days passed before the gang got in touch again.'

Trilling interrupted. 'Was the caller male or female?'

'Male, sir.' Greenleaf had studied the case file well over the previous hour. He knew that he was leaving just enough out so that the Commander would ask him questions. He already knew the answers to those questions. It was an old trick which made you look not-quite-perfect but not too far off it either.

'And the gang?'

'La Croix Jaune: Yellow Cross. Nothing much about them on the files. Probably a splinter group from one of the other terrorist organisations. The name may be some obscure joke to do with the Red Brigade. They came on the scene in '85 and seemed to disappear again in '88. In fact, there are doubts they ever existed at all as a group. The name may just be a cover for two or three criminals working together. Two kidnaps and two armed bank robberies. They were never identified, let alone captured. The only time a bank camera caught them they were masked.'

'You say two or three members?'

'That's all Christina Gibson saw. They kept her blindfolded most of the time, and at others they were dressed in balaclavas and sunglasses. But she was fairly sure there were two men, one taller than the other, and one woman, as tall as the men but slimmer.'

Trilling nodded thoughtfully. 'So what happened?'

'Mr Gibson cooperated throughout with the police. It was an international effort by then, as far as these things go. Two Special Branch men were flown out to assist. Matt Duncan and Iain Campbell. The kidnappers—'

'Anyone else?'

'Sorry, sir?'

'The British contingent: did it include anyone else?'

'Not on record, sir.' Greenleaf frowned. This was the first question to have stumped him. But Trilling was smiling, nodding to himself.

'That means nothing,' he said quietly. 'Go on.'

'Well, sir, the kidnappers wanted dollars, but we asked Mr Gibson to persuade them to take sterling. He told them dollars would take some time, while he had the sterling to hand. They agreed. So we put together thirty grand's worth of notes. The intention was to catch them cold, but there was a shoot-out and they got away. The girl was released, but the money had flown with the gang.'

'Clumsy.'

'Agreed. The Italians reckoned they wounded one of the gang, but nothing came of it. And the money disappeared, despite a check by all clearing banks. The notes on Crane's body are the first to have surfaced.'

'Poor choice of word,' commented Trilling. 'Still, good work, John.'

'Thank you, sir.'

'Yes, very good work. So, what do we make of it?'

'Well, it links Crane to a terrorist group, which indicates arms smuggling rather than drugs.'

'All it links him to, John, is dirty money. You can buy dirty money for fivepence in the pound. It's a cheap way of paying someone a large sum when you're not bothered what happens to the person afterwards.' Trilling thought for a moment. 'You know, I'm not at all sure that we've been given a level playing field here.'

'Sir?'

'It all smacks of the cloak-and-dagger brigade. Who did you say contacted us in the first place?'

Christ, what was his name? Barrow ... Beardsley ... Barkworth ... 'Barclay, sir.'

'Barclay. Never heard of him. But he's one of Joyce Parry's. I wonder what Joyce is playing at? I think I'd better have a word with her.'

He was about to pick up his receiver when there was a knock at the door. Greenleaf rubbed his stomach to stop it from rumbling. It was quarter to one, and so far today all he'd had was five cups of coffee.

'Come in.'

It was Trilling's secretary. She was holding two sheets of paper, stapled together. 'Mr Doyle's report, sir.'

'Thank you, Celia.' Trilling held out his hand, took the report and laid it on his desk, on top of Greenleaf's own report. Greenleaf stared at the closely typed top sheet. He was oblivious to Celia's smile, or the closing of the door after she left. He kept hearing her words: Mr Doyle's report ... Mr Doyle's report. When Greenleaf looked up from the desk, he saw Commander Trilling studying him.

'Efficient, isn't he?' Trilling mused.

'Very, sir. But how ... ?'

'Oh, quite simple really. Doyle requested a laptop computer. He's taken it with him. Clever devices, they work on rechargeable batteries you know. Sizeable memory, too. I can never get on with the screens on them, but some people can.'

'So Doyle's writing his report as he goes?'

'That's it. Then he plugs the laptop into a modem, presses a few buttons, and his copy arrives at a computer here. All we have to do is run off a hard copy.' He patted Doyle's report, then lifted it up. 'Now, let's see what he's got to say for himself.' But instead of reading, he looked at Greenleaf over the paper. '*If* there's a case to investigate, John, I want you and Doyle to work on it together. Understand? *Together.* Do you think you can manage that?'

'Of course, sir.'

Trilling continued to look at him. 'Good,' he said, before turning his attention to the report.


Dominic Elder was a large man, larger than Barclay had expected. That surname, Elder, had put him on the wrong track. He'd expected a hunched, defeated figure, the sort who had been elders at his mother's Presbyterian church. But Dominic Elder was large and fit and strong. He'd be about fifty, a year or two older than Joyce Parry. His face had been handsome once, but time had done things to it. He looked out of place in the garden of the pretty cottage, on his knees and planting out seedlings in a well-kept vegetable-bed.

'Mr Elder?' Barclay had driven slowly down the lane, and had parked right outside the gate before ejecting *Il Trovatore* from the cassette player. But, even as he pushed open the gate, the man in the garden seemed not to acknowledge his presence.

'Mr Elder?' Barclay repeated. 'Dominic Elder?'

'That's me, Mr Barclay,' the figure said, rising stiffly to its feet and brushing soil from its hands. 'Who did you expect to find?'

'There's no number or name on the gate,' Barclay explained. 'I wasn't sure I had the right house.'

Elder looked around him slowly. 'You may not have noticed,' he said in his quiet, deep voice, 'but this is the only house there is.' He said it slowly, as if he were explaining something to a child. His eyes fixed on Barclay's as he spoke. He was massaging his back with the knuckles of one hand. 'I suppose you were recruited straight from university, yes?'

Barclay made a non-committal gesture. He wasn't sure where this was leading. He'd had a long drive, and an exasperating one. Roadworks, wrong turnings, and trouble with the car's third gear. It kept slipping back into neutral. On top of which it was twenty-eight degrees, and he needed a drink.

'Yes,' Elder was saying, 'straight from university. What did you study?'

'Electronics.'

'"Oh, brave new world."' Elder chuckled. 'So they put you into surveillance first, did they?'

'Yes, but—'

'But it was routine and boring. You wanted out.'

Barclay shuffled his feet. Maybe Elder was astute, but then again maybe he'd learned all this from Joyce Parry. Barclay wasn't impressed by tricks.

'And eventually you got your transfer.' Elder checked the dirt beneath his gardener's fingernails. 'What school did you go to?'

'I really don't see what . . .' Barclay sighed. Losing his patience wouldn't do any good. Besides, this man was an old friend of Mrs Parry's. It might pay to humour him. 'It was a comprehensive,' he conceded. 'I *suppose* that's what you want to know.'

'Scottish?'

'I was born there.'

'But you moved away when you were young. The name's right, but there's not much of an accent left. Father in the armed forces?'

'RAF.'

Elder nodded. He checked his fingernails again, then

55

stretched a hand out towards Barclay. 'Pleased to meet you, Mr Barclay.'

Barclay thought about refusing the handshake, but eventually gave in. Elder's grip was a lot firmer than he'd expected. He did his best to squeeze back.

'A rough journey, eh?' Elder commented. 'I was expecting you three-quarters of an hour ago, allowing for one stop at motorway services.'

'Roadworks,' Barclay explained. 'And my gearbox is playing up.'

'Been to Wales before?' Elder was walking back towards the cottage. Barclay followed him.

'Only to Llandudno.'

'Strange choice.'

'It was a day trip. We were on holiday in Southport.'

'Strange choice. This was when you were younger?'

'Eleven or twelve, yes. Why do you say "strange"?'

'Most families with children would choose Blackpool or Morecambe. I've always thought Southport very . . . reserved. Was there much to do there?'

They were at the front door now. It was already open, and Elder wandered inside and along the narrow hall. 'I don't remember,' Barclay said. 'Some would say there's not a lot to do in rural Wales either.'

'They'd be right.' At the end of the hall, Elder entered the kitchen and stood in front of the sink, rinsing his hands. Barclay, who had followed, felt awkward standing in the doorway. 'That's why I'm here,' said Elder. 'To enjoy my twilight years.'

'Twilight? But you're only—'

'Fifty. Like I say, twilight. In our profession.'

*Our*. For the first time, Barclay felt a little of his hostility fall away.

'Take my advice, Mr Barclay, set your sights on

retirement at fifty. Maybe even at forty-five. I know, it all seems a long way off. What are you ... late-twenties?'

'Twenty-five.'

'Twenty-five then. In a few more years, you'll begin to notice things. You'll notice your reactions slowing – almost imperceptibly, but with the proper equipment you can measure the decline. You'll start to feel aches and pains, twinges. Try testing your memory, speed and accuracy of recall. Do it every six months or so and chart your decline.'

'Very comforting.'

Elder, drying his hands on a teatowel, shook his head. 'Not comforting, no. But by being aware of your limitations, you may save your own life. More important still, you might just save other people's. Think about it. Think about our profession. That's all I'm saying.' He reached a hand behind his back and rubbed at it slowly, thoughtfully. 'Tea? Or would you prefer a beer?'

'Something cold would be gratefully received.'

'I think I've some bottles in the fridge. We can take a couple into the living-room. It's cooler in there.'

Cooler and darker. There were windows only to the back and side of the cottage, and these were part-overgrown with ivy. The room was small and comfortable. It had a messy, lived-in look, like a favourite pullover. The walls were whitewashed stone, and against one stretched a series of chipboard and melamine bookcases, standing at crazy angles due to the weight of books pressing down on them over the years. On a low tile-topped table sat a range of bottles – gin, Pimm's, whisky, vodka – full or nearly full. Various knick-knacks filled the window ledges and a few of the spare shelves. The room also contained TV, video, a hi-fi, half a wall of classical LPs, a sofa, and two armchairs. Elder made for one of these. Again, he made no motion, no gesture to help Barclay decide what to do. Should he opt for the other chair or the sofa? He decided on the chair, and sank slowly into it, looking round appreciatively at the room. Yes, comfortable. But dusty, too. There were edges of fluff where the carpet met a chair or a bookcase. There was a layer of dust on the video recorder, and another covering the front of the hi-fi.

Well, thought Barclay, let's try playing him at his own game. He swallowed a mouthful of cold beer and said: 'You're not married, Mr Elder?'

But Elder was nodding. He waved his left hand towards Barclay. There was a ring on the wedding-finger. 'Didn't you notice? I suppose you've got computers to do that sort of thing for you.'

Barclay knew now what Joyce Parry had been getting at when she'd talked of Elder as though he were some dinosaur from the ancient past. He'd retired only two years ago, yet his ideas were Stone Age. Barclay had come across them before, these troglodytes who thought the Enigma code-breaker was a bit too high-tech to deal with. They belonged to old spy novels, left unread in second-hand bookshops.

'A penny for them,' Elder said, startling Barclay.

'Oh, I was just wondering about your wife.'

'Why?'

'Curious, I suppose.'

'We're separated. Have been for years. No plans for divorce. Funny, we get on fine when we're not living together. We can meet for dinner or the theatre.'

'And you still wear your ring.'

'No reason not to.'

Barclay noticed a small framed photograph on one of the shelves. He got up the better to study it. A young girl dressed in pale colours. A big gap-toothed grin and short

58

black hair. It looked like an old photo. He waited for Elder to say something, but Elder was ignoring him.

'Your daughter?' Barclay offered.

Elder nodded. 'Deceased.'

Barclay put the photograph back carefully. 'I'm sorry,' he said. 'How did she—'

'So,' Elder interrupted, 'how's Joyce Parry?'

'Fine.' Barclay sat down again.

'It was nice to hear from her. We haven't really kept in touch.' A pause. 'We should have. Have you worked it out yet?'

'Worked out what?'

Elder smiled. 'Something we all used to wonder: whether she's an iron fist in a velvet glove, or a velvet fist in an iron one.'

Barclay smiled back. 'Both have the same effect, surely?'

'Not when the gloves are off.' Elder took another mouthful of beer. 'So,' he said, sounding suddenly businesslike, 'you're here to tell me something.'

'Well, yes.'

'Something about Witch.'

'We don't know that yet, even supposing Witch exists . . .'

'She exists.'

'She?'

'She, Mr Barclay. One woman.'

'I thought it was a group.'

Elder shook his head. 'That's what the department thought at the time. It's what Joyce believes to this day. It's not a gang, Mr Barclay, it's an individual, an assassin.'

'And female?'

'Female.'

'Because of the Hiroshima murder?'

59

'No, not just that. Hiroshima was merely her entrance. And now something similar has happened?'

'Two boats, one either side of the Channel—'

'Yes, so Joyce said. One off Calais, the other near Folkestone . . .'

'The *Cassandra Christa*.'

'What?'

'The English boat, it was called the *Cassandra Christa*.'

'Cassandra . . . extraordinary.'

Barclay didn't follow. 'You know it?'

But Elder shook his head. 'I meant the parallel. You didn't have a classical education, Mr Barclay?'

Barclay's voice was as cold as his drink. 'Apparently not.'

'Cassandra,' Elder was saying, 'was the daughter of Priam, King of Troy. The god Apollo endowed her with the gift of prophecy . . . but not of being believed.'

Barclay nodded slowly, smiling. 'And you're Cassandra, Mr Elder?'

His eyes twinkled. 'In the present case, yes, perhaps I am.' He paused. 'Mr Barclay, do you know *why* Joyce has sent you here?'

Barclay took a deep breath. 'To be honest, off the record, no.'

'Me neither. I admit I'm intrigued. Are Special Branch investigating the sinkings?'

'Yes.'

'They'll probably plump for an arms shipment. Believable scenario. Strange, if it *is* Witch . . .'

'Yes?'

'She's a quick learner, Mr Barclay. That's why she's survived so long. We haven't seen hide or hair of her for a couple of years. I thought maybe she'd retired. Yet here she is, announcing herself loud and clear. You see, she didn't use that particular trick again. She tends not to use the same trick twice, ever. She enters and leaves countries in different ways, using different disguises, different means of killing her victims. Now she seems to have returned to her original calling-card. Why?'

'Maybe she's run out of ideas, gone back to square one.'

'Maybe.'

'Mr Elder, you say this group ... you say *she's* an assassin.'

'Yes.'

'For money, or for an ideal?'

'Both. Having an ideal costs money.'

'And what is her ideal?'

Elder shook his head. 'If I knew that, I might have caught her by now.' He sat up suddenly. 'There are two ways of doing this, the fast and the slow. I'd prefer the slow. Do you have any plans for this evening?'

'No.' This was a lie, but Barclay was intrigued.

'Then I'll cook some supper. Come on.' He rose to his feet. 'Let's see what needs picking in the garden.'

The evening stayed balmy, and they were able to eat at a picnic table in the back garden. Apart from the immaculate vegetable plot, the garden itself had been left wild. But there was order in the wilderness. The phrase that sprang to Barclay's mind was: the organisation of chaos.

He didn't know what to make of Elder. Partly, he thought the man intelligent, cautious, impressive; partly, he thought him just another old service crank. The story he told seemed harshly at odds with the scenery surrounding them as they sat into the twilight and beyond.

'Hiroshima was the first,' Elder said, almost drowsily. 'Except that it wasn't. That sounds like a riddle, but I'll

61

explain it as I go along. I filed the report on the Hassan killing.'

'Yes, I read it.'

'But of course, I couldn't know then . . . well, nobody could know about Witch. Then there were other incidents, other operations. Most of them terrorist-related. I like to imagine Witch as a *pure* terrorist.' He smiled. 'I'm sure she isn't though.' He seemed to be drifting away. Barclay feared the man was about to fall asleep.

'And after Hassan?' he asked.

Elder stirred himself. 'After Hassan . . . well, there was an Italian kidnapping. A British businessman, working for some chemical conglomerate. They took his daughter. I was sent over there to liaise with police. It was an utter farce. The gang got away, *and* with the ransom.'

'The daughter?'

'Oh, freed. But she's been a nervous wreck ever since, poor child.'

'You said a gang: not Witch then?'

'Not just Witch, no. Two men and a woman. You see, this was her training period, a term of probation on the one hand and learning on the other. She didn't work alone in the early days.'

'And since?'

'Since?' Elder shrugged. 'The problem is that there's so little evidence. Seven armed robberies on the Continent . . . three assassinations. Many more assassination attempts, either foiled or botched. And always a woman mentioned afterwards, maybe just a passing note in somebody's report, but always a woman, a tall young woman. The most extraordinary story concerns a NATO General.' Elder toyed with his fork. 'It was hushed-up at the time, for reasons you will appreciate. He was an American based in Europe, but had to fly out to . . . let's just say Asia . . . as part of a very sensitive delegation.

This General, however, had a taste for violent, forced sex. Oh, he was willing to pay. He'd made several pimps and madams very wealthy in his time. He was intrigued by stories of a very special prostitute. The rougher things got, the better she liked it. That was the story.' Elder paused and glanced around his garden, either appraising it or else playing for time, wondering how to phrase what came next. 'He was discovered lying naked on a bed with his head severed from its body at the neck. The head had been placed between his legs. In effect, the corpse was giving itself a blow job.'

Now Elder looked towards Barclay. He was smiling.

'I never said Witch didn't have a sense of humour,' he said. Then he rose from his chair and walked into the house.

Barclay found that his hand was shaking just a little as he picked up his glass. This was his third glass of wine, on top of two beers. His third and last glass, otherwise the trip back would be fraught. He looked at his watch. It was getting late. He'd have to start off in the next hour or so anyway. He still didn't know what he was doing here. He was still intrigued.

Something exploded on the table. Looking round, he saw Elder standing just behind him. The man had approached in absolute silence. And on the table sat a fat document wallet, its flap open, spewing paper and glossy photographs across the table-top.

'The Witch Report,' Elder said, sitting down again.

'I was told there wasn't a file on Witch.'

'Joyce told you that? Well, here's one I made earlier.' Elder slapped the file. 'What I've been telling you so far are the facts, such as they are. *This* is the supposition. And it begins several years before the Hassan killing. It begins in 1982, when the Pope visited Scotland.' Elder was reaching into the file. He drew out three large black and white photographs. 'There was another tourist in Edinburgh that summer. Wolf Bandorff.' Elder handed the photo over. It was a close-up of a crowd scene, picking out three or four people, focusing on two of them. A young couple. The man had a long thick mane of hair and wore circular spectacles. He was looking over the person in front of his shoulder. He looked to Barclay like a postgraduate student. Beside him was a girl with long straight black hair and dark eye make-up. In the 60s, she might have passed for a model.

'You won't have heard of Wolf,' Elder was saying. But he waited until Barclay had shaken his head. 'No, thought not. He'll be in some computer, and that excuses us our bad memories and failure to learn. He was a West German terrorist. I say "West" because this was in the days before glorious unification, and I say "was" because he's currently serving a sentence in a maximum security prison outside Hanover. German intelligence tipped us off that he was in the UK. There were a few false starts before we found him in Edinburgh. As soon as he knew we were on to him, he disappeared, along with his girlfriend there. These photos are the slim prize for our time and effort.'

Barclay put the photographs down and waited for more. Elder dug into the file again and produced a single photograph of similar size. 'The girlfriend was Wolf's acolyte. You know what acolyte means?'

'Someone who's learning, isn't it?'

Elder's eyes seemed to sparkle in the disappearing light. The garden was illuminated now chiefly by lights from inside the cottage. 'That's right,' he said softly. 'Someone who's learning. In the early days, she attached herself to men, to the leaders of the various groups. That way she learned all the quicker, and gained power and influence too. That way, she gained *contacts*.' Now he handed over the photograph. 'This was taken just under four years ago, after the Hassan killing and the Italian kidnap. It was taken during Operation Warlock.'

Barclay looked up. 'Warlock?'

'Named by someone with an interest in role-playing games. And not very apt, since we soon found we were dealing not with a man but with a woman, apparently working alone. If there's any pattern to the way she works, I'd say she joins or puts together a group, then plans something with some financial reward – a bank robbery or kidnap or paid assassination. Then she uses her share to finance her . . . other activities. For example, the NATO General. No group ever claimed responsibility. There's no information that any group wanted him dead specifically.'

'A feminist assassin,' mused Barclay.

'That may not be so far from the truth.'

'And this is her?' Barclay waved the photograph.

'*I* think so. Others aren't convinced. I know Joyce thinks Witch is a group, and I know others think that too. Sticking to facts, this picture was taken at a rally by the opposition leader in one of the least stable South American countries.'

It was another crowd picture, focusing on a young woman with a dark tanned face but bleached and cropped blonde hair. Her cheeks were plump, her eyes small, her eyebrows almost non-existent.

'We knew there was a plot to assassinate him. It would have been against everyone's interests if such a plot had succeeded. There was concerted effort to stop the attempt taking place.'

'Operation Warlock.'

'Yes, Operation Warlock. After this rally and despite all our warnings, there was a motorcade. He died a few hours later. Poison. A pin-prick was found on the back of his hand. Among those who "pressed the flesh", so to speak, was a young supporter with bleached hair. Despite those distinctive looks, she was never seen again.'

Barclay turned the photo towards Elder, who nodded slowly back at him before sliding the Wolf Bandorff photo across the table.

'Look again, Mr Barclay. Look at Wolf's acolyte.'

'You think they're the same person?'

'I'm sure of it.' Elder watched as Barclay compared the two photographs. 'I see you're not convinced.'

'I can't really see any resemblance.'

Elder took the photos from him and stared at them. Barclay got the impression the older man had done this many times over the years. 'No, maybe you're right. The resemblance is *below* the skin. And the eyes of course. That look in the eyes ... I know it's her. It's Witch.'

'Is that how she got her name? Operation Warlock?'

'Yes. From warlock to witch, once we knew the sex.'

'But there's no proof it was the woman who killed the—'

'Not a shred of proof. I never said there was. Suppositions, Mr Barclay.'

'Then we're no further forward really, are we?' Barclay was in a mood to wind things up. What had he learned here tonight? Stories, that's all. Merely stories.

'Perhaps not,' Elder said ruefully. 'You know best.'

'I didn't mean—'

'No, no, I know what you meant, Mr Barclay. You think this file represents the most tenuous speculation. Maybe you're right.' He stared at Barclay. 'Maybe I'm being paranoid, a symptom of the whole organisation.'

There was silence between them, Elder still staring. Barclay had heard those words before. Suddenly he

66

realised they were *his* words, the ones he'd used at his selection-board.

'You,' he said. 'You were on my interview panel, weren't you?' Elder smiled, bowing his head a little. 'You didn't say a word the whole time, not one.'

'And that unsettled you,' Elder stated.

'Of course it did.'

'But it did not stop you making your little speech. And as you can see, I was listening.'

'I thought I knew your name, I wasn't sure how.'

Elder had begun slotting the photos back in their proper places inside the file. Barclay realised suddenly just how much this file meant to Elder.

'Mr Elder, could I take your report with me to look at?'

Elder considered this. 'I don't think so,' he said. 'You're not ready yet.' He rose and tucked the file beneath his arm. 'You've got a long drive ahead. We'd better have some coffee. Come on, it's too dark out here. Let's go inside where it's light.'

Over coffee, Elder would speak only of opera, of *Il Trovatore*, of performances seen and performances heard. Barclay tried consistently to bring the conversation back to Witch, but Elder was having none of it. Eventually, Barclay gave up. They moved from opera to the cricket season. And then it was time for Barclay to leave. He drove back to London in silence, wondering what else was in Dominic Elder's file on Witch, wondering what was in Joyce Parry's files on Elder. The word acolyte bounced around in his head. *You're not ready yet.* Was Elder inviting him to . . . to what? To learn? He wasn't sure.

He brightened when he remembered that this was Friday night. The weekend stretched ahead of him. He wondered if he'd be able to put Witch, Elder, and the American General out of his mind. Then he recalled that he himself had set these wheels in motion. *He* had noticed the original report on the sinkings. *He* had contacted Special Branch.

'What have I let myself in for?' he wondered as the overhead sodium arc came into view, the light emanating from London.

# The Operating Theatre

# Friday, Saturday, Sunday

Idres Salaam-Khan – known to everyone simply as Khan – had a good life. Khan knew it, and Khan's chauffeur-cum-bodyguard knew it. A good life. As a senior official (though not a director) of a small, anonymous bank, his salary was kept undisclosed. It managed to bury itself amidst still larger figures on the yearly accounting sheet. But whatever it was, it was enough to bring to Khan the simple and not so simple pleasures of life, such as his Belgravia mews house (a converted stables) and his country house in Scotland, his BMW 7-Series (so much less conspicuous than a Rolls-Royce) and, for when conspicuousness was the whole point, his Ferrari. These days, though, he did not use the Ferrari much, since there wasn't really room in it for his bodyguard. These were uncomfortable times, against which luxury proved a flimsy barrier. A bodyguard was some comfort. But Khan did not look upon Henrik as a luxury; he looked upon him as a necessity.

The small anonymous bank's small anonymous head-quarters (Europe) was in London. The clients came to it precisely because it *was* small and anonymous. It was discreet, and it was generous in its interest rates. High players only though: there were no sterling accounts of less than six figures. Few of the customers using the bank in the UK actually ever borrowed from it. They tended to be depositors. The borrowers were elsewhere. In truth, the largest depositors were elsewhere too, but none of this bothered the UK operation.

Certainly, none of it bothered Khan, whose role at the bank was, to many, such a mystery. He seemed to spend three days there each week – Tuesday, Wednesday, Thursday – with Friday to Monday being spent elsewhere, most often these days in Scotland. He liked Scotland, finding it, like the bank, small and anonymous. The only thing missing, really, was nightlife. Which was why he'd decided, this trip, to bring his own nightlife with him. She was called either Shari or Sherri, he'd never really worked it out. She seemed to respond to both names as easily as she responded to questions like 'More champagne?', 'More smoked salmon?', and 'Another line?'

Khan had effortless access to the most exotic drugs. There were those in the London clubs who would have given their eye-teeth for his contacts. But Khan merely smiled with lips tightly shut, heightening the mystique around him. To have answered 'diplomatic baggage' would have burst the bubble after all, wouldn't it?

In the clubs he frequented, Khan was always 'Khan the banker'. Few knew more about his life than that simple three-word statement. He always either brought with him, or else ended the evening with, the most beautiful woman around. He always ordered either Krug or Roederer Cristal. And he always paid in cash. Cash was his currency, crisp new Bank of England notes, and because of this he found favour with every club owner and restaurateur.

He was an acknowledged creature of the night. There were stories of champagne at dawn in Hyde Park, of designer dresses being delivered out of the blue to Kensington flats – and fitting the recipient perfectly. There were gold taps in his Belgravia house, and breakfast was actually *delivered* from a nearby five-star hotel. But Shari or Sherri was the first person to take the trip to Scotland with him. She was an agency model, with no bookings all week. She was, with a name like that, naturally American – from Cincinnati. Her skin was soft and very lightly tanned, and she just loved what Khan did to her in bed.

There was a problem though. It was a long and tiring drive to the Scottish residence, situated just outside Auchterarder and not a ten-minute drive from Gleneagles Hotel. Henrik and Khan had driven it in the past, but recently Khan had opted for the bank's private twelve-seater plane which was kept at an airfield to the south-west of London. It could be flown to a small airfield adjoining Edinburgh Airport, from where it was an hour by hired car to Auchterarder. The plane usually stood idle anyway, with a pilot on permanent contract, and Khan reckoned all he was costing his employers were some fuel and the pilot's expenses in Edinburgh. But this week, the plane was booked. Two of the bank's South-East Asia personnel were in Britain, and the plane was required for trips to Manchester, Newcastle, and Glasgow.

However, the airfield's owner, recognising valued custom, asked if he might be of assistance to Khan. There was an eight-seater available which could be hired for fifteen hundred pounds a day, the fee to include a pilot's services. The airfield owner stressed that fifteen hundred was cheap these days, and Khan knew this to be the case. All the same. He would be charged per day, and staying in Scotland from Friday through Monday . . .

'Would the pilot be willing to fly us up there then bring the plane back the same day, and return to Edinburgh to collect us on the Monday?' Khan listened to the silence on the other end of his car-phone. The airfield owner was considering this proposition.

'I suppose that'd be all right,' the man answered at last.

'And the charge would be for the two days only?'

'I don't know about that, Mr Khan. See, if he's got to pick you up on the Monday, that means he's tied up. He can't take any other work.'

'I see,' said Khan. 'I'll get back to you.' And he terminated the call. He considered for a moment, then placed another call, this time to the Edinburgh airfield. 'It's Mr Khan here. Would it be possible to hire a small plane, a six-seater would suffice, to bring some people back from Edinburgh to London on Monday?' He listened to the answer. 'And how much would it cost?' he asked. 'Two thousand? Yes, thank you. That's a definite booking. It's Khan. K-h-a-n. I'll be arriving in Edinburgh this afternoon. I can pay the deposit then, if that's all right. I don't suppose there would be a cash discount?'

As he said this, he tried to make it sound like a joke. But it was certainly not taken as a joke at the other end of the line. There was an agreement. A ten percent discount for cash, and no receipts issued. Khan rang off, and rang the English airfield again. 'I'll take the plane and pilot for today only. One way. Fifteen hundred pounds as agreed.' Again, he terminated the call and sat back in his seat. The BMW was entering Jermyn Street. Khan needed some shirts.

Rich people are often those who are most canny with their money. At least, the people who stay rich are, and Khan had every intention of both him and his bank remaining wealthy. He was a born haggler, but only when it mattered. It was not, for example, worth asking for a cash discount on a bottle of Krug or a club membership. This would merely make one look cheap. But in business, haggling was an ancient and honourable adjunct. He didn't really understand the British reserve in this matter. He enjoyed the London markets, where stall-holders would cajole people into buying by adding another bunch of bananas to the box they were already holding. And another bunch . . . and another . . . until suddenly some invisible, unspoken point was reached, and several hands shot out holding money. Of course, only one of them was chosen.

Londoners, native Londoners, working-class Londoners, were excellent hagglers. Often it was trained out of them, but many retained the habit and the skill. Just look at the City, at the young brokers who were just as likely to come from the East End as from Eton. These people were a pleasure to do business with. Khan totted up that he had just saved £2,300, either for the bank or for himself (depending on how it swung). He was pleased. But then, what was £2,300? The cost of a single bottle of Petrus at some wine merchants. The cost of an adequate vintage in several London restaurants. The cost of thirty shirts: a scant month's worth. Of course, because the Edinburgh end of the deal involved no receipts, there could be no allowances against tax either . . . but then Khan and his bank were not worried by UK taxation laws.

'The parking looks difficult,' Henrik called from the driver's seat. 'Shall I drop you off and drive around the block?'

'Okay. I shouldn't be more than twenty minutes.'

'Yes, sir.'

The car stopped, blocking the narrow street. Behind it, a taxi sounded its horn. Khan stepped slowly from the back of the BMW and gave the taxi driver a cool gaze. The pavements were wet, but drying fast. The summer shower was over, and the sun had appeared again. Steam rose into the sky. Khan walked on leather soles and heels through the steam and into the shop. The shop was another saving. He had found that, due to his 'regular shape', tailored shirts fitted him no better than a decent ready-made. There were four customers in the shop, each busy with an assistant.

'With you in a moment, sir,' someone said to Khan, who bowed his head in acknowledgement. He was in no hurry. He slipped his hands into his trouser pockets and examined the collar-sizes on the rows of wooden shelves. The hand in his left pocket touched something small and cold: an alarm. If he pressed its round red button, Henrik would arrive with all speed. This, too, Khan did not perceive as a luxury.

They flew up to Scotland over the west coast. The plane's interior was cramped yet somehow comfortable. There was something reassuring about the closeness of proximity. Henrik shifted seats half a dozen times, when he was not dispensing drinks. There was a cool-box on board, in which had been placed two bottles of champagne, several rounds of smoked salmon sandwiches, and small cocktail packets of pistachios and almonds. Plastic cups for the champagne though: an obvious oversight. Khan handed two cups to Henrik.

'Ask the pilot if he'd like one.'

'Yes, sir.'

The pilot could be seen, there being no curtain between cockpit and passenger deck. This annoyed Khan, too, though it could hardly be said to be the pilot's fault. Henrik returned with the two beakers. He was grinning.

'Not while he's driving, Mr Khan, but he thanks you for the thought.'

Khan nodded. Sensible, really, but then some of the pilots he'd had in the past were not what one would call top-flight. They were getting old and getting fat. Fat pilots worried Khan. They should be full of nervous energy, wiry as a result. He'd waited until well into the flight before offering the champagne, just to see if the pilot's will would crack. It hadn't.

Khan looked across to Henrik. He too was showing signs of the good, easy life. He was paid well for his services, and those services so far had not exactly taxed him, either physically or mentally. When Khan had hired him, Henrik had been muscular; almost muscle-bound. Working weights and hoping to turn pro, paying his way by acting as bouncer for a West End club owner. Khan had asked the club owner's permission before approaching Henrik with an offer of a job. The chauffeur's role hadn't appealed to the Dane, but he'd taken the job anyway. He was not stupid. He knew that as bodyguard he would have to accompany Khan just about everywhere: everywhere glamorous, everywhere expensive, everywhere that was Somewhere.

But too many hours in the driving seat were taking their toll. Henrik was still big, still strong, but there was excess flesh now, too. Khan, who worked out each day, appreciated Henrik's problem; it was one of mental application. The Dane was no longer hungry. Look at him, champagne in both hands, sipping from one cup then from the other, gazing out of the window down on to the visible landscape. Khan was aware that Henrik might have to go. There might be a termination of contract, the hiring of someone new, someone strong but hungry. Would he perhaps keep Henrik on as driver? He was a good, safe driver after all. But no, that would be to denigrate the man, to humble him. More importantly, it might well make Henrik bitter. And a bitter man was an enemy. It didn't do to employ potential spies, potential adversaries. No, Henrik would have to go. Soon. There was that new doorman at the Dorica Club . . .

'This is great, really great.' Shari or Sherri slumped her head against Khan's shoulder. She was dressed well. He'd been relieved when they'd stopped the car outside her block and she'd opened the door and started down the steps, smiling, waving, carrying two large holdalls . . . and above all dressed well. Discreetly sensual. Not too much make-up, not too much perfume. A clinging red dress which just met her knees. Her tanned legs did not need covering. Her shoes were red too. She knew how well her blonde hair and high cheekbones suited red.

'You're very special,' he told her now, rubbing one smooth knee. It was true: they were *all* very special.

'Touching down in ten minutes,' called the pilot. One bottle of champagne was still unopened, the sandwiches barely touched.

'You're special too, Khan,' said Shari or Sherri.

'Thank you, my dear.' He patted the back of her hand, which lay on his right thigh. 'I'm sure we're going to have a wonderful time.'

'Yes,' she said. 'Me too.'

Across the aisle from them, Henrik drained first one beaker and then the other. His chin dropped against his neck as he stifled a belch.


A wonderful time. Well, yes, at first it was. But it struck Khan that there was something not quite right. The time was wonderful but not perfect. It wasn't that he was worrying about bank business. The bank was always in and on his mind, even on these trips north. Scotland was not a refuge. There were computers and modems and faxes and telephones in his house. A call might come on his portable phone during lunch or dinner, or to his bedside telephone in the middle of the night. New York might call to warn of an incoming fax, for his eyes only. Seoul might need information. Karachi, Lahore, Patna,

Bombay, Bangkok, George Town, Shanghai ... not everyone appreciated what the local hour was when they called. If it was the middle or the beginning or the end of their banking day, then it was Khan's banking day too.

But no, it was nothing to do with business. Business was not a problem. Was the problem Shari or Sherri? Ah, yes, maybe. Maybe that was it. She did love what he did to her in bed ... and elsewhere in and out of the house. Her American accent grated, but only a little. She was not over-talkative, which was a relief to him. And she looked good all the time. She made herself presentable. What then?

Well ... There came a time when, sated, he liked his women to open themselves up a little to him, to tell him about their lives. Normally, he was uninterested in pasts, but there was something about the aftermath of the sexual act. He liked to listen to their stories then, and file them away. So that he could assure himself he had been fucking someone's history, a real flesh and blood human, and not just a beautiful dummy.

And it was here that Shari or Sherri had disappointed him. She had disappointed him by being at first vague, and then by making obvious mistakes. For instance, she told him about a childhood incident when a boy neighbour had lifted up her skirt and slipped his hot little hand inside her pants. She told the story twice, and the first time the boy's hand had gone down the front of her pants, the second time the back. Khan hadn't commented, but it had made him wonder. He made her work harder, recalling more and more of her past for him. He got her to go over the same story twice, once at breakfast and once over dinner, checking for mistakes in the retelling. There were one or two, not significant in themselves.

He remembered how he met her. In a club. She'd been with a friend, a male friend, an admirer perhaps. She'd caught Khan's eye several times, and he'd held her glances, until eye contact between them became more prolonged and meaningful. He was a sucker for this kind of conquest, the kind where he almost literally tore a woman from another man's arms. By the end of the evening she was at his table, and the other suitor had vanished. It had been easy, and she'd been ravishing, and he'd felt the sweet, warm glow of success.

He knew she worked as a model. Well, he knew she *said* she worked as a model. He'd once picked her up outside a prestigious model agency off Oxford Street, but then when his car had arrived she'd already been waiting on the pavement, hadn't she? How was he to know that she'd ever actually been inside the building? What really did he *know* about her? Precious little, it suddenly seemed to him. He'd liked that in the past, had preferred it. Keeping things casual, no hint of a more meaningful, a more lasting relationship. But now . . . Suddenly he wanted to know more about her. What was her last name? Kazowski? Kaprinski? Something East European. She told him she'd changed it to Capri for modelling purposes. Shari Capri or Sherri Capri. Stupid name. Stupid names.

And another thing, wasn't she overfriendly towards Henrik? With her 'Thank you, Henrik' whenever she stepped into or out of the car. Her smiles to him. The way she lightly touched his arm if she wanted to ask him something. Checking that she was in the bath, Khan strode quickly to his study, unlocked the door (he was never so foolish, so trusting as to leave it unlocked, but then locks were easy to pick, weren't they?), and made for his desk. He glanced at it, looking for signs that things had been moved, pages turned over. Nothing. He checked his computer for a certain phone number, then picked up the telephone and dialled London. An 081 number, Outer London. There was a young firm used by the bank sometimes. They were dynamic, and they got results. Nobody wanted to know *how* they got results, but they got them. There was no one in the office, but as he'd expected a recording gave him another phone number where he could reach one of the partners. He entered this number onto his computer for future reference, then dialled it. The call was answered almost immediately.

'Hello, is that Mr Allison? It's Khan here. I'm calling from Scotland. There's a job I'd like done. Private, not on the bank's account. I want you to check on a Miss Sherri S-h-e-r-r-i or Shari S-h-a-r-i Capri C-a-p-r-i. I'll give you her home address and where she says she works. I want anything on her you can find. Oh, and Mr Allison, she's up here with me, so there should be no problems. I mean, you won't bump into her should you happen to . . . well, you know what I mean. Her home address? Yes, of course . . .'

Afterwards, he felt a little relieved. Allison was *extremely* capable, ex-CID. And his partner Crichton had a pedigree which took in both the Parachute Regiment and the SAS. Yes, a trouble shared *was* a trouble halved. Khan felt better. So much so that he was able to put his troubles out of his mind for quarter of an hour, time spent in the bathroom with a wet and so very slippery Shari or Sherri Capri . . .

On their last evening, they dined in. There was a local chef who, on days off, could occasionally be persuaded to cook for Khan and his guests.

Usually, Khan reserved this treat for larger dinner parties. But on Sunday morning news came through of a spectacular deal which had been concluded by the South-East Asia personnel during their whistlestop tour of the British Isles. A great deal of money would be travelling from the UK to the bank's South-East Asia office, and it would travel via the London office where a certain amount, as always, would be held back in the name of handling fees. A sum slightly in excess of one million sterling.

It was a job well done, and Khan, who had played no part in it, felt a little of its success rub off on him. A quick call to the chef, Gordon Sinclair, had secured his services, and when all was said and done it was practically as cheap as eating out since this way Khan would drink champagne, wine and spirits from his own well-stocked cellar. And at the end of the evening it was always pleasant to share a malt with Gordon and talk about food and the appreciation of food. Gordon knew that Khan had contacts in London, that he had eaten in all the top restaurants and was on first-name terms with many of the restaurateurs and chefs – not merely in London but, it seemed, all over. And Khan knew that Gordon had itchy feet, that the only thing tying him to Scotland was his Scottishness. He would have to flee soon if he were really to start – the term came to Khan with a smile – *cooking*: a quality London restaurant, where he could make a name for himself, and then his own restaurant under his own name. That was the route to success.

They would talk about these things and more. Perhaps Shari would be listening, or perhaps she would have retired for the night, to be joined by Khan later.

Yes, it was Shari, not Sherri. Shari Capri. Allison had phoned with this information, and with a few other snippets. But as he pointed out, weekends weren't the best time to track down information, especially not from places of employment. Come Monday, he could work on the model agency, but not before. It was half in Khan's mind to ask if he'd considered breaking and entering, but such a question would have been in considerable bad taste besides which, if his phone were bugged, he could be accused of incitement to commit a criminal act. That would never do. So he had to accept what scant information Allison had gleaned, and wait until Monday. By Monday he would be back in London, he would have said goodbye to Shari, with promises of phone calls and meetings for dinner – promises he seldom kept as a rule. But it might be that he'd have to keep tabs on her for a little while longer, just until he knew the truth.

'More wine, Shari?'

They were alone in the dining room. The kitchen was a long way away. Henrik, dismissed for the evening, would be in one of the bars in Auchterarder. He'd told Khan about a barmaid with whom he'd become friendly. So it was just Shari and Khan, and, his presence no more than a distant clang of pots and sizzle of fat, Gordon Sinclair. And Gordon's girlfriend, who had come to help him in the kitchen. She would leave before dessert was served, while Gordon would linger, clearing up a little and loading his excess ingredients back into the boot of his small sports car. Khan hadn't met the girlfriend before. She was attractive, if a bit red in the cheeks. Very Scottish: shy, elusive even. Plump too, or at least well-rounded. Khan had the idea that Gordon and she might make a go of a restaurant together. Perhaps she was the knot which tied him to the area. Khan was beginning to form an idea about a restaurant, financed by him and run by Gordon and his girlfriend . . .

'Yes, please,' said Shari. 'This is delicious.'

Trout in almonds. Local trout, naturally, with the cream sauce flavoured by a little island malt. The sauce succeeded in not overpowering the delicate fish. The julienne of vegetables remained a little overcooked for Khan's tastes, but he knew Shari liked them soft almost to the point of mush. She retained the annoying American habit of cutting and spooning everything up with the use of just her fork.

'Delicious,' she said again.

He looked at her and smiled. Maybe he was becoming paranoid. Maybe there was nothing to worry about. Look at her – beautiful, fragile. Everything about her was surface. She couldn't possibly be hiding anything from him. No, he was being stupid. He should forget everything and just enjoy this final night with her.

'Yes, it is delicious, isn't it?' he said, pouring a little more Meursault. Meursault was a little rich for trout on its own, but the sauce both deserved and could cope with it. He knew Gordon liked to surprise him, but Khan guessed some prime beef would be next (albeit in a sauce of exotic provenance), followed by an Orkney cheese and freshly made crannachan. And the beauty was that all the mess in the kitchen and the plates and things in the dining-room could be left just as they were. Mrs MacArthur would come in on Monday afternoon and tidy the lot up.

Before he'd employed her, and again twice since, Khan had had Mrs MacArthur checked over by a detective agency in Dundee. The agency reckoned that not only was she clean, she was practically unbribable. So Khan didn't mind that she held a set of keys to the house and to the alarm system. Besides, she never entered the study, which was kept on a separate alarm circuit anyway (to which Khan and the local police held the only keys).

'Delicious,' he said, raising his glass as if in a toast.

It was one of those special pubs where at weekends after

closing time the lights are turned off and the regulars drink on in darkness. But not on a Sunday. Some traditions held fast on a Sunday, and the pub closed at ten-thirty sharp. Which suited Henrik really, since he'd offered to drive Nessa home and she had laughingly accepted.

'Though it's only a five-minute walk,' she'd added.

'Well, we can always drive home the long way.'

She'd said nothing at that. He'd been waiting outside in the rented Ford Scorpio, the stereo playing, engine running. She said goodnight to the barman, who was locking up, then walked smartly to the edge of the kerb. Henrik was already out of the car, so he could hold the passenger door open for her. She gave him a funny look.

'Thank you, kind sir,' she said.

He got back into the driver's seat. 'Where to?' he asked her.

'Home, of course.'

'*Straight* home?'

She gave him the look again. 'Not necessarily.'

They stopped by a field just off the dual carriageway to the south of the town, and stayed there half an hour or so, chatting, kissing. They were as clumsy as teenagers, even with the seats tilted back. Eventually she laughed again and loosed herself from him.

'I'd better get back. My mum'll be getting worried.'

He nodded. 'Okay.' They drove more or less in silence after that, except for her few directions. Until eventually they arrived at the stone bungalow.

'This is it. Thanks for the lift.'

'I'll be back again next week probably. What about dinner?'

'Dinner?'

'At the hotel if you like.'

'Depends on my shifts really.'

'Maybe I can phone you at the pub?'

She thought this over. 'Yes, okay,' she said. 'Do that.'

'Goodnight, Nessa.' He pulled her to him for a final kiss, but she wriggled free and glanced out of the window.

'My mother might be watching. Night, Henrik.' And she relented, pecking him on the cheek. He watched her as she opened and closed her gate, gave him a final wave, and climbed the steps to her front door. He thought he saw a curtain twitch in one of the unlit windows. The hall light was on. She closed the door softly behind her. Henrik slipped the gear lever into the Drive position and started off. At the end of her road, he ejected Barry Manilow from the tape-player and pushed home some heavy metal, turning the volume all the way up. He drove through Auchterarder's dark deserted streets for some time with the driver's window down, grinning to himself. Then he headed home. No doubt he would have to lie in bed and put up with all that squealing and squawking from Khan's room, all the grunting and puffing. He wondered if it was a put-on, maybe a recording or something. Was it supposed to impress him? Or did neither party realise he had ears?

Mind you, she was a particular beauty, this present catch. And the way she looked at Henrik himself . . . the way she touched him, as though wanting to assure herself that his build was a fact and not some fantasy. Yes, maybe when Khan had finished with her, maybe there'd be room for Henrik to move in. He knew where she worked in London. He knew where she lived. He might just happen to be passing. He was pretty sure she'd make even more noise with him than she did with Khan. Yes, pretty damned sure. His grin was even wider as he drove through the gates of the walled and detached house.

He locked the high metal gates behind him. The chef would be long gone. There was no sign of another car. A short gravel driveway led to the front of the house. The place looked to be in darkness. It was only ten to twelve. Maybe they'd finished and were asleep. Maybe he wouldn't have to resort to vodka to send him into oblivion. He left the car at the top of the drive rather than parking it in the small garage. He stood for a moment, leaning against the cooling body of the car, listening to the silence. A rustling of trees, a bird in the distance, maybe even some frogs. But that was all. And it was so dark. So utterly dark, with the stars shining high in the sky. So different from London, so quiet and isolated. Certainly isolated. They'd talked of keeping guard dogs which could prowl the garden around the house, but then who would feed them and look after them? So instead there was the alarm system, linked to the local station *and* to Perth constabulary (the latter for times when the former was closed or unmanned).

His eyes having adjusted to the dark, Henrik walked to the front door and opened it, then locked it behind him, using the mortice deadlock as well as the Yale. The light was on at the far end of the hall, where the central alarm system was contained in a metal box secured to the wall beside the door to the kitchen. He used one key to open the box, and another to turn on the system. The bedrooms upstairs were en suite, so he set the pressure-pad alarm for the whole house. No need for anyone to leave their rooms before morning. In the morning, the first person up would have a minute to deactivate the alarm system before the bells started ringing both outside the house itself and inside the police station.

Now, having turned on the system, he had a minute to get to his room, a minute before it was fully operational. He headed for the stairs. There was a soft buzzing from the alarm box which told him it was working. When the buzzing stopped, the various window devices and movement-sensitive beams and pressure-pads woke up for the evening. Silence upstairs, and no light from Khan's bedroom. Henrik switched off the hall lights and closed his door behind him.

She knows the house almost as well as she knows the surrounding area. In the past two days she's been here half a dozen times, and twice at the dead of night, the witching hour.

She's been in the grounds, and has peered through windows into rooms, through the letterbox into the hall. She has seen that the alarm box sits at the end of the hall, attached to the wall. She knows the kind of alarm it will be. She has checked door and window locks. She has even gone so far as to pass an angled mirror on the end of a stick through the letterbox, the better to see the locks from the inside. All has proven very satisfactory. The nearest house is half a mile away. There are no alarms in the garden, no infra red beams which, when broken, would turn on floodlights. No lights at all to complicate her approach. No cameras. No dogs. She is especially pleased that there are no dogs.

The gates are high and topped with spikes, but the wall is a pathetic affair with broken bottle-glass cemented to its top. Too pathetic for it to have been Khan's work. It must already have been in place when he bought the house. The glass has been worn smooth over the years. She won't even bother to cover it with a blanket before she climbs into the garden.

But first, there is the alarm system. She straps on a special climbing-belt – the sort known to every telephone engineer – and attaches spiked soles to her shoes. The spiked soles are for wear by gardeners so they can aerate their lawns. She has modified the spikes only a little. She drove to a garden centre outside Perth for the spike-shoes, and bought a lot of other stuff as well, stuff she didn't need, bought solely to disguise this singular purchase. She passed two garden centres before reaching Perth. Police might investigate one or two garden centres, but she doubts they would go much further afield.

She is now standing beside a telegraph-pole in a field across the lane from Khan's house. She knows this is a dangerous period. She will soon be visible from the house. She checks her watch. Two. The bodyguard locked up two hours ago. They will rise early tomorrow to catch their plane back south. Or rather, if things go as intended, they won't.

She waits another minute. What moon there is disappears behind a hefty bank of cloud. She ties her belt around the pole as well as herself, grips the pole, hugging herself to it, and begins to climb. Eventually, she knows, twenty-odd feet up, there will be foot-holds to help her. But for now she has only her own strength. She knows it will be enough. She does not hesitate.

At the top of the pole, beneath the wires themselves, sits a large junction box containing the thinner wires running back to homes in the area. She thinks Khan's alarm system works via telephone lines. From what she's seen of it, it looks just the type. If it doesn't . . . Well, she will fall back on other plans, other options. But for now she has to keep busy, working fast while the moon stays hidden. She slips a pencil-thin torch into her mouth, holding it as she would a cigarette, and, by its light, begins to unscrew the front from the junction box.

Terrorists aren't just people who terrorise. They are people who hunger for knowledge, the knowledge of how things work. In knowing how things work, you discover how society works, and that knowledge can help cripple society. She knows she can disrupt communications, bring transport systems to a halt, generate mayhem by computer. Given the knowledge, anything can be achieved. The junction box holds no surprises for her, only a certain measure of relief. She stares at the confusion of wires for a moment, and knows that she can stay with plan one.

There is a distinct colour-coding for the wires from Khan's alarm system. The puzzle is that there seem to be two sets. One for the main house . . . The other? A room inside the house, perhaps, or a garage or workshop. She decides to take both sets out with her neat rubber-handled wire-clippers. It was a good alarm system, but not a great one. A great alarm system would send a constant pulse to the outside world. And if that pulse were interrupted, *then* the alarm bells would ring. Cutting the wires would cause the alarm to sound in the distant police station. But such systems are unreliable and seldom used. They are nuisances, sounding whenever a fluctuation in current occurs, or a phone-line momentarily breaks up. Society demands that alarms not be a nuisance.

There were times when Witch worried about society.

The job done, she slipped slowly back down the pole and untied her harness at the bottom, putting it back in her heavy black holdall along with the spikes and her tools. Now for the wall. She clambered up and sat on the top for a second, studying the windows in the house, then fell into the dark garden. She had climbed the wall precisely twelve feet to the left of the gate, so that she fell onto grass and not into shrubbery. She'd decided to enter the way most burglars would – by the back entrance – not that she was intending to make this look like a burglary. No, this was to be messy. Her employers wanted her to leave a message, a clear statement of their feelings.

The kitchen then, its door bolted top and bottom with a mortice lock beside the handle. The bedrooms are to the front of the house. She can make a certain amount of noise here. Silence, of course, would be best. Silence is the ideal. In her holdall is a carefully measured and cut piece of Fablon, purchased at a department store in Perth. Ghastly pattern and colour, though the assistant had praised it as though it were an Impressionist painting. Witch is surprised people still use it. She measured the kitchen windows yesterday, and chose the smaller for her purpose. Slowly, carefully, she unpeels the Fablon and presses it against the smaller window, covering it exactly. In the department store she also purchased some good-quality yellow dusters, while at a small hardware shop the keen young assistant was only too pleased to sell some garden twine and a hammer to a lady keen to stake out her future vegetable plots.

She takes the hammer from her holdall. She has used some twine to tie a duster around the head. Out of the spare cuts of Fablon she has made some makeshift handles, which she attaches to the sheet of Fablon stuck to the window. She grips one of these handles as, softly, near soundlessly, she begins to tap away at the glass, which falls away from the window-frame but stays attached to the Fablon. Within three minutes she is lifting the whole window out from its frame, laying it on the ground. The alarm is just outside the kitchen door. If she'd set it off, it would probably be buzzing by now. But she can't hear it. She can't hear anything, not even her heart.

Upstairs, Henrik is asleep and dreaming in Danish. He's dreaming of barmaids with pumps attached to their breasts, and of flying champagne bottles, and of winning a bodybuilding contest against Khan and the pre-movie star Schwarzenegger. He drank one glass of neat vodka before retiring, and watched ten minutes of the satellite movie on his eighteen-inch television before falling asleep, waking half an hour later just long enough to switch off the television.

He sleeps and he dreams with one hand tight between his legs, something he's done since childhood. Girlfriends have commented on it, laughed at it even. If he catches himself doing it, he shoves the hand under a pillow, but it always seems to creep south again of its own volition.

The barmaids are singing. Topless for some reason, and singing in a language he doesn't understand. His name? His name? Can they possibly be singing . . . his name?

'Wake up!' A whisper. A woman's urgent hiss. His eyes open to blackness and he tries to sit up, but a feminine hand pushes at his chest, and he sinks back down again. The hand remains against his chest, rubbing it. A silky-smooth hand.

Shari's hand.

'What is it?' he hisses back. 'What's the matter, Shari?'

Her face seems very close to him. 'It's Khan. He's sound asleep . . . as usual. He just doesn't . . . I don't want to put him down or anything, but he just doesn't *satisfy* me.'

Topless barmaids . . . breasts. Henrik gives a groggy half-smile in the dark. He reaches a hand to where he imagines her chest is. He's not sure whether he finds it or not. She's wearing her clothes . . . maybe some sort of nightdress, a baby-doll or something.

'I knew you'd come,' he whispers. 'I was going to call on you when we got back to London. Khan's a shit, he'll dump you the minute the plane lands.'

92

'I know.' Her hand rubbing him, rubbing in wider circles, taking in shoulders and down over his stomach. Feels good. 'He doesn't understand how I like it.'

'Like it?'

'Sex.' A low guttural sound, more moan than whisper. 'I love it.' Still rubbing, smooth hand. 'I like it tied up. Khan doesn't like that, but it's such a turn on. What about you, huh? Is it a turn on for you?'

'Sure.' He's waking up now. *Tied up?*

'Want to try? I've got some of Khan's ties. Want to try it with *his* ties?'

'Why not?' Her hand is insistent on him now. She moves one of his arms, then the other, until his hands are behind him, grasping at the bedposts. He realises now that *she* wants to tie *him* up . . . not what he had in mind, but all the same . . . And in fact she's already busy. It's easy for her to slip the ties around his wrists.

'Not too tight are they?'

'No.' Lying. His wrists feel like the circulation's been cut.

And around his feet too, so he is splayed and naked on the bed. He knows he's in good shape, but sucks his gut in a little anyway. He's stiff as a beer-pump himself now. Damn, he'll make her bells ring, little Shari's bells ring. Oh Christ, but if she calls out . . . what if Khan hears? He's a pretty light sleeper, what if he bursts in while he's lying here all trussed . . .

Bells . . . make her bells ring . . .

*How come she hasn't set off the alarm system?*

He's forming the question when he hears tape being torn, and next thing her hand is over his face, wrapping tape around his mouth, around the back of his head, mouth again, and again, and again. Jesus fucking Christ! He grunts, struggles. But then he hears a cli-chick, and another, and another, and another. Four. And he's not being held by ties any more. Something cold instead. And then the light goes on.

It takes his eyes a second or two to deal with the difference. He sees himself naked, and the handcuffs around his ankles. They're around his wrists too, pinning him to the bedposts top and bottom. No problem. He can contract himself and snap the god-damned bedposts off if he has to. Idiot that he was in the first place. Khan'll kill him for this. But who is the woman? The woman dressed in black, who's standing there at the foot of the bed. He hasn't been able to focus on her yet, but now she's stepping forwards and

Thwock!

One blow to the right temple with her hammer, and it's back to the barmaids for Henrik. Witch looks down on him and smiles. Well, what's the point of working if you can't have a little fun?

Across the corridor and down the hall, two people are asleep in a large rumpled bed. The whole room smells of perfume and bath-soap and sex. Their clothes are distributed across the floor without any discernible pattern or progress. The man is naked and lies on his side without any covering. The woman lies on her front, hair tangled across the pillow. She is covered by a white sheet, and her left arm hangs limply down from the edge of the bed, fingernails grazing the carpet. No fun and games here. Now the work begins in earnest. The arm is actually a bonus, lying bulging-veined like that. She uses the pencil-thin torch to help her prepare and test the syringe, which she then jabs home into one of Shari Capri's veins, just where the forearm meets the elbow. Not merely asleep now but unconscious. An explosion wouldn't wake her. Gunshots would cause no flickering of her eyelids. She'll wake up in the morning, glueymouthed, thirsty, with a sore head most probably.

These will be the least of her problems.

Now only Khan remains. He seems to be sleeping peacefully. She wonders what he's dreaming of. What *do* you dream of when you have everything? You dream of more. Or else the terror of losing everything you've got. Either would be appropriate, considering what is about to happen, and *why* it's about to happen. Witch squats on the floor, her face in line with Khan's. She's not six feet from him – not quite close enough for him to take a waking, desperate lunge at her, but close enough so that she can study him. And studying him, he becomes less human to her, and less human still. He becomes a motive, a deal, a set of crooked figures on an accounting sheet. He becomes her pay-off.

'Mr Khan,' she says softly. 'Mr Khan.' An eye opens to a slit. Her voice is as casual as any nurse's would be to the patient who's come out of the operating theatre. 'Time to wake up now, Mr Khan.'

The difference being, of course, that now Khan is awake, the operating theatre waits for him. Witch, smiling, already has the good sharp knife in her hand. It flashes through her mind that she has been in Britain exactly a week.

Happy anniversary.

# The Protean Self

# Monday 8 June

'So how was France then?' Greenleaf was smiling. Some might have called it a grimace.

Doyle smiled too: with pleasure. '*Mag-ni-fique*, John. Just *mag-ni-fique*. Here . . .' He reached into a carrier bag. 'Have a bottle of beer. I've another 199 of them in the garage at home.'

Greenleaf accepted the small green bottle. 'Thanks,' he said. 'I'll savour it.'

'You do that, John. That's one franc's worth of best Alsace lager in there. Four-point-nine alcohol, so take it slow, eh?' And Doyle gave Greenleaf a big wink.

I don't really hate him, Greenleaf thought suddenly. He's smarmy all right, but I wonder how seriously he takes himself. Maybe the whole thing is just him sending himself up. I don't really hate him. It's just gentle loathing.

'So,' Doyle was saying, looking around him at the office. 'The place didn't crumble in my absence? I'm hurt. I used to think I was the only thing holding this place together.'

'We do our best, Doyle. It's not easy, but we do our best.'

'Good man. So, what did you get in Folkestone?'

'Some cod and a couple of bloaters.'

Doyle laughed for a full fifteen seconds. 'Christ, John, I think a bit of me's rubbing off on you. Don't ask me which bit, mind.'

'As long as I don't catch anything.'

'There you go again! Catch anything. You're pinching all my best lines.'

'Lines, eh?' Even Greenleaf was smiling now: also with pleasure. 'Can I take it I'm part of a running gag about fish?'

'Bear in mind one of the poor sods who got blown up was called Perch.'

'Yes, I met his mother.'

The smile vanished from Doyle's face. 'Yes, doesn't do to joke, does it? So, what did you *really* find in Folkestone?'

'Haven't you read the report?'

Doyle wrinkled his nose. 'Give me the details. I'll read it later.'

'Well, I found pretty much what you said I would. Looks like it was an explosion all right. Guy's business was in trouble, he was open to any kind of offer. They found two grand on him. I managed to trace the notes.'

Doyle's eyes opened wide. 'Yeah?' Greenleaf nodded. 'Well, good for you, John. Good for you. And?'

'Old notes. Part of a ransom paid to some kidnappers in Italy five years ago.'

'What?'

'It's all in my report.'

'Maybe I'd better read it after all.'

'So what about Calais?'

'Not a lot to tell really.'

'I saw the stuff you sent through by modem on Friday.'

Doyle shrugged. 'Something to impress the old man. A bit of technology. There wasn't much substance to what I sent.'

Greenleaf nodded. This was true. What's more, it was a shrewd observation of Trilling, who had slavered over the print-out more for what it *was*, the manner of its transmission, than for what it contained.

'Still,' said Doyle, 'sending it as it happened meant I had the weekend clear. I found this great restaurant, five courses for a tenner. You should nip over for—'

'Doyle! Greenleaf! In my office!'

They looked at one another for a silent moment. Greenleaf spoke first.

'Sounds like the headmaster wants to see us.'

'John,' said Doyle, 'you took the words right out of my mouth.'

It occurred to Greenleaf that the reason he was feeling so . . . so damned *mellow* this morning was the weekend he'd just spent with Shirley. A glorious weekend. On Saturday they'd gone shopping at Brent Cross and bought a new dining-room suite, the one she'd been nagging him about for months. The summer sales had suddenly seen it reduced in price by twenty-five percent, and Greenleaf, seeing this as a reward for his previous prudence, had agreed they should buy the thing. They'd celebrated with dinner at an Indian place near their home, then watched half a video before going to bed. And on Sunday, waking late, they'd taken a picnic to Trent Park . . . All very different to Doyle's weekend, he was sure, but he felt the better for it.

'Sit down, please,' said Commander Trilling, himself already seated. He didn't look in the best of humours. His *Financial Times* sat folded, apparently unread, on a corner of his desk. 'I've just had a long chat with Mrs Parry over at Spook City. It seems I was right. She's been holding out on us.'

'Tut tut,' commented Doyle.

'Yes,' said Trilling. 'This double sinking is, apparently, a near copycat of a sinking several years ago off Japan.'

'Japan?' This from Greenleaf.

'Japan,' said the Commander. 'A terrorist entered Japan and then blew up the boat which had taken her there.'

'*Her?*' From Doyle.

'Her,' said Trilling.

'Which group, sir?' asked Greenleaf.

'Mrs Parry's more than a bit vague on that. She's sending over a courier with what information there is. The pair of you'd better study it. Makes sense if you think about it. Terrorists kidnap a girl, then the ransom money turns up after the Folkestone explosion. Simplest explanation is that someone from the original terrorist group has entered Britain.'

'And,' added Doyle, 'the "someone" in question also carried out an assassination in Japan.'

'Quite so.'

'Political?'

'Not entirely. A peace campaigner. The rumour, according to Mrs Parry, is that some arms dealers might have chipped in to hire a killer.'

'Nice people to do business with,' said Doyle.

Greenleaf said nothing. He was noting how Trilling harped on that *Mrs*. He really *was* pissed off with Parry.

'So now,' the Commander was saying, 'there's a good possibility that a terrorist, a hired assassin, is somewhere in the country. Maybe a woman. And she's been here for a few days now, while Mrs Parry has withheld vital information from us.'

Greenleaf: 'So by now she could be anywhere.'

'Anywhere.'

'And her target?'

Trilling shrugged. 'That's our next line of inquiry. Always supposing we *are* dealing with an individual – of whatever sex. Parry herself only sounds half-convinced, but the original theory starts with a retired agent called

Dominic Elder. I know Elder of old. He's prone to exaggeration but basically sound.'

'So what do we do, sir?'

'I want you to put together a list of possible targets, political or otherwise. Including peace campaigners, journalists, judges, anyone of influence really. A lot of it will already be in the files, it's just a matter of collation.'

'The summit's the obvious contender,' said Doyle.

'Unfortunately that's true.'

'Do we have a description of the woman?'

'Not one that would help.'

'It's not much to go on, is it?'

'No,' said Trilling, 'it's not. But we've got the point of landing, and that's a start.'

'Depends, sir,' said Greenleaf. 'She may have left the boat at any point along the coast.'

'Well, let's take it that she ... or *he* ... or *they* ... didn't. Let's start with a three-mile strip either side of Folkestone. Either there was a car waiting, which would make sense, or else the terrorist walked into town.'

'Or away from it.'

'Or away from it,' agreed Trilling. 'Whatever, it was well past midnight. At that time of night, anything arouses interest. A parked car on a deserted road ... someone walking along that road ... maybe even someone coming ashore. Let's get men on to it, asking questions, stopping drivers. Put up checkpoints on all the roads into Folkestone, and especially after midnight. Stop every driver and ask them if they saw anything suspicious. Most vehicles that time of night will be lorries, so check haulage firms, delivery vans, the lot.'

'That's a ton of work, sir.'

'I know it is. Would you rather we let this person take a pot-shot at a visiting dignitary? Think what it would do to the tourist trade.'

'It'd make the roads a bit quieter,' commented Doyle, and received a filthy look from Trilling.

'Maximum effort, gentlemen, starting now. As soon as the courier arrives, I'll let you have copies of whatever there is. Remember, maximum effort. Whatever it takes.'

'Whatever it takes, sir,' agreed Doyle.

'Sir, what about a name for the operation?'

'For what it's worth, Parry and her crew used the name Witch.'

'But that's not the name of the gang?'

'No, it's just something Dominic Elder thought up.'

'What about Operation Bedknobs then?' Doyle suggested. 'You know, *Bedknobs and Broomsticks*.'

'Or just Witch Hunt,' Greenleaf added.

'I don't like the connotations of witch hunt,' commented Trilling. 'And Bedknobs is merely stupid. Let's go with Broomstick. Operation Broomstick. Now, both of you, get sweeping!'

In unison: 'Yes, sir.'


She sat staring from her desk, staring towards and out of her open door. It had been an uncomfortable conversation, and thinking back on it Joyce Parry realised that she might have phrased things differently; that she might, unusually for her, have played it all wrong. There were strong ties between her department and Special Branch. The secret services held no powers of arrest, and depended on Special Branch help in that, as in many other things. It didn't do to fall out. Especially not with Bill Trilling, who was a crotchety sod at the best of times, and not the easiest person either to work or merely to liaise with.

No, she'd played him all wrong. She'd tried to soothe things, to work *around* the problem. Best just to have dived in, admitting a cock-up, giving assurances that it wouldn't happen again. A little bit of grovelling and Trilling would have been satisfied. But having seen her grovel once, wouldn't he have demanded more? She didn't like to look weak. She certainly didn't like to look weak to people like Trilling. No, in the long run she'd probably done the right thing. She'd been strong and she'd tried to be diplomatic, and he would remember that. Always supposing one or both of them kept their present jobs . . .

*If* the woman Dominic Elder called Witch had entered the country, and *if* she carried out an assassination, then questions would be asked of the security and intelligence services. There could be no doubting where the buck would stop: it would stop with Bill Trilling and with her. But Trilling had a trump card. His men had been sent to investigate the double sinking without knowing of the possible link with the Japanese sinking six years before. So the buck came, finally, to Joyce Parry. In her defence, she could point out that it was six years ago, that it was merely a notion that had come into her head. There was nothing to prove that Witch was in Britain. Probably, there would be no proof until she or he or they made her or his or their move. But by then it would be too late. Of course, Barclay should have spoken to her before contacting Special Branch. He'd take a certain portion of the blame, but not enough to save her from forced resignation . . . She shivered at the thought. She'd worked so hard to get here, harder than any man would have had to work to achieve the same high office.

She didn't need Bill Trilling as an enemy; she needed him as a friend. But she was damned if she'd crawl or beg or even simper. She'd be herself. If he helped, he would help because it was in everyone's interests for him to and not because she'd asked him 'please'. Yes, she was stubborn. Dominic had always said it was her least alluring attribute.

He was one to talk.

Did Dominic hold the key? She should talk to him anyway about his meeting with Barclay. She wondered what he'd made of Michael Barclay . . . She thought she knew the answer, but it would be interesting to hear it. Besides, Dominic knew such a lot – or thought he did – about Witch. She needed friends. She needed people working *for* her rather than against her. If Witch was in the country, and if Witch was going to be caught, she could ignore nobody.

She picked up her receiver and, from memory, dialled his number. For her efforts, she got a constant tone: number unobtainable. She checked his phone number on the computer: she'd transposed the last two numbers. She dialled again. This time, he picked up the telephone on the first ring.

'Hello, Dominic, it's Joyce.'

'Yes, hello. I thought you'd call. I've been thinking about you.'

'Oh?'

'You just can't get the staff these days, can you?'

'I take it Barclay didn't meet with your approval?'

'Let's say he strikes me as . . . naive.'

'Weren't we all once?'

He ignored this. 'I blame computers. People sit in front of them all day thinking they're the answer.' Joyce, staring at his phone number on her computer screen, smiled at this. 'They're just the *tools*. People don't go out into the world any more.'

'I don't remember going out into the world.'

'Oh come on, Joyce, you were a field agent for – what? – five years?'

'And much good did it do me.'

106

'It broadened your mind.'

'I had to be broad-minded, Dominic, working with you.'

'That joke's a decade old, Joyce.'

'Then let's change the subject. I take it you weren't able to help Barclay?'

'He wasn't able to focus on what I was telling him.'

'So you did tell him about Witch?'

'I told him *all* about Witch. Much good will it do any of us. Joyce, if you need my help, I'm here. But I can be anywhere you want, just say the word.'

'I may take you up on that, Dominic.'

'Do.'

'I'm not sure there's funding for a freelancer.'

'I don't want money, Joyce. I want *her*.'

Joyce Parry smiled. Yes, he was committed all right. More, he was obsessed. Was she merely opening an old wound, or could she help him exorcise the ghost?

'I'll call you,' she said merely. 'Meantime, any suggestions?'

'I take it Special Branch are covering this end of things?'

'At the moment, yes.'

'Then at the moment, I'd leave them to it. What about sending someone to Calais?'

'Why?'

'It was her leaping-off point this trip. Someone may know something.'

'Special Branch already sent someone.'

'What? Some detective from New Scotland Yard? Spoke French did he? What was he looking for? How long was he there?'

Still sharp, Dominic. Maybe this *will* be good for you. God knows, you're not old enough for the cottage-and-garden routine, she thought. 'I believe he stayed there overnight, and he spoke a little French.'

'One night? Dinner at his hotel and a few gifts for his mistress. He'll have listened to what the local *gendarmes* tell him, then reported it back verbatim. It's hardly what you'd call Intelligence.'

'So you think we should send one of our own?'

'Yes.' A pause. 'Send Barclay.'

'Barclay?'

'Why not? He speaks French, and travel *does* broaden the mind.'

'I thought you said you didn't like him?'

'I don't recall saying anything of the kind. Remind me to play back the tape I'm making of our conversation, just to check. No, but let's say I think he could do with some . . . training. On his feet, so to speak, rather than with them stuck beneath a terminal screen. Terminal being the operative word.'

Joyce Parry smiled at the pun, whether it was intended or not. 'I'll think about it,' she said. 'I hope you're not up to your old tricks, Dominic.'

'Old tricks?'

'Using people, getting them to run your errands.'

'I don't know what you mean.'

She saw that Barclay himself was standing in her doorway, ready to report on his meeting with Elder. 'I'd better go. Talk to you later.'

'Joyce, I'm serious about wanting to help. You know that.'

'I know. 'Bye.' She put down the receiver. '*Bonjour, Michael*,' she said. '*Comment ça va?*'

Greenleaf was back at his desk barely quarter of an hour when the phone call came from Folkestone. It was Chief Inspector Rennie.

'Inspector Greenleaf?'

'Yes, Chief Inspector. What can I do for you, sir?'

'Might be nothing. We've been talking with Mr Crane's employees, present and past.'

'Yes?'

'One man, a Mr McKillip, said something quite interesting. I thought you might like to talk to him yourself . . .'

It was a slow drive to Folkestone. Roadworks and holiday caravans. But Trilling had been adamant: Greenleaf should go straight away. God knew, they'd been moving through treacle these past few days, ever since the original phone call from Michael Barclay.

Mike McKillip wasn't at the police station. He'd got tired of waiting and had gone home. It took Greenleaf a further twenty minutes to locate McKillip's house from the directions given him at the police station's front desk. You take a left here, then a right at the chip shop, then third on the left past the postbox . . . What chip shop? What postbox? McKillip was watching TV when Greenleaf finally arrived, hungry and parched. McKillip lay slumped along the sagging sofa, guzzling beer from the tin. He did not offer the policeman any, nor did he bother switching off the TV, or even turning the sound down. He just kept complaining about how the firm was going to the wall now that Crane was dead, and what was he supposed to do for work around these parts, and who'd have him at his age anyway when there were younger men out there?

Mike McKillip was thirty-seven. About six foot two tall, Greenleaf would guess, and probably fifteen stones. It wasn't a *fit* fifteen stones, but it was weight, weight to be thrown about, imposing weight. Which was why George Crane had paid him twenty quid to drink in a pub one lunchtime.

'What did he tell you, Mr McKillip?'

'Just that he had to talk business with some geezer, and the geezer might turn nasty. He didn't say why or anything, just that it might turn nasty. I was supposed to stand at the bar and have a drink, not stare at them or anything, just casual like. But if anything happened . . .' McKillip punched a meaty fist down into the soft fabric of the sofa.

'And did anything happen?'

'Nah. Soon as I saw the geezer I thought, *He's* not going to give any trouble. Big . . . tall, I mean. Though I've seen more meat on a butcher's pencil.' Another huge slurp of beer. Christ, Greenleaf would murder for a drink.

'Anything else about the man?'

'Fair hair, I think. Youngish, early-thirties. Going a bit thin on top. *Seriously* thin on top, now that I think about it. They had one drink, bit of a natter. I wasn't watching particularly. The geezer wasn't to know I was there. I just did me drinking. Easiest score I've ever made, I can tell you.' A low throaty chuckle. The can was empty. He crushed it and placed it on the carpet beside three other derelict cans, then gave a belch.

'Did Mr Crane say anything afterwards?'

McKillip shook his head. 'Looked pleased as punch though, so I asked him if it had all gone off all right after all. He said yeah, it was fine. That was the end of it, far as I was concerned.' He shrugged. 'That's all.'

'Which pub was this?'

'The Wheatsheaf.'

'At lunchtime, you say?'

'That's right.'

'Would you know the man again, Mr McKillip?'

'No sweat. I've got a memory for faces.'

Greenleaf nodded, not that he believed McKillip . . . not

as far as he could throw him. He was desperate to be out of here, desperate to assuage both thirst and hunger. He swallowed drily. 'You hadn't seen him before?'

'Nor since.'

'How was the meeting arranged?'

'I don't know. Christ, man, I was just the muscle. I wasn't the boss's lawyer or anything.'

'And you didn't see anything change hands between Mr Crane and this other man?'

'Like what?'

'Anything. A parcel, a bag, some money maybe . . .?'

'Nah, nothing. They'd cooked something up all right though. The gaffer was chipper all that afternoon and the next day.'

'When was this meeting exactly, Mr McKillip?'

'God, now you're asking . . . No idea. Weeks ago.'

'Weeks?'

'Well, a couple of weeks anyway, maybe more like a month.'

'Between a fortnight and a month. I see. Thank you.'

'I told them down the station. I said, it's not much. Not worth bothering about. But they had to report it, they said. You come down from London?' Greenleaf nodded. McKillip shook his head. 'That's my taxes, you know, paying for all this farting about. Not that I'll be paying taxes much longer. *You'll* be paying my dole instead. That wife of his is winding the company up. Bloody shame that. If there'd been a son . . . maybe he could have made a go of it, but not her. Bloody women, you can't trust them. Soon as your pocket's empty, they're off. I'm speaking from experience, mind. Wife took the kids with her, back to her mum's in Croydon. Good luck to her. I like it fine here . . .'

'Yes,' said Greenleaf, rising from the tactile surface of his armchair, 'I'm sure you do, Mr McKillip.'

McKillip wished him a good drive back as Greenleaf made his exit. He got back in his car but stopped at the first pub he saw and drank several orange juices, using them to wash down a cheese and onion sandwich. Too late, he remembered that Shirley hated it when his mouth tasted of onion. Afterwards, he headed back to the police station where he made arrangements for an artist to make an appointment with McKillip. They'd get a sketch of the stranger in the pub. It might come in handy. Then again . . . Still, best to be thorough. Christ knows, if Doyle had come down here, he'd return to London with an oil painting of the man.

In his flat, Michael Barclay was busy packing for the trip to Calais. He'd pack one item, then have to sit for a while to ponder the same question: why me? Those two words bounced around in his brain like cursors gone mad. Why me? He couldn't figure it out. He tried not to think about it. If he continued to think about it, he'd be sure to forget something. He switched on the radio to take his mind off it. There was music, not very good music, and then there was news. It included a story about some banker murdered in his bed. Barclay caught mentions of handcuffs and glamorous models. Well, you could tell what *that* particular dirty banker had been up to, couldn't you? Handcuffs and models . . . some guys had all the luck.

Michael Barclay went on with his packing. He decided to take his personal cassette player and some opera tapes. It might be a long crossing. And he tried out a few sentences in French, desperately recalling the work he'd done for A Level (C grade pass). Christ, that had been seven years ago. Then he had a brainwave. On the bookshelves in his study, he eventually tracked down an old French grammar book and a pocket French-English dictionary, both unused since schooldays. They, too, went into his case. He was pausing for coffee when he caught the next lot of news headlines. It seemed the banker had been found *handcuffed* to the model, that she'd been hysterical and was now under heavy sedation. Michael Barclay whistled.

Then he zipped up his case.

# Tuesday 9 June

When Greenleaf arrived in the office that morning, Doyle was waiting to pounce.

'You are not going to believe this,' he said. 'I could give you five thousand guesses and you still wouldn't guess.'

'What?'

Doyle just leered and tapped the side of his nose. 'The Commander wants us in his office in five minutes. You'll find out then.'

Greenleaf suffered a moment's panic. He was going to be carpeted for something, something he either hadn't done or didn't know he had done. What? But then he relaxed. Doyle would have said something, something more than he'd hinted at. And besides, they hadn't put a foot wrong so far, had they? They'd set up the Folkestone operation, and they'd made good progress with the list of possible assassination hits. They'd started with 1,612 names on the list: 790 individuals (MPs, military chiefs, senior civil servants, prominent businessmen, etc.), 167 organisations or events (such as the summit meeting), and 655 buildings and other landmarks, everything from Stonehenge to the Old Man of Hoy.

This was an extensive, but not an exhaustive, list. It had been designed by the Intelligence department known as 'Profiling' to encompass the most likely terrorist targets in the UK. The details of Witch sent by Joyce Parry to Special Branch had also gone to Profiling, and they'd used these details to begin whittling the list down.

Events and individuals were Witch's specialities; even at that she usually targeted an individual at an event rather than the event itself. Profiling had spoken by phone with Dominic Elder, who had agreed with their assessment. They were looking for an event, where a specific individual would be targeted.

Usually, a sitting of Parliament would be top of the list. But not this month. This month London was hosting something even bigger, and Greenleaf himself had compiled a report on its security.

Doyle had pointed out though that they couldn't know there was an assassin actually at large until *after* a hit had been attempted, successful or not. All they had so far was theory, supposition, and precious little fact. All they had was coincidence. Joyce Parry and her department had been at their cagiest. What reports had been sent over were full of 'might haves' and 'could bes' and 'ifs'. Riddled, in other words, with get-out clauses. Only Elder seemed sure of his ground, but then it was all right for him, he was out of the game.

Greenleaf mentioned this again as he waited with Doyle outside Commander Trilling's door. Doyle turned to him and grinned.

'Don't worry, John. We've got confirmation.'

'What?'

But Doyle was already knocking on and simultaneously opening the door.

'Come in, gentlemen,' said Commander Trilling. 'Sit down. Has Doyle told you, John?'

Greenleaf cast a glance towards his 'partner'. 'No, sir,' he said coldly. 'He's not seen fit to let me into the secret.'

'No secret,' said Trilling. 'It was on last night's news and it'll be on today's. Well, the bare facts will be. We've got a little more than that.' He glanced over a sheet of fax paper on his desk. 'A man's been murdered. A banker, based in London.'

'Murdered, sir?'

'Assassinated, if you like. No other motive, certainly not burglary. And the world of business espionage doesn't usually encompass slaughter.'

'Killed to order then.'

'You could say that,' Doyle said. He sat well back on his chair, with legs apart and arms folded. He looked like he was having a good time.

'Who was he exactly, sir?' asked Greenleaf.

'A Mr Khan, senior banking official for a small foreign bank based in London.'

Greenleaf nodded. 'I heard it on the radio. Killed up in Scotland, wasn't he?'

'Yes, he has a house up there, near ...' Trilling examined the fax sheet again. 'Auchterarder,' he said, and looked up at Greenleaf. 'Gleneagles, that sort of area.'

'"Senior banking official" you said. What precisely does that mean, sir?'

Trilling sighed, exhaling peppermint. 'We're not sure. Nobody seems to know what Mr Khan's role was in this bank of his. Serious Fraud Office investigated the bank, but even they're not sure.'

'He was a fixer,' said Doyle bluntly.

'I'm not sure that description takes us much further,' Trilling complained. 'Whatever his job entailed, it seems to have made him enemies.'

'How professional was the hit, sir?'

'Very.'

'But not without its funny side,' added Doyle.

Greenleaf looked at Trilling. 'Funny?'

'Doyle has a strange sense of humour,' muttered

Trilling. 'The murder took place sometime during Sunday night. Mr Khan was due to fly back to London yesterday morning. He has a cleaning lady tidy up after him—'

'Wiping the leftover coke off the hand-mirror, that sort of thing,' said Doyle.

Trilling ignored the interruption. 'A Mrs MacArthur tidies for him. She has her own key. But she was surprised to arrive at the house yesterday afternoon and find Mr Khan's car still in the drive. She went inside. There was no noise, but as she climbed the stairs she could hear sounds of a struggle in the room occupied by Mr Khan's chauffeur—'

'Bodyguard,' said Doyle.

'—a Danish gentleman. She went into his room and found him handcuffed to his bed, and trying desperately to free himself. He'd been gagged.'

'*And* he was stark bollock naked,' added Doyle.

'She didn't have any way of freeing him, so she went in search of Mr Khan. She suspected a robbery, and there was a phone in Mr Khan's bedroom. When she arrived, she found Mr Khan's girlfriend weeping and frantic. One of her wrists had been chained to the bedpost. The other was handcuffed to one of Mr Khan's wrists. Mr Khan himself was dead, tongue cut out and throat cut. The poor girl had to wait for police to release her. She's under sedation in hospital.'

'Christ,' said Greenleaf.

Doyle was chuckling. 'Isn't it a beauty? It'll be all over the papers. You couldn't keep it quiet if you tried. Blonde beauty driven mad in corpse-chaining horror. That's what the assassin wants, of course.'

'Why?' Greenleaf asked numbly.

'Easy,' said Doyle. 'It's a message, isn't it? Like sticking a horse's head in somebody's bed. Shock value. It scares people off.'

'But scares them off what?'

Trilling cleared his throat. 'I heard from Mrs Parry earlier this morning. It seems that her organisation had been ... using Mr Khan.'

'Using him?'

'As a source of information. Mr Khan was skimming a certain amount from his bank without anyone's knowledge. Parry's agents found out and Khan was ... persuaded to exchange information for silence.'

'Complicity,' corrected Doyle.

'That's a long word for you, Doyle,' warned Trilling. 'I'd be careful of long words, they can get you into trouble.'

'Come on, sir, it's the oldest blackmail scam in the book. Sex and money, the two persuaders.' Doyle turned to Greenleaf. 'Khan's bank's been laundering money for years. Terrorist money, drug money, all kinds of money. Parry's lot have known about it for just about as long as it's been going on. But it's *convenient* to have a dirty bank, just so long as you can keep tabs on its business. That way you know who's doing what to whom, how much it's making them, and where the money's going. They've had Khan in their pocket for over a year.'

'So Khan feeds titbits of information ...'

'In return for Parry's lot keeping quiet about his skim. Nice and easy, and nobody gets hurt.'

'Unless you're found out,' said Greenleaf.

'Unless you're found out,' agreed Trilling. 'If you're discovered – or even simply *believed* – to be an informant, suddenly you've got a lot of enemies. Ruthless enemies, who will pay not only for your elimination, but will demand something more.'

'A very public execution,' said Doyle.

'To scare off other potential informers,' Greenleaf added, completing the deductive process.

'Exactly,' said Trilling. 'We can't know which particular group of investors ordered the assassination, but we can be pretty sure that they wanted it to be newsworthy, and newsworthy they got.'

'And we think the assassin is Witch?' Greenleaf surmised. Trilling shrugged his shoulders.

'There's no modus operandi for us to identify the present hit against. The killer was clever and well-informed. An alarm and a window were taken out, a fit young man overpowered. What we do know, from the Dane, is that we're looking for a woman.'

'Description?'

Trilling shook his head. 'It was dark. He didn't see anything.'

Doyle leered again. 'She didn't chain two wrists and two ankles to bedposts in the dark without him waking up. It was a sucker punch, sir.'

'That's not what the Dane says.'

'With respect, sir, bollocks to what the Dane says. He was awake, and she suckered him.'

'How?' asked Greenleaf. Doyle turned towards him so suddenly, Greenleaf knew he'd been waiting for the question to be asked.

'A woman comes into your bedroom and says she wants to tie you up. You fall for it. Why? Because you think she's got some rumpy in mind. The stupid bugger's supposed to be a bodyguard, and he lets some bird he's never seen before tie him to a bed. Sucker punch. Maybe she slipped him a couple of thousand on the side, make the whole thing more ... palatable.'

'There you go again, Doyle. Stick to *short* words.' Trilling shifted in his chair. 'But we're checking him anyway. We don't think he was in on it, but you can never be sure. He did receive a nasty blow to the head, not far off being fatal according to the hospital.'

'What else have we got, sir?'

'Not much. Not yet. But the assassin did leave some clues behind.'

'What sort of clues?'

'Things required to do the job. The handcuffs for a start, six pairs. You don't just place an order for six pairs of handcuffs without someone raising an eyebrow. Then there was some . . .'

'Sticky-backed plastic,' offered Doyle helpfully. 'That's what they used to call it on *Blue Peter*.'

'Probably bought locally. There's a murder team busy at the scene. They'll do what they can, ask around, check the various shops . . .'

'You don't sound too hopeful, sir.'

'I'll admit, John, I'm not. This was a pro, albeit one with a warped sense of humour. She won't have left many *real* clues, though Christ knows how many red herrings we'll find. And even if we trace the stuff back to a shop, what will we get? A general description of a female. She can change her looks in minutes: wig, hair-dye, make-up, new clothes . . .'

Shape-changer, thought Greenleaf. What did you call them? Proteus? Now that he thought of it, why weren't there more women con artists around? So easy for them to chop and change disguises: high heels and low heels, padding round the waist or in the bra, hair-dye . . . yes, a complete identity change in minutes. Trilling was right.

'But at least now, sir,' he offered, 'we know we *are* dealing with a woman, and we know she *did* land in the country. At least now we've got two facts where before we only had guesses.'

'True,' agreed Commander Trilling.

'But at the same time,' added Doyle, 'she's finished her

job before we've even had half a chance. She could already be back out of the country.'

'I don't think so,' Greenleaf said quietly. Doyle and Trilling looked at him, seeking further explanation. He obliged. 'You don't hire an outside contractor for a single hit like this. And nobody's going to blow up two boats just because they're on a job to bump off a solitary banker. It has to be bigger, don't you think?'

'You've got a point,' said Trilling.

'I've trained him well, sir,' added Doyle. 'Yes, doesn't make much sense, does it? Unless the whole thing is one *huge* red herring, keeping us busy up in Jockland while Witch is busy elsewhere.'

'Could be,' said Greenleaf. 'But there's something else in one of those reports, the ones Mrs Parry sent over. Something said by that man Elder. He points out that Witch often kills for money in order to finance another operation. What is it he says?' Greenleaf threw his head back, quoting from memory. 'To finance her "pursuit of a pure terrorism, untainted by monetary, political or propaganda gain".' He shrugged self-effacingly. 'Something like that.'

'As I say, sir,' Doyle said to Trilling with a wink, 'I've trained him well.' And turning to Greenleaf: 'You're doing fine, John. Just remember who it was taught you everything you know.'

'How can I forget?' said Greenleaf.

The final edition of the day's *Evening Standard* ran with the story, as did other evening papers throughout the country. In Edinburgh and Glasgow, copies of those cities' evening offerings were snapped up. Radio news expanded on their previous day's coverage of the murder. Nor did television show much restraint as more details were leaked. Diversions had to be set up either end of the lane, to stop the curious blocking the road outside Khan's house.

In the field across from the house, a sky-platform, the sort used by firemen tackling fires and by council workers changing the lightbulbs in street-lamps, stood parked beneath a telegraph pole. The platform had been elevated to the height of the top of the pole, so that two CID men (afraid of heights and gripping on to the safety bar) could be shown by a British Telecom engineer just how the alarm wires from Khan's house had been severed. Prior to this, forensic scientists had taken the juddering trip to the top of the pole, dusting the junction box and photographing sections of the wooden pole itself, picking out the holes made by climbing-spikes and the chafing of the wood made by some sort of harness. The engineer was clear in his own mind.

'It was another telephone engineer,' he told the murder squad detectives. 'Had to be. He had all the gear, and he knew just what he was doing.' The detectives didn't bother telling him that he'd even got the sex wrong. They were keen to get back to Dundee, back to their watering holes where ears would be keen to hear the details. They pitied their poor colleagues who'd been sent to track down Fablon and garden twine, leaving no general store or garden centre unturned. But at least garden centres were sited on terra firma, and not forty feet up in the air . . .

In London, Joyce Parry sat in a railway station buffet, drinking tea and deep in thought. During her many telephone conversations that day and the evening before, no one had uttered much by way of condolence regarding Khan. He was a loss, but only as a merchant-able item, not as a human being. His information had been useful, of course, but it could be gained in other

122

ways. GCHQ already provided a lot of data – Khan's snippets had often served only to confirm or consolidate what was already known. Intelligence services in other countries, for example, passed on information about the bank's operations abroad. Joyce Parry hoped the bank would not find itself in trouble because of Khan. One bad apple shouldn't be allowed to ... She'd already had to divert the attention of the Serious Fraud Office. If the drug barons and crime cartels moved their money out of the bank ... well, then the security services would have to start all over again, locating the new bank, shifting spheres of operation so that the new bank was part of the orbit. Time-consuming, expensive, and prone to losses.

No, Joyce Parry hoped things would stay as they were. She hoped upon hope.

And she drank her tea, though 'tea' was not the most suitable description for the liquid in front of her. On the menu the drink was described as fresh-leaf tea. Well, it had been fresh once upon a time, she supposed, in some other country.

After her hectic morning – so many people who needed to be notified of Khan's demise and of the manner of his dying – she'd found time in her office for a moment's reflection ... again, curiously enough, over a cup of tea. She'd reflected, then she'd made yet another call.

To Dominic Elder.

'Dominic, it's Joyce.'

'Ah, Joyce, I was beginning to wonder ... Can I assume something has happened?'

'A killing.'

'Someone important?'

'No.'

'Someone murdered to order?'

'Yes.'

'I thought that's how it would be. She's just earned the money she needs for her own future hit.'

'What makes you so sure it was Witch?'

'You wouldn't have phoned otherwise.'

She'd smiled at that. So simple. 'Of course,' she'd said. 'Well, it was a woman. We don't have a description.'

'It wouldn't matter if you did,' he said calmly.

'No.'

'So what now?'

'Special Branch are checking—'

'Yes, fine, but what now?' The voice not so calm any more. 'The police can check till Doomsday. They'll find only as much as she wants them to.'

'You don't think Witch's job is finished?'

'Joyce, I don't *think* it's even begun . . .'

The door of the buffet opened, interrupting her reverie. He was carrying a suitcase which he placed on the floor beside her booth before sliding on to the seat opposite her.

'Hello, Joyce. I was expecting more of a welcome.'

'Your train's early. I was going to wait for you on the platform.'

He smiled. 'I was being ironic.'

'Oh.' She looked down at her hands. They lay palms down on the table-top, either side of her cup. Then she slid one of them across the table towards him and lightly touched his fingers. 'It's nice to see you again, Dominic.'

'Nice to be here. How's the tea?'

She laughed. 'Terrible.'

'Thought as much. What about a drink?'

'A drink?'

'It's what people do in pubs.'

'A drink.' She thought for a moment. 'Yes, all right.'

'You can even treat me to dinner if you like.'

124

She almost winced. 'Sorry, Dominic, previous engage-ment.'

'Oh.'

'Official business. I can't worm out of it this late on.'

'No problem. I shall dine alone in the teeming city. Is Delpuy's still open?'

'Delpuy's? God, I don't know. I mean, I haven't been there in – well, since well, not for ages.'

'I'll give it a try. Did you find me a room?'

'Yes. Quite central, quite reasonable. I can drop you off if you like.'

'Is there time for that drink?'

'Just about.'

'Then what are we waiting for?' He slid back out of the booth. She pushed the tea aside and stood up too. For a moment they were inches apart, facing one another. He leaned towards her and pecked her on the cheek before picking up his case. 'After you,' he said.

Making to unlock her car-boot, she dropped her keys and had to bend to pick them up. Elder was asking her a question, but she didn't catch it.

'Sorry?' she said.

'I said, who's my contact at Special Branch?'

'Contacts. There are two of them, Doyle and . . . Greenleaf, I think the other one's called.' She thought again of the tea, fresh-leaf. A bit like green-leaf . . . She unlocked the boot and opened it. Elder heaved in his case.

'I've heard of Doyle. He's pretty good, isn't he?'

'I wouldn't know. They both work for Trilling.' She slammed shut the boot.

'Bill Trilling? Jesus, is he still around?'

'Very much so. I should warn you, he's not best pleased with us just at the minute. I'll tell you about it en route.' She unlocked the car and eased herself into the driver's seat, fumbling in her bag for her glasses. As they fastened their seatbelts, their hands touched. She started as though from a static shock. She couldn't help it. She'd thought she could handle this with her usual ... well, whatever it was. But it was turning stupid. Meantime, Elder had asked another question.

'Sorry?' she said.

'Trouble with your ears, Joyce? That's twice I've had to repeat myself. I said, how's young Barclay getting on?'

'I don't know. Okay, I suppose.' She started the car. The sooner she'd delivered him to his hotel room, the better.

Better for all concerned.

'You sent him, didn't you?' He framed it as a question, but really it was a statement.

'Yes,' she said, reversing the car out of its parking space. 'I sent him.'

'Good.'

'Let's get one thing straight from the start, Dominic. You're here in a consultative capacity. I don't want you going rogue, and I don't want you ...'

'Manipulating others to serve my needs? Dumping them afterwards?' He was quoting from memory; she'd given him this speech before. 'You're pre-judging me, Joyce.'

'On past experience.' She felt more confident now, more like herself. She knew that given free rein Dominic would have the whole department looking for ghosts. He'd tried it before. 'Why the interest in Barclay?'

'*Am* I interested?'

'You wanted him sent to France. That smacks of the old Dominic Elder.'

'Maybe he reminds me of someone.'

'Who?'

'I'm not sure. Tell me about our friend Khan.'

126

Elder listened as she spoke, his eyes on the world outside the car. A tedious evening might lie ahead, and he had grown to loathe London, yet he felt quite calm, quite satisfied for the moment. He rubbed against the back of the seat. When Joyce had finished talking he was thoughtful for a moment.

'The model interests me,' he said.

'How so?'

'Witch must have had inside information. She knew where Khan was going to be, and she seems to have known he'd have company. It can't have been the bodyguard, she damned near killed him. We should be asking questions about the model.'

'Okay. Anything else?'

'Just the obvious question really.'

'And what's that?'

He turned to her. 'Where exactly did they find Khan's tongue?'

Calais was grim. Bloody French. They waited, seemingly with infinite patience, while he tried in his stumbling French to ask his questions, then it turned out half of them spoke English anyway. They would stare at him and explain slowly and carefully that an English policeman had already asked them these questions before. One of them had even had the gall to ask, at the end of a particularly fraught session, if Barclay wasn't going to ask him about the financial affairs of the sunken boat's skipper.

'The other policeman,' explained the Frenchman, 'he thought this was a very important question to ask.'

'Yes,' said Barclay through gritted teeth, 'I was just getting round to it.'

'Ah,' said the Frenchman, sitting back, hands resting easily on thighs. There could be no doubt in anyone's mind: this young man was a tyro, sent here for some mysterious reason but certainly not to gain any new information. There was no new information. Monsieur Doyle, the boisterous drinks-buying Englishman, had covered the ground before. Barclay didn't feel like a tyro. He felt like a remould tyre – all the miles had been covered before he'd appeared on the scene. He was driving an old circuit, a loop. No one could understand why. Not even Barclay.

Well, maybe that wasn't exactly true. At first, despite his puzzlement, he'd felt pleased. He was being trusted on a foreign mission, trusted with expenses and with back-up. He was going 'into the field'. He couldn't help feeling that Dominic Elder was somewhere at the back of it. Then he saw what it was, saw what was behind the whole thing.

He was being punished.

Joyce Parry was punishing him for having gone behind her back to Special Branch in the first place. He had blotted his copybook. And his punishment? He would follow in the footsteps of a Special Branch officer, unable to find fresh or missed information, expendable.

Yes, there was no doubt about it. This was the penance expected of him. So he kept his teeth gritted as he went about his business.

'But the other policeman, Monsieur Doyle, he already ask this!'

'Yes, but if you could just tell me again what it was that made you . . .'

All day. A long and exhausting day. And not a single grain of evidence or even supposition to show for it. There wasn't much to the centre of Calais. It had taken him an hour to explore what there was. There wasn't much to the centre, but the place stretched along the coast, a maze of docks and landing bays, quaysides, jetties and chaotic buildings, either smelling of fish or of engine oil.

That's why it had taken him so long to track down the people he wanted to question: the boatmen, the port authorities, people who'd been around and about that evening when the boat carrying Witch had chugged out to sea. It was no wonder the men he spoke to weren't enthusiastic, when he himself showed about as much enthusiasm as a netted cod. In short, he'd completed a poor day's work, and still with a number of people on his list, not yet found. He'd try to wrap it up tomorrow morning. Before lunchtime. The sooner the better.

It was six now. He'd been warned that the French did not eat dinner before eight o'clock. Time for a shower and a change of clothes back at his hotel. Really, he should head back out to the docks after dinner: there were a couple of names on his list who worked only after dark and whose home addresses no one seemed willing to divulge.

'*Sur le bleu*,' one man had told him, tapping finger against nose. On the blue: the French equivalent of the black economy. These men would work for cash, no questions asked or taxes paid. Maybe they had daytime jobs. But they were on the sidelines. Doyle had spoken with them and learnt nothing. How could men working '*sur le bleu*' afford to see anything or hear anything? They didn't exist officially. They were non-persons at the docks. All of this Doyle had put in his report, a report Barclay had read. It was a thorough report, certainly as good as the one Barclay himself would write. But it was also a bit pleased with itself, a bit smug: I've covered everything, it seemed to suggest, what did you expect me to find?

Barclay's hotel lay in a dark, narrow street near the bus terminus. There was a small piece of waste ground nearby which served as a car park (at each car owner's risk). Barclay had taken out European insurance before crossing the Channel, and he half-hoped someone *would* steal his creaky Fiesta with its malfunctioning gearbox. To this end, he gathered together his opera tapes and carried them in a plastic bag. He didn't mind losing the car, but he didn't want his tapes stolen too . . .

His hotel was in fact the two floors over a bar, but with a separate smoked-glass door taking residents up the steep staircase to the rooms. He'd been given a key to this door and told that meals were served in the bar. Between the smoked-glass door and the stairs there was another door of solid wood, leading into the bar. He paused, having pressed the time-controlled light-switch, illuminating the staircase with its grey vinyl wallpaper. He could nip into the bar for a drink: a cognac or a pastis. He could, but he wouldn't. He could hear locals in there, shouting the odds about something, their voices echoing. Two or three of them, the bar empty apart from them. He started to climb the stairs, and was halfway up when the lights went off.

He wasn't in complete darkness. A little light came from the downstairs door. But not much. There was another light-switch on the landing, just beside the huge potted plant and the framed painting of some anthropomorphic dogs playing pool. He climbed slowly, hand brushing against the horrible wallpaper with bristly vertical stripes, more like carpeting than anything else. The sort of carpeting that gave you an electric shock if you wore the wrong kind of shoes. Just along the wall a little . . . light-switch somewhere around here . . . ah, yes, just . . .

His fingers pressed against something. But it wasn't the switch. It was warm, soft, yielding. It was a hand. He started and almost fell back down the stairs, but another

130

hand grabbed his arm and pulled him upright. At the same time, the lights came back on. The hand his own hand had touched had already been resting on the light-switch. He found himself facing a young woman, small, with short black hair and very red lips. Her face was round and mischievous. She smiled wryly.

'*Pardon*,' she said: the French word, not the English. He attempted a light laugh which came out as a strangled snuffle. Then she brushed past him and descended the staircase. He watched her go. She was wearing baggy trousers and a sort of cotton blouson, the trousers dark blue and the blouson sky blue. And lace-up shoes, quite rugged things. Her fingers touched the stair-rail as she went. At the bottom, unexpectedly, she turned back and caught him looking at her, then opened not the door to the street but the one leading into the bar. The voices from inside were amplified for a moment, then the door closed again, muffling them.

'Christ,' he said to himself. He walked unsteadily along the corridor and was just trying to fit his room-key into the lock when the lights went out yet again.

Inside the room, he threw his bag of cassettes on to the carpet and sat down on the springy bed. Then he lay back across it, left hand gripping right wrist and both resting on his forehead. He should make a start on his report, at least get his notes in order. But he kept seeing the girl in his mind. Why had she given him such a start? He managed to smile about it after a bit, rearranging his memory of the incident so that he came out of it in a better light. Well, at least he hadn't tried to say anything in his inimitable French.

He had a shower, humming to himself all the time, then dried himself briskly and lay back down on the bed again. After a moment's thought, he reached down beneath the bed and pulled out a bulging cardboard document wallet marked in thick felt pen with the single word WITCH. It had arrived by motorbike courier at his flat in London, less than half an hour before he'd been due to leave to catch the ferry. A large padded envelope, and the helmeted rider saying: 'Sign here.' He'd torn the envelope open, not knowing what to expect – certainly not expecting Dominic Elder's crammed but meticulously organised obsession. There was a note pinned to the dog-eared flap: 'I have the feeling your need will be greater than mine. Besides, I know it by heart. I'll be in touch. Good luck. Elder.'

Biked all the way from deepest south Wales to London. The bike charges must have been phenomenal, but then Barclay surmised that the department would be paying.

He'd read through the file on the trip across the Channel. It contained plenty of detail; the only thing missing was factual evidence that any of the operations and incidents outlined in two dozen separate reports had anything to do with an individual codenamed 'Witch'. It seemed to Barclay that Dominic Elder had latched onto any unsolved assassination, any unclaimed terrorist outrage, and had placed the name Witch beside it. A woman seen fleeing the scene . . . a telephone call made by a female . . . a prostitute visited . . . a girl student who disappeared afterwards . . . these shadowy, ephemeral figures all turned into the same person in Elder's mind. It smacked of psychosis.

Barclay wondered why. He wondered what had spurred Elder on, why had the mere *idea* of Witch gripped him in the first place? He got the feeling Elder knew more than he was saying. Flicking through the file for a second time, he caught a single mention of Operation Silverfish. It was noted in passing, no more. Operation Silverfish. No clue as to what it was, just that it had occurred two years before. The year, in fact, that Elder had 'retired' from the department. The year, too, that Barclay had joined: they'd missed one another by a little over five weeks. A slender gap between the old and the new. He would ask someone about Silverfish when he got back. Joyce Parry perhaps, or Elder. It might be that he could access the operation file without prior consent anyway. He'd be back tomorrow, back to the reality of technology, back to his role as Intelligence Technician.

His phone buzzed. This in itself was surprising: the apparatus looked too old to be functional. He picked up the receiver.

'Hello?'

'Barclay? It's Dominic Elder. I said I'd be in touch.'

'How did you get my . . . ?'

'Joyce passed it along. I'm in London now. Anything to report?'

'Nothing Special Branch haven't already found.'

'Flagging already, eh?'

Barclay bristled. 'Not at all.'

'Good. Listen, Special Branch are policemen, they've got policemen's minds. Don't get stuck in their rut.'

Barclay smiled at the image, remembering his retread tyre. 'You'd advise lateral thinking then?'

'No, just *deep* thinking. Follow every idea through. All right?'

'All right.'

'I'll call again tomorrow. And listen, don't tell Mrs Parry. It would only get us both into trouble.'

'I thought you said she'd given you this number?'

'Well, she told me which hotel you were in. I found the number for myself.'

Barclay smiled again. Then he remembered something. 'I've been reading the file, I wanted to ask you about Operation Silver—'

'Talk to you soon then. 'Bye.'

The connection was dead. It was as though Elder simply hadn't heard him. Barclay put the receiver back. He was quite getting to like Dominic Elder.

He had brought a couple of paperbacks with him, expecting to have time to kill. He'd been struggling with one of them for weeks, Thomas Pynchon's *Gravity's Rainbow*. A computer buff friend had recommended it. He'd unpacked the book and left it on the bedside cabinet, beside his French Grammar and travel alarm. He picked up the book now. He still had an hour before wandering off in search of dinner. Maybe he could pick up the thread of Pynchon.

He opened it where his leather bookmark rested. Jesus, was he really only up to page forty-nine? He read halfway down the page, sure that he'd read this before. He was much further on . . . page sixty-five or seventy at least. What was the bookmark doing left at a page he'd read before? He thought for a couple of minutes. Then he examined the corners of the book. There was a slight dent to the bottom right-hand corner of the cover, and to a few of the pages after it. The book had been bought new, pristine. The dent was the kind made by dropping a book. Picking it up to flip through it . . . dropping it . . . the bookmark falling out . . . replaced at random . . .

'Jesus,' he said, for the second time in an hour.

Dressed for dinner, in lightweight cream suit and brown brogues, white shirt and red paisley tie, Barclay opened the door to the bar. It was busier, five men leaning against the bar itself and deep in discussion with the hotelier who filled glasses as he spoke. Barclay smiled and nodded towards him, then made for a table. There was only one other person seated, the young woman from the landing. He pulled out a chair from opposite her and sat down.

'Do you mind if I join you?' he asked.

'*Comment? Vous êtes anglais, monsieur?*'

'*Anglais, oui.*' He stared at her without blinking. 'Are you staying here, *mademoiselle? Restez-vous ici?*'

She appeared not to understand. The hotelier had come to the table to take Barclay's order. '*Une pression, s'il vous plaît.*' Barclay's eyes were still on her. 'Would you like another?' She had an empty glass in front of her. She shook her head. The hotelier moved back to the bar.

'So,' said Barclay quietly, 'did you find anything interesting in my room?'

A tinge of red came to her cheekbones and stayed there. She found that she could speak English after all. 'I did not mean to . . . I thought I would wait there for you. Then I changed my mind.'

'But we bumped into one another on the stairs. Why not introduce yourself then?'

She shrugged. 'It did not seem the right moment.'

He nodded. 'Because I would know you'd been to my room?'

'It was the book, yes?' She needed no affirmation. 'Yes, the book was stupid. I thought it would . . . pass time.'

'It was clumsy certainly.' His beer arrived. He waited till the hotelier had returned once again to the bar before asking, 'How much did you give him?'

'Nothing.' She dug into the pocket of her blouson. 'I had only to show him some identification.' She handed him a small laminated card, carrying a photograph of her with her hair longer and permed into tight curls. Her name was Dominique Herault. As she handed the card to him, he checked her fingers. She wore four ornate but cheap-looking rings; there was no ring on her wedding-finger.

'DST,' he read from the card, and nodded to himself. Direction de la Surveillance du Territoire, the French

135

equivalent of MI5. Parry had warned him that once DST knew a British agent was on his way to France (and she would have to inform them – it was a matter of protocol) they would almost certainly send one of their agents to 'assist' him. He handed back her card. 'You're not quite what I had in mind,' he said.

'You were expecting perhaps Peter Sellers?'

He smiled. 'No, no, I was just expecting someone more . . . mature.' She raised an eyebrow. 'I mean,' he went on, 'someone older.'

'Ah,' she said. 'No, Mr Barclay, you are not senior enough to merit someone . . . older.'

'*Touché*,' he murmured, raising his glass to his lips.

Now it was Dominique Herault's turn to smile.

'So,' he went on, having swallowed the ice-cold beer, 'now that you've ransacked my room, I suppose that puts us on a footing of mutual trust and cooperation.'

'I was only—'

'Waiting for me. Yes, you said. Forgive me, but in Britain we normally wait *outside* a person's room. We don't break and enter.'

'Break? Nothing was broken. Besides, MI5 is famous for its breaking and entering, isn't it so?'

'Once upon a time,' Barclay replied coolly. 'But we draw the line at sinking Greenpeace ships.'

'That was the DGSE, not the DST,' she said, rather too quickly. 'And it too was a long time ago. What do you say . . . water under the bridge?'

'Ironic under the circumstances, but yes, that's what we say. Your English is good.'

'Better than your French, I think. I saw the grammar book in your room. It is for children, no?'

He shifted a little, saying nothing.

Her finger drew a circle on the table-top. 'And do you

think,' she said, 'you can find anything in Calais which we might have overlooked ourselves?'

'I didn't know you were interested.'

'French people were killed, Mr Barclay. Killed by a bomb, a terrorist bomb, we think. Naturally we are interested.'

'Yes, I didn't mean—'

'So now you will answer my question: do you think you can find anything we might have overlooked?'

He shook his head.

'No,' she agreed. 'And let me make some guesses. You have been talking to ... sailors. Just as the Special Branch agent did. You have been interviewing all the people *he* interviewed. You have read the local police report. You have been concentrating on the boat, on the people who died on it, on people who might have seen it. Yes?'

'Basically correct.'

'Yes. We made the same mistake. Not me, I was not involved at the beginning. But now I am here to ...'

'Assist?' he offered.

'Assist, yes, I am to assist you. So, what I say to you is ...' She leaned forward and lowered her voice. 'You are not thinking about this the right way.'

'I'm not?' He tried to keep the acid out of his voice. She was shaking her head, deaf to nuance.

'No. The way to work is backwards, backwards from the departure of the boat.'

'Yes, that's what I've been—'

'*Further* back. Much further.'

'I'm not sure I understand.'

'I will tell you.' She checked her watch. 'You are dressed to go out. You're eating out?'

'Yes.'

She was on her feet. 'I know a good restaurant. Not

here, out of town a few kilometres. We can take my car.'
She called over to the hotelier. 'I've told him to put my
drink and yours on your bill.'

'Thank you. So kind.'

She stared fixedly at him through narrowed eyes.
'Irony?' she guessed at last.

'Irony,' he admitted.

She had a Citroën 2CV, not a recent model. The sides of
the car were dented and scraped from years of Parisian
lane-discipline. The suspension was like nothing Barclay
had ever experienced, and she drove like a demon. The
last time he'd been thrown about like this had been on a
fairground ride. She yelled to him over the noise from the
motor, but he couldn't make out a word. He just nodded,
and smiled whenever she glanced towards him. His
responses seemed enough.

By the time they arrived at what looked like someone's
cottage, deep in the middle of nowhere, he felt that he
would never eat again. But the smells wafting from the
kitchen soon changed his mind.

'My employers' treat,' she said as they took their seats
at a cramped table for two. Menus the size of the table's
surface were handed to them, and she immediately
ordered two Kirs before gazing over her menu at him.

'Shall I order?' she asked. He nodded his head. Her
eyelashes were thick but not long. He was still trying to
work out whether she dyed her hair. And her age, too,
he wondered about. Somewhere between twenty-one
and twenty-eight. But why not twenty or twenty-nine?
She kept her head hidden behind the menu for a full
minute, while he looked around him at the diners
occupying every other table in the place. There had been
no sign that their table had been reserved, and she'd said

nothing to the waiter about a reservation, but he wondered all the same . . .

At last she put down the menu. 'You eat meat?' she asked.

'Yes.'

'Good, here in France we are still a little . . . recidivist about vegetarianism.'

'Recidivist?'

She looked appalled. 'That is not the right word?'

He shrugged. 'No idea,' he told her. 'Not only is your French better than mine, I'm beginning to wonder about your English, too.'

This remark seemed to cheer her enormously. She straightened her back and gave another red-lipped smile.

'For that,' she said, 'I order the *second* cheapest bottle of wine rather than the cheapest.'

'Your employers are very generous.'

'No, they are very literal-minded, like security organisations all over the world. Do you enjoy Thomas Pynchon?'

'I don't even *understand* Thomas Pynchon.'

Barclay was remembering that, foreign territory or not, he had the ability to charm if nothing else. She was still smiling. He thought she probably was charmed.

'Do you ever read Conan Doyle?'

'What, Sherlock Holmes? No, but I've seen the films.'

'The books, the stories, they are very different to these films. Sherlock Holmes has an exaggerated power of deductive reasoning. He can solve any case by deductive reasoning alone. To some extent, Mr Conan Doyle has a point.' She paused, suddenly thinking of something. 'The Mr Doyle from Special Branch, do you know him? Is he perhaps related to Mr Conan Doyle?'

'I don't know him, but I shouldn't think so.'

She nodded at this, but seemed disappointed all the

same. 'You know,' she said, 'Mr Conan Doyle was interested in deductive reasoning, yet he also believed deeply in spiritualism.'

'Really?' said Barclay, for want of anything better to reply. He couldn't see where any of this was leading.

'Yes,' she said, 'really. I find that strange.'

'I suppose it is a little.'

The waiter had appeared, pad and pen at the ready. To Barclay's mind, it seemed to take a lot of talking for the meal to be ordered. There was much discussion, back-tracking, changing of mind. And glances from both Dominique and the waiter towards him; even, at one point, a conspiratorial smile. The waiter bowed at last and retreated, accepting Barclay's unused menu from him with exaggerated courtesy. A new waitress had arrived with two glasses of Kir.

'Cheers,' said Dominique, lifting hers.

'*Santé*,' replied Barclay. He sipped, sounded his appreciation, and put the glass down. A basket of bread now arrived, courtesy of the original waiter. At a nearby table, something sizzling was being served on to two plates. The diners at surrounding tables looked eagerly, unashamedly, towards the source of the sound, then exchanged remarks about the quality of the dish. When Barclay looked back at her, Dominique was staring at him from behind her tall glass.

'So,' he said, shifting his weight slightly in the solid wooden chair, 'what were you saying about Conan Doyle?'

'Not Conan Doyle, Sherlock Holmes. Deductive reasoning. This is my point. We should be working backwards, asking ourselves questions, and deciding on probabilities. Don't you agree?'

Lateral thinking, following an idea all the way

140

through ... that was how Dominic Elder had put it. Barclay nodded. 'So what would *you* do?'

She leaned forwards, resting her elbows on the table-top. 'The assassin, we think probably she is a woman, yes?'

'Agreed.'

'Now, think of this: how did she come to arrive in Calais?'

'By train or by road.'

'Correct. Which is the more probable? Road. *Perhaps* she came from Paris. But trains are very public, aren't they? While assassins are not. So, it is *more* probable that she arrived by road. Yes?'

He shrugged. 'If you say so.'

'Then either she drove or she was driven. She is said to enjoy working alone. An independent woman, self-sufficient.' She paused, waiting for his nodded agreement that she had chosen her words correctly. 'Probably therefore,' she went on, 'she did not have an accomplice. She may have hitch-hiked, or she may have driven to Calais by herself. Yes?'

'Yes.'

'Now, the easiest hitch-hiking is by lorry. Lorry drivers will more probably pick up hitch-hikers than will car drivers. I know this from experience.' A flickering smile at this, but she was too busy concentrating on her English for the smile to last. 'So,' she said, 'this woman probably either hitch-hiked by lorry or else drove here herself.'

Barclay, slow at first, was picking it up quickly. 'So we shouldn't be talking to fishermen,' he said, 'we should be talking to lorry drivers?'

'Freight terminals, haulage firms, yes. And also, we should check for abandoned vehicles. Cars left in car parks or set fire to in fields, that sort of thing. There is always the chance she arrived here by other means . . .'

'But the laws of probability dictate otherwise?'

She took a second or two translating this. 'If you say so,' she said finally, just as the tureen of soup was arriving.

# Wednesday 10 June

The fair had yet to open for the day, but the front of Barnaby's Gun Stall had been unlocked and drawn back. The machine-gun had been connected to its compression pump, and it had been loaded with pellets too. Keith was now fixing a three-inch square target (half the size of the usual scorecards) to the heart of the life-size metal figure. He glanced back warily to where she was standing, balancing the gun's weight in her hand, finding its fulcrum. Rosa's girl: that's who she'd always been, Rosa's girl. Little was ever said about her. There were shrugs, and the acceptance that she had once been part of the fair. Keith couldn't remember that far back. But he knew he fancied her now. Which was why he didn't mind opening the gun range for her, even though the locals might complain about the noise this early in the day. She'd even put her two one-pound coins down on the counter.

'Don't be daft,' he'd said. But she'd shaken her head.

'Keep it, I'm quite well off at the moment.'

'Lucky for some.' So Keith had pocketed the money.

He stuck the last pin into the last corner of the target. She was already lining up the gun. He could feel its sights on him like a weight pressing the back of his head. The compressor was hissing somewhere behind him.

'Okay,' he cried. 'That's it.' And he stumbled backwards away from the silhouette.

But still she did not fire. She stood there, her eye trained along the sights, the barrel of the gun barely wavering by a millimetre. Then she pulled the trigger. There was furious noise for ten seconds, then blessed silence. Keith stared at where dust was rising from in front of the silhouette figure. The edges of the paper target were still intact, like a window-frame. But everything inside the frame had been reduced to a haze in the air.

He gave a loud whistle. 'I've never seen shooting like—'

But when he turned around she had vanished. The machine-gun was lying on its side on the counter. Keith whistled more softly this time, grinning at the target and rubbing his chin. Then he stepped forward and began carefully removing the tacks from the corners of the target. He knew exactly what he was going to do with it.


Thinking back on the evening, running the dialogue through his head, Barclay saw that there had been a great deal of competitiveness during the meal. Which wasn't to say that it hadn't been fun.

He was breakfasting – milky coffee and croissants in the hotel bar – while he waited for Dominique. She'd driven him back last night with beady determination. She was probably half his weight, yet she'd drunk the same as him during dinner. She'd dropped him off outside the hotel, waving and sounding her horn as she sped off. And he'd stood there for a moment, searching for his door-key and wondering if he should have said something more to her, should have attempted a kiss.

'Not on a first date,' he'd muttered before dragging the key out of his pocket.

A shower before breakfast, and he felt fine. Ready for the day ahead. He even noticed how a Frenchman, eating breakfast standing at the bar, dunked his croissant into his coffee. So when Barclay's croissants arrived

144

without butter, he knew just what to do with them, and felt unduly pleased with himself as he ate.

The door opened and in breezed Dominique. Having met the hotelier yesterday, she was now on hailing terms with him, and uttered a loud '*Bonjour*' as she settled into the booth.

'Good morning,' she said.

'Hello.'

She looked as though she'd been up for hours. She had clipped a red woollen head-square around her throat with a gold-coloured brooch. The scarf matched her lipstick, and made her mouth seem more glistening than ever. White T-shirt, brown leather shoulder-bag, faded blue denims turned up at bared ankles, and those same sensible laced shoes. Barclay drank her in as he broke off a corner of croissant.

'Thank you for last night,' he said. He had rehearsed a longer speech, but didn't feel the need to make it. She shrugged.

'Come on,' she said, looking down meaningfully at his cup, which was still half full. 'We've got a lot of work ahead of us.'

'Okay, okay.'

'Now listen, I've been thinking.' She took a deep breath before continuing. 'I'm looking for my sister. That's the story I will tell to the drivers. She has run away from home and I think maybe she is heading for England.'

'That's good, we'll get their sympathy if nothing else.'

'Exactly, and they may like the idea of two sisters. It may make them remember something.'

'You're speaking from experience?' She narrowed her eyes and he nodded. 'Yes,' he admitted, 'irony, sort of.'

'Well, anyway, it's true.'

'And what role do I play?'

'You are like The Who's Tommy: deaf and dumb.'

'And blind?'

'No, but just let me do all the talking. Yes?'

'Fine by me.'

'Now *hurry up.*' And to help, she seized the last piece of croissant, drowned it in his cup, then manoeuvred the whole dripping concoction across the tabletop and into her mouth.

'Shall we take my car?' he suggested.

'I'm from Paris,' she snapped. 'Why would I be driving a British car?'

'I won't say another word,' he said, following her to the café door.

It was every bit as tiring and frustrating as the previous day, but with the bonus that *she* was doing all the work while he loitered in the background. Dominique took the freight-men's comments and double entendres in good part, even though Barclay himself felt like smashing some of them in the mouth. But though she listened, there didn't seem much to learn. No driver knew anything. If she had a photograph of her sister, perhaps, a picture they could keep . . . ? Maybe something of the both of them in their swimming costumes . . . ?

General laughter and guttural speech, slangy, spoken at furious speed. Barclay caught about a quarter of it and understood less than that. They ate at the French equivalent of a greasy spoon: a dingy bar which, hazy with smoke, still served up a more than passable five-course meal. Barclay ate three courses, pleading that he was still full from the previous evening. From a booth in the post office in town, Dominique made several telephone calls, paying the counter staff afterwards and asking for a receipt.

Then there were more firms to check, more fake

questions to ask, always to more shakes of the head and shrugs of the shoulders. He saw her spirits flag, and suddenly he knew her. He knew her for what she was. She was young and hungry like him, keen to succeed, keen to show up the flaws and weaknesses of others before her. She wasn't here to 'assist' him: she was here to make her mark, so that she could climb the rungs of the promotion ladder. Watching her work, he saw an emptiness at his own core. Watching her fail to get results, he became more determined that they shouldn't give up.

Until suddenly, at five o'clock, there were no people left to ask. They had exhausted the possibilities. Or rather, they had exhausted one seam; but there was another seam left to mine, so long as her spirits were up to it.

Over a glass of wine in a bar, he gave something equating to a pep talk. It half-worked. She agreed to give it another hour or so. Then he would take her to dinner – on *his* firm this time.

They made for the police station, and there asked at the desk about abandoned vehicles. Inspector Bugeaud, who had already spent more time than he cared to remember helping the DST, Special Branch, and Barclay, groaned when he saw them. But he was persuaded to look in the files. He came up with only two possibilities. A motorbike stolen in Marquise and pushed off a cliff several kilometres out of town, and a car stolen in Paris and found by a farmer in some woods, again several kilometres out of town.

'Stolen in Paris?' Dominique said, her eyes glinting. The Inspector nodded.

'This car,' said Barclay, 'where is it now, Inspector?'

Bugeaud checked the paperwork. 'Back with its owner,' he said.

'Was it checked for fingerprints?' Dominique asked. She had risen onto her tiptoes. Barclay got the feeling that in another location, she might actually have been jumping up and down with excitement. But here she managed to retain a measure of composure.

The Inspector shrugged. 'Why bother? It wasn't damaged, except for some paint scraped off by the trees. The owner was happy enough to know its whereabouts. End of story.'

'I don't think so,' said Dominique with a slow shake of her head. 'I don't think it's the end of the story at all, Inspector.' She turned towards Barclay. 'I think it's just the beginning.' She slapped the file. 'Can I please have a photocopy of the relevant details, Inspector? *Two* photocopies.' (Another glance in Barclay's direction.) 'No, best make it three. My superiors will want to take a look. I'll see that your help is reported back to them, too.'

'Don't bother,' said Bugeaud, retreating back upstairs to turn on the photocopier. 'I prefer the quiet life.'

That night, after another large meal, Barclay telephoned London from his room. His call was transferred to a private house – there were sounds of a loud dinner party in the background – where he was able to speak to Joyce Parry. He gave her what news he had, playing down Dominique's role, feeling only a little like a snake as he did so. She sounded thoughtful rather than enthusiastic.

'It's an interesting idea,' she said, 'a car stolen in Paris . . .'

'Yes, ma'am.'

There was silence. 'What do the DST think?' Joyce Parry asked at last.

'They're heading back to Paris to do some checking.'

'Fair enough. So you'll be back here tomorrow?'

He swallowed, ready with his story but still nervous.

'I'd rather stick close to this, ma'am,' he said. 'It seems to me that we and DST are coming at this from different angles. They're worried that Witch may have had help in France. They want to cut any future aid-route. They're not bothered by the fact that she's now in England. Left to themselves, they may not ask the right questions.'

An excruciating pause, background laughter, then: 'I see. Well, all right then, off you go to Paris. Call me from there.'

'Yes, ma'am.' *Just* keeping the excitement out of his voice.

'And don't play silly buggers with your expenses. I don't want to see receipts from the Moulin Rouge. Okay?'

She was making a joke of it. She'd believed him. Well, and why not? Dominic Elder had said it might work. Elder had called only twenty minutes ago, while Barclay and Dominique had been drinking and scheming in the hotel bar.

'Understood,' said Barclay, ringing off before she could change her mind. Dominique was waiting for him downstairs.

'Well?' she said.

He was very casual, shrugging his shoulders as he slid into the booth. 'It's settled.' He picked up his beer. 'I'm coming to Paris.'

She nodded, managing to seem neither pleased nor displeased.

'Now,' he said, 'what about a nightcap?'

She looked at him strangely. 'Nightcap?' she repeated.

'A final drink before retiring,' he explained.

'Oh.' She nodded thoughtfully. 'Yes, why not? But remember, Michael, we are not celebrating . . . not yet. These are still—'

'Probabilities, I know. But whatever they are, they're

better than nothing. They're certainly better than being stuck in an office in London.' He found himself believing this, too. The office was no longer a safe haven. It seemed boring, a place without possibilities. Besides, he *had* to go to Paris, didn't he? He'd found a lead, something Doyle had missed. Who knew what else he might find if he stuck close to Dominique? It was difficult work, but someone had to do it.

'Have you ever been to Paris before?' she asked.

'Once or twice.'

'With lovers?'

'That's classified information.'

She laughed. 'I will show you Paris. You will love it.'

Barclay was signalling to the barman. 'Is that your deductive reasoning again?'

'No,' she said, finishing her drink, 'just instinct.'

# Thursday 11 June

The first meeting between the two Special Branch detectives and Dominic Elder could not be considered a success. It wasn't helped by the attendance, for part of the time, of Joyce Parry and Commander Trilling, who looked to be conducting their own personal Cold War.

But it was Doyle who really set the tone. Introduced to and shaking hands with Elder, his first question was: 'So, Mr Elder, and how long have you been on the pension?'

Elder ignored this, but Doyle just couldn't let it go. His contributions to the discussion were peppered with references to 'the retired gentleman', 'the ex-agent', 'the man from the country' and so on. The more he went on, the more fixed became Elder's smile. Greenleaf tried jolting Doyle's mind on to another track, getting him to talk about Calais, about the Folkestone operation, but nothing could deter Doyle. Nothing could rob him of his simple pleasures. He even, as Elder had judged he would, came up with a crack about Elder's name: 'Perhaps,' Doyle began one loud sentence, 'I shouldn't say this in front of my *elders*, but—'

Dominic Elder had been waiting. 'Elders and betters, Mr Doyle. I believe that's the phrase.'

He wasn't smiling any more.

Greenleaf twisted in his seat as though trying to avoid a shrewdly placed drawing-pin. He had spent most of the previous evening boning up for this meeting, ensuring he was word perfect. He had learned the case notes off by heart, wanting to look good in front of Parry and Elder.

But now he seemed the unwilling referee in a tag-team wrestling match, trapped between Parry and Commander Trilling grappling in one corner of the ring, and Doyle and Elder in the other. He knew he wouldn't make any friends if he attempted to make the peace, so he sat quiet in his chair, reciting inwardly his litany of dates, times, officers' names, interviewees . . . Until finally it was too much for him. He thought he was going to burst. He did burst.

'As you know,' he began, 'we've got officers on the ground around Folkestone, stopping drivers and asking questions. Nothing as yet, but it's early days. While we're waiting, the least we could do is study the security procedures for, say, the top three targets on the list, by which I mean next week's nine-nation summit, the Houses of Parliament, and Her Majesty the Queen.'

'God bless her,' said Doyle.

'Since security is in place, and is constantly monitored and tightened around the last two, perhaps we can concentrate our efforts on the summit. I know there has already been considerable liaison between Special Branch, the security services, and the secret services of the countries taking part. But maybe if we put our heads together and study the available commentaries, we can decide a) whether the summit is a likely target for the assassin, and b) *how* she might strike. If we know how she's going to strike, we can work out *where* she's going to strike, and perhaps even *when*. As you may know, I've already done some work on the summit security arrangements, but as you also know nothing is ever the last word. In some ways, I'd even say the summit is *too* tempting a target. On the other hand, we've got this.' He waved in front of him an artist's impression of the man George Crane had met, the man described by McKillip. The others in the room had an identical xerox. 'We could concentrate our efforts on finding this customer. Maybe he'd lead us to Witch.'

Suddenly, the flow ceased. Greenleaf was himself again, and found himself looking at the intent faces around him. He swallowed. 'I . . . uh . . .' He looked to Trilling. 'That's how I see it, sir.'

'Thank you, John,' said Trilling quietly. Doyle was sitting arms folded, lips pursed, eyes on his own navel. He looked like he might laugh, might shoot his 'partner' down, but he didn't get the chance.

'They're as good as any ideas I've heard so far,' commented Elder, 'and better than most.' He nodded in Greenleaf's direction.

'Agreed,' said Joyce Parry.

'What about Khan's bodyguard and the woman?' Elder asked.

Doyle answered. 'They were interviewed in Perth.'

'Are they back in London?'

Doyle shifted a little in his seat. 'They've left Perth.'

'You can't find them?' Elder suggested.

Now Doyle sat up straight. 'The bodyguard's okay.'

'The woman then?'

Now Doyle nodded. 'She gave a false address. We're on to it though, don't worry.'

Joyce Parry saw that Elder had no more questions. 'I've another meeting to go to,' she said. 'I'd better say my piece before I go. We've got a man in Calais, Michael Barclay.'

Doyle started. 'I've already covered Calais.'

Joyce Parry ignored the interruption. 'He telephoned last night with new information.'

(Greenleaf noticed how Dominic Elder perked up at this, enjoying Doyle's discomfort. If truth be told, Greenleaf himself enjoyed it just a little, too.)

'Rather than confining himself to the details of the

woman's *departure* from Calais,' Parry went on, 'Barclay concentrated on her mode of arrival at Calais.'

'I checked that,' snapped Doyle.

Again, Parry ignored him. 'He went to the local police and asked about vehicles which had been abandoned or destroyed in and around the town. The police came up with two possibilities, and one of these was a car stolen in Paris several days before and found hidden in a patch of woodland. Barclay is now on his way to Paris to ...' (consciously, she chose Doyle's own word) '... to *check* the details of the theft. That's all. Now, if you'll excuse me, gentlemen?'

'Yes,' said Trilling. He rose to his feet and collected his things together. He too was due in another meeting.

Greenleaf was studying Dominic Elder. An impassive face, not old, certainly not past it despite Doyle's jibes. The problem with Doyle was, there was too much on the surface. He presented far too much of himself, or his image of himself, to the outside world. Which was dangerous, since it made him easy to 'read'. Greenleaf was willing to bet Elder could 'read' Doyle. Look at how quickly he'd come back over the elder jibe. Anticipation. He wondered just what Elder made of *him*, especially after that outburst. He didn't know what had made him do it, but he had a sneaking feeling it was all Shirley's fault. He'd been trying to concentrate all last night, concentrate on learning his facts. And she'd had the telly on – louder than necessary. He'd pleaded with her to turn it down, and she'd had a go at him.

'What's the point of all that swotting? Trying to impress the teachers, is that it, John? Give up, you're too old. That sort of stuff is for schoolboys. You're a grown man. Initiative, that's what impresses people in a grown-up. Memory-men are freaks, the sort of thing you might see at Blackpool or on the telly.' Then she'd subsided, touching his arm. 'John, love, you're not in Special Branch because you're good at studying. You're there because you're good, full stop. Now take a break from that and come and sit with me. Come on.'

It was the most she'd said to him in days, ever since the picnic really. They'd talked themselves hoarse the rest of the evening. God, what a relief it had been. But he'd lain awake long after Shirley had drifted off to sleep. He could hear her words. And he was afraid, afraid that the only thing he *was* good at was the learning and spouting of facts and figures. He'd been called a 'copper's copper' in the early days. But initiative . . . when had he ever really shown any of that? He was a 'company man', and initiative was for lone wolves like Doyle, the sort who got into all sorts of trouble but usually ended up with a result along the way. So he'd been sitting there, alternately bursting to recite his facts and desperate to show his initiative. Initiative had won, for a change . . . and no one had minded. It sounded like this Barclay character – the one who'd contacted Special Branch in the first place – it sounded like *he* was showing initiative too . . .

As Parry and Trilling left the room – not together but one after the other, with a decent pause between – Doyle handed him a scrap of paper. He unfolded it. It read: 'What are you looking so fucking smug about?'

He looked back at Doyle and shrugged his shoulders. There was no malice in the note, and no necessity for it. It was a public gesture, meant for Elder. The message to Elder was clear. It was two against one now, Doyle and Greenleaf were a team. Greenleaf didn't want this. It wouldn't help to isolate Elder. So, dropping his pen and stooping to retrieve it, he scraped his chair a little further along the table, away from Doyle, making the seating arrangement slightly more triangular. Elder noticed, but his face showed nothing. As the door closed, leaving the three of them together, there was another silence until Doyle broke it, directing his words at Greenleaf.

'Come on then, Sherlock, you seem to know all about it. What's the game plan?'

'We could start by taking a look at the Conference Centre and surrounding area.'

'Join the queue, you mean? The place is already swarming with Anti-Terrorist Branch, sniffer-dogs, bomb experts . . .'

'Not to mention a few dozen . . . delegates from the other countries,' added Elder.

'Yes,' agreed Doyle, 'we've already got security men checking the security men who're checking security. What more can *we* do?'

'I didn't mean to imply,' said Elder, 'that we shouldn't get involved. Everyone should be notified that Witch may pay a visit.'

'What, work them up good and proper?' Doyle was dismissive. 'They'd start shooting at shadows. The American lot are edgy as it is. Someone sent a threat to their embassy: the President gets it, that sort of thing.'

'We needn't alarm them,' said Elder quietly. 'But they should be informed.'

Greenleaf was about to agree when there was a knock at the door. It opened, and a woman announced that there was a telephone call for Mr Doyle.

'Won't be a minute,' he said, getting up and leaving the room. Only then did Greenleaf notice that the conference room itself contained no telephones. On cue, Elder seemed to read his mind.

'Phones are receivers,' he explained. 'They can be bugged.'

Greenleaf nodded at this. He did not know what he had been expecting of the building. It appeared much the same as any other civil service admin block . . . or police admin block come to that. Yet it was, as Doyle had commented on the way there, CDHQ – Cloak & Dagger Headquarters.

'So,' said Elder conversationally, 'whose idea was the name?'

'The name?'

'Operation Broomstick.'

'Oh, that. Commander Trilling.'

Elder nodded. 'Bill Trilling's a tough old bull, isn't he?'

Greenleaf shrugged.

'When did he stop smoking?'

'About seven months back.'

'Remind me to buy some shares in whoever manufactures those mints of his.'

Greenleaf smiled, then checked himself. He didn't want to appear disloyal. 'The Commander's all right,' he said.

'I don't doubt it. Not slow to take offence though, wouldn't you agree?'

'Unlike Mrs Parry, you mean?'

'Oh, no, I wasn't . . . never mind.'

There was quite a long pause. Elder had turned to his case-file and was browsing through it.

'How long have you been retired?' Greenleaf asked.

'Two years.' Elder's eyes were still on the file.

'Enjoying it?'

'Yes, thanks.'

'So why are you here?'

Now Elder looked up. 'Because I'm interested. I wrote the original Hiroshima summary . . .'

'Yes, I know. And you've been interested in Witch ever since. If I didn't know better, I might even say you're a fan.'

Elder nodded. 'Oh, I'm a fan all right. Look at the Khan hit. Don't you find it in some way admirable? I mean, as

157

a *professional*. There is something to admire in perfection, even when it's the perfection of the enemy. Somehow, I can't see Mr Doyle planning and executing anything with the same degree of . . . élan.'

'His bark's worse than his bite.'

'I sincerely hope not. If we *do* locate Witch, his bite will have to be very fierce indeed.' Elder wagged a finger. 'And so will yours, Mr Greenleaf. It doesn't do to ignore the facts of the Khan assassination. Witch is utterly ruthless.'

'Not *so* ruthless. She didn't kill the bodyguard and the girlfriend.'

'No, quite. I've been wondering about that.'

'Oh?'

'Leaving the bodyguard alive is the only evidence we have that the assassin *was* a woman.'

'You think she wanted us to know? That wouldn't make sense, would it?'

'I suppose not. But then blowing up both those boats hardly "makes sense".'

'Tying up loose ends? Maybe the crews knew something we don't.'

'Possibly.' Elder didn't sound enthusiastic.

'Well,' said Greenleaf, 'why *does* she want us to know she's here?'

'Maybe she's issuing a challenge.'

'To you?'

'Yes.'

'You think she knows about you?'

'Oh, she knows all right, believe me.'

'How?'

Elder shrugged.

'Then how can you be so sure?' Greenleaf persisted.

Another shrug. 'I just am, Mr Greenleaf. I just am.

What you said about the summit being almost *too* tempting ... there may be something in that.'

Another knock at the door. Someone opened the door from the corridor, and someone else bore in a tray of mugs.

'Mrs Parry said you'd likely be needing some tea,' the man announced. He placed the tray on the table. The tea was already in the mugs, but the tray also held a bowl of sugar, jug of milk, and plate of biscuits.

'Thanks, Derek,' said Elder. The man smiled.

'Didn't think you'd remember me.'

'Of course I remember you. How're things?'

'Not so bad.' The man lowered his voice a little and wrinkled his nose. 'It's not the same these days though,' he said. 'Not like it was.' His partner, waiting in the corridor with his hand still on the door handle, gave an impatient cough. The man winked at Elder. 'I'll leave you to it then,' he said, closing the door after him.

'Anyone would think you'd been retired twenty years,' Greenleaf said.

'All the same,' said Elder, lifting one of the mugs, 'he's got a point. I've only been back one full day and I've noticed changes. More machines and less staff.'

'You mean computers?' Greenleaf poured milk into his chosen mug. 'They're a boon. All the sifting that Profiling had to do to produce the target list, it only took a few hours.'

'The problem is that the operatives tend to speed up too, making errors or creating gaps, where patience and plodding really *are* necessary virtues.' Elder thought of a comparison Greenleaf could relate to. 'It's like running a murder inquiry without the door-to-door. Nothing beats actually talking to someone face-to-face. You get an inkling, don't you, whether they're telling the truth or not? I've seen people beat lie-detector tests, but I've never seen them get past a shrewd interrogator.'

'I'll take your word for it,' said Greenleaf, raising the mug to his lips.

The door burst open. This time it was Doyle. His eyes darted around excitedly, eventually alighting on the last mug of tea.

'Great,' he said. He lifted the mug and gulped from it, not bothering with milk or sugar.

'What is it?' said Greenleaf, recognising in Doyle the symptoms of some news. But knowing Doyle, it would take an age to extract the actual information.

And indeed, he shook his head as he drank, until he'd finished the tea. He went to his chair and gathered up his papers. Only then did he pause, studying the two seated figures.

'Come on then,' he said.

'Where?'

'You can stay here if you like,' Doyle said.

'For Christ's sake, spit it out, will you?'

Doyle's eyes twinkled. 'Say please.'

'Please,' said Greenleaf. Somehow, Elder was managing to stay calm and silent, nibbling on a biscuit between sips of milky tea.

Doyle seemed to consider. He even glanced over towards Elder who certainly wasn't about to say 'please'. Then he placed his papers back on the desktop and sat down again, but resting on the edge of the chair only.

'That phone call was Folkestone. They've traced a driver who says he gave a lift to a woman.'

Elder put his mug down on the table.

'Really?' said Greenleaf. 'That night? What time?'

There was a scraping sound as Dominic Elder pushed back his chair and stood up, collecting together his own sheaf of paper. 'Never mind questions,' he said authoritatively. 'We can ask those on the way. Come on.' And with that, he strode to the door and out of the room. Doyle grinned at Greenleaf.

'Thought that might get him going.'

For one stomach-churning second, Greenleaf thought Doyle had just played some monstrous practical joke. It was a hoax, there was no driver, no sighting. But then Doyle too got to his feet. 'What are you waiting for?' he called back to Greenleaf as he made for the door.


Sitting in the police station, smoking his sixteenth cigarette, Bill Moncur was regretting ever opening his mouth. It was like his mate Pat had told him: say nowt at no time to no one. When he was a kid, there'd been a little china ornament on the mantelpiece at home. It was called The Three Wise Monkeys. They sat in a row, one seeing no evil, one hearing no evil, one speaking no evil. But one day Bill had picked the ornament up, and it had slipped out of his hand, smashing on the tiles around the fireplace. When his mother came through from the kitchen, he was standing there, hand clamped to his mouth just like the third monkey, stifling a cry.

He thought of that ornament now, for some crazy reason. Maybe the same crazy reason he'd said 'yes' to the policeman's question.

'Hello, sir. We're just asking drivers about a woman who might have been hitching along this way a couple of weekends back, late on Sunday the thirty-first or early Monday the first. Don't suppose you were along this way then, were you?'

Why? Why had he opened his big mouth and said, 'Yes, I was.' Why? It was just so . . . stunning. He'd never felt important like that before, included like that. He'd been stopped before by similar checkpoints, usually trying to find witnesses to a crash or a hit-and-run. He'd never been able to help in the past. He'd never been able to involve himself. Not until now.

Say nowt at no time to no one.

See no evil, hear no evil, speak no evil.

'Yes, I was. I picked up a hitch-hiker, too. Young woman. Would that be her, do you think?'

The constable had said something like, 'Just wait there, sir,' and then had retreated, off to have a word with his superior. Right then, right at that precise moment, Bill Moncur knew he'd said the wrong thing. He'd a load to deliver to Margate, and after that he'd to head for Whitstable and Canterbury before home. A busy schedule. Why hadn't he just shaken his head and driven on? Another van, which had been stopped in front of him, now started off again. His boss would give him hell for this. Why didn't you just keep your trap shut, Bill? His van was still revving. He could scarper while the copper was out of sight. But not even Bill Moncur was *that* stupid. They were looking for a young woman. Maybe she'd gone missing, been raped. Couldn't have been the woman he picked up, could it? Must be somebody else. Oh Christ, but what if it *was* her? What if she'd been found dead in a ditch somewhere, and here he was saying he'd given her a lift. He'd be a suspect, the sort you heard about on the news. A man is helping police with their inquiries. Well, that's what *he* was trying to do, but out of public-spiritedness, not because he had anything to confess or anything to be guilty about. Okay, so he skimmed a bit off his company. He might use the van for a bit of business at nights and weekends, but never anything outrageous. Not like Pat, who'd taken *his* van over the Channel one weekend and used it for smuggling back porn mags, videos, fags and booze. It was like one of those old mobile shops in the back of Pat's van, but he'd shifted the lot before Monday morning, and with four hundred quid clear profit in his pocket. But Jesus, if he'd been caught . . . caught using the firm's van . . .

'Hello, sir.' There were two of them standing there, the constable he'd spoken to before and now this plain-clothes man, reeking of ciggies and CID. 'My colleague tells me you may have some information for us?'

'Yeah, that's right, but I'm a bit pushed just now, see. Deliveries to make. Maybe I could come into the station later on, like. Tomorrow morning, eh?'

The CID man was gesturing with his arm, as if he hadn't heard a word Bill had been saying. 'You can park just over there, sir. In the lay-by, other side of the police car. We'll have a little chat then, eh? Don't want to hold up the vehicles behind.'

So that was that. He'd shoved first gear home and started off. Even as he moved slowly forwards, he thought: I could still run for it. He shook the thought aside. He had absolutely nothing to hide. It wouldn't take him five minutes to tell them his story, and after that he could bugger off again. Maybe they'd take his name and address, maybe they'd get back to him later, but for today he'd be back on the road. With luck, he could push the speedo to 70 or 80 on some stretches, make up the time easy. Wouldn't it be funny if he got stopped for speeding? Sorry, officer, I was helping your colleagues with their inquiries and I sort of got behind on my deliveries.

He pulled into the lay-by at quarter to eleven. Now, as he sat in the police station and lit his seventeenth cigarette – seventeenth of the day – it was quarter past one. They'd brought him a filled roll, egg mayonnaise, disgusting, and a packet of spring onion crisps. By dint of putting the crisps *in* the roll, he managed to force it all down. He thought, not for the first time: On a normal run I'd be in the Feathers by now, supping a pint and tucking in to one of that big bird Julie's home-made stews. Full of succulent carrots and little bits of onion. No gristle on the meat either. Beautiful. Egg mayonnaise and bloody crisps. Bill Moncur and his big bloody mouth.

They'd let him call the office. That hadn't been much fun, even though the CID man had explained that everything was all right, that he wasn't in any trouble or anything, but that he'd have to stay at the station for a little while longer. The firm were sending someone else out, some relief driver (it might even be Pat). The van keys were at the desk. The relief would pick them up and do the run for him. The relief driver would stop at the Feathers to chat up Julie and watch the way she pulled a pint with her manicured, painted fingernails on the pump.

How much fucking longer? he said to himself. There were four empty polystyrene cups in front of him as well as the empty crisp packet, cellophane from the roll, brimming ashtray, ciggies and lighter. He used the tip of his finger to pick up a few crumbs of crisp from the desktop, transferring them to his mouth. They'd be along in a minute to ask him if he wanted more coffee. He'd tell them then: 'I'm not waiting any fucking longer. You can't keep me here. If you want me, you know where to look. I'm in the phone book.'

That's what he'd say. This time. This time he'd really say it, and not just think it. Bonny girl they'd sent in last time to ask about the coffee, mind. Took his mind off it for a moment, so that he forgot to ask in the end. No, not ask, *demand*. It was his *right* to walk out of there whenever he felt like it. He'd only been in a police station twice in his life. Once when he was thirteen, and they found him staggering pissed out of his head along the main road. They took him back to the station, put him into a cell, stood him up, and kneed him in the nuts until he threw up. Then they left him for an hour before kicking him out. Could hardly walk straight for days after that ... which was ironic, as Pat said, since they'd picked him up in the first place for not walking straight.

That was once. The second time, they raided a pub during a brawl, and though he'd taken hardly any part in it he was dragged down to the station with the rest of them. But the barman, Milo, had put in a word for him, so they'd let him go with a caution.

That was twice. Hardly premier league, was it, hardly major crime? Were they holding him so they could look him up in their records? Maybe they were seeing if he had any priors for rape or murder or abduction or anything. Well, in that case he'd walk when they'd finished checking. How long could it take?

Of course, he did have *something* to hide. For a start, if it got back to his boss that he was out in the van on a Sunday night ... well, bosses tended to have inquiring minds in that direction. But his boss wouldn't find out, not unless the police said anything. He could always tell them he was in his car rather than the van anyway ... but no, it didn't do to lie when the truth wouldn't hurt. If they caught him lying, they might wonder what else he was hiding. No, he'd tell them. He was using the van to help out a friend. And indeed this was the truth. His neighbour Chas played keyboards in a sort of country and western band. They'd been playing a Sunday night gig at a pub in Folkestone, and he'd been acting as Road Manager, which meant picking up the PA from Margate and taking it back to Folkestone. It was all a fuck-up in the first place, that's why he'd had the drive to do. The band's own PA had blown half a dozen fuses or something, and a friend of Chas's who had a residency in

Margate had said the band could borrow *his* band's gear on the proviso that they brought it back the same night.

Stupid, but the gear was good stuff, a few thousand quid's worth, and the guy didn't want it out of his sight overnight. So, for fifty quid and a few drinks, Bill had driven to Margate, picked up the gear, brought it to Folkestone, sat through the gig, then hauled it back to Margate again before returning to Folkestone, absolutely knackered. It was a lot of work for fifty quid, but then Chas was a mate, and besides, Bill liked being a Road Manager. He'd have liked to play in a band himself had he been what you would call musical. Musical he was not. He'd tried auditioning as a vocalist once – not in Chas's band, in another local outfit – but the ciggies had shot his voice to hell. Like the band's leader said, his timing and pace were superb, and he'd plenty of emotion, but he just couldn't 'hold a tune'. Whatever that meant.

The door opened and in walked the same CID man who'd spoken to him in the lay-by.

'Well about bloody time,' said Bill. 'Listen, I can't hang around here any longer, and I'm—'

They kept filing into the room, three of them as well as the CID man. The room, which had been so empty before, now seemed overfull.

'These gentlemen have driven down from London to see you, Mr Moncur,' said the CID.

'Bit pokey in here, innit?' said one of the men. He looked to Bill Moncur like an old boxer, semi-pro. The speaker turned to the CID man. 'Haven't you got an office we could use?'

'Well . . .' The CID man thought about it. 'There's the Chief's office. He's not around this afternoon.'

'That'll do us then.'

The other two Londoners were silent. They seemed

happy enough to let their colleague do the talking. They all trooped out of the interview room and along to a more spacious, airier office. Extra chairs were carried in, and the CID man left, closing the door behind him. The oldest of the three Londoners, craggy-faced and grim-looking, had taken the chair already behind the desk, a big comfortable leather affair. Moncur was sitting in the other chair already in place on the other side of the desk. He kept looking to Craggy Face, who seemed like the boss, but he still wasn't speaking. The one who'd done all the speaking, and who now remained standing, started things off.

'We're Special Branch officers, Mr Moncur. I'm Inspector Doyle, and this' – with a nod to the third man, who had taken a seat against the wall – 'is Inspector Greenleaf. We're particularly interested in what you told Detective Sergeant Hines. Could you go through your story again for us?'

'You mean I've been kept in here waiting for you lot to arrive from London? You could have asked me over the phone.'

'We could have, but we didn't.' This Doyle was a short-fuse merchant, Moncur could see that. 'The sooner we have your story, the sooner you'll be out of here. It's not as if you're in any trouble . . .'

'Tell that to my gaffer.'

'If you want me to, I will.'

The third Londoner, Greenleaf, had picked up a briefcase from the floor and rested it on his knees. He now brought out a twin cassette-deck, an old-fashioned and unwieldy-looking thing. The other one was speaking again.

'Do you mind if we record this interview? We'll have it transcribed, and you can check it for mistakes. It's just a record so we don't have to bother you again if we forget something. Okay?'

'Whatever.' He didn't like it though. The man with the briefcase was plugging in the deck. Positioning it on the desk. Checking that it worked. Testing, testing: just like Chas at a sound-check. Only this was very different from a sound-check.

'You were out on a run in your van, Mr Moncur?' asked Doyle, almost catching him off-guard. The interview had started already.

'That's right. Sunday night it was. Last day of May.'

'And what exactly were you doing?'

'I was helping a mate. He plays in a band. Well, their PA had broken down and I had to fetch another from Margate, see. Only, after the show, the guy who owned the PA wanted it delivered back to him. So off I went to Margate again.'

'Were you alone in the van, Mr Moncur?'

'At the beginning I was. Nobody else in the band could be bothered to—'

'But you weren't alone for long?'

'No, I picked up a hitch-hiker.'

'What time was this?'

'Late. The dance the band were playing at didn't finish till after one. Then we had a few drinks ...' He caught himself. 'I stuck to orange juice, mind. I don't drink and drive, can't afford to. It's my livelihood, see, and I don't—'

'So it was after one?'

'After two more like. After the gig, we'd to load the van, then we had a drink ... yes, after two.'

'Late for someone to be hitching, eh?'

'That's just what I told her. I don't normally pick up hitch-hikers, no matter what time of day it is. But a woman out on her own at that time of night ... well, that's just plain bloody stupid. To be honest, at first I thought maybe it was a trap.'

'A trap?'

'Yeah, I stop the van for her, then her boyfriend and a few others appear from nowhere and hoist whatever I'm carrying. It's happened to a mate of mine.'

'But it didn't happen to you?'

'No.'

'Tell me about the woman, Mr Moncur. What sort of—'

But now the man behind the desk, the one who hadn't been introduced, now *he* spoke. 'Before that, perhaps Mr Moncur could show us on a map?' A map was produced and spread out on the top of the desk. Moncur studied it, trying to trace his route.

'I was never much good at geography,' he explained as his finger traced first this contour line, then that.

'These are the roads here, Mr Moncur,' said the man behind the desk, running his finger along them.

Moncur attempted a chuckle. 'I'd never make it as a long-distance driver, eh?' Nobody smiled. 'Well, anyway, it was just there.' A pen was produced, a dot marked on the map.

'How far is that from the coast?' asked Doyle.

'Oh, a mile, couple of miles.'

'All right.' The map was folded away again. The questioning resumed as before. 'So, you saw a woman at the side of the road?'

'That's right.'

'Can you describe her?'

'Long hair, dark brown or maybe black. I didn't have the lights on in the cab, so it wasn't easy to tell. Sort of . . . well, I mean, she was quite pretty and all, but she wasn't . . . she wasn't anything out of the ordinary.'

169

'What about height?' This from the one behind the desk.

'I dunno, average. Five-seven, five-eight.'

'A little taller than average, maybe,' he suggested. 'What was she wearing?'

'Jeans, a jacket. She looked cold.'

'Did she seem wet?'

'Wet? No, it wasn't raining. But she looked cold. I turned the heating up in the cab.'

'And what was she carrying?'

'Just a bag, a haversack sort of thing.'

'Anything else?'

'No.'

'Was the haversack heavy?'

A short nervous laugh. 'I don't know. She heaved it into the van herself.'

The man behind the desk nodded thoughtfully.

'Okay, Mr Moncur,' Doyle continued. 'Is there anything else you can tell us about her appearance? Her shoes for example.'

'Never noticed them.'

'Was she wearing make-up?'

'No. She could have done with a bit. Pale face. I suppose it was the cold.'

'And her accent, was it local?'

'No.'

'But English?'

'Oh, yeah, she was English. Definitely.'

'Right, so you picked her up. You've given us her description. What did you talk about?'

'She wasn't all that talkative. I got the idea she was doing a runner. Well, that time of night . . .'

'Running from whom exactly?'

'Boyfriend probably. She wasn't wearing any rings,

not married or anything. I reckoned boyfriend. She looked like she'd been crying.'

'Or swimming,' from behind the desk.

'At that time of night?' Bill Moncur laughed again. Again, nobody laughed with him. 'We didn't talk that much really. I thought that if she got to talking about it, she'd burst into tears. That was the last thing I wanted.'

'So would you describe her as ... what? Sullen?'

'No, not sullen. I mean, she was pleasant enough and all. Smiled a few times. Laughed at one of my jokes.'

'Where was she headed?'

'She said Margate would do. At first, anyway.'

'She didn't specify her destination?' asked Doyle, but now the quiet man, Greenleaf, the one with the cassette-deck, spoke.

'What did you mean, "at first"?'

'Well, when we got a bit closer, she asked if I was going through Cliftonville. To be honest, I wasn't, but she looked washed out. So I asked her if that was where she wanted dropping off, and she nodded. It wasn't much out of my way, so I took her there.'

'Cliftonville. Somewhere specific in Cliftonville?'

'No, anywhere along the front seemed to suit her. She wasn't bothered. I thought it was funny at the time. I mean, saying where you want to go, then not really minding whereabouts you're dropped off once you get there. Maybe she was going to run away with the circus, eh?'

'Maybe.' This from behind the desk again. 'I'd like to hear anything she said to you, Mr Moncur, anything you can remember. It doesn't matter how trivial you think it was, whether it was just yes or no to a question or whatever. *Any*thing she said to you, I'd like to hear it.'

So he'd to go over the whole journey. It took the best part of half an hour. They'd to put in fresh tapes at one point. He noticed that they were making two copies of the interview. Finally, he asked a question of his own.

'What's she done then? What's so important?'

'We think she's a terrorist, Mr Moncur.'

'Terrorist?' He sounded amazed. 'I don't hold no truck with that sort of—'

'You might not *hold* any truck,' said Doyle, 'but you had one *in* your truck.' And he grinned. Bill Moncur found himself unable to smile back. 'Get it?' Doyle asked Greenleaf.

'I get it, Doyle,' said Greenleaf.

'You said she had long hair,' the man behind the desk interrupted. 'How long?'

Moncur tapped his back with a finger. 'Right down to here,' he said.

'Could it have been a wig?'

Moncur shrugged.

Now Doyle came up to him, leaning down over him, grinning. 'Just between us, Bill, man to man like, we all know what it's like driving a lorry ... picking up a woman. Did you ... you know ... did you ... ?' Doyle winked and leered. But Moncur was shaking his head.

'Nothing like that,' he said.

Doyle straightened up. He looked disappointed. He looked at Moncur as if he might be gay.

'Not that I wouldn't have or anything,' Moncur protested. 'But that time of night ... I was absolutely shattered. I couldn't have got it up for a centrefold.'

Doyle still looked dubious.

'Honest,' said Moncur.

'Well,' said the one behind the desk, 'no need to dwell on that.'

Then came the crusher.

'Mr Moncur,' he continued, 'we'll have to go to

172

Cliftonville. We need to know exactly where you dropped her off.'

'Fine, okay.' Bill Moncur nodded enthusiastically. They were leaving! He'd be out of here in a minute. 'When you go into the town,' he said, 'you head straight for—'

'You don't understand, Mr Moncur. Directions won't do. We need you there with us to show us the spot.'

'What?' It dawned on him. 'Cliftonville? *Now?* Aw, for Christ's sake.'

They busied themselves with locating a detailed map of Cliftonville, ignoring Bill Moncur's protestations. The CID man, DS Hines, appeared again to see if they needed a car. No, the one car they already had would be enough. And then the pretty WPC put her head round the door, smiling at Moncur. He blessed her for that smile.

'Need any tea or coffee here?' she asked.

'Not for us, thanks. We've got to be going. Come on, Mr Moncur. We'll take the same route you took that night. That way, you can show us where you picked up Witch.'

'Picked up which what?'

The one from behind the desk smiled for a moment. 'A slip of the tongue,' he said, motioning towards the doorway with his arm. 'After you.'

Eventually, at the end of his gruelling day, a police car took Bill Moncur back to Folkestone.

Elder, Doyle and Greenleaf remained in Cliftonville, their unmarked car (Doyle's car, still messy from his French trip) parked in the forecourt of a small hotel. They'd booked rooms for the evening, despite having brought nothing with them, no change of clothes, no toothbrushes ... It was Elder's decision, but the Special

173

Branch men were happy to go along with it, Greenleaf despite the facts that a) he'd have to call Shirley to tell her, and b) he'd be sharing a room with Doyle. They visited a chemist's and bought toiletries, before rendezvousing in the hotel lounge. It was just the right side of salubrious, with a tropical theme to the furnishings which extended to an island mural on one wall. A long time ago someone had painted white seashells on the dark green linoleum floor. They had the place to themselves. Greenleaf couldn't imagine why.

'It's important,' said Elder, 'not to let the trail grow colder than it already is. That means working through this evening.'

'Fine,' said Doyle, 'but am I being stupid or was the last sighting of Witch in Auchterwhatsit, six hundred miles north of here?'

Elder smiled. 'You're not being stupid, Mr Doyle, but there's something we've got to ask ourselves.'

Doyle said nothing, so Greenleaf provided the answer.

'Why did she specifically want to come to Cliftonville?'

'Exactly, Mr Greenleaf. I mean, look at the place. It's quiet, anonymous. It's perfect for her.'

Now Doyle spoke. 'You think she's got a contact here?'

Elder shrugged. 'It's possible her paymaster met her here with final instructions.'

'You don't think she's *here* though?'

'Mr Doyle, as my old Aberdonian tailor used to say, discount nothing.'

Doyle thought about this for a moment, realised a joke had been made, and laughed. Greenleaf didn't: his mother had come from Aberdeen.

'So what do we do this evening?'

'We cover as much ground as possible. That means splitting up. I'd suggest one of us makes contact with the local police, one asks around in the pubs, and one asks

taxi drivers and so on. We're talking about the wee sma'
hours of a Monday morning. A woman dropped off and
having, presumably, to walk to some destination. A late-
night patrol car may have spotted her. Taxi drivers may
have slowed to see if they had a fare. Were there any
nightclubs emptying around the time she arrived?
Someone may, without knowing it, have seen something. Perhaps she'd prearranged her late arrival with a
hotel or boarding-house. Or maybe some early-day
fisherman saw her – we can't possibly cover all the
angles, that's where the local police will come in.'

'We should set up a Portakabin on the front, put up
posters: have you seen this woman, that sort of thing.
Ask everybody who passes . . .'

But Elder was shaking his head. 'No, Doyle, that's
precisely what we don't want.'

'Because,' Greenleaf added, 'if she *is* still around here,
we don't want to chase her away.'

'Precisely. Softly softly, as the saying goes. Now, sitting
here like this, we're already losing valuable time. Let's
get down to some *real* work.'

Walking through the blowy streets that night, his feet
swelling in his shoes, Dominic Elder was worried. It
wasn't Greenleaf and Doyle who worried him. They
seemed capable sorts, if slightly curious as a twosome.
Well, perhaps not. It was the old interrogation two-step:
bad guy and nice guy. It could be a useful combination.

Elder did something he hadn't done in years. He
bought some cod and chips. The meal came on a
polystyrene tray with a small wooden fork, the whole
wrapped in a custom paper bag. Different to the way
Elder remembered it: greasy newsprint coming off on his
hands, picking at the fish-flesh with his fingers. The cod
had texture but no flavour at all. And the chips tasted

mass-produced. There was a regularity about their size which depressed him, but it did not worry him.

Witch worried him.

He could almost smell her, almost taste her behind the seaside flavours and aromas. She had been here. And not long enough ago for her taint to have left the place. Was she still here? He didn't think so. But if the hunt started to close in on her, she might just come back. A safe port in a storm. This had been her first lair on arriving in England. It would have meaning and resonance for her. Wounded, she might come crawling back. It would do no harm for Elder to learn the ground, her home-ground. So he walked, stopping to talk with people. Was the bakery all-night? It was, but the shift didn't come on till eleven. He could come back and ask his questions then. As he walked, he became more comfortable with his story. She was his daughter. She'd run away, and he wanted to find her. Doyle and Greenleaf were to tell similar tales in the pubs and clubs, with the necessary alteration turning Witch into their sister rather than daughter.

Elder knew he was getting old. Despite living in the country, tonight was as much walking as he'd done in a year or more. Doyle and Greenleaf were younger, fitter and faster than him. They'd be fast making a life or death decision. Would he be too slow? Say he came up against Witch, came up against her again. Would she be so much faster than him? Or was she ageing too? No, not judging by the Khan assassination. If anything, she was sharper than ever, damn her. He'd been rusty at the police station, interviewing the lorry driver. He'd asked leading questions rather than waiting for Moncur to tell his version. That was bad. *That* worried him.

Something else worried him, too. She wouldn't have come to Britain unless she was after very big game indeed. He didn't know why he felt this, but he did. Britain was enemy territory to her, Elder's territory. He couldn't help but think of the whole thing on the personal level. Which was dangerous. Things might start getting out of perspective. He might start reading too much or not enough into certain situations. He wished he knew who her target was. It crossed his mind – it had crossed his mind all week – that maybe *he* was her target. But, really, this was nothing but ego. It didn't make sense. He was no threat to her. He was in retirement, off the scene. Unless ... unless there was something in his file on her, something he'd overlooked and which could be dangerous to her. Well, Barclay had the file now; maybe *he* would see something, something Elder couldn't see.

Her target had to be the summit. But wasn't it at the same time just too obvious, as Greenleaf had hinted? All those heads of state ... But look at the challenge it presented to her. The security services of nine countries would be there, protecting their leaders. Over seven hundred and fifty security personnel in total (the majority supplied, of course, by the host nation), and more if you counted the uniformed police officers who would line the routes, holding back traffic and the public. Oh yes, it was a challenge all right, but then challenges had never been Witch's thing. She worked on a smaller scale. Yes, there was the Pope, but they'd scared her off there with fewer personnel. Besides, that was Wolf Bandorff's plan, not hers. Kidnappings, peace campaigners ... these were her arena. Would she bother, these days, with a head of state?

God alone knew. God, and the woman herself.

*Dominic Elder. A priest's name. You should have been a priest.* That's what she'd told him. Remembering, he rubbed his back.

177

He had come to the outskirts of the town. The wind was sharp and salty, the sea a distant clash. Maybe a storm was coming. The wind, though sharp, was warm. Clouds moved fast against the sky. He paused to rub at his back, and stared at the spotlit frontage of a small pub. Pubs were Doyle's and Greenleaf's territory. But all the same, the vinegary chips had left him with a dry throat. He stared at the pub's name.

The Cat over the Broomstick.

The name decided him. He pushed open the door and entered smoke and noise. It was a young people's pub. Jukebox, video games, loud conversations peppered with swearing, and necking in the few dark corners available. He hesitated, but walked up to the bar anyway. The youth in front of him, being served with seven pints of lager, wore a denim jacket with its arms shorn off, and beneath it a leather jacket, arms intact. Elder recognised biker gear when he saw it. A biker pub then, the dull offspring of the original Hell's Angels. Someone behind him called out 'Hey, Grandad!' to snorts of laughter. Elder stood his ground. The pints had been loaded onto a tray, the tray taken away. The barman was Elder's age, and sweating. He wore an apologetic look for his new customer, a look which said, 'It's business. If they weren't spending money here they'd be doing it somewhere else.'

'Whisky, please,' said Elder, 'a double.'

He wondered if Doyle and Greenleaf had made it out this far yet. Somehow he doubted it. They'd most probably have a drink in every pub they visited ... He gave the barman a fiver and, while waiting for his change, added plenty of water to his drink from a jug on the bar.

'I'm looking for my daughter,' he told the barman. But as he started to speak, a particularly thunderous track started on the jukebox, gaining a roar of approval from the drinkers.

'What?' said the barman, leaning his ear towards Elder.

'My daughter!' Elder yelled. 'I'm looking for her.'

The barman shook his head, and then jerked it towards one of the loudspeakers. The message was clear: We'll talk when the music stops. He went off to serve another customer. Another tray was needed. At one point, the barman twiddled with a knob mounted on the wall behind the optics. He did this as the song was ending. Another started up, but not so loud any more.

'Turn it up, Joe!'

'Come on, Joe, we can hardly hear it!'

'Crank it up!'

He shook his head and smiled. 'In a minute,' he called. 'Just give me a minute's rest, eh?'

There were groans but nothing more. Joe the barman came back to Elder.

'Now then, you were saying . . . ?'

'I'm looking for my daughter. She's run off and I think maybe she . . . she might have come down this way.'

'Are you Mr Elder?'

Elder's knees almost collapsed under him. 'What? How . . . yes, yes, I'm Dominic Elder.'

The barman nodded and moved back to the optics. On a shelf sat a letter, which he lifted and handed over the bar. Elder's hand didn't quite tremble as he accepted it.

'She left it for you.'

On the white envelope was printed MR DOMINIC ELDER. Elder knew the score. He knew he shouldn't touch it. It should go straight into a polythene bag for forensic analysis, for checks on fibres, saliva used to stick the envelope down . . . the arcana of the forensic arts. But then Elder was a retired member of the security services.

He might forget procedures, mightn't he? He tore open the envelope. Inside was a single folded sheet of lined writing-paper on which was scribbled a handwritten message. He looked around him. Joe the barman had gone off to serve yet another thirsty client. Then he read.

'Don't bother. When it's time, I'll find you. W.'

He read it again . . . and again . . . and again.

'Don't bother. When it's time, I'll find you. W.'

The 'I'll' and the 'you' had been double-underlined. *I'll* find *you*. Yes, but only when it was time. There was something else to be done first. The Khan assassination? Or something on a grander scale? He managed a wry smile. Oh, she was clever. She'd known Elder might well become involved . . . she'd even guessed that he might track her as far as Cliftonville. So she'd gone into an aptly named pub and left a note for him. She couldn't know it would reach him of course. But if it did . . . Yes, it seemed her style all right. But she'd slipped up, too. The note was handwritten. It wasn't much, but it was something. He looked about for the telephone, and found that there was a booth next to the toilets. He slipped the letter back into its envelope, put the envelope in his pocket, and made for the booth.

Doyle and Greenleaf weren't yet back at the hotel, so he tried the police station. No, the two gentlemen had called in, but there'd been no one available to help them. They'd arranged a meeting with Inspector Block in a pub somewhere . . . probably the Faithful Collie. Yes, he had the telephone number.

So he tried the Faithful Collie. Calling to a pub from a pub: talk about a noisy line! *I'll* find *you* . . . Eventually he got the barman in the Faithful Collie to understand. There was a yell, another yell, and finally Greenleaf answered.

'Is that you, Mr Elder?'

'She's left a message for me in a pub.'

'What? I didn't make that out.'

'Witch has left me a message.'

A burly biker roamed past on his way to the toilets. Another came out. They exchanged handslaps.

'How do you know?' Greenleaf was asking.

'Because a barman just handed it to me.'

'What does it say?'

'It says I'm not to look for her, she'll find me when she wants.'

'We've got to get it down to a lab ...' The fact suddenly struck Greenleaf. 'Oh,' he said, 'you've opened it.'

'Obviously.'

'You shouldn't have done that.'

'I realise ...'

'Still, not much we can do now. Which pub?'

'The Cat over the Broomstick.'

'You're kidding. You think she's guessed about Operation Broomstick?'

'I don't know. She knows we call her Witch.'

'We'll be right over.'

'Is Doyle sober?'

'He will be. Give us ... I don't know, depends how far we are from you.'

'Is Inspector Block still with you?'

'Yes, I'll bring him along too.'

'Fine. But be warned, this is a Hell's Angels' watering-hole.'

'Funny pubs you choose, Mr Elder. Is it the leather you like or what?'

Elder smiled but said nothing. He put down the receiver and went back to the bar, where his whisky was still waiting. Joe the barman was waiting too.

'Can you tell me anything about her?' Elder asked.

181

Joe shrugged. 'Came in about a week ago. Said she was on the move, keeping away from an older man.'

'How did she look?'

'Fine. Tired maybe. And she had a sprained wrist. That's why she got me to write it.' He looked along the bar to his right. 'Coming, Tony.' He went off to serve the customer. But Elder followed him.

'What do you mean?'

'I mean she'd sprained her wrist. She had a bandage on it. So she couldn't write. She thought for some reason you'd come looking for her in here. I told her we didn't usually cater to . . . older men. Well, you can see that for yourself. But she seemed to know . . . well, you're here, so it looks like she was right.'

'She didn't write the note then?'

Joe shook his head. 'One pound thirty-five please, Tony. No, like I say, I'd to write it for her. She told me what to put. Looks like she doesn't want to be found, Mr Elder, not yet any road.'

'Yes,' he said, 'looks like.'

A sprained wrist . . . couldn't write. She was cunning all right, and at the same time she was playing with him. If he found the note, she must know he would talk to the barman. And if he talked to the barman, he would find out the handwriting wasn't hers. If she'd *really* wanted to lead him a dance, she'd have asked someone else to write the note, so Elder wouldn't know that it *wasn't* her writing . . . Yes, she was playing games. This was so different to the Witch of old. What had happened to her? Had she gone mad? Was she on a suicide mission? What had happened? This wasn't the old Witch at all.

And yet, obviously it *was* the old Witch – as shrewd and as deadly as ever.

'I'll have another whisky when you're ready,' he told Joe the barman. 'And have one yourself.'

'Thanks, I will,' said Joe, making for the optics and once more turning up the volume. He received the cheers from the bar with a little bow from the waist.

Looking back on a startling day, it still seemed to Barclay that the most startling thing of all had been Dominique's driving in central Paris.

They set off from Calais in her car, leaving his in the police station car park, his packed bag locked in the boot. He brought to Dominique's car a single change of clothes, the Witch file, and a couple of opera tapes. During the drive, and above the noise of the engine and the rather extraordinary ventilation system (a single flap between dashboard and windscreen), they planned their next moves.

'His name,' Dominique yelled, 'is Monsieur Jean-Claude Separt. I know of him actually. He is a cartoonist. He draws stories.'

'You mean strip cartoons?'

'Cartoons in a strip, yes.'

'For a newspaper?'

'No, he makes books. Books of strip cartoons are very popular in France.'

'What sort of stuff does he do?'

'Political cartoons, or cartoons with a political point. He is left-wing. More than that I can't tell you until we get to Paris. There will be information on him when we get there.'

'What about his car?'

'It's curious, he reported it missing only *after* it was found. Doesn't that sound strange to you?'

'A bit. What's his story?'

She shrugged, pulling out to overtake a lorry. The 2CV barely had enough power to pull past the long, fuming vehicle. A car bore down on them, but Dominique shot

183

the 2CV back into the right-hand lane with two or three seconds to spare. The blood had vanished entirely from Barclay's face.

'I don't know yet,' she continued, as though nothing had happened. 'We shall have to ask him ourselves . . .'

The car didn't have a tape-deck, but it did have a radio. Dominique found a jazz station and turned the volume all the way up, so the music was just about audible above the engine. She beat her hands against the steering-wheel.

'In your room,' she yelled, 'I saw your cassettes – classical music.'

'Opera,' he corrected.

She wrinkled her nose. 'Jazz,' she said. 'Jazz is the only music in the world, and Paris is the capital!' She signalled, slipped the gear down into third, and roared out to pass another lorry.

In Paris, she first headed for her office, Barclay remaining in the car while she sprinted to the building, and, moments later, sprinted out again. She threw a file on to his lap, slapped his hand away from the radio (he'd been trying to find a classical station), and slammed shut the driver's-side door. Then she indicated and screeched back into the traffic again, horns sounding all around them.

'They had it waiting at reception for me,' she said of the file. 'Read it out while I drive.'

So, in his stilted French, he read from the report, thankful for it since it served to take his eyes off the madness all about him. Lunchtime in Paris. He'd been here for weekends before, and even then had marvelled at the ability of the local drivers to squeeze five-abreast into a three-lane road without scraping up against each other. Meanwhile, as he read, Dominique translated some of the more difficult sentences into English, until at last he'd finished the report on the life and career of the cartoonist Jean-Claude Separt and they were pulling into a narrow street, the buildings tall on either side, blocking out the light and a good deal of the city's noise. There were shops and offices at ground level, dingy-looking things with unwashed windows. But the storeys above were apartments, some with small verandahs, all with dusty shutters, the paint flaking off, some slats missing or hanging loose. Dominique double-parked the 2CV alongside a venerable-looking low-slung Citroën.

'Come on,' she said.

'Where?'

She motioned upwards. 'This is where I live ... my home. I have to change my clothes.' She pulled at the material of her jacket. She was smiling. 'Coming?'

He nodded. 'Sure,' he said. His heart started pumping a little faster. 'Sure,' he repeated, getting out of the car.

'Stairs only,' she warned him. 'No elevator.'

The place smelled a bit like the London Underground. He couldn't think why. It was a smell like burnt oil, and lurking beneath it dampness and rot. He got the feeling that if he touched the dark green walls, a residue would come off on his fingers.

He was behind Dominique, carrying her small suitcase. He watched her body as she climbed the winding stairs.

'Next floor,' she said, a little breathlessly.

'Right, okay.' But it wasn't okay. Her case was heavier than he'd expected. What did she have in there, a couple of sub-machine guns?

And then they were standing facing one another outside an ornate front door. She smiled, catching her breath. He smiled back, concentrating his eyes on hers, trying not to show how hard he was breathing after the climb. She brought a key out of her bag and opened the door.

He looked into a well-kept if old-fashioned hall. The carpet was faded. So were the furnishings. Was there a radio playing in the distance?

'*Mama*,' called Dominique. '*C'est moi.*'

Briskly, she took the case from him and walked up the hall.

'*C'est toi, Dominique?*' came a wavering voice from behind one of the doors. Barclay still stood in the hall, drinking in this unexpected reality. Dominique waved for him to follow her, then opened a door at the end of the hall.

In the living-room sat Madame Herault. But she stood to receive her foreign visitor, and switched off her radio too. She looked like her daughter, but was between thirty and forty years older. She patted her hair and said something about how Dominique should have warned her. To which Dominique replied that if she had warned her mother, her mother would merely have tired herself out cleaning and making cakes and dressing herself up, when they were only staying for fifteen minutes or so. Then Dominique said she had to go to her room and change. Barclay was made to sit on the huge springy sofa which reminded him unnervingly of the 2CV's suspension.

'Keep Mama company, will you?' Dominique asked in English. 'I won't be long. Oh, and if she offers you some of her calvados . . . refuse it.'

And with that she was gone. Madame Herault, still standing, asked him if he would like something to drink? He didn't, but nodded anyway, since Madame Herault fixing him something to drink was preferable to Madame Herault sitting expecting him to make conversation with her. Then he remembered the warning about the calvados.

'*Pastis, s'il vous plaît,*' he said.

But a drink was not enough. He would have something to eat, too, wouldn't he? Barclay shook his head, patting his stomach.

'*Complet,*' he said, hoping it was the right word.

She persisted, but he persisted too. Just a drink, a drink would be very good.

'Calvados?' Madame Herault asked.

Barclay shook his head. '*Pastis, s'il vous plaît,*' he insisted.

So off she went to fetch him a pastis. He released a great intake of air, and smilingly chastised himself for his original thoughts regarding Dominique's intentions. The room was comfortably old-fashioned, exuding what seemed to him a particularly French sort of genteel shabbiness. The ornaments were too ornate, the furniture too bulky. The dresser was enormous, and should have stood in a chateau entrance hall rather than a second-floor Parisian apartment. He wondered how they'd got it into the room in the first place. The obvious answer seemed to be: through the large windows. A block and tackle job from street level. Yes.

God, he thought, what am I doing here? I should have stayed in the car. She's been teasing me, hasn't she? She could have said it was her mother's place. She could have told me her mother would be home. Instead of which, Dominique had let him think his own thoughts, teasing him. Little vixen.

Madame Herault carried a tray back into the room. Barclay had risen from the sofa and was examining some framed photographs on top of an upright piano. There was one of a man in police uniform.

'*Mon mari,*' explained Madame Herault. '*Il est mort.*'

She placed the tray on a footstool. There was a long slim glass containing an inch of pastis and a single ice-cube. There was also a jug of water, and a saucer on which sat some plain biscuits. She motioned with the jug and poured until he told her to stop. Then she handed him the glass and picked up the photograph, giving him some long story of which Barclay made out probably most of the relevant facts. Monsieur Herault had been a policeman in Paris, a detective. But a terrorist bomb had blown him up ten years ago. He'd been helping to evacuate shoppers from a department store where a bomb was said to be hidden. But it had gone off sooner than expected . . .

She gave a rueful smile and picked up another photograph, a beaming schoolgirl.

'Dominique,' she said, quite unnecessarily. Barclay nodded. She looked up at him. '*Très belle.*' He nodded again. For want of anything else to add, he gulped at the drink. Mother of God, it was strong! He lifted a biscuit to disguise his discomfort. But the biscuit disintegrated in his hand, falling like bits of bomb-blast to the floor.

Madame Herault apologised and went to kneel to pick the pieces up, but Barclay was already down on his knees, his fingers trying to lift the tiny pieces without them splintering further.

And that was the scene which presented itself to Dominique when she entered the room. The crumbs collected, more or less, Barclay got to his feet and helped Madame Herault to hers. Dominique had changed into a knee-length skirt, showing off legs which, even in the dim light of the apartment, Barclay could see were tanned and smooth. She had a jacket slung over her shoulder, and wore a crisp white blouse with a small gold cross on a chain around her neck.

'Drinking in the middle of the day?' she chided him.

'We've still got a lot of work to do, Michael, remember?'
Then she said something in a rush of French to her
mother, and her mother replied in an even faster rush,
her cadences soaring and plummeting. He finished his
drink while the conversation went on, noticing Dominique glancing towards him from time to time. When he
made to replace the empty glass on the tray, she
signalled, with the slightest jerk of her head, that it was
time to go. This was actually hard to achieve, since
Madame Herault seemed to have a lot she still wanted to
say to him, and there were hands to be shaken, cheeks to
be kissed.

'*Oui, Mama, oui,*' Dominique kept saying, her exaspera-
tion increasing. Finally, they were at the front door, and
with a final push from Dominique herself Barclay found
himself on the stairs and starting his descent. But
Madame Herault came to the stair-head and continued
to call down instructions to her daughter.

'*Oui!*' Dominique called back. '*Bien sûr! D'accord. A ce
soir, Mama! Ce soir!*'

The street, the dull claustrophobic street, seemed
suddenly a huge and necessary release, a refuge. Even
Dominique sighed and fanned her face with her hand
before getting back into the car. She didn't say anything
as she keyed the ignition, checked behind her, and
started off along the street. But, edging out into the
traffic at the end of the road, she remarked simply, 'That
was my mother.'

'Really?' replied Barclay.

His irony escaped her. 'Yes, really.'

'She was charming, so like her daughter.'

She pursed her lips. 'I should have warned you.'

'Yes, you bloody well should.'

She laughed. 'Tell me, Mr Michael Barclay, what were
you thinking?'

'When?'

'When I led you up the stairs.'

'I was wondering why the stairwell smelled like the London Underground.'

The answer surprised her. She glanced at him. 'Really?' she asked.

He nodded. 'That's what I was thinking,' he said. And he kept his eyes on the windscreen, well away from her bare tanned legs as they worked brake, clutch and accelerator.

'Mama kissed you twice,' Dominique mused. 'I think you made an impression of her.'

'An impression *on* her,' Barclay corrected.

'Well, anyway,' Dominique added with a smile, 'you made an impression.' And she laughed, suddenly and brightly.

By a strange twist of fate, Jean-Claude Separt's apartment-cum-studio was the sort of place Barclay had imagined Dominique's apartment would be. It was obvious that cartoonists, even (especially?) left-wing cartoonists, could live very comfortably in France. The apartment took up the whole top storey of a sandblasted block near Odeon.

'*Très cher, très chic,*' Dominique kept saying as they made their way up in the lift to the penthouse. They'd spoken about Separt on the way to Paris, talking about the garret he would inhabit, vermin-ridden and with unsold tracts and pamphlets piled to the ceiling. Preconceptions were there to be broken. Here was the second (only the second?) shattered preconception of the day.

Barclay knew his place. He was Dominique's colleague, a police officer from England (but not London; nowhere as important as London) on an exchange programme and spending the day with Dominique, who was herself a lowly police officer, a trainee in one of the administrative departments. They were here to interview Monsieur Separt regarding the theft of his motor vehicle, for a scheme called, as far as Barclay could work it out, the Vehicle Repatriation Register Survey. Well, something like that. Dominique had prepared some questions, and had written them down on a sheet of paper attached to a clipboard. She looked the part, he decided. Her clean, efficient clothes were just a bit *too* clean and efficient – the sort of outfit a trainee would wear when wanting to impress with the notion that they wouldn't stay a trainee forever. And she'd got rid of her lipstick, so that her face was a little plainer. It was perfect.

So was Separt's apartment. He was fat and greying with cropped hair and a grizzled beard. He wore faded denims, baggy at the knees and ankles, but tight at the stomach. He wore a short-sleéved striped shirt, and his eyes glinted from behind thick-lensed glasses. A strong yellow-papered cigarette either hung from his mouth or else from his fingers. And he lit a new cigarette with the dying embers of each old one.

Having ushered them in, Separt flapped back to his working-desk. 'I won't be a second,' he said. 'Just the finishing touches to a face . . .'

The bulk of the apartment was taken up by a single, huge thick-carpeted room. At one end stood a series of architect's tables over which hung anglepoise lamps. Here, Separt worked on his cartoons. On shelves behind him along the walls were various tools, old comic books, magazines, disparate newspaper cuttings. Pinned to the walls were photographs of politicians, some of them subtly and tellingly altered by the cartoonist. Barclay laughed at one of his country's own Prime Minister, showing the premier emerging from a bowl of soup. Written at the bottom was 'Prime Minestrone'.

Separt seemed inordinately pleased at Barclay's response. He chuckled and went back to inking some wild hair on his latest caricature.

There was a computer close by, which Barclay studied too. He thought maybe it would be a Paintbox, one of those extraordinary machines used by some artists and graphic designers. But it was just a plain old personal computer.

At the other end of the room, Dominique had already settled on the extremely long sofa. Empty wine bottles and beer bottles were strewn around the floor, and ashtrays brimmed with cigarette ends and the roaches from several joints. Separt, who had known from their intercom conversation that two police officers were on their way up, didn't seem bothered in the slightest. Two walls of the room were made up of windows, one side opening onto a small rooftop patio. The view of the city was breathtaking.

'How can he work with a view like that in front of him?' Barclay marvelled. Dominique translated the question, and Separt, who had thrown down his pen with a flourish, beamed again before saying something.

'He says,' Dominique replied, 'that he no longer sees the view. It is something for visitors, that's all.' Separt and Barclay shared a smile, and Separt motioned for his English guest to sit on the sofa beside Dominique. Barclay did so, and Separt, ignoring the spare chair, flopped on to the floor in front of his visitors, resting with legs out, one foot over the other, hands stretched behind him so he sat up. He had an impish look, as though every moment of his life was both revelation and opportunity for humour. But Barclay noticed that Dominique pressed her knees together and kept them like that, and he wondered if there were some more sordid reason for Separt's choice of seat . . .

His French was coming on fast, and he understood most of the dialogue which followed.

'Your car was stolen, monsieur,' Dominique began, her pen held above the clipboard.

'Of course, otherwise you would not be here.' Separt beamed again.

'Of course,' said Dominique. She was a good trainee police officer. But Barclay wondered how she would have talked her way out of it if Separt had asked for identification. They'd considered the question on the way over here. Considered it, and come to no solution.

'We'll handle it when the time comes,' she had said, leaving it at that.

'But you are one of the lucky few,' she was saying now, 'who not only have their car stolen, they also have it recovered.'

'So I understand. But it's an old car.' He shrugged. 'It would not have been a catastrophe if the car had disappeared from my life for ever!'

'You reported the car missing quite late, I believe?'

'No, not late, just before midday I think.' He chuckled again.

Dominique managed the faintest of official smiles. 'I meant, monsieur—'

'Yes, yes, I know what you meant.' Another shrug. 'I reported it stolen when I realised it had been stolen. You've seen the parking around here, mademoiselle. A nightmare. I had parked the car around the corner in Rue des Fêtes. It was not visible from the apartment.' He laughed, gesturing towards the huge windows. 'Unlike most of the motor vehicles in Paris.'

She smiled a cool smile, scratched on the pad with her pen. 'You were ill, is that correct?' This much they had read in the Calais police report.

Separt nodded. 'I wasn't out of the apartment for four days. Some sort of bug, I don't know exactly.'

'What did the doctor say?'

'Doctors?' He wrinkled his face. 'I can't be bothered with doctors. If I get better, I get better; and if I die, so be it. I'd rather give my money to tramps on the street than hand any over to a doctor.'

'And the tramps might give you a more accurate diagnosis,' added Dominique, causing Separt to collapse into a laughing fit, which then became a coughing fit. He rose to his feet, shaking his head.

'You are making my day, believe me,' he said. 'I must write that down. It's a good idea for a cartoon. Give the money to the beggars instead of the doctors, and the beggars give you a diagnosis – on the state of society's health.'

Barclay and Dominique sat silently while he went to his work table and wrote something on a sheet of paper, which he then tore from its pad and pinned to the wall.

'You know,' he called, 'my best ideas come this way – from other people. I feel a little guilty sometimes, I do so little work myself.'

When he returned, he chose the chair rather than the floor, sinking into it and crossing his ankles. Now that he was seated on a level with her, Dominique relented and released the pressure on her knees.

'So the car could have been taken any time during those four days?' she asked.

'That's right. I went outside on the fifth day, and I was puzzled at first, I wondered if I'd parked it where I thought I had. I walked around all the neighbouring streets. No sign. So I called the police.'

'This was on the first of June?'

'Was it? I'll take your word for it.'

'According to the records it was.'

'Then it was.'

'But your car's outside now?'

'And as rusty as ever. There are a few scratches on it that weren't there before. Well, to be honest maybe they *were* there before – it's hard to tell.'

'Nothing missing from the car?'

'No.'

'And nothing there that wasn't there before?'

He laughed again. 'You mean, did the thief *leave* me anything? No, not a sou.'

'Why do you think someone would steal a car from this arrondissement and take it to Calais?'

Separt shrugged. 'Joy riding. They may have been all over the place, and just run out of petrol there. Or maybe they were considering a trip to England, but changed their minds. Something like that, I imagine.'

Dominique nodded. 'On the whole, monsieur, you're happy to have your car returned?'

Separt gave this a little thought. 'On the whole, I suppose I am. Not that it would bother me unduly if someone stole it again ... Listen, I'm being rude, can I get you a glass of wine?'

'That's very kind, but we've already taken up enough of your time. We appreciate your talking to us like this.'

'Not at all.'

Dominique rose to her feet. Barclay rose too. He was glad they didn't have to drink anything. His head still ached from the pastis. Separt seemed disappointed that they were leaving so soon.

'When the survey is complete,' Dominique said, 'I may have to return with a few final follow-up questions ... without my colleague here, I'm afraid.'

'Oh, yes?' said Separt. 'You'll be welcome any time, believe me.'

Barclay had never seen anyone chatting up an

on-duty policewoman before. Trust the French. Separt took Dominique's hand and brushed his lips against it. Then he shook Barclay's hand warmly. A few words of English came to the cartoonist.

'Urrr . . . good luck, chum. Have a nice day.'

'*Merci*,' said Barclay. He waved a hand around him. 'You have a beautiful home.'

Nodding, grinning, laughing to himself now and then, the cartoonist showed them out of the apartment. When Dominique and Barclay were alone in the lift, and it had started its descent, he turned to her.

'Seemed like a nice chap,' he said.

'And genuine?'

'Not entirely.'

'A complete fake. He was worried as hell, that's why he kept laughing like that. Nervous laughter.'

'You think he knows something? So what do we do now? Keep a watch on him?'

She bit her bottom lip. 'Better than that, I would like to bug him. But I don't think my superiors would allow it.'

'Why not?'

'Separt's politics. If a bug was discovered, the left would have a . . . what do you say?'

'A field day?'

She nodded. 'A field day.'

Barclay had a thought. 'What if you *didn't* bug him?' he said.

'What do you mean?'

'Do you know how to make a listening device?'

'No.'

He nodded. 'What if someone created a bug of their own? Not the French security service. Maybe the British.'

She gasped. 'You're mad. If it got back to your superiors . . .'

196

'Or if it got back to *your* superiors that you'd helped me . . .'

They were both silent for a moment, considering these thoughts. Then Dominique turned to him. 'What would you need?'

'A shop selling electronic parts, an enthusiast's shop. And entry to Separt's apartment, preferably when he's out.'

'We can find such a shop,' she said. 'As for entry to the apartment, did you notice, he does not have a burglar alarm?'

'I didn't notice, no.'

She nodded. 'And only two locks on the door. It shouldn't be difficult. After all, I got into your hotel room, didn't I?'

'I thought you said . . . ?'

'The manager? No, he told me your room number. I went upstairs to see if you were in. You weren't, so I opened your door.'

'Where did you learn tricks like that? Part of the training?'

She shook her head. 'My father taught me,' she said quietly. 'A long time ago.'

One phone call to a friend who was a 'buff', and Dominique had the address she needed. The shop was a wonderland of chips and processors and wiring and tools. The assistant was helpful too, even though Dominique had trouble translating some of Barclay's requests into French. She wasn't sure what a soldering-iron was, or what it might be in French. But eventually Barclay had just about everything he needed. It wouldn't be craftsmanship, but it would do the job.

'And maybe some computer disks too,' he said. He

inspected the available stock and picked out the type he needed. 'A couple of these, I think.'

They returned to Dominique's apartment where the spare bedroom was handed over for his use.

'My very own workshop,' he said, getting down to work. Work stopped quite quickly when he found they'd forgotten to buy a plug for the soldering-iron. He removed the two-pin plug from the room's bedside lamp and attached it to the soldering-iron. Then he had to borrow a pair of tweezers from Dominique, and a small magnifying-glass (which she used for reading) from Madame Herault.

As he worked, he could hear Dominique and her mother talking in the living-room. Whenever Madame Herault spoke too loudly, her daughter would 'shush' her, and their voices would drop to a whisper again. It was as if he were the surgeon and this some particularly difficult operation. It wasn't really. It was the sort of stuff any teenage kid could accomplish with the aid either of inspiration or the plans from a hobby magazine. It took Barclay just over an hour. The wire he was using was no thicker than thread. He feared it would snap. Using runs of shorter than a centimetre, he dropped countless pieces and then couldn't find them, so had to cut more tiny lengths.

'A kid would have a steadier hand,' he muttered. But at last he was finished. He washed his face, splashing water into his bleary eyes, then had tea with Dominique and her mother. Then, with Dominique in her room and Barclay outside the front door, they tested the two small devices. Their range was not great. He hoped it would be enough. A neighbour passed him as he was standing in the stairwell with the receiver. He smiled at her, and received a mighty and quizzical frown in return.

'All right,' he said at last, after Dominique had hugged him briefly for being a genius, 'now it's your turn.'

But before they left, he tried telephoning Dominic Elder at his London hotel. He didn't know why exactly. Maybe he just wanted the assurance he felt Elder would give. But Elder wasn't there.

They drove back to Separt's block and squeezed the car into a parking space, then Dominique went to the phone-box on the corner and tried Separt's number. She returned quickly.

'An answering-machine,' she said. 'And I don't see his car anywhere.'

'That doesn't mean he's out. He may just be working. Did you see his car when we were here earlier?'

'To be honest, no. It may be parked in another street.'

'So what now?'

'We'll have to try the intercom. If he answers, that's too bad.' So they walked to the front door and tried the intercom. There was no reply. 'So now we know he's out,' she said.

'Which doesn't get us *in*.'

He looked up and down the street. A woman was heading in their direction, pausing now and again to chastise her poodle about something it either had or had not done. 'Back to the car,' he said. They sat in the car and waited. 'When I call you, don't come,' he ordered. While Dominique puzzled over this, the woman stopped finally at the front door to the block, and then opened the door. Barclay sprang from the car and held the door open for the woman, who was having trouble persuading her poodle to enter the building.

'*Merci, madame,*' Barclay said. Then he called towards the car: '*Dominique, ici! Vite!*' Dominique sat still and looked at him. She had changed, back at her apartment, into faded denims and T-shirt, and she was wearing her

199

lipstick again. She now checked her lipstick in the rearview mirror, ignoring his calls.

Barclay made an exasperated sound and shrugged to the woman. But now the woman was inside the building and making for the lift. 'Ici, Dominique!' Barclay glanced behind him, saw the lift doors close with the woman and her dog inside, and now gestured for Dominique to join him. She lifted the plastic bag from the back seat and got out of the car. He gestured her through the door, and it locked behind them. They waited for ages while the lift took its cargo to the third floor, paused, then started down towards them. After their own ascent, the lift opened on to Separt's private floor. There were two doors, one unmarked, the other belonging to Separt's apartment. Dominique got busy on this door. She had brought some old-fashioned-looking lockpicks with her from her apartment. No doubt they had belonged to her father before her. Barclay had his doubts whether they would be up to handling modern-day locks. But within two minutes, the door was open.

'Brilliant,' he said.

'Quick, in you go.'

In he went. It was his job now. Hers was to stand by the lift. If it was called for, if it started back up from ground level, then she'd call to him and he'd clear out. What they would do after that was unclear to him. 'We'll think of something,' she'd said. 'Don't worry.'

Don't worry!

Well, after all, what was there to worry about? He was only bugging someone's private home, having broken into it. That was all. And in foreign territory, too. And without permission from Joyce Parry. That was all. It was a breeze ...

The telephone was on the floor beside the desks, next to the answering-machine. He unscrewed the receiver and fixed the small transmitter in place, screwing the receiver shut again and shaking it to check it didn't rattle before replacing it in its cradle. Then he placed another transmitter down at the other end of the room, stuck to the underside of the sofa. Recalling how Separt liked to sit on the floor, he slouched on the floor himself. No, the bug wasn't visible. He'd no way of knowing if either bug would work. In theory they would, but in practice? And as for getting them out again afterwards . . .

Now he went to the computer. It was switched on, which saved a bit of time, but also indicated that Separt wouldn't be gone for long. He opened the box of computer disks beside the terminal. There were half a dozen disks, none bearing helpful markings. He pulled his own disks out of his pocket. The shop assistant had formatted them already, and Dominique had given him some French computer commands. The keyboard was slightly different from British models, but not so different. It didn't take long to copy a couple of Separt's disks.

A hiss from Dominique at the open door. 'Lift's coming!'

He closed the disk box and checked the screen display. There was no indication that he'd accessed the computer. Dominique was calling out floor numbers as he took a last look around. It might be another resident. The lift might stop before the penthouse. But it didn't look like it was stopping.

'Two . . . three . . .'

He was out now. She closed the door and did what she had to do with her picklock. Just the one lock needed reworking, the other being a Yale-type which had locked itself on closing.

He looked at the lift. 'Four,' he said. 'Five. Christ, Dominique, it's this floor next!'

She swivelled from the door and pushed him back-wards. His back hit the landing's other door, which opened, and suddenly he was on the emergency stair-well, his kidneys colliding with the banister. He gasped while Dominique pushed the door closed again, just as the ping of a bell from the landing signalled the arrival of the lift. They both held their breath and listened as Separt unlocked his door. He closed it behind him, and all was quiet again.

'He didn't notice anything,' she hissed, leaning her head against Barclay's shoulder. 'He's gone inside. Come on.'

They crept stealthily down one flight of stairs, entered the fifth floor landing, and summoned the lift from the floor above to take them to ground level. Back in the 2CV they smiled at one another, releasing the tension.

'That was *too* close,' Barclay said.

Dominique shrugged. 'I have been in tighter places.'

'Tighter spots,' Barclay corrected. But when she asked him what was wrong with the way she'd phrased it, he couldn't think of an answer.

Then came the moment of truth. He switched on the receivers. There were two, each with its own local frequency. One would pick up the telephone, one the bug under the sofa. They might jam or feed back on one another, but he didn't think so. A more real problem was that they might pick up other frequency-users: local taxis, CB radios . . . The signal was weak. A hiss, nothing more. Then the sound of a cough. Dominique thumped him on the shoulder in triumph.

'That's him!' she said. Then she clamped her hand over her mouth. Barclay laughed.

'He can't hear you, don't worry,' he said. Now came the sound of music. Classical music. Separt hummed along to it. Actually, it occurred to Barclay that there was a chance Separt *could* hear them if he happened to put his ear close enough to the microphones while they were talking: these things had a way of working in both directions. Headphones were microphones, too.

'Now,' Dominique was saying, 'all we can do is wait.'

'And hope,' added Barclay.

'Hope?'

'That he doesn't find the bugs.'

She was dismissive. 'Don't worry about that,' she said. 'If he finds them, we'll . . .'

'I know, I know: we'll think of something.' He turned to her. 'Tell me,' he said, 'did you *know* there were stairs behind that door?'

She smiled. 'Of course.'

'You might have—'

'Warned you? Yes, I forgot. Pardon me.'

'I'm not sure I can,' said Barclay. She leaned over and gave him a peck on the cheek. She was wearing perfume. He hadn't really noticed before. He looked in the rearview mirror and saw lipstick on his cheek. He smiled, and did not wipe it off.

After an hour, Dominique got bored. 'Nothing's happening,' she said.

'I can see you're not a cricket fan.'

'Cricket? You mean the English game?'

'Surveillance requires patience,' he said.

Well, so he would guess at any rate. He'd never actually been on a proper surveillance operation, had never been active 'in the field'. He'd always been what could be called a backroom boy. But he'd read about 'the field' in novels. He supposed the novelists must know. Besides, he was quite enjoying the music Separt was playing. Ravel.

Dominique opened her door. 'I'll get us some coffee and a sandwich,' she said.

'What happens if there's some action while you're away?'

'You'll still be here.'

'Yes, but I don't understand French. If anyone telephones ...'

She thought about this, then collapsed back into her seat with an exasperated sound and slammed shut her door.

'I'll fetch us something to drink if you like?'

She gripped the steering-wheel. 'I'd get even *more* bored on my own. Besides, I'm not really thirsty.' Her pout turned her into a teenager again. What was her age? 'Listen,' she said suddenly, springing forward. Separt's phone was ringing. Barclay sat up straight in his seat. This was his bug's first trial. The music was being turned down. Barclay placed a finger to his lips, warning Dominique not to speak. The phone stopped ringing.

'*Allo?*' Separt's voice.

'*C'est Jean-Pierre.*' The caller was loud and clear – much to Barclay's relief. Dominique was listening intently to the conversation, mouthing the words silently as though learning them off by heart. She signalled for a pen and paper. He took his pen and diary from his inside pocket and handed them over. She opened the diary at November and began to write. After a few minutes of pretty well one-sided conversation, the call was terminated. But Dominique wrote on for another minute or so, reaching December, then read back through what she'd written, altering some words, adding others.

'*Eh bien,*' she said. 'That was lucky.'

'How?'

'When Separt went out, he was trying to find the

caller. But the caller was not at home, so he merely left a message asking him to call back. This he has done.'

'And?'

She smiled. 'I don't think we fooled him completely. He wanted to tell the caller all about us. Why would the police do such a survey? What could it mean? The caller was very interested.'

'Did they say anything specific about Witch?'

'Do not rush me. No, nothing about Witch. They were very . . . careful. A care that is learned over years. You might even say a *professional* care. They talked around the subject, like two friends, one merely telling his story to the other.'

'You think Separt knows about the bug?'

She shook her head. 'If he knew, he would have warned the caller, and the caller would not have given away his location.'

'You know where he is?'

She nodded. 'Pretty well. He said Separt had just missed him. He'd been across the street in Janetta's.'

'Janetta's?'

'It sounds like a bar, yes? Perhaps Janetta's is not the name of the bar but of the woman who runs the bar. We will find out, but it might take some time. I think this Jean-Pierre knows something.'

'Such as?'

'Monsieur Separt reported his car missing *after* the assassin landed in England. I think someone persuaded him to . . . to turn the other cheek while the car was taken. He was not ill. He was waiting until it was safe to report the vehicle stolen. Why do you smile?'

'You mean turn a blind eye, not turn the other cheek.'

'Do I?'

He nodded slowly. 'Okay, so now we track down

Janetta's.' He paused, wriggling in his seat. 'Or do you want to stick around here?'

'No.' She checked her watch and turned towards him. 'Tonight, you will sleep with me.' The look on Barclay's face alerted her. 'I mean,' she said quickly, 'you will sleep at the apartment. Mama will insist that we dine with her. Don't worry, she is a very good cook. And after dinner . . .'

'Yes?'

'Maybe you will show me your file on Witch. We are partners now after all, aren't we?'

'I suppose we are,' said Barclay, wondering what he would elect to tell Joyce Parry about all of this. She'd be expecting him back soon, maybe as soon as tomorrow morning. He'd have to think up a story to tell her, something convincing. Dominique seemed to read his mind.

'Your employers will allow you another day in Paris?' she asked.

Barclay slapped a confident look onto his face and said nonchalantly, 'Oh, yes.'

But inside, he couldn't help wondering.

# Friday 12 June

Elder telephoned Joyce Parry just before breakfast. Smells of bacon-fat and frying tomatoes wafted up to his room as he made the call.

'Joyce? Dominic here.'

'Who else would have the . . . consideration to call at this hour?'

She sounded sleepy. 'Sorry,' he said, 'did I wake you?'

'Just give me the news.'

He wondered idly whether she'd spent the night alone, as he had. 'I've been sent a note,' he said.

'From whom?'

'Witch.'

'What?'

'Not what, who: Witch.'

'Don't get smart, Dominic. Tell me.'

'Just that. A note warning me to stay away.'

'You personally?'

'Me personally.'

'Was it delivered?'

'She left it at a pub, The Cat over the Broomstick.'

'What?'

'That's the name of the pub. I think she left it on the off-chance.'

'You don't think she's following you?'

'No.'

'But she knows you're after her.'

'I'm not even sure about that. Could just be a shrewd guess. She may not know I've retired.'

'Have forensics had a—'

'They're checking it this morning. I don't expect they'll find anything. She left the note with a barman. Doyle and Greenleaf are interviewing him this morning. We had a word with him last night, but today they're really going to put him through it. For what it's worth.'

'Meaning?'

'Meaning she got *him* to write the note for her. Pretended her wrist was sprained.'

'Clever girl.' Joyce Parry almost purred the words.

'Few more like her on our side,' Elder conceded, 'and we might still be an Empire.'

There was a choked sound as Joyce Parry stifled a yawn. 'Description?' she asked at last.

'Come on, Joyce, wakey wakey. She could have changed her looks a dozen times since then. No description the barman can give is going to be valid.'

'You sound disheartened.' She almost sounded concerned.

'Do I?' He managed a smile. 'Maybe it's because I haven't had breakfast yet.'

'What's stopping you?'

'I thought you'd want to—'

'And now I *do* know. So go and have your breakfast. And Dominic . . . ?'

'Yes?'

'Don't do too much. Rely on Greenleaf and Doyle, that's what they're there for.'

'You mean I should ask them to push my bath-chair?'

'I mean it isn't all on *your* shoulders. You're not a one-man band.'

'I have a strange feeling of déjà vu . . .'

'Don't joke about it! I warned you at the start of—'

'Operation Silverfish, I know.'

'And I'm warning you now. You didn't listen then.

208

But listen now, Dominic: if I get any hint that you're going solo on this, I'll send you back to the valleys. Understood?'

'Jesus, next time I'll phone *after* we've both had breakfast.'

'Do you understand me?'

He punched his pillow before replying. 'Yes, Joyce,' he said sweetly, 'loud and impeccably clear.'

'Good. Now go and eat, there's a good boy.'

'Yes, Joyce. Thank you, Joyce. Oh, one last thing. How's the kid doing?'

'I take it you mean Barclay. He's in Paris, following a lead.'

'Really?'

'You sound surprised.'

'I am. Pleasantly so. Field experience, Joyce. There's no substitute for it.'

'I don't recall it doing *you* much good on Silverfish.'

There was a moment's silence. He was waiting for her to apologise. She didn't.

'Goodbye, Joyce,' he said. 'Oh, hold on. Did you ever find out where Ms Capri found Khan's tongue?'

'Between her thighs,' Joyce Parry said quietly.

'Exactly. Remember the rough trade NATO General? Same modus operandi. It goes all the way back, Joyce, just like I told you.'

He put down the receiver. Then, going over the conversation again as he knotted his tie and slipped on his jacket, he smiled to himself. Same old Joyce. Prudent and cautious. She hadn't got where she was today by going out on a limb. He'd always been the limb-creeper. And damn it, some things just didn't and couldn't change. He'd spoken to Barclay quarter of an hour ago. He knew what Barclay had done; he'd have done the same himself. Elder was smiling as he left his room, locking the door after him.

He was impressed to find that Greenleaf and Doyle had already eaten and were on their way to the police station, where Joe the barman had agreed to meet them. So he took breakfast alone, staring out of the window at the early sunshine, thinking about his garden. A drinking companion, Tommy Bridges, had agreed at short notice to water the garden as necessary. But Tommy's memory wasn't so hot these days – too many bottles of rum had cascaded down his throat; perhaps Elder should phone and remind him. But according to the paper, it had rained in south-west Wales yesterday, with more to come today. He hoped his seedlings wouldn't be drowned.

After a filling breakfast and too much weak coffee, he headed back on to the streets, stomach swilling, and decided to concentrate his efforts on the town centre. Witch's note had been a nice shortcut in one respect, in that they now knew she'd been here, had spent at least a little time here. But exactly *where* had she stayed? Doyle was to spend today organising door-to-door enquiries of the resort's hotels and guest houses. Officers were being drafted in from Margate, but Elder doubted they'd be enough. They might have to start recruiting further afield. The problem with that was that it increased the visible presence, and while it was unlikely Witch *was* still here, it might be that too many coppers suddenly appearing on the streets would scare off accomplices or witnesses.

He'd stressed to Doyle that it had to be low-key. Doyle in turn had argued that low-key was slow, and speed was of the essence. In a hostage situation, Doyle would not hesitate to kick the door down and go in shooting. Megaphone diplomacy, waiting it out, these were not his style. And it niggled Elder, for maybe Doyle was right at that. Greenleaf, the quiet one, had made no comment. He'd been fairly docile ever since his outburst at that first meeting in London. If careful Greenleaf, rather than wham-bam Doyle, had been sent to Calais in the first place, perhaps there would have been no new lead for Barclay to find. Now that he thought about it, Joyce hadn't said what was happening in Paris. Keeping it close to her chest, in case nothing came of it: prudent and cautious. And he, Elder, hadn't asked, hadn't probed. Another slip-up on his part, and Joyce would doubtless realise it.

He'd been too long out of the game, it was true. Whatever his failings, someone like Barclay at least had youth on his side. Elder stopped on the pavement and considered this. Yes, he'd wanted Barclay sent to France because he'd thought it would teach the young man a lesson. But what kind of lesson: the useful kind, or the cruel kind? He wasn't sure now. It seemed so long ago. He was standing outside a butcher's shop, busy despite the early hour. Inside the large plate-glass window was displayed an array of red, glistening meat, grey sausages, pink pork loins. The butcher and his young assistant were working speedily, chatting all the time with the customers, who were also passing the time talking among themselves. Pleasures of the flesh-ing.

Then his eyes focused on the window itself. There was a small poster advertising a craft exhibition. And on the glass door to the shop, a door wedged open, there was a larger poster advertising a travelling fair. He'd passed similar flysheets last night during his walk, but he hadn't actually seen the fair itself. He recalled someone saying, 'Maybe she was going to run away with the circus . . .' Moncur the lorry driver had said it. A travelling fair. Night-people. Maybe one of them would have seen

211

something. She'd been making for Cliftonville, and there'd been a fair here. Now she'd gone, and so it seemed had the fair. Elder walked briskly into the shop.

The women stared at him suspiciously as he failed to join the queue. Instead, he leaned over the counter.

'Excuse me, that fair . . .' He pointed to the poster on the door. 'Is it still in town?'

The butcher, busy wrapping a package, glanced at the door. 'Don't know, sorry,' he said, taking a pencil from behind his ear. 'Now, Mrs Slattery, is that it?' The woman nodded, and he began totting up figures on a scrap of paper. 'That's four pounds and fifty pence then,' he said.

'Cleared out at the beginning of the week,' said a voice from the queue. Elder turned towards it.

'Do you know where they were headed next?'

Mutters and shakes of the head. 'Someone down on the front might know. A landlord, someone like that.'

'Yes,' said Elder. 'Thank you.' A woman was coming into the shop.

'Hello, Elsie,' said a voice from the queue. 'Here, any idea where that fair was off to?'

'Same as every year,' said Elsie authoritatively. 'Brighton.'

She wondered why the man beamed at her before rushing out of the shop. 'You get some funny types,' she said, 'this time of year. Some right funny types.' Then she sniffed and joined the end of the queue, where there was valuable gossip to be exchanged and the man was soon forgotten.


Madame Herault and Barclay were getting along like the proverbial house on fire. Despite the language barrier, despite barriers of age and culture, they knew one thing: they both liked to dunk their croissants in their coffee.

They sat together at the table in the kitchen. Now and then Madame Herault would call for Dominique, and Dominique would call back that she'd be there in a moment. There was a news programme on the radio, the presenters talking too fast for Barclay to make much sense of any of the stories. Madame Herault commented from time to time before shrugging her shoulders and returning to her coffee. She pushed the basket of croissants and chocolatines closer to him, exhorting him to eat, eat. He nodded and smiled, smiled and nodded. And he ate.

He'd spent a restless night in the spare room. Dominique's bedroom was through the wall from his, and he could hear her old bed creaking and groaning. His own bed was newer, more solid. It was also short, so that he couldn't lie stretched out unless he lay in a diagonal across the bed. His feather-filled pillow smelt musty, as did the sheets and the single blanket. Finally, he shrugged off sleep altogether and got up. He still had a lot of bits and pieces left over from his shopping trip to the electronics store. He plugged in the soldering-iron and hummed an aria or two from *The Marriage of Figaro*, waiting for it to warm ...

Now here she came, into the kitchen. Madame Herault gave an insulted gasp. Barclay almost gasped too. Dominique was dressed in winkle-picker black-buckled boots, black tights, black leather mini-skirt, a white T-shirt torn at the armpits and spattered with paint, and more jewellery than Barclay had seen outside a department store. Her eyes were surrounded by thick black eyeshadow and her face was dusted white, making her lips seem redder than ever before. She'd teased her hair up into spikes, brittle with gel or hairspray, and she wore three earrings in either ear.

Her mother said something biting. Dominique ignored

213

her and leaned past Barclay to grab a chocolatine. With it in her mouth, she went to the stove and poured coffee from the ancient metal percolator, then dragged a chair out from beneath the table and sat down between her mother and her guest. Barclay tried not to look at her. He kept his eyes on the tabletop, on her mother, on the pans and utensils hanging from the wall in front of him. He could smell patchouli oil. He could feel his heart pounding. She really did look incredible. It was just that she wasn't Dominique any more.

She was wearing her disguise.

'I telephoned a colleague,' she informed Barclay in English. 'He's checking on possible Janettas. With luck there won't be more than one or two.'

He nodded. 'I've made a wire,' he said.

'A wire?' Flakes of pastry escaped from her mouth.

'A bug for you to wear, so I can listen.'

She swallowed some coffee. 'When did you make it?'

'During the night. I couldn't sleep.'

'Me neither. I was reading your file. It was interesting. I would like to meet Mr Dominic Elder.'

Madame Herault, who had been muttering throughout and averting her gaze, now said something aloud, directed at her daughter. Dominique replied in similarly caustic tones then turned to Barclay. 'My mother says I am insulting her in front of a guest. I've told her all the women dress like this in London. She's waiting for you to agree.'

Barclay shrugged and nodded. Madame Herault pursed her lips and stirred her coffee-cup, shaking her head. The rest of breakfast was passed more or less in silence. After breakfast, Dominique and Barclay retired to the spare room.

'We need some tape,' he said.

'I'll bring some.'

214

She was back within a minute, holding a roll of thick brown packing tape.

'Just as well your T-shirt's baggy,' said Barclay. 'Otherwise, anyone could see you're wearing a wire.'

She stood with the transmitter in her hand. There wasn't much to it – a length of wire connecting a small microphone at one end to a transmitter at the other. It was bulkier than Barclay would have liked, and at the same time it was more delicate, too. His soldering wasn't perfect, but it would hold . . . he hoped.

'Lift your shirt at the back,' he ordered. She did so, and he stood behind her. Her skin was very lightly tanned, smooth, broken only by a pattern of variously-sized brown moles. She was not wearing a bra. This is work, he told himself. Just work.

He tore off a length of tape with his teeth and placed it over the wire, pushing it on to her back so that the transmitter hung free below the tape itself. Then around to her front, the T-shirt lifted still higher so that he could make out the swelling shadowy undersides of her breasts. Work, work, work. He ran the wire around to her smooth stomach, wondering whether to place the microphone just above her belly-button, or higher, in the hollow of her sternum.

'Having fun down there?' said Dominique.

'Sorry, I'm considering placements.' He touched her stomach then her sternum with the tip of his forefinger. 'Here or here?'

'Ah, I see. High up, I think. Unless the man is a midget, the microphone will be closer to his mouth.'

'Good point.' He tore off more tape and secured the microphone in the cleft just below her breasts. Then he used more tape to attach the wire to her side. 'Okay,' he said at last. 'Just try not to wriggle or bend over. He might hear the tape crinkling.'

She dropped her T-shirt and examined herself in the mirror, twisting to see if the wire was visible through the cotton. She stepped over to the window, then walked back slowly towards Barclay. He shook his head.

'Can't see a thing,' he said.

'What if I stretch myself?' She thrust back her shoulders and stuck out her chest. Barclay still couldn't see any sign either of brown tape or of black wire. And as for the slight bulge of the microphone itself . . .

'If you do that,' he said, 'I don't think Jean-Pierre's eyes are going to rest *between* your breasts so much as *on* them.'

She thumped his shoulder. 'You are teasing,' she said. He was about to deny it when there was a sound from the hall: the telephone was ringing. Dominique dashed out of the room to answer it, spoke excitedly, then dashed back.

'The fifth arrondissement,' she said. 'A street in the Latin Quarter. There is a bar called Janetta's.'

'Sounds good. Lift your T-shirt again. After all that running around, I want to check the tapes are still fast.'

'Fast?'

'Still stuck down.'

'Okay.' She lifted the T-shirt. 'But listen,' she said, 'there's more. In the same street lives an Australian, an anarchist. Called John Peter Wrightson. He's lived in France for years. You see?'

'John Peter, Jean-Pierre.'

'Yes! It makes sense, no?'

'Separt's caller didn't sound Aussie to me.' She shrugged. The tape had held fairly well. He just hoped she didn't sweat. 'Okay,' he said, 'you can drop the shirt. It looks okay.'

'You sound like a doctor.'

He smiled. 'Your . . . colleague, he sounds as if he's on the ball. I mean, he sounds efficient.'

'It was easy for him. The bar was in the directory. Then he entered the street name into the computer just to see if there was any further information. Monsieur Wrightson's name came on to the screen.'

'Speaking of computers . . .'

'Everything is being printed out at my office. We can pick up copies later today. That was a clever trick you played.'

He shrugged. 'A computer makes it easy.' Not that he imagined Separt would keep anything important on the disks. Dominique looked ready to go. 'We haven't tried out the transmitter yet.'

'They worked yesterday. This one will work today. I trust you.'

'That's another thing. We've got to go back to Separt's apartment and get those two—'

'Later, later.' She grabbed his hand. 'Now let's hurry, otherwise Mama will wonder what we're doing in here.' And she giggled as she led him down the hall, yelling a farewell to her mother. Then she stopped. 'Wait a moment,' she said returning to her bedroom. When she appeared again, she was pinning an Anarchy badge to her T-shirt.

'Nice touch,' he said.

The punk driving the 2CV certainly attracted stares from male drivers whenever she stopped at lights or was caught in a jam. Barclay had to give her credit. If – when – Separt and Jean-Pierre spoke again, their descriptions of the two women who visited them would be difficult to reconcile into a single individual. The winkle-picker heels even made her a good inch taller. Her hair was the same colour as yesterday, but that was the only area of

217

comparison. In all other details, she was a different person.

They'd agreed that she would visit Jean-Pierre alone: Barclay would stick out like a sore thumb. Dominique could disguise herself, but there was no disguising Barclay. She would visit alone, but Barclay insisted that she would wear a wire, so that he could listen from the car. He didn't want her getting into trouble.

They went over Dominique's story again on the way there. The fact that Jean-Pierre might well be the anarchist John Wrightson gave them a new angle to work from. They added it to her story, making slight alterations. The street they finally entered was squalid and incredibly narrow, or rather made narrow by the lines of parked cars either side, leaving a single lane with no passing places. A car in front of them – and thankfully travelling the same direction as them – hesitated by a gap between two of the parked cars, considered it but moved on. It was a gap just about big enough for a motorbike or a moped, but not for a car.

'We're in luck,' said Dominique, passing the gap and then stopping. 'Here's a space.'

'You've got to be kidding.'

But she'd already pushed the dashboard-mounted gear-stick into reverse, and craned her neck around to watch through the rear window as she backed the car in towards the kerb, turning the steering-wheel hard. Barclay watched through the front windscreen and saw that they were a centimetre from the car in front. Then there was the slight jolt of a collision: they had hit the car behind. But Dominique just kept reversing, pushing against the car behind, then easing down on the clutch and turning the steering-wheel hard back around. This time, edging forwards, her front bumper touched the car in front and pushed it forward a couple of centimetres.

'In Paris,' she said, 'we park with the handbrake off.'

'Right,' said Barclay. The 2CV was now parked, kerbside, a couple of inches from the car in front, and the same distance from the car behind. He tried not to think about how they would make a fast getaway.

'That's Janetta's,' said Dominique. 'You see? With the PMU sign.'

Barclay saw. 'It doesn't look particularly open.'

'It's open,' she said. With nice timing, the door of the bar was pulled from within, and a fat unshaven man wearing blue workman's clothes and a beret came sauntering out. He looked like he'd had a few drinks. It was quarter to ten. The door jangled closed behind him.

'So it's open,' he said.

'Monsieur Wrightson lives this side of the street, across from the bar. Number thirty-eight. Oh, well.' She took a deep breath. She did look a little nervous. It struck Barclay that maybe she too was getting out of her depth.

'Be careful,' he said as she opened the door.

'I'll be careful,' she said, closing the door after her. She came round to his side of the car and opened the door to say something more. 'If anything *does* happen to me . . .'

'Yes?'

'Please, look after Mama.' Then she closed the door again, gave him a big grin and threw him a kiss, before turning on her noisy heels and making for number thirty-eight. He wondered if that extra wiggle of her leather-clad bum was for him, or whether she was just getting into her part. Then he reached for his receiver, switched it on, and waited.

She had to climb two flights to the door marked WRIGHT-SON, J-P. She spoke in a low voice as she climbed.

'I hope you can hear me, Michael. This is a very dirty stairwell, not at all like Monsieur Separt's. It makes me

219

wonder what the two men could have in common, one living in luxury, the other in squalor. What do you think? Their politics, perhaps? Ideals can bridge gulfs, can't they?'

She paused outside the door, then pressed the buzzer. She couldn't hear anything from inside, so she knocked with her closed fist instead. And again. And again. There was a noise from within, a creaking floorboard, someone coughing. The door was unlocked.

'*Qui est . . . ?* Jesus Christ!' The man who stood there was scrawny, no fat at all on his body. He wore only tight grey underpants, and had a cigarette hanging from one corner of his mouth. He stared hard at every inch of the girl in front of him. 'Jesus Christ,' he said again. Then he lapsed into French, and Dominique was sure in her mind. When she spoke, she spoke in English.

'Ah . . . I am looking for Diana.'

'You speak English?' He nodded, scratching himself. Then he frowned. 'Diana? Never heard of her.'

'Oh.' She looked crestfallen. 'She told me she lived here.'

'*Here?*'

She nodded. 'I think so. She told me her address and I forgot it. I was drunk a little, I think. But this morning I wake up and I think I remember it. I dreamed it, maybe.'

'You mean this building?'

She shook her head, earrings jangling against each other. 'This floor.'

'Yeah? Well, there's old Prévost across the hall . . . but he hasn't set foot outside since '68.' Wrightson smiled. He was still studying her, appraising her. 'Anyway,' he said, 'come in. Can't remember when I last saw a punk.'

'Is it not still the fashion in England?'

'I wouldn't know, *chèrie*. I'm not English, I'm Australian.'

220

Dominique looked excited. 'Yes!' she said. 'Diana told me there was an Australian!'

'Yeah?' He frowned again. 'Beats the hell out of me.'

'You do not know her?'

He shrugged. 'Describe her to me.'

He had led her through a hall resembling a warehouse. There were boxes of flysheets, teetering piles of books, and the walls were covered with political posters. One of the posters showed a scrawled capital A over a circle.

'Anarchy,' she said, pointing to it. 'Just like my badge.'

He nodded, but didn't say anything. Maybe she'd been a bit too heavy-handed. She tried to slow her pulse-rate, keeping her breathing regular. She stared at another poster, another artfully scrawled circle but this time with a capital V on the top of it.

'*V for Vendetta*,' he explained. 'It's a comic book.'

'It looks like the anarchy symbol upside down.'

'I suppose it does.' He seemed pleased by the comparison.

The room they entered was stuffy, and seemed to double as living-room and bedroom. There were more boxes here, books, more mess. A woman, not too young, was sitting up inside a sleeping-bag on the floor, long brown hair falling down over her naked chest. She looked like she was in the process of waking up.

'Dawn, go make some coffee, girl.'

'Jesus, J-P, I made it yesterday.' Her accent was American. Wrightson growled at her. 'What time is it anyway?'

'Nearly ten,' Dominique answered after Wrightson had shrugged his shoulders.

'Middle of the damned night.' The woman looked about her until she found some tobacco and a paper, rolled herself a cigarette, then stepped from the sleeping-bag and walked through to the kitchen. Wrightson watched her depart.

'No shame, these Yanks,' he said. 'Speaking of which . . .' He wandered over behind the sofa and pulled a pair of jeans from the floor, shaking them free of dust before putting them on. Then he sat down again, resting on the arm of the sofa. Dominique was still standing. 'You were describing Diana to me,' he said.

'Oh, well, she's tall, short dark hair. English, I think. She has very . . . uh, piercing eyes.'

He thought for a moment, then shrugged. 'You say her hair's short? Pinned up maybe?'

'Pinned up, yes.'

Another moment's thought. 'Where did you meet her?'

'Outside the Louvre, beside the pyramid. She was sitting by herself, watching the fountains. I was bored. We talked a little. I liked her.'

He drew on his cigarette, blowing the smoke out through his nose. He was studying her very closely. 'What was she wearing?'

Dominique made a show of remembering. 'Black jeans, I think. A T-shirt, I don't remember what colour.'

'Sunglasses?'

'No. Maybe she had some in her pocket.'

'Mm-hmm.'

The woman, Dawn, had come back and was pulling on her clothes. She examined Dominique, saw the badge. 'Anarchy,' she said, nodding.

'What's your name, *chèrie?*' Wrightson asked.

'Françoise.'

'Like Françoise Sagan?'

'Yes, I suppose so.'

'Are you an anarchist, Françoise?'

She nodded. He gestured towards the boxes.

222

'Take some literature with you. Maybe you'll have read it before, maybe not. And leave an address and phone number. If Diana comes here, I can tell her where you are.'

'You know her then?'

He shrugged. 'Maybe. Maybe not.'

'I already gave her my phone number, outside the Louvre. She never got in touch. She said she would. We had a drink together . . . I liked her.'

She hoped she sounded and looked in as much despair as she felt. Wrightson was suspicious, of course he was. He was also very careful. She should have realised that from his telephone conversation with Separt. Only that one word – Janetta's – had given him away. She had another thought, too: maybe there was another Janetta's in another street with another Jean-Pierre living across the road. Maybe, but she didn't think so. This *felt* right. She walked across to the boxes and pulled out a pamphlet – wordy, written in slightly imperfect French.

'Make Françoise some coffee, too,' Wrightson said to Dawn, who was making for the kitchen again. Then he came over towards Dominique and put an arm around her shoulders. She flinched. What if he felt the transmitter?

'Easy,' he said. 'It'll be all right. You'll find other . . . women friends. I know lots of girls like you, Françoise, believe me.' His proximity disgusted her. She could smell his sweat, the rancid nicotine breath. Then she saw some cartoon books and moved away from him, picking one up. It was by Separt.

Wrightson followed her. 'You like his stuff?'

She shook her head. 'Too tame.'

He looked disappointed. Obviously, he'd just been about to claim friendship with the great cartoonist.

Below the cartoon book there was a newspaper. She picked it up, too.

'You read the London *Times*?' she said.

'Just the crossword. I enjoy a challenge.'

'The pages are torn.'

He winked. 'It saves on toilet paper.'

She gave a small laugh.

'That's more like it,' he said. 'How old are you, Françoise?'

Barclay had told her on the way that she would pass for eighteen. 'Nineteen,' she said, just to be safe.

'It's a good age to be. Have you got a job?'

'No.'

'Where do you live?'

'With friends. Some HLM housing . . .'

'Do *you* enjoy a challenge, Françoise?'

She frowned. 'I don't understand.'

Wrightson waved some of his pamphlets at her. 'I need help distributing my . . . literature. It's late-night work, you understand? Not much pay, but maybe you'd be interested.'

'Maybe.'

He nodded. She saw him for what he was, a cunning man but also stupid. A user of women, hiding his true feelings and desires behind political slogans. She'd met his type before.

'Leave me your phone number,' he said.

'We don't have a phone.'

The eyes narrowed. 'You said you gave it to Diana?'

She was ready for this. She nodded. 'The number of a club where some of us go. Everybody knows me there.'

'Okay, which club?'

She was ready for this too. Her night had been busy with plans, with dress rehearsals. 'L'Arriviste,' she said. 'Rue de la Lune, second arrondissement.'

He nodded. 'I'll remember that.'

Dawn appeared with three filthy mugs, brimming with black coffee. 'There's no sugar,' she said.

'Then we drink it black and bitter,' said Wrightson, taking a mug, 'like our thoughts.'

Dawn thought this over, then smiled towards Dominique, a smile full of admiration for Wrightson. But she was also warning the young pretender, the arriviste: 'He's *my* property.' Dominique drank to it.

They talked politics over the coffee, and she managed to sound less knowledgeable than she actually was. She also made sure to express her naivety, leading Wrightson to give speech after speech. The more he spoke, the less he asked, and the less he asked the more comfortable she felt. Yes, his ego was his fatal flaw. It had made him blind to the motives of others. All he cared about was himself. She had heard better speeches in the bars of schools and polytechnics.

The coffee finished, she said she had to go. He pressed her to stay but she shook her head. So he put together a bundle of stuff, photocopied single sheets, folded pamphlets, a couple of posters, and thrust it into her hands. The paper everything was printed on was cheap scratchy stuff, some of it off-white, some yellow. She thanked him.

'Just read,' he said. 'And pass on the message.'

'Message?'

He tapped the pamphlets. 'Tell your friends.'

'Ah, yes, yes, of course.'

She said goodbye to Dawn, and Wrightson saw her to the door, his hand rubbing her shoulder again, creeping down to graze against the bare skin of her arm. Then, as he opened the door, he put his hand on the back of her head and pulled her to him. With her hands full of paper, she couldn't push away. He planted a kiss on her lips, his tongue probing against her gritted teeth. Then he pulled away, leaving her gasping.

As she ran (as best she could in her heels) down the stairs, she could hear him laughing. Then he slammed shut the door, and it boomed and echoed like cannon-fire all the way out to the street.

Barclay could see that she was in a furious temper. She threw the bits of paper on to his lap, got behind the steering-wheel, and shunted her way out of the parking space and into the road.

'You were in there for hours,' he said into the silence. 'What happened?'

'Didn't you hear?'

'Only up to where he had Dawn go make you coffee.'

'He put his arm around me.'

'Probably pulled loose a connection. You'll have to tell me the rest.'

'First I need a drink. I need to get rid of the taste in my mouth.' She reached under her T-shirt and ripped off the transmitter, tossing it on to Barclay's lap beside the bits of paper.

She was quiet all the way to her favoured corner bar, where she collapsed into one of the terrace chairs and ordered a *pression*. What the hell, it had just gone eleven. Barclay ordered one too. She still didn't seem to want to talk, so he glanced through the literature she'd thrown at him, and which he had brought with him to the café.

'Well, well, well,' he said, holding one pamphlet up for her to see. It was concerned with 'European Freedom Fighters'. There was mention of the Italian group Croix Jaune, and of the German Wolfgang Bandorff. There was, to Barclay's eyes, a *lot* about Wolfgang Bandorff, with a final call to all 'lovers of freedom' to follow Bandorff's dicta, to motivate and mobilise and to let 'actions speak where the mouths of the oppressed are gagged'.

'Interesting,' said Barclay. He'd got Dominique's attention. She read through the pamphlet, but didn't speak until the beer had been placed in front of her, demolished, and another one ordered.

'Bandorff was mentioned in the Witch file,' Barclay reminded her.

'Yes, he was in Scotland when the Pope visited.'

'It can't be just coincidence.'

Dominique didn't say anything. She was running her tongue over her gums, as though washing them clean of something.

'So what happened up there?' he asked.

Her second beer arrived, and this time she drank it slowly, taking her time as she told him all about John Peter Wrightson.


Roadworks impeded Elder's progress on the route to Brighton. There were times when it seemed to him the whole road network of England was being coned off and dug up. He was sure he could remember a time when there'd been no contraflows. But of course there'd been less traffic then, too. It was taking him a little while to get used to Doyle's car. It was fast and certainly nippy in traffic, but the clutch seemed to have a mind of its own. Doyle had complained when Elder asked for his car. But it was only reasonable. They'd travelled down in the one car – Doyle's – and now that car was needed. Besides, as Elder pointed out, Doyle was staying in the town. What did he need his car for? And if a car *were* needed, he could always borrow one from the police.

'So what's stopping you doing that, too?' Doyle had said.

'I'm in a hurry.'

'I can't see there's any rush.'

Elder had already filled both Doyle and Greenleaf in on his planned trip, and the reasoning behind it, so he stayed silent and let Doyle have his grumble. As ever, Greenleaf wasn't saying much. The silent type.

They looked like they'd been working together on interrogations for years. They looked confident, successful. They looked like a team.

'If you scratch it,' Doyle said at last, digging his hand into his trouser pocket, 'if you so much as fart on the seat-fabric . . .' He held the keys in the air for an instant, not letting Elder have them.

'Understood,' he said. 'It'll get a full valet service before I bring it back.'

Doyle spoke quietly, spacing each word. 'Just bring it back.'

Elder nodded. 'Will do.' He reached out his hand and took the keys from Doyle.

There was nothing for him to do in Cliftonville anyway. The note was already in the forensic lab. The paper and envelope would be analysed, since Witch rather than the barman had provided them. Sometimes you could tell a lot from a sheet of paper: brand used, batch number, when produced, where stocked. Same went for fibre analysis. They would take the envelope apart with surgical precision, just in case there was a fibre or anything similar inside, anything that could tell them anything about Witch.

Joe the barman had been little help. And so far no one they'd spoken to had seen or heard anything that Sunday night. The thing to do was get the local police involved and have them do the leg-work. Time was pressing. They needed to be in London. The summit would start on Tuesday; hardly any time at all to recheck security. A few of the delegations, Elder knew, had already arrived. Most would arrive over the weekend. The last to arrive, the Americans, would touch down on Monday morning. Thirty secret servicemen would protect the President. But they couldn't protect him from a single sniper's bullet, from a well-placed bomb, from most of the tricks Witch had learned.

Sitting in a slow-moving queue, Elder leaned forwards the better to scratch his back, just where it itched. He'd had the itch for a long time. It hadn't really bothered him in Wales, not often, but now it had started up again. There was just something about a traffic jam that set it off. At least, he kidded himself it was the traffic jam.

Finally, he reached the outskirts of Brighton. He knew the town well, or had known it well at one time. He used to have a friend just west of the town in Portslade, beyond Hove. A female friend, the partner in a veterinary practice. He remembered her bedroom faced onto the sea. A long time ago ... He made friends with difficulty, kept them with even more difficulty. His fault, not theirs. He was a slovenly correspondent, forgetful of things like birthdays, and he found friendship at times a heavy baggage to bear. That was why he hadn't made a good husband: he didn't make a good friend in the first place. He sometimes wondered what kind of father he'd have made, if Susanne hadn't been taken from him.

He drove through Brighton until he hit the seafront. There was no sign of a travelling fair. He couldn't see any posters, either. Nothing to say whether it had been and gone, or was still to arrive. Nothing. But what he did notice were kids – kids lounging about, kids with nothing to do. School-leavers, probably, their exams over. Or the unemployed youth of the town. There were tramps too, and younger men, somewhere between school-leaver and tramp. They tried begging from passers-by, offering swigs from their bottle as trade. Living in rural Wales,

Elder was accustomed to the occasional hippy convoy, but nothing like this. The unemployed men he knew in his local village had been hard-working men who wanted to get back into hard work.

He drove slowly all the way along the front and back, studying the faces he saw. The world was changing; time was slipping into reverse. It was like the 1920s and 30s, or even the Victorian world described by Dickens. In London, he'd seen teams of windscreen washers, something he'd only before seen on American TV dramas. Young men – predominantly black – would wait at traffic lights and, when the lights turned red, would wash windscreens, then ask to be paid. One group Elder had seen had brought a sofa to the kerbside, so that they could relax in comfort between shifts. He wondered how much they made. He'd arrived in London without his car. A car would have protected him from the worst of it, from the beggars waiting for him in underpasses, the buskers in the Underground, the cardboard boxes which had become people's homes. That hopeless, toneless cry: 'Spare change, please, any spare change. Spare change, please, any spare change.' Like rag and bone men expecting society's leftovers.

Finally, having twice driven the length of the promenade, he pulled in at the kerb, near a group of teenagers, and wound down his window.

'Oi, oi!' cried one. 'Here's a punter looking for a bit of bum action! Go talk to the man, Chrissy!'

The one called Chrissy spat on the ground and gave Elder a baleful look.

'I'm looking for the fair,' Elder called from the car. 'Is there a fair in town?'

'You're after kids, is that it? We know your sort, don't we?' There were grins at this. Elder tried to smile back, as though he too were enjoying the joke.

'I'm just looking for the fair,' he said, making it sound like a not unreasonable request.

'Marine Parade,' said one of the crowd, waving a hand holding a can of beer in the direction of the Palace Pier.

'Yes,' said Elder, 'but that's a permanent fairground, isn't it? I'm looking for a *travelling* fair.'

'Sorry I spoke. Here, give us five quid for some chips, guv.' The youth was slouching towards him, hand held out. Elder didn't see anything dangerous in the young man's eyes; just an idiot vacancy. He knew pressure points which would have the youth dancing in agony within seconds. He knew how much pain the body could stand, and how much less the mind itself could stand. He knew.

Then he sighed and handed over a five-pound note.

'The fair,' he said.

The youth grinned. 'There's a fair up on The Level. Know where that is?'

Yes, Elder knew where it was. He'd practically driven past it on his way down to the shore. He didn't recall seeing a fair, but then he hadn't really been looking.

'Thank you,' he said, driving on. Behind him, the youth was fanning himself with the banknote. Already his friends were gathering round like jackals.

The front at Brighton was all pebblestone beach and inescapable breeze, fun-rides and day-trippers. But further up the town's hill, past the Pavilion and the shops, was a large, flat, grassy park called The Level, criss-crossed with paths. Locals walked their dogs here, children shrieked on swings. And every year there came a fair. He wondered that he'd been able to miss it, but then he'd presupposed any fairground would be stationed along the promenade, where the pickings were richest. There weren't as many stalls and rides as he'd been expecting. The usual waltzers and dodgems and rifle-ranges, ghost train, kiddies' rides, hot dog stalls. But no big wheel or dive-bombers, nothing that he would call a big attraction. Marine Parade had stolen a march on the travelling fair.

And everything was closed, save a couple of the kiddies' rides which were doing desultory business. A monkey swung down over the children on one ride, operated by a sour-looking woman. The trick seemed to be that if a child pulled the tail off the monkey, the child got a free ride. Something like that. The fair proper would no doubt open up later on in the day. He parked Doyle's car at a safe distance from The Level itself – he didn't want errant hands wiping candy floss on it – and walked back. One ride was discharging its cargo. The woman who operated both ride and monkey came out of her stall to collect the money from the few kids waiting for the ride to start up again. She wore a leather bag slung around her neck, the sort conductors still used on some London buses. Elder noticed that the rides were old, certainly older than their cargo. There was a horse, a racing car with a horn, a tiny double-decker bus, a sort of ladybird from which most of the paint had flaked, a jeep with movable steering-wheel, and a spaceship. There was heated competition for both the spaceship and the racing car.

'Excuse me,' he said to the woman, 'where can I find whoever's in charge?'

'That's me.' She went on taking money, dispensing change.

'No, I mean in charge of the fair as a whole.'

'Oh?' She gave him the benefit of a two-second glance, then sighed. 'What's wrong now?'

'Nothing.'

'Are you council?'

'No, nothing like that.'

232

'What then?'

He paused. 'If you'd just tell me where I can find . . .'

Having collected all the fares, she moved past him. 'Mind yourself,' she said. 'If you stay on there, you'll have to pay same as the rest.' Back in her perspex-fronted booth, she turned on a tape-recorder. A pop song blasted out of the speaker overhead. Then the carousel started to turn, and she tugged her left arm, jiggling the monkey up and down, comfortably out of reach of the squealing children. Elder stood his ground by the open door. The children were waving at their parents as they spun slowly past them. One of the kids looked petrified, though he was trying not to show it. He gripped on to the steering-wheel of his jeep, hardly daring to take a hand off to wave, despite the cajoling of his mother. Fear, Elder was reminded, was utterly relative, a shifting quantity.

As the allotted time of the ride came to its end, the woman lowered the monkey so that a girl could whip off its tail. Then she pulled the monkey up again and hooked her end of its line over a nail on the wall of her booth, holding it there. The music was turned down, but not off, the ride came to a stop, the parents collected their children. The boy from the jeep looked pale. The woman looked at them through the perspex window, then turned to Elder.

'Still here?'

He shrugged. 'I've nothing better to do.'

'Sure you're not council?' He shook his head and she sighed again. 'Try the caravan behind the waltzers,' she said. 'The long caravan, mind, not the little one.'

'And who am I looking for?'

'His name's Ted. That's all, just Ted.'

And indeed it was.

'Just call me Ted,' the man said when Elder appeared

at the caravan door and asked for him. They shook hands.

'I'm Dominic Elder.'

'Pleased to meet you. Now, Mr Elder, what seems to be the problem?'

'No problem, I assure you.'

'Good, pleased to hear it. In that case, why don't you come in?'

The caravan was large but cramped, the result of too many ornaments on too many occasional tables. Glass clowns seemed to predominate. There was a small two-seater sofa, and two armchairs, re-covered in an orange-coloured flowery print. Ted nodded towards a chair.

'Take a pew, Mr Elder. Now, what can I do for you?'

It wasn't until Elder was seated that he saw it was Ted's intention to continue standing, arms folded, ready to listen. Elder admired the man's grasp of psychology. Standing, he had authority over the seated Elder. They were not equals. That, at least, was the ploy. Ted might not be the man's real name. He was in his 50s, and wore his hair slicked back, his sideburns long: a Teddy Boy look. Perhaps the name had stuck. There was doubtless a comb in the back pocket of his oily denims.

'I'm looking for my daughter,' Elder said.

'Yes? In Brighton is she?'

'I don't know. I *think* she was in Cliftonville.'

'We were there the other week.'

Elder nodded. 'She's keen on fairs, I thought maybe somebody might have seen her wandering around . . .'

'How old is she, Mr Elder?' There was sympathy in Ted's voice, but not much. He was still suspicious.

'She's twenty-nine,' Elder said. Ted looked suitably surprised.

'So it's not a case of the kid running away with the

fair?' he said, more to himself than to Elder. 'Twenty-nine, eh? Got a photo of her?'

'Not on me, no. I was in Cliftonville, and when I heard about your fair, well, I rushed down here without thinking.'

'Twenty-nine . . . and she likes fairs, you say?'

'I'm afraid she's . . . well, she's a little *backward*, Ted. An accident as a child . . .'

Ted raised a hand. 'Say no more, Mr Elder. Understood. Well, I can certainly put the word about. You'd better give me a description.'

'Of course. She's slim, five foot ten inches.'

'Tall then?'

'Tall, yes.'

'Go on.'

'Well, the problem is . . . she may have disguised herself. You know, dyed her hair, bought a wig. Her hair's usually short, dark brown.'

'Doesn't matter really. A woman her age, hanging around the rides, someone'll have clocked her. Are you sticking around Brighton, Mr Elder? Only, there's a few more fairs on the go – Eastbourne, Guildford, Newbury – I could give you the names of some people to talk with . . .'

'That's very kind of you, Ted.'

'Hold on, I'll get a bit of paper.'

He went through to another room, probably his office. Elder thought about getting to his feet but decided that his best bet was to stay seated, that way he could be fairly sure of maintaining the sympathy vote. The standing/sitting psychology only worked if, when you were standing, the person who was seated was trying to be your equal. But Elder, in confessing to having a 'backward' daughter, had relinquished such a role, placing the burden of responsibility on the 'stronger' Ted.

It was the sort of stuff you learned early on in Elder's profession. Another trick of the tradecraft.

The door to the caravan opened and a woman clambered aboard. She seemed surprised to see Elder. He took her for Ted's wife until she spoke.

'Sorry, is Ted about?'

'Here, Rosa,' called Ted, emerging from his office. He pointed a biro at Elder. 'This is Mr Elder. His daughter's run away. Last seen in Cliftonville. He was wondering if we'd come across her.'

'Oh dear,' said the woman. She perched herself on the edge of an armchair. 'What's her name, lovey?'

'Diana,' said Elder.

Ted laughed. 'Trust Rosa to get down to nuts and bolts. I clean forgot to ask you what she was called. Mr Elder, this is Gypsy Rose Pellengro, mistress of the crystal ball.'

Elder nodded his greeting towards Gypsy Rose, and she smiled back.

'Diana,' she said. 'It's a lovely name, sir. Your wife's choice or yours?'

Elder laughed. 'I can't honestly remember. It was a long time ago.'

'Mr Elder's daughter is twenty-nine,' Ted informed Gypsy Rose. He had settled at a table, slipped on a pair of half-moon glasses, and was scratching on a piece of notepaper with his pen.

'Twenty-nine?' said Gypsy Rose. 'I thought she was—'

'Me, too,' said Ted. 'Preconceptions, Rosa. You see, Mr Elder, we get a lot of parents coming to us. Oh, yes, a lot. Their kiddies have gone missing and they're desperate to find them. One woman . . . up in Watford, I think it is . . . she's been coming to see me for six or seven years. Very sad, clinging to hope like that.'

'Sad,' echoed Gypsy Rose.

'Diana's tall and slim,' Ted informed Gypsy Rose, 'and she's maybe got short dark hair. I don't suppose she came to you for a consultation while we were in Cliftonville?'

'No.' Gypsy Rose shook her head. 'No, I'd have remembered someone like that.'

Like what? thought Elder. The description was vague to the point of uselessness.

'Well, ask around the other stalls, will you, Rosa?' Ted had taken off his glasses and risen from his chair. He handed Elder the slip of paper, which Elder read. Four different fairs in four locations, with dates and a contact name for each.

'Thank you very much,' Elder said, pocketing the note.

'They're not as big as this, mind. We all join up for the bigger events. Tell them Ted sent you, they should see you right.'

'Thanks again,' Elder said. He reached into his pocket and brought out a small notebook and a pen. 'I'm staying at a hotel in Cliftonville. I may have to move on, but they can forward any messages to me.' He wrote down the telephone number, tore out the page, and handed it to Ted.

'If I hear anything, I'll let you know,' said Ted.

'I'd be very grateful.' Elder rose to his feet. 'It's been nice to meet you,' he said to Gypsy Rose.

'Likewise.'

Ted saw him to the door. The two men shook hands.

'Mind how you go, Mr Elder,' said Ted. 'And good luck.'

'Thanks,' said Elder. 'Goodbye.'

He walked with care across the snaking lengths of power-cable, squeezed between two closed stalls, and was back on the road again. He wandered the length of the fair, and stopped beside the caravan belonging to

Gypsy Rose Pellengro, reading the citations pinned to the board beside her door. He peered in through the window. The interior looked neat and plain.

'She'll be back in five minutes!' someone yelled from further along. Elder walked towards the voice. A middle-aged man was unhooking chains from in front of the ghost train. Already, two young children, brother and sister, stood waiting for the ride to open. Elder nodded a greeting at the man. 'Thanks,' he said, 'maybe I'll come by later.'

'Please yourself.' The man looked at the children and jerked his head towards the carriages. 'On you go then, hop in.' They fairly sprinted for the train's front carriage. The man smiled, watching them go. Then he headed for his booth, leaning into it. 'Hold tight,' he warned. 'Or the goblins'll grab you.' He grinned towards Elder. 'And being grabbed by the goblins,' he said, 'is no laughing matter.'

Elder obliged with a laugh, then watched as the train jolted forwards, hit the doors, and rattled its way through them into darkness. The doors swung shut again, showing a picture of a leering demon.

'Your two, are they?' the man asked.

'No,' said Elder, listening for shrieks from the interior.

'No?' The man sounded surprised. 'I thought they were. If I'd known, I'd have had the money off them first.'

Elder brought out some coins from his pocket. 'They can have this ride on me anyway,' he said, handing over the money. Then he moved off again, passing rides and booths and Barnaby's Gun Stall. Outside the Gun Stall, which was locked shut, there was a wooden figure, its sex indeterminate. Pinned to the centre of its chest was what remained of a small paper target, only the four right-angled edges left. Above this, taped to the figure's head, was a crudely written message: 'A young lady did this. Can YOU do better?' Elder smiled.

A voice came from behind him. 'Well, could you?'

He turned. A young man was standing there, head cocked to one side, hands in the greasy pockets of his denims. Elder looked at the target.

'Probably not,' he said.

'Come back in an hour, guv, and you can see if you're right. Only two quid a go.'

'The young woman ... she must have been quite something.'

The man winked. 'Maybe I'm lying, eh? Maybe I just tore the middle out myself.' And he snorted a short-lived laugh. 'Open in an hour,' he repeated, moving away. Elder watched him go.

A travelling fair. What connection could Witch possibly have with a travelling fair? None that he could think of. *I'd have remembered someone like that.* Rosa Pellengro had sounded very sure of herself. Very sure. But then she *was* supposed to be a clairvoyant. He wondered if it was worthwhile keeping a watch on the fair. Maybe Witch had been here. If so, she might come back or she might not.

He was in a thoughtful mood as he reached Doyle's car. Two gulls cackled somewhere in the distance. They had left generous gifts on the windscreen and bonnet. Elder sighed. Time to find a car-wash.

'I'm glad you've called,' Michael Barclay said into the receiver.

'And who was that delightful French lady?' Dominic Elder asked.

'My colleague's mother.' Just then Dominique herself came into the hall and handed Barclay a glass of cold beer, with which he toasted her. It had been another long day.

'Since you're glad I called,' Elder went on, 'I take it you're either in trouble or you're on to something.'

'Maybe both,' said Barclay. 'When I bugged Separt's apartment, I copied some of his computer disks.'

'Clever boy.'

'I bet Mrs Parry would say something different. Anyway, we've been reading through them. Mostly ideas for cartoon strips, but there's a lot of personal correspondence too, including a couple of letters to Wolf Bandorff.'

'Well well.'

'Discussing some project of Separt's, a cartoon book about Bandorff's career.'

'The world is a strange place, Michael. So what does this tell us?'

'It connects Separt to Witch's old teacher.'

'It does indeed. It's almost as if she's living her life again backwards.'

'Sorry?' Barclay had finished the beer. He held the cold glass against his face, like a second telephone receiver.

'She started her life in Britain, but early on joined Bandorff's gang. The link seems still to be there.'

Barclay still wasn't sure what Elder was getting at. 'You told me,' he said, 'always work the idea all the way through.'

There was a pause. 'You're thinking of taking another trip?'

'Yes. Do you think I could get it past Mrs Parry?'

Elder considered this. 'To be frank, almost certainly not. It's getting too far out of our territory.' He paused. 'Then again, maybe there's just a chance.'

'How?'

240

Elder's voice seemed to have faded slightly. 'You've lied to her before, haven't you . . . ?'

Dominique had already made *her* necessary telephone calls, and now all Barclay had to do, before taking her to dinner, was make one call himself. To Joyce Parry.

Elder was right, he'd lied to her before. Well, he'd been economical with the truth, say. But this time he was going to deliver a whopper. He went over his story two or three times in his head, Dominique goading him into making the call right now and getting it over and done with. At last he picked up the phone.

'Joyce Parry speaking.'

'It's Michael Barclay here.'

'Ah, Michael, I wondered where you'd got to.'

'Well, there's a bit of a lull here.'

'You're on your way home then?'

'Ah . . . not exactly. Any progress?'

'Special Branch and Mr Elder are still in Cliftonville. A lorry driver picked up a hitch-hiker and dropped her there, did you know? Anyway, it seems a note was left for Mr Elder at a pub in the town.'

'A note?'

'Vaguely threatening, signed with the initial W.'

'God, that must have shaken him up a bit.' He swallowed. He'd almost said, He didn't tell me.

'He seemed very calm when I spoke to him. Now then, what about you?'

He swallowed again. 'DST are keeping watch on a couple of men. One of them, the one who had his car stolen, he's a left-wing sympathiser. He didn't report the car stolen until *after* the explosions on the two boats. DST think that's suspicious, and I tend to agree with them.'

'Go on.'

'This man has made contact with an anarchist. We

. . . that is, DST . . . think the anarchist may know Witch. They think maybe the anarchist persuaded the other man to turn a blind eye while his car was taken.'

'Not to say anything, you mean?'

'Yes, until *after* Witch was home and dry . . . so to speak.'

'You sound tired, Michael. Are they treating you all right?'

He almost laughed. 'Oh yes, no complaints.'

'So what now?'

'As I say, they're keeping a watch on both men. I thought I'd give it until Monday, see if anything happens.'

'A weekend in Paris, eh?'

'A working weekend, ma'am.'

'I don't doubt it.' Her tone was good-humoured. Barclay hated himself for what he was doing. But it had to be done. No way would she sanction a trip to Germany, especially when explaining the trip would mean explaining how he'd come upon Separt's correspondence and Wrightson's leaflets.

'Okay, take the weekend,' Joyce Parry was saying. 'But be back here Monday. The summit begins Tuesday, and I want you in London. God knows, we'll be stretched as it is.'

'Yes, ma'am.'

'And let me know the minute you learn anything.'

'Of course.'

'And Michael . . . ?'

'Yes, ma'am?'

'You've already proved a point. You found something Special Branch missed. Okay?'

'Yes, thank you, ma'am. Goodbye.'

He noticed that his hand was shaking as he replaced the receiver.

'Well?' asked Dominique. Barclay wiped a line of perspiration from his forehead.

'I can stay on till Monday.'

Dominique grinned. Somehow, Barclay didn't share her enthusiasm. 'Good,' she said, 'we can start for Germany in the morning. The interview is arranged for two o'clock on Sunday.' She noticed his pallor. 'What's wrong, Michael?'

'I don't know . . . It's not every day I put my career on the line.'

'How will your boss find out? She won't. If we find nothing, we *say* nothing. But if we find *some*thing, then we are the heroes, yes?'

'I suppose so.'

'Cheer up. You are taking me to dinner, remember?'

He gave a weak smile. 'Of course. Listen, any chance that I can wash these clothes?' He picked at his shirt. 'Remember, I only brought the one change with me.'

She smiled. 'Of course. We will put them in the machine. They will be dry by morning. All right?'

He nodded.

'Good, now I will get changed. You, too.' She skipped down the hall to her room, calling back after her: 'Rendezvous in twenty minutes!'

After a moment, Barclay walked slowly back to his own room, his feet barely rising from the floor. Behind Dominique's door, he could hear her humming a tune, the sound of a zip being unfastened, of something being thrown on to the bed or a chair. In his own room, he fell onto the bed and stared at the dusty ceiling, focusing on one of its dark cobwebbed corners.

How did I talk myself into this?

Perhaps Witch *had* been in touch with Bandorff recently. But why should Bandorff admit it or say anything about it or them about it? Although he knew what he was doing, and knew that Dominique and he were making the decisions, he couldn't help feeling that Dominic Elder was an influence too, and not entirely a benign one. He wished he knew more about the man. He knew almost nothing about him, did he? All he knew was that Elder had pulled him into this obsession – an obsession Barclay himself had recently termed a psychosis.

'I'm mad,' he said to the ceiling.

But if he was, Dominique was mad too. *She'd* been the first to phone her office, securing clearance for herself and Barclay to go to Germany. He'd missed most of that call actually: he'd been busy in the toilet. He'd emerged again as she was dialling Germany, dialling direct to the Burgwede Maximum Security Prison, just north of Hanover.

'It's fixed,' she said after dialling, waiting for an answer. 'My office has given me clearance. I just have to . . .'

And then she lapsed into German, talking to the person on the other end of the phone. Barclay heard her mention the Bundesamt für Verfassungsschutz, Germany's security service, the BfV. Even in German, she was able to charm whoever she was speaking with. She laughed, she apologised for her accent and her lack of vocabulary (not that either, to Barclay's ear, needed apologising for). And eventually, after some quibbling, she had a day – Sunday – and a time – two in the afternoon.

For a meeting with the terrorist Wolfgang Bandorff, Witch's old lover.

She looked distinctly pleased with herself when she came off the phone, and hummed a little triumphant tune.

'What was that about the BfV?' asked Barclay.

'Michael, you are so . . . astute. That was my one little white lie. I told Herr Grunner I had liaised with the BfV. I think this means he takes me more seriously.'

'Don't tell me, when we turn up there, I'm going to pretend to be a German secret agent?'

'Of course not, Michael. But sometimes bureaucracy has to be . . .' She sought the word.

'Got around?' he suggested.

She liked that, and nodded. 'Yes,' she said, 'like swerving to avoid another car, yes?'

'Bobbing and weaving, ducking and diving.'

As now, hours later, staring at the cobwebbed ceiling above his bed, he feels his stomach diving. He might not be able to keep anything down at dinner. Maybe he'll have to cry wolf on the whole thing. Let Dominique cover herself with glory; he could ship out on the first hovercraft or cross-Channel ferry. But he knows he won't. He can't. He's already told Joyce Parry too many white lies.

So they're going to Germany, driving there in the awful 2CV. Hanover wasn't just across the border either. It is hard driving. And both of them out of their territory – even Elder had said as much. He didn't think they'd learn anything from Bandorff. And they'd have to be careful, too. If he found out how keen they were to track down Witch, he might start throwing them off her scent, laying false trails.

Jesus, what if this whole thing was an extended false trail? No, no, best not to think about that. She couldn't be that clever, could she? No one was *that* clever, clever enough to lay a trail backwards through Europe, a trail with a trap lying at the end of it.

Jesus, don't think about it!

Dominique came in unannounced. She looked sensational, in a clinging woollen red dress and black tights. She wasn't wearing shoes or make-up yet.

'I thought you were being quiet,' she said. She closed the door, before settling herself on the edge of his bed. 'What's the matter?'

'Pre-match jitters.'

'What?'

'It's a football term. The nerves you get before a game.'

'Ah.' She nodded understanding and took his hand in hers. 'But I am nervous, too, Michael. We must plan carefully what we will say to Herr Bandorff. We must . . . like actors, you know?'

'Rehearse.'

'Yes, rehearse. We must be word perfect. We will set off in the morning, and stay overnight at a hotel. We will rehearse and rehearse and rehearse. The leading man and leading woman.' She smiled, and squeezed his hand.

'It's all right for you,' said Barclay, 'your department's behind you. I've lied through my teeth to mine.'

'Because you want to stay with me, yes?'

He stared into her eyes and nodded. She stood up, dropping his hand.

'And you are right to stay with me,' she said. 'Because I am going to find out about this Witch woman, I am going to discover all about her from Herr Bandorff. Just you wait and see. Besides, Mr Elder is behind you.'

'Yes, and pushing hard.'

She was at the door now, opening it. She turned back to him. 'Rendezvous in five minutes,' she said, 'whether you're ready or not.'

And with a final carefree smile, she was gone. Barclay sat up on the bed, clasping his arms around his knees. From the living-room came the sound of an accordion. Madame Herault was listening to her radio. Madame

Herault, who had already lost a husband to the terrorist threat, and whose daughter now might be in danger. He got up off the bed and stood in front of the dressing table, where the Witch file sat surrounded by bits of wire and solder, unused diodes and broken bits of circuit-board. He touched the cover of the file for luck.

Back in her room, Dominique studied herself in her mirror. Her employers had attached her to Michael Barclay because she was persistent. She had been brought up to be stubborn in pursuit of her goal, and her goal had been an assignment. She wanted to prove herself. How could you prove yourself in an office? She touched a framed photograph of her father. He had proved himself on the streets of the city, not behind a desk. He was her hero, and always would be, his life snuffed out by terrorists. And now she was in pursuit of terrorists, of people like those who had murdered her father. She kept her mind focused on that fact.

She didn't mind cutting corners. She didn't mind lying to her employers. She gave them daily reports on the British agent's actions and whereabouts. As long as he was around, she was to stick close to him, nothing more than that. They did not know how fascinated she had become, fascinated by this creature called Witch, conjured up from scattered events and rumours. It was as though the creature stood for all the terrorists in the world. Dominique wanted to get closer to it still. She examined her hair, her face, her body, and she smiled. She knew she was just about beautiful.

She knew too that Witch, not she, was the real *femme fatale*.

She had spent much of the past few days in London, watching. At times she had been a tourist, clutching her street-map and her carrier bag from Fortnum's, her head arched up to take in the sights, while those around her kept their eyes either firmly straight ahead or else angled downwards, checking the paving stones for cracks to be avoided.

At other times, she'd been a busy office worker, rushing with the best of them, with only enough free time for a lunch of a takeaway burger. And she'd been unemployed, too, with too much time on her hands, sitting against a wall with her knees hugged to her beneath her chin. All these things she had been. Nobody paid much attention to her several incarnations. To passers-by, the tourist was merely another obstacle in their way as they manoeuvred past her while she stood in Victoria Street, staring up in the direction of Westminster Abbey. And as the office worker ate her burger, seated in the plaza between Victoria Street and Westminster Cathedral, only one young man attempted to chat her up. But he was in a hurry, too, and so a single shake of her head was enough to deter him.

While the unemployed girl, the pale and tired-looking girl – well, everybody chose to ignore her existence. She was moved on once or twice by doormen and police officers. The police asked her where she stayed.

'Lewisham.'

'Well, bugger off back there then. And don't go hanging around Victoria Station either. We'll be along there in an hour, and if you're still there we'll take you down the nick. All right?'

She sniffed, nodded, picked up her cheap blue nylon shopping-bag. There were tears in her eyes as the policemen moved away. An old man took pity on her and handed her a one-pound coin. She took it with muttered thanks. She wandered off towards Victoria Station, where, in a toilet cubicle, she stripped down and swapped her clothes for another set in the shopping-bag. Then the shopping-bag itself was folded and slipped into a better-quality bag, along with the clothes. At the wash-basin, she combed the snags out of her hair, washed her face, dried it, and applied make-up. Girl about town again. In the station concourse, true to their word but half an hour ahead of schedule, the two police constables were passing through. She smiled at one as she passed them. He smiled back, and turned to watch her go.

'Thought you'd cracked it there,' his colleague said.

'Some of them just can't resist the uniform.'

Girl about town went back to Victoria Street, walked its length, pausing only outside the building which was 1–19 Victoria Street, headquarters of the Department of Trade and Industry. She had a momentary feeling of claustrophobia. She was within a five-minute walk of the Houses of Parliament, Westminster Abbey, Westminster Cathedral, New Scotland Yard, the Queen Elizabeth II Conference Centre. Not much further to Whitehall, Downing Street, Buckingham Palace even ... So many targets to choose from, all so convenient. One really *huge* device and you could wreak mayhem.

It was an idle thought, an idle moment, the stuff of crank anarchists' dreams, anarchists like John Wrightson. She let it pass and checked her watch. Quarter to six. Friday evening at quarter to six. The offices had started their weekend evacuation at four-thirty. Pubs and wine-bars would be filling. Train carriages would be squeezing in just one last body. The discharge of the city. It was hard to tell, but she thought she probably had another ten minutes. She didn't like the thought of loitering, not in her girl about town disguise. But of course, if anyone should ask, she was waiting for a boyfriend who worked for the DTI. She was respectable. She wasn't suspicious. She rose onto her tiptoes then rocked back onto her heels. Waiting for her boyfriend. A few drinks after work, then a meal, maybe a film . . . no, not a film: she didn't know what films were on where. A meal, one of the little Chinese restaurants off Leicester Square. Then back to his place . . . The perfect start to the weekend.

Another five or ten minutes. She hoped to God she hadn't missed her quarry. It was unlikely. The first day Witch had spotted her, she'd worked till six-thirty, the next day six-fifteen. She would knock off early on a Friday, of course she would. But not that early. She had an important position. Let the others in the office leave her behind, she'd be the last out, feeling virtuous, another hard professional week over. Maybe a last-minute task would keep her. Maybe she'd been taken ill and had gone home early . . .

Witch had spent some time choosing. She was a fussy shopper. There had been false starts: one woman was perfect in build and face, but too junior. Witch needed someone with a modicum of clout, the sort of person the security guards would look up to. Another woman had seemed senior enough for the purpose, but she was also too striking, the sort of person people would notice, so that they'd notice, too, if she went missing for a few days or if someone else brandished her security pass.

Security. She'd wandered into one of the DTI buildings at lunchtime one day. There were seats in the reception area, tedious-looking literature to pass the time. A businessman sat leafing through the contents of his briefcase. A young man stepped from an elevator and called to him. The businessman shook hands with the young man, the young man signed him in at the desk, a chitty was given to the businessman, and both headed for the elevator again.

'Yes, miss?' the security man called from behind his large desk.

There were two of them seated behind the desk. The one who had called to Witch, and another who was talking with another colleague, a black woman. Witch approached the desk and smiled.

'I'm meeting my boyfriend for lunch.' She looked at her watch. 'I'm a bit early. Is it all right if I wait?'

'Of course, miss. If you'll just take a seat. You can call up to him if you like, maybe he can knock off early.'

She smiled gratefully. 'No, he's always complaining I'm too early for things.'

'You're not like my wife then,' said the security man, laughing, turning to share the joke with his colleagues.

'I'll just wait for him,' said Witch.

So she sat in the reception area, watching the civil servants come and go. Most were going – it *was* lunchtime – but a few were already returning with sandwiches and cans of soft drinks. As they passed the security desk, heading for the elevators, some merely smiled and nodded in the direction of the guards, some showed passes, and some just glided by without acknowledging the guards' existence – which was also the guards' response to the flow: they barely looked up from their desk. The legitimate workers had a breeziness about them. Yes, breeziness was the word. It was the feeling that came with a certain power – the power to move past an official barrier which kept others out, the power of belonging.

If she moved breezily, holding her pass out like every other day, would the guards look up? And if they did, would they go any further? Would they frown, ask her to step over to the desk, scrutinise her pass? She doubted it. They'd blink. She'd smiled at them so she must know

251

them. They'd return to their telephone call or their tabloid newspaper or the conversation they were having.

What alerted them to strangers were the movements of the strangers themselves. Someone pushed open the glass door slowly, uncertainly. They hesitated once inside, looking around, getting their bearings. And they walked almost reluctantly towards the desk, where the guard, who had caught these signs, was already asking if he could help. Yes, visitors gave themselves away. If they knew the layout, if they breezed towards the elevators rather than staring dumbly at the desk . . . *anyone* could walk into the building. Anyone could take the elevator to any floor they liked, floors where ministers and senior civil servants might be meeting.

Oh, how Witch loved a democracy. They took their freedoms too easily, treated them too casually. This wasn't security; it was the opposite of security. It was a soft job, and the guards were happy to acknowledge this. She got up from her seat and walked one circuit of the reception area, then stood by the glass door. When the guards were busy, she pushed the door open and walked back out on to the street, sure that they would have forgotten her existence by the time the next tea-break came.

How long had she been waiting now? Maybe her fears of an illness were well-founded . . . Ah, but no . . . here came the woman now. Calling back over her shoulder to the security guard. Then pushing open the heavy glass door. Outside, she stopped and took a deep invigorating breath. Her weekend started here, started now. She held two briefcases, one a plain brown attaché case – her own – the other looking like an expensive school satchel, made from black leather and bearing a small crown insignia above the name-plate. This was government property, and a sign that she wasn't just some clerical worker. She had achieved a good grade, not quite senior but certainly on her way there. She was vivacious, full of life and hope. She made friends quite easily. The security guard would know her name. Yet she didn't seem to go out much. She shared a house with two other young professional women in Stoke Newington. Perhaps the house was rented, or perhaps they'd clubbed together and bought it between them before the government had changed the law on mortgage tax relief. Some things, even Witch couldn't be sure of.

She travelled to work by overland railway and tube. She travelled home the same way. It was a fairly hellish journey, and the later she worked or stayed on in town, the less teeming the crowds were on the trip home. So, one night, she'd hung around for an hour in a nearby wine-bar, having a drink with some of the other office staff. They were celebrating someone's birthday. But she hadn't stuck around for the Indian vegetarian meal. She'd kept looking surreptitiously at her watch. She'd made her apologies at half-past seven.

No boyfriend to meet, despite the nods and winks and oohs of her colleagues, just the tube and train and the short walk home. To stay in all the rest of the evening, as all her other evenings, watching TV.

Wondering what her weekend plans would be, today, after all three women had left for work, Witch had entered their house. Inside, she'd found a pleasant surprise: the other residents were going away for the weekend. There were signs of planned departure: packed and half-packed bags, raids on the bathroom toiletries. They'd tried to pack this morning before leaving for work, but had blearily only half succeeded. Only Christine Jones's room was tidy. No luggage there.

In the kitchen was the brochure for a Welsh campsite. Its telephone number had been ringed. Obviously it was there in case Christine needed it: Christine's idea probably. She seemed so much more organised than her housemates. And on a wall calendar was marked a time this evening when 'Garry and Ed' would be calling. Another look in the housemates' bedrooms confirmed that Garry and Ed were the boyfriends. The four of them were off to Wales on a camping expedition. Lovely.

Witch wondered how Christine Jones would spend her weekend. There didn't seem any clues that she was planning to go away, or to have someone over, or to hold a party, even a dinner party. She was doing German at night school, and it looked like part of her time would be spent catching up on her assignments. There were also three fat and newly borrowed library books to be read, and a video club membership card was handy on the coffee table in the living-room, in case she wanted to rent a film or two . . .

There'd be a spot of shopping on Saturday morning. Not having transport, she tended to use the local shops – though someone in the flat had access to a car, since there had been supermarket buying in bulk, shown in the contents of the refrigerator. Christine Jones wouldn't go hungry, not for food. But it wasn't party food, not social food; it was fast food, the stuff of days spent doing homework and nights spent watching TV.

One of her housemates, Tessa, kept a diary, and recent entries, when not running on about Garry and his physique and his bedroom athletics, showed concern for 'Chris', who had split up with a boyfriend several months before and seemed to have just lost interest . . .

'Hope she'll be okay this weekend,' the entry ended. Witch was tempted to take up a pen and add: 'She'll be fine, honest.'

She didn't.

When the mail arrived, she glanced at it, leaving it

untouched on the hall floor. Then, having satisfied herself with the layout of the house, she left it as neatly as she had entered it, and walked back to the railway station, a lazy stroll, nothing better to do, just whiling away the hours ...

Until now. As she follows Christine Jones along Victoria Street, she's thinking, ticking things off on a list in her mind. Christine knows the guard, but that probably doesn't matter. Another of the DTI buildings further along Victoria Street would do just as well, once Witch has a security pass. She's studying the way Christine moves, the way she walks, how far she places one foot in front of the other, the way she turns her head when she wants to cross the road. None of this is necessary – she doesn't intend to impersonate Christine Jones after all – but it is useful and it is interesting. Witch is learning to move like a professional woman, a woman on the way up in the civil service. She's thinking too of the evening ahead, of what must be done immediately, and what can be left till later. And, briefly, she's thinking of Khan, of how pleased her employers were, how generous. And she spares a thought, too, for Dominic Elder and all the other people who may be chasing her shadow just now. She's thinking all these things, but her walk is that of the girl about town, making her way home.

Home to Stoke Newington. Directly home. Poor Christine Jones, her eyes fixed on yet another book, a fat paperback this time. (She's almost finished it. Probably she's already looking forward to the three fat library books waiting for her at home.) No after-work drinks for her. Probably she wants to make it back to the house before her housemates leave. Sending her best wishes with them. Yes, better to return to a few minutes of

255

chaotic farewell than to an absolute forty-eight-hour emptiness. Poor Christine Jones.

She stops in at a newsagent on the way home. She buys a couple of magazines, and then, biting her lip guiltily, adds several chocolate bars to her purchases. Comfort food. The newsagent puts the whole lot into a white paper bag. It is awkward to carry. She might stop for a moment, open her satchel, and place the magazines and sweets inside, but she's hurrying now. Bloody London bloody public bloody transport. The bane of her existence. Late home as usual. It's nearly seven. The girls will be leaving soon. Yes, the car is parked outside the house. A tanned young man is carrying out two suitcases.

'Hello, Garry,' says Christine.

Garry lifts the cases higher. The action shows off his physique. 'Look at this,' he says. 'You'd think we were off for a fortnight on the QE2. I wish now I was staying behind with you, Chris. We could get nice and cosy, eh?'

'Leave my flatmate alone!' yells Tessa from the front door, half-jokingly at least.

The other housemate emerges with more bags. Behind her, her boyfriend is manoeuvring a large suitcase out of the door.

'We'll never get it all in!' calls Garry.

'As the actress said to the bishop,' retorts his friend. The girls laugh, the way they're supposed to. This is fun. Christine's smile is fixed. Witch can see that she is in a quandary. She's holding the paper bag to her, while she wonders whether to offer the chocolate to the foursome for their journey, or whether to say nothing about it. Witch is surprised, but pleased too, to see that self-gratification wins. Christine keeps the chocolate to herself.

Witch has passed the scene now, eyes on the cracks in

the pavement ahead. She's on the other side of the street from them, but not quite invisible enough. Garry gives her a half-hearted wolf whistle, almost drawing unwanted attention. But no one seems to pay him any heed. The cases *will* all go in, but only if some of the bags sit on the floor in the back and under the driver's and front-passenger's seats, and even then it's going to be tight.

'As the actress said—'

A thump silences the end of the sentence. Witch has turned the corner now. She stops, pretending to rummage in her bag for something. The car doors are opening, closing, opening again. Kisses and hugs are exchanged.

'It's only for the weekend,' complains Garry as the housemates make their farewells. 'It's not like a fortnight on the QE2 or anything . . .'

The doors close. All four of them. The engine starts with a throaty roar. Not one to hang about, the driver lets the tyres squeal as he releases the handbrake, and he fairly races to the end of the road, signalling left, turning left, and revving away in the opposite direction from Witch.

Moments later, the front door of the house closes, leaving Christine Jones indoors on her own.

Witch waited at the corner for a few minutes, not looking in her bag any more but waiting for a gentleman friend. She peered up this road and down along that, searching for him. And glanced at her watch, for the benefit of anyone looking from their windows. Not that anyone did. They minded their business and got down to the proper work of the evening: watching the television.

A few people hurried past, refugees from the latest train, she guessed. They looked worn out and glanced at her, nothing more. Nobody smiled, nobody offered a chat-up line or a joke or a 'Can I help you?' The time passed without incident.

She walked back around the corner then started into a brisk run, clutching her carrier bag to her to stop the contents from spilling out. She ran up to the gate, pushed it open, climbed the steps noisily, and rang the doorbell.

Christine Jones had hardly had time to start her first chocolate bar of the evening. She'd taken off jacket and shoes, nothing more. She opened the door wide, then looked disappointed.

'Have I missed her?' said Witch, panting, trying to catch her breath.

'Who?'

'Tessa, only there was something I wanted to give her.' She winked. 'For the weekend, if you know what I mean.'

'You just missed her,' said Christine. 'Funny, I thought maybe that was her coming back to say she'd forgotten something.'

'Oh shit!' Witch threw back her head and exhaled noisily. 'Shit, shit, shit.' Then she caught herself, grinned. 'Sorry, you must be Chris. She's told me about you. I'm Anna.'

'Hello, Anna. Do you work beside—? God, listen to me.' Christine rolled her eyes. 'Do you want to come in? You look like you could use a drink.'

'Too right I could.'

'Me too. After all, it *is* the weekend.'

Christine Jones stepped back so Witch could walk into her home. Then Christine closed the door. Witch was standing, waiting. 'Along here,' said Christine, signalling with the chocolate bar, leading her towards the living-room. 'You didn't say, do you work beside Tessa?'

'Well, sort of, yes.'

As Christine pushed open the door to the living-room, Witch hit her at the base of the skull. Christine froze for a moment, then fell forwards, turning sideways as she did so, so that her left shoulder hit the rug first, her head following it with an almighty thump.

She was aware that she couldn't move, aware too of a heat-source near her face. She opened her eyes to agony, the blood beating in her head. Immediately she opened her eyes, a hand descended on to her mouth, the thumb hooking itself under her chin. The side of the hand left just enough room below her nose to allow her to breathe. She looked up into the eyes of the woman who had tricked her way indoors. And she knew why she couldn't move.

Witch had tied Christine Jones to her own bed, using pairs of grey tights. There was an electrical socket just beside the bed, hidden behind the bedside cabinet. A clock-alarm and a reading-lamp had been plugged into the double socket. She'd unplugged the lamp and plugged in the iron, turning the heat all the way up. Now, while one hand gagged Christine Jones, the other gripped the handle of the iron and held it close to her face. Witch turned away from Christine and spat on to the dull metal face of the iron. Her saliva sizzled and bubbled.

'A nice hot iron,' she said quietly. 'You've got to be careful with a hot iron. Place it on the wrong kind of material and you can do terrible damage. Place it on *delicate* material, and you can ruin the material forever.' Christine's nostrils flared as she fought for breath, hyperventilating.

'Now,' said Witch, 'I'm going to take my hand away from your mouth. You could scream if you wanted to, but I'm not sure anyone would hear. There's no one else in the house, your windows are double-glazed and shut tight, and your room's on the end of the house. A good solid end wall rather than a connecting wall. No neighbours to hear. You understand what I'm saying? If you scream, nobody will hear, and you might startle me. I might drop the iron. I don't think you'll scream. I don't want to hurt you. It's not necessary to hurt you. I just need you to answer a few questions about your work.' She paused. 'Now, do you want me to repeat anything I've said?'

Beneath the pressure of her hand, Witch felt Christine Jones try to shake her head. She brought the iron down until it was inches above Christine's face, causing the young woman to screw shut her eyes. The iron went 'click' occasionally, its light coming on to show that it was heating up again, then another 'click' as maximum heat was achieved and the light went off, the iron starting to cool . . .

Witch lifted away her hand. Christine gulped in air, licked her lips. There was sweat on her face. She suddenly started thrashing, but Witch had expected this and sat still on the edge of the bed, waiting for the thrashing to stop. The bonds were holding. Christine calmed down.

'Oh God,' she said, trembling. 'Oh God, I'm sorry. I didn't mean to do that.'

Witch smiled. 'It's all right, Christine. It's only natural. Chain up any animal and it'll do the same thing . . . for a moment or two, until it realises it really is chained.'

'How do you know who I am?'

'I've been watching you. I'm interested in where you work.'

She seemed confused. 'DTI?'

'Yes, all those buildings along Victoria Street.'

'What about them?'

'I want you to tell me about them, anything you know, no matter how trivial.'

'What? Is this some kind of—' But of course it wasn't a joke. She could feel the heat of the iron. No, whatever else this was, it wasn't a joke.

'Take it floor by floor,' said Witch, 'starting with the ground.'

'Why? I don't understand.'

'You don't *need* to understand. All you have to do is tell me.'

'About the buildings?'

'Yes, about the buildings.' Another click from the iron. 'Take it floor by floor,' Witch repeated.

Christine Jones took it floor by floor.

After a while, Witch saw that she didn't need the iron. She rested it on its end on the bedside cabinet. She even left the room long enough to fetch water and paracetamol from the bathroom. It didn't look as though Christine had struggled at all during her absence, but of course she had. Witch merely smiled.

'I know how to make a knot,' she said.

'Why do you want to know all this?' asked Christine.

'Open wide,' said Witch. She held a tablet above Christine's mouth, and, when the mouth with its good solid teeth opened, she dropped the tablet in, placing the cup of water against her bottom lip and pouring some in. Christine swallowed the tablet, and Witch repeated the process.

'You're bound to have a sore head,' she said. 'It'll wear off in time. No lasting effects, I promise. I know how to hit people, too.'

'You know a lot,' said Christine, refreshed by the water. She'd been talking for over an hour.

'Knowledge is power,' said Witch quietly. Then she smiled. 'And I'm power-crazy, Christine. You're an intelligent woman. By now you're beginning to guess *why* I might want to know so much about Victoria Street. You won't say anything, because if you did, you think *I* might think I'd have to silence you. Permanently. Am I right?' Christine said nothing: answer in itself. 'Well, don't worry. I don't kill people for pleasure, only for profit.' She paused, seeming to think of something. Then she came to herself. 'And there's no profit in killing you, Christine. But I can't have you telling anyone either.'

'I wouldn't tell, I'd keep my mouth—'

Witch shook her head. 'So I'm going to have to hide you somewhere until this is all over. Probably Wednesday. It's not a long time, Friday night until Wednesday. It'll be uncomfortable, but no more than that. Now, because of this, because you're going to be my . . . guest over the next few days, I need some more information, different information this time.'

'Yes?'

'Who's your doctor, Christine?'

'My doctor?' Witch nodded. 'Doctor Woodcourt.'

'Male or female?'

'Female.'

'With a practice where?'

'Ebury Road . . . just at the end of the street.'

'And does Doctor Woodcourt know you?'

'Know me?'

'Do you visit regularly? Would she know you to look at?'

'I went a year or so ago for some jabs, holiday vaccinations. But now that I think about it, some locum saw me. I can't think when I last saw Doctor Woodcourt . . . maybe two years ago, when I was going on the pill.'

'Two years is a long time. I don't think she'd recognise you, do you?'

262

'Probably not. I don't see what—'

'On Monday morning, I'm going to call in sick to your office on your behalf. You're allowed several sick days before you need notification from your doctor.'

'A sick-line, yes.' And then Christine Jones saw. 'You'd pretend to be me? Just to get a sick-line?'

'It shouldn't come to that. Three days should suffice. What about your housemates?'

'What about them?'

'They'll be worried if you suddenly disappear.'

'Not them. I don't think they'd bother. I go away with my boyfriend all the time without saying anything.'

'But you've split up with your boyfriend.'

'How do you know that?'

Witch smiled. 'And you're lying about your housemates. They'll be worried if they don't hear from you.' She reached into her bag and produced a card of some kind. Christine saw it was a postcard. There were four separate views on the front and some writing: 'Greetings from Auchterarder'. Witch untied Christine's right hand. 'I want you to send them a postcard.' The card, which had been sitting on the bed, slipped off on to the floor. Before she realised the enormity of her mistake, Witch had leaned halfway towards the floor to retrieve it.

Christine's free hand shot to the bedside cabinet and snatched at the iron, stabbing at Witch with it. But Witch was too quick. She leapt from the bed and stood at a safe distance.

'Get out!' screamed Christine. 'Go on, get out of here!' Then she started to yell at the top of her voice. 'Help! Someone, please! Help!'

There was no time for indecision. Witch turned and left the room, closing the door after her. Christine might stop yelling for a moment to listen for sounds of her leaving. At the bottom of the stairs, Witch walked along the hall, opened the front door, checked that no one was in the street, then slammed it shut. On tiptoe, she walked back along the hall to the cupboard beside the living-room door, the cupboard under the stairs. Christine would have put the iron down so that, with her one free hand, she could untie her other bonds. They were difficult knots. It would take her some seconds.

The switch on the fusebox went from On to Off. The lights went off. The noisy fridge clunked to a halt. The display on the bedside clock went blank. Christine realised what was happening and started yelling again. Witch was climbing the stairs, her eyes cold and hard. She opened the door to Christine's room. The evening was still light, even though Witch had closed the curtains. There was the beginning of an orange glow from the street-lighting. They stared at one another, Witch utterly silent, Christine almost hoarse from shouting, and crying too. Of course, Christine knew that the iron she was again holding, the only thing that held Witch at bay, was cooling and would not get hot again. If she put it down, she could untie the knots, but if she put it down . . .

She did what Witch had hoped she would. She grew frustrated. And she tried to throw the iron not at Witch – Christine was cleverer than that – but at the window. But the plug held in the socket and the iron fell to the floor with a dull thud. It took two seconds for Witch to reach the bed, raise a fist, and strike Christine Jones back into unconsciousness.

Stillness. Peace. She peered out through the curtains. Someone in the house across the street was staring from their window. Someone else joined them, then they gave up and turned away. She had to act fast now. Things were becoming dangerous. She went to the fusebox and turned it back on. Then, in the living-room, she made a telephone call.

'It's me,' she said into the receiver.

'I was wondering when you'd call.' He pronounced the final word as 'gall'.

'I need a package picked up,' Witch said. 'A large package. I'll give you the address. The package needs to be stored for a few days. Can you do that?'

'It's in one piece, is it? Damaged goods might be a problem.'

'It's in one piece.'

'All right, give me the address.'

She did so.

'We need to meet,' said the voice, a European voice, Dutch perhaps.

'Monday,' she said. 'I'll call you. The package needs to be picked up within the hour, sooner if possible.'

'To Stoke Newington? Twenty minutes.'

'Good.' She put down the telephone. She returned to Christine's room and opened the wardrobe. On top was a small suitcase, which she lifted down. She began to pack clothes, enough for a few days' travel. Good clothes, too, including the smartest-looking dress. She also packed make-up, and a few toiletries from the bathroom. Christine seemed to keep her things in a wash-bag. The wash-bag and its contents went into the case. Shoes, too. And one of the fat new library books.

She took her own carrier bag downstairs and placed it next to the front door. Beside it she left Christine's attaché case and satchel, having first checked that her security pass was in the satchel, along with other documentation allowing access to canteens, clubs, sports facilities. She stared for a moment at the photograph on the security pass. The photo showed head and shoulders only, as these things always did. Another lapse: anyone with similar facial features could use another person's card, even if, like Witch and Christine, one of them was a good four inches taller than the other.

With make-up and a little hairdressing, she could pass for Christine Jones. She felt sure of it. She looked again out into the street. No signs of police or even curious neighbours. If anyone had heard the cries, they were ignoring them. Witch lifted the postcard from beside Christine's bed, took up a pen, and printed the message: HARD WORK BUT FUN. SEE YOU SOON. C. She then also printed the address of the house, leaving the space for names blank. An envelope on Christine's study-desk gave her the correct postcode. She reread the card. It was by no means perfect, but it would have to suffice . . . under the circumstances. The card had already been stamped with a Scottish-issue stamp, the lion rampant in one corner. She'd been so careful in Auchterarder. So careful. The card was delicious. Elder and company wouldn't see it till afterwards, till long after she'd gone.

The case was all packed. Time to tidy up. She put the iron back where she'd found it, and plugged the lamp back in. She reset the time on the clock-alarm, and went through to the other bedrooms to do the same. There was a humming from one bedroom. It was a computer, its screen white and blank and flickering, sitting on a large table. It had been left on. She ejected the disk, found the start-up disk, and rebooted the system. Then she put the original disk back in. Had it been set at the menu screen? That would make sense, nobody would leave it halfway through a file when they were going off for the weekend. Unless . . . She looked down the file names on the menu. One caught her eye: CHRIS. BYE. She opened the file. It was a message, short and to the point:

WHAT ARE YOU DOING IN HERE? DON'T YOU DARE READ MY LETTERS!!

Witch smiled. It was a message left for Christine. She began typing, her fingers efficient.

WOULDN'T DREAM OF IT! ANYWAY, GOT A CALL THIS EVENING. SOMEONE'S DROPPED OUT OF A CONFERENCE AT GLENEAGLES, AND DTI WANT ME TO GO!

She pondered the exclamation marks: were they Christine's style? Yes, probably. A woman on the way up in the civil service, and now a chance to shine at an important conference ... yes, they were excusable. Witch typed on.

OFF TOMORROW MORNING, BACK LATER IN THE WEEK, CHRIS.

She saved, and considered leaving the screen on. But Christine wouldn't, not all weekend with no one in the house. So Witch ejected the disk and switched off the computer. She reset the room's clock-alarm and, with a last look around, headed for the stairs. There was a soft knock at the door.

'Yes?'

'Come to pick up a package,' called the voice. Witch opened the door and stood back so that the two men could enter the hall. One of them carried a long, flat-packed section of cardboard.

'Upstairs on the right,' said Witch. 'And listen ...' She handed one of the men the postcard. 'This has to be posted by Monday morning in Scotland, to arrive here Tuesday or Wednesday morning.'

'No problem,' said the man, taking the card from her and slipping it inside his shirt. 'Might even manage it tomorrow.' Then the two men went upstairs. Minutes later, they appeared at the top of the stairs grappling with a large cardboard box, no longer flat-packed. Inside, Christine Jones would be trussed like a Christmas bird, knees tucked up into her chest, plastic restraining cords wrapped around her, arms tied against her sides. The human body, positioned just right, could make a smaller

267

package than might be imagined. The box was barely four feet long.

They brought her downstairs slowly, careful not to topple or trip. Witch held open the door for them, and held the suitcase out towards the man at the back. 'This too,' she said. 'It can stay with her.' The man took the case with difficulty by its handle, but said nothing. Witch closed the door after the men. She watched from the upstairs bedroom window as they loaded the van, got in, and drove off. The street still did not stir. It took more than odd comings and goings to produce a reaction here. Now, alone in the house, Witch went about her final tidying-up. She untied the tights from the bedposts and put them back in Christine's drawer, then straightened the bed. Having made sure things looked neat and tidy, she went back downstairs and picked up her bags. She let herself out and closed the door behind her. Then she took out Christine's bunch of keys and locked the mortice. There, just the way Christine would have left the place. Yes, she'd been in a hurry. Yes, the conference had come as a surprise. But she'd still left the house without fuss or undue mess. A very proper young woman.

Then Witch remembered the trick with the iron, and the way Christine had screamed the place down. She didn't blame her; she blamed herself. Next time, she'd have to do better. Get everything ready *before* loosing the knot around the hand.

Preparation, that was the secret. Be prepared. She'd learned her lesson. She was just glad she hadn't had to learn it the hard way. Christine Jones was still alive. Witch was still unscarred. She knew why she'd made the mistake, too. Her mind was running along two parallel roads, with occasional jolts from one road onto the other. In those moments, she was weak. She knew she couldn't afford any weakness. She was taking a risk this time, bigger than any she'd taken before. The deceit was greater, the sense of treachery more impending. If she double-crossed them ... *when* she double-crossed them, they would be far from pleased. They'd perhaps send another assassin after her. She smiled at that. Who would they hire? Who would take the job? The answer to the second question was obvious: if the price was right, *anyone* would take the job, no matter how dangerous.

Witch closed the gate. A police car was drawing up on the other side of the road. One of the officers called to her. She crossed the road towards the car. The policeman sat with his elbow resting on the sill of his wound-down window.

'Sorry to trouble you, miss. There's been a report of some screaming or yelling. Heard anything?'

Witch thought for a moment. 'I don't think so,' she said. Then she smiled. 'Hard to tell in this street though. They're always yelling at each other.'

The policeman smiled back and turned to his colleague. 'It was number twenty-seven made the call, wasn't it? Better go have a word.' He turned back to Witch and nodded in the direction of Christine Jones's house. 'You live there?' Witch nodded slowly. 'Well, that's one to cross off the list then, eh?'

'Yes,' said Witch. 'I've just locked the place up. I'm going away for a few days.'

'Lucky you. Anywhere nice?'

'Scotland.'

'Locked all your windows?'

'Of course.'

'Burglar alarm?'

'We don't have one.'

He puckered his lips. 'Think about getting one, that's my advice. Well, thanks anyway.'

'You're welcome,' Witch answered politely, crossing the road again and walking on steady legs in the direction of Stoke Newington railway station.

The policeman turned to his companion. 'Travels light, doesn't she?' he said.

# Saturday 13 June

'What are we looking for?'

Joyce Parry was not best pleased at being summoned to her own office on a Saturday morning, and all because Elder didn't like using computers. She sat at her desk in front of the terminal while Dominic rested his hands on the back of her chair and leaned his head close to her right shoulder.

'Someone this end helped her enter the country,' he answered. 'She's travelling, she's hiding, she's already had help on the Khan hit. There *has* to be someone else, however loose a tie they might be.' He checked that he wasn't about to give away more than he should know. 'Your man Barclay has found a link between Witch and two men in Paris.'

'DST found it, he's just tagging along.'

Elder looked at the back of her head. 'Whatever,' he said. 'I'm wondering if there's another terrorist loose over here, someone she knows she can call on for help.'

'You want to access MI6's files?'

'Yes.'

'How wide a search?'

'I'm still thinking about the American woman, Khan's lover.'

Parry nodded. 'It's a starting point.' She half-turned to him. 'Could be a long day.' She didn't sound angry with him any more. He squeezed her shoulder and she began tapping in her security code. Then she had a thought,

271

and swung her chair towards the telephone. 'I'd better just clear this with my oppo.'

After a short conversation, she was back at the screen. Moments later, the first file appeared – a brief description and history with a head and shoulders picture. Elder wanted to study every one of them as they came up. After a dozen or so, Joyce smiled at the screen. He saw the reflection of her face there.

'What's so funny?'

She shook her head. 'Nothing. It's just a bit like old times.'

A few dozen files later, Elder made her go back a couple of files. It wasn't a woman's face on the screen, it was a man's, going bald.

'Someone we should know?' Joyce asked.

'Someone we *do* know.'

The phone rang, and she swivelled towards it, leaving him staring at the picture on the screen.

'It's for you,' she said.

He tore his gaze away and took the receiver from her. 'Hello?'

'It's Doyle here.'

'Good, I think I've got something for you.'

'Me too.' There was a pause. He was waiting for Elder to ask, so Elder obliged.

'And what would that be?'

'Khan's tart, Shari Capri. I know who she is.'

It was oppressively hot in Trilling's office. Outside there was a generous summer's day. The building was quiet, it being the weekend. Yet here they were – Dominic Elder, Doyle and Greenleaf, and Trilling himself – stuck in darkness behind a firmly shut door and closed venetian blinds.

'It's the bleedin' black hole of Calcutta,' Doyle said,

shifting on his chair. Doyle, Greenleaf and Elder sat on a row of three stiff-backed chairs facing the wall behind Trilling's desk where a white screen had been erected, the sort used for slide-shows and home movies. Not that anyone bothered with Super 8 any more; it was all videos these days.

'When does the usherette come round?' Doyle asked, changing his metaphor but not the irritation in his voice. He had something to say and he wanted to say it, but first there was all this to be gone through. Trilling was behind them, fiddling with a slide projector which had been set up on a tripod. Its piercing beam shot between Greenleaf's left and Doyle's right shoulder and wavered against the screen as Trilling made adjustments to height and attempted to level the slightly askew – 'pissed' was Doyle's word – beam.

'Can I help you with that, sir?' asked Greenleaf, not for the first time.

'Perfectly capable myself,' muttered Trilling, also not for the first time. He was grinding a peppermint to powder between his teeth.

Elder was thinking of Joyce Parry. They were dining out together tonight, a celebration of their morning's work and, as Elder put it, a chance to relax before the storm came. He'd chosen a small, intimate restaurant near Kew Gardens, and he'd been in luck: a booking had just fallen through, there was a spare table.

He wondered now why he'd chosen *that* particular restaurant. The answer, of course, was its intimacy. It was a restaurant for seduction. The fact that it was run by an apparently brilliant young chef had little to do with it. He wanted Joyce to get his message, loud and clear, which meant soft lighting and low music . . .

'That looks about right,' said Trilling.

'Maybe move the tripod an inch to the left, sir,' commented Greenleaf.

Lab analysis of Witch's letter to Elder had thrown up nothing, not even saliva on the flap: Barman Joe told them she'd dabbed her finger into her drink and wet the seal with that. The lab confirmed that the drink had been neat tonic water with a slice of lemon. Joe's session with the two Special Branch men had been long, but totally unproductive. She'd only come into the bar the once, and he hadn't seen her around before or since. An artist drew up a sketch from Joe's description, and this had been run off for the officers whose job it now was to check hotels, boarding-houses, taxi-ranks, and so on. The sketch had been turned into a small wanted-style poster. Information wanted on the whereabouts of this woman. Details were given beneath the drawing itself: approximate age, height, what she'd been last seen wearing.

The van driver, Bill Moncur, who'd given her the lift from Folkestone to Cliftonville said all she'd had with her was the one rucksack of stuff, and it hadn't looked full, yet already she'd worn two outfits – the one described by Moncur and the one described by Barman Joe. Maybe she'd done some shopping in Cliftonville. Shops, too, would be shown the artist's impression. The poster would go up in clubs and pubs, on the off-chance that some pissed late-night punter had seen her.

The drawing had been shown to Moncur, who had shrugged. 'Hard to tell,' he'd said. 'Maybe it's the same woman, maybe not.'

More copies had been made, too, of the drawing of the man Mike McKillip had seen his employer talking to in the bar. To be shown around Cliftonville at the same time as the Witch drawings. Yes, they were going through the procedures, the correct and proper routine.

But Elder thought he had something better than an artist's impression.

Greenleaf had suggested yet another line of inquiry: travel. She'd travelled from Cliftonville to Scotland. How? She wouldn't still be hitching, not now that the hunt was on for her. Too open, too public. Which left several options: public transport, a bought or hired car, or an accomplice. Train stations were being checked, booking clerks questioned. Bus company offices would be next, then car-hire firms, then car dealers. She would need fake documents for these last two, and Elder reckoned there was a better chance that she was actually using train or bus or plane or, most likely, a combination of these. He didn't think she'd be using an accomplice to chauffeur her around. She liked working alone too much.

Auchterarder did not have a railway station. However, buses passed through it, and nearby Gleneagles *did* have its own small railway station, an echo of the days when visitors would arrive by train for their holiday there. Maybe some still did.

It was true that they hadn't given Auchterarder much thought. They'd been too busy further south. But the town wasn't populous, and Elder knew the Scots to be a curious race, in the sense that they liked to know all about strangers. So now a team was being despatched north – a proper team, not just local CID and the like. They knew what questions to ask, and where to ask them. In a town that small, Elder reckoned Witch wouldn't have opted for staying at a hotel or B&B. She just about had the cheek to check into Gleneagles itself, and this option would be checked. But he thought the likeliest bet was that she'd slept rough, out in the countryside around the town. Which meant checking camp-sites, showing her sketch to farmers ... She'd travelled further afield than anticipated. The Fablon she'd used was only available in that part of the world, according to the makers, from a store in Perth. The store had been visited. Yes, they did sell that particular design, but no, no one remembered serving anyone with it, let alone someone of Witch's description.

Another dead end, but it opened other routes. How had she travelled to Perth? Had she bought any other materials there? Had she stayed there for any time? The local CID were now busy finding answers to these questions. Patience and manpower were the necessities. But they were already stretching things to the limit and beyond. This close to the summit, they should be focusing in, instead of which the hunt seemed to be spreading wider and wider. He thought for a moment of Barclay. He hoped he would be all right. No, that wasn't exactly true: he hoped he would get results.

The summit started on Tuesday, meaning Witch was probably already in town calculating her plan of attack and her escape routes. She'd have more than one escape route. Unless this really was to be her swansong, her kamikaze trip. Elder was beginning to wonder. He'd stared long and hard at the drawing of her conjured up by the police artist's hand and Barman Joe's memory, trying to place the face . . . failing . . .

'Here we are,' said Trilling. There was no longer white on the screen in front of them, but colour. Greenleaf adjusted the focusing before sitting down. 'Thank you, John.'

In focus, the slide showed a man leaving a building. It had been shot with a powerful zoom, looking down from an angle. Probably taken, thought Elder, from the second or third storey of the building across the road from where the man was emerging. There was a car standing at the kerbside and he was heading purposefully for it, his lips pursed. In the second slide he was looking to his right, and in the third to his left, checking both ways along the street as he stooped to get into the passenger seat. A careful man, quite a nervous man. He had blond hair, but was mostly bald. What was left of his hair he wore quite long, in strands which fell down around his ears and over the back of his neck. His face was pale, cheekbones prominent. He didn't have much in the way of eyebrows.

'We don't know his name,' said Trilling. 'Or rather, we know too many of them – at least a dozen aliases in the past three or four years, and those are only the ones we know about.'

'So who is he?' asked Doyle, wanting Trilling to get on with it. Trilling did not reply. Instead, the projector clicked its way to slide number four. Same man, at a café table, enjoying a joke with an olive-skinned man.

'The Arab gentleman is known as Mahmoud. He works for an arms dealer. Or should I say, he works for the owner of an import-export business located in Cairo.'

'I went there once on holiday,' commented Doyle. 'You think the traffic's bad here . . .'

Cli-chack, cli-chack. Slide five. A street scene. The camera had just about managed to focus on a conversation between two men who looked to be arguing about something. The bald blond, and this time a small fat Asian-looking man.

'Spokesman for a now-defunct terrorist group. This is a rare photo of him, made more rare by the fact that he died last year. *Not* natural causes.'

Cli-chack. Slide six. Cli-chack. Slide seven. And so it went. In a few of the photos, the bald blond had disguised his appearance. There was a particularly risible hairpiece. There were sunglasses, of course, and what looked like an authentic moustache. Eventually, the slides came to an end.

'So he doesn't mix with royalty,' said Doyle. 'But, with respect, sir, who the hell is he?'

Trilling switched off the projector. Greenleaf went to the window and tugged up the venetian blinds. Elder walked to the projection screen and stood in front of it.

'He's a go-between,' he said. 'Just that. He has made a profession and a reputation out of liaising between people – terrorist groups and arms suppliers, crooked politicians and drug dealers, all sorts of organisations. He's worked in India, Czechoslovakia, Beirut, Austria, Egypt, Colombia . . .'

'A one-man United Nations.'

'I think *divided* nations would be nearer the mark, Doyle. He's Dutch, that much we're sure of. These slides came courtesy of MI6, who were given them by the Dutch authorities. There was, and still is, a long-term operation to arrest this man.' He paused.

'But not,' suggested Trilling, 'until his usefulness is past.'

'I can't comment on that,' said Elder.

'What do you mean, sir?' Greenleaf asked Trilling.

'I mean,' Trilling was happy to explain, 'just now they keep a watch on him, and they learn what he's up to. They amass information about all these groups he seems to work for. He's more useful as an unwitting source of information than he is behind bars.'

'The old story,' Doyle said simply.

'The old story,' Elder agreed.

'Like with Khan,' Doyle added.

'I can't comment on that either,' said Elder with a smile.

'So anyway,' said Greenleaf, 'what about him?'

'Two things,' Elder said. 'One, he's in Britain. That, at

any rate, is what the Dutch think. His trail's gone cold, and they'd quite like to pick it up again.'

'As if we don't have enough on our plates,' said Doyle.

'I don't think you quite see,' Elder told him.

'Oh? What don't I see? We're up to our arses in the summit and Witch and everything . . .'

'And so,' said Elder quietly, 'is the Dutchman. My second point. Think back to the description of the man Crane was seen having a drink with. Do you remember?'

Ever-ready Greenleaf supplied the answer. 'Fair and balding, according to Mr McKillip.'

Elder nodded, while Doyle took it all in.

'It does seem a mighty coincidence,' said Trilling. He handed a copy of the McKillip drawing to Doyle so that Doyle could take in the resemblance for himself.

'It could well be that this Dutchman is the link between the assassin and her paymasters,' said Elder.

'You mean her paymasters on the Khan hit?'

Elder shook his head. 'Nobody brings an expensive assassin like Witch into the country for a hit like that. There's another job, and *those* paymasters will have supplied the Dutchman.'

'I thought,' said Greenleaf, 'she did one paid hit to finance her own private vendettas, isn't that what you told us?'

'Yes, but aspects of this operation make it unique. It doesn't quite fit her previous profile.'

Doyle was pinching the skin at the bridge of his nose. 'So now you're saying we change tack completely? Leave Witch and start looking for this Dutchman? New posters made up, more questions at hotels and boarding-houses . . .'

'Starting here in London,' Greenleaf added. 'It's the obvious place.'

'Which is probably precisely why he'll be based

elsewhere,' said Elder. 'Somewhere out in the suburbs, pretending to be the rep for a Dutch company or something.'

Doyle counted on his fingers. 'Saturday, Sunday, Monday. Three days before the summit opens. It's too much ground even to *start* to cover.'

'So what should we do? Ignore the information?'

'You know that's not what I'm saying.'

'I *know* what you're saying, Doyle. You're saying you object to the workload, you object to grafting all weekend – again. You're tired and you need a break. Am I right?'

Doyle shifted his weight on the chair.

'We all need a break,' Trilling said quietly. Then he smiled. 'Maybe our Dutch friend will be *precisely* the break we need.'

Only Greenleaf laughed at the pun, and then not for long.

'Find the Dutchman,' said Elder levelly, 'and we find who Witch's target is. He's almost bound to know. We may even catch Witch herself.'

Trilling nodded. After a moment, Doyle nodded too. He looked around at the three faces.

'Well?' he said, rising to his feet. 'What are we waiting for? I'll just phone my bird and tell her I'm not available for lechery this weekend.'

Greenleaf sighed. 'And I suppose *I'd* better phone Shirley. I've hardly seen her recently. She'll go spare.'

'And I,' said Trilling, 'have to cancel a race meeting I was supposed to be attending. You see, we all make sacrifices.'

Elder was pleased, but didn't let it show. He was wondering how he would break it to his colleagues that he had to make a progress report to Joyce Parry this evening, a briefing he just couldn't cancel. Then Doyle remembered something.

'Oh,' he said, 'I know who the American bird is. An old mate of mine, Pete Allison – I used to work with him in CID, he runs his own security firm these days. He phoned me to say he'd been working for Khan, trying to find out about Shari Capri.'

'Why did he want you to know?'

Doyle shrugged. 'He was a bit sweaty about Khan being bumped off like that. He thought it through and decided he'd better come clean.'

'So what did he find?'

'She's a hooker, not a cheap one. That was all crap about her being a model. The story Pete heard is that another security firm had hired her to sniff around Khan.'

'Commercial espionage?'

Doyle nodded. 'Women and money, that's what it boils down to in the end. Another bank wanted to know what Khan's bank was up to, so they hired themselves a spy.' He turned to Elder. 'You still think she was working with Witch?'

Elder shrugged. 'Maybe not. But Witch *did* know a lot about Khan's movements. Maybe she had the Dutchman put a bit of money about, ask a few questions.'

'The security firm?'

'That'd be my guess. Someone there would have known what Ms Capri knew. Any idea where she is?'

'Not a clue. Want me to push it a bit further?'

Elder shook his head. 'It's a dead end. I'm sure she only took the job because she knew it would stretch us, lead us away from the real action. No, she's *here* now. Let's remember that and act on it.'

They left the office as a team.

The first thing to be done was to distribute photos of the Dutchman to police stations in central and greater London. The weekend wasn't really the time to accomplish this, but they did their best. A computer was used to create an A4-sized poster containing a description of the Dutchman and his photograph. The quality of reproduction of the photo left a little to be desired, and Elder doubted that, faxed, it would remain recognisable.

'The woman who really knows this machine is on holiday,' was the excuse offered.

'Then bring her back.'

They brought her back, and she sharpened the image to Elder's satisfaction, after which they laser-printed a few dozen copies. As well as police stations, the first target remained the Conference Centre itself. The description would go to every delegation, and to the various security organisations involved in the summit. The Dutchman probably wouldn't risk getting close to the summit itself, but the warning was worth making. Here was someone tangible for everyone to keep an eye open for. Here was something to keep them on their toes. Here was, at the very least, a *photograph*.

The day passed quickly. Doyle was sent to have a word with his snitches and least salubrious contacts.

'Bit out of their league,' he said, 'but you never know.'

There were Dutch-style pubs and Dutch restaurants in the capital. Greenleaf went to talk with owners, staff and regular clients. Again, they could be pretty sure that the Dutchman would steer clear of such places. Again, it was still worth a try.

Elder thought of his own contacts in London . . . and came to the conclusion that none of them was left; none, at least, who could be of any possible use. Apart from Charlie Giltrap. He wondered if Charlie was still around. He wasn't in the phone book, and a check showed that he wasn't unlisted either. Not that either of these meant anything. It was over two years since he'd seen Charlie, over two years since Charlie had given him his last, near-fatal tip-off.

'Just popping out for a minute,' he said. He made for the nearest newsagent's where he flicked through a listings magazine, concentrating on 'Events'. Sure enough, there was a record buyers' mart in London today, and ironically it was taking place at Westminster Central Hall, within spitting distance of the Conference Centre and not a five-minute walk from where he was standing. He put the magazine back on the rack and set off. It was just another long-shot . . . either that or fate.

At the Central Hall, he paid his entrance money and squeezed into a mayhem of noise and too many people crammed into the narrow aisles. Most of the music seemed to be heavy metal, not what he'd been expecting. The clientele was young and bedenimed and greasy-haired. They were listening to tapes on personal cassette-players before deciding whether to buy. Rare LPs were displayed against walls, some of the asking prices reaching three figures. A young woman, a heavy metal fan by the look of her, was attracting attention and comment as she browsed, apparently unaware of the hungry stares behind her. She was wearing a tight red leather skirt, zipped up both sides, and a black leather jacket. Elder found himself examining her too. He was looking for someone he knew beneath all that make-up and dishevelled hair. He failed to find her.

A few old-timers, and he put himself in this category, did their best to move through the crush, seeking out stalls selling older stuff: 50s and 60s music. He did one circuit of the hall without seeing Charlie Giltrap. And then, in a corner, stooped as he rifled through a cardboard box full of LPs, there he was. Grinning, Elder tapped him on the shoulder.

Charlie Giltrap turned around, his fingers still keeping his place in the box. Then his eyes opened wide and he let the records fall back, both his hands coming round to clasp Elder's.

'Dom! Where the hell did you spring from?' He was pumping Elder's right hand with both of his own, his grin near-toothless, cheeks slightly sunken where the extractions had been made. His eyes were dark-ringed, nose red-veined. Typically, he wore clothes too young for him: faded, patched denims, cheesecloth shirt, and a leather thong around his neck. His long grey hair was tied back in a ponytail.

'You never did send me your address, you bastard,' he said.

'I didn't have an address for *you*, remember,' replied Elder. 'But as it happens, I *did* send you a note.'

'Yeah?'

'Care of your father.'

A snort. 'That explains it then. Mind like a sieve. He probably chucked it out without telling me.'

'How is he?'

'Six feet under, God rest his soul. Went last Christmas.'

'I'm sorry.'

'Comes to us all, Dom. Maybe if I start smoking forty a day I'll live to be eighty-six like him. He used to say he'd smoked so much he'd been *cured*.' Charlie's laughter spluttered out of him.

'Yes, I remember,' said Elder.

'How are you doing anyway? What brings you back to the Smoke?'

'Work brings me back, Charlie.'

'Yeah, didn't think you'd just want to talk over old times.'

284

'Still get out and about, do you?'

'Not as much as before, but I keep my hand in.' Charlie winked. 'Let me settle up here and we'll go for a drink, yeah?'

Charlie turned back to the stall-holder. Elder noticed that half a dozen LPs had been lifted from the box and placed flat down on top of another box. Charlie picked them up and handed them over. The stall-holder totted up the prices and put them in a plastic carrier.

'Thirty quid, mate,' he said. Charlie handed over a fifty and, waiting for his change, turned to Elder.

'This place has gone right downhill, Dom. All hip-hop records and thrash bootleg tapes.'

'So I noticed.'

'Thing is, it's about the only place in London where you can still buy LPs. The shops all sell CDs, bigger mark-up, see. Phasing out vinyl. It's a catastrophe.' He took his change and his albums. 'Cheers, mate. See you next time.'

'Right you are, Charlie.'

Charlie and Elder squeezed back through the crowds in the aisles until they reached the doors to the lobby. Elder noticed that the heavy metal girl was standing chatting to some friends. As she laughed, he saw she was about ten years too young to be Witch ...

'What a relief,' said Charlie, glad to be out of the crowd. 'My motor's parked round the side of the cathedral. Come on.'

'Where are we going?' asked Elder. Charlie looked at him.

'We're going to find you a pint of Young's best,' he said.

Elder laughed. 'I haven't had any of that in over two years.'

'You used to knock it back.'

'So where do we find Young's round here?'

'It's in a few places. The best I've tasted's in Soho.'

They drove into the middle of Soho and, the car park being full, cruised until they found someone pulling away from a parking meter.

'God bless you,' Charlie called to the departing car, slipping his own resprayed Escort into the space. Elder noticed that Charlie hid his LPs under the driver's seat, and then unslotted his radio and did the same with it.

'These days . . .' he said, simply, locking the car. He put some more money in the meter and led Elder into the dark interior of a pub. No jukebox, no television, no video games, and only a single fruit-machine.

'It's an oasis,' commented Elder, who thought such pubs no longer existed in London.

'It gets noisy at night,' said Charlie, ordering two pints of Young's Special. The beer when it came was dark and rich. 'Just like my landlord,' said Charlie. They perched on stools at the bar and exchanged histories of the past two years. Charlie had cut down on cigarettes and also on drugs and drink.

'Doctor's orders,' he said. He thumped his chest. 'Dodgy bellows, plus high blood pressure.'

Meantime, his album collection had risen from three thousand to nearer five, most of the records bought secondhand, few of them more contemporary than 1972.

The conversation was stilted, awkward. They were at the same time recalling past events and attempting to evade making mention of them. They both knew they were doing this, and smiled a few times in embarrassment as the conversation lapsed into silence.

'So,' Charlie said at last, 'what can I do for you, Dom?'

Dominic Elder ordered two more pints and a couple of filled rolls. 'I'm looking for a Dutchman,' he said.

'Uh-huh.'

'I thought maybe you could do your sniffer-dog routine.'

'Long time since anyone's said that to me: sniffer-dog. Private matter, is it?'

'No, strictly company business.'

'Uh-huh.' Charlie sipped his drink thoughtfully, then shook his head. 'I'm not sure, Dom. I mean, after that last time ...'

'This is a team effort.'

'Yeah, but so was *that*. Didn't stop you going off and ... I don't know. I'd be worried, that's all.'

'About me?' Elder smiled. 'I'm touched, Charlie, but I meant what I said, this time it's a team effort.'

'No individual skills, eh? Playing for the team.'

'That's right.'

'Yeah, well ...' He straightened his back, scratched his nose, slumped again, studying his glass. 'All right then, can't do any harm. Mind, I don't have the eyes and ears I once had.'

'Just do what you can.' Elder handed over one of the descriptions of the Dutchman. Charlie read through it.

'Dutch pubs?' he said.

'We're already covering them.'

'Clubs, restaurants?'

'Those too.'

'Wonder if he's hired a car while he's here ...'

'We'll check.'

Charlie nodded. He refolded the piece of paper and put it in his back pocket. 'Like I say, Dom, I'll do what I can.'

'What's the going rate these days, Charlie? I'm a bit out of touch.'

'You and me both. We'll sort the money out later. Don't worry, there's a discount for friends. Where can I find you?'

Elder gave the name of his hotel.

'Using your own name?' asked Charlie. Elder nodded, then thought: I shouldn't be, though. I shouldn't be using my own name. How long would it take her to find him, phoning all the hotels alphabetically, asking for him at reception? A day, two at most . . . if she wanted to, if she didn't have anything else to keep her busy.

'Have another?' said Charlie. Elder shook his head.

'Better get back,' he said. 'I want a clear head for tonight.'

'Oh, yes? Still up to your old tricks, eh? Who is she?'

'Never mind.'

'Dinner, is it?' Elder nodded. 'Listen, do me a favour. After you've bought the forty-quid bottle of wine and you're tasting it, just ask yourself this: does it taste any better than the pint I had this afternoon? I can tell you now what the answer'll be.'

Elder laughed. 'You're probably right, Charlie.'

'That's me, Dom, a right Charlie. Come on, I'll give you a lift back.'

Joyce Parry came naked from her bathroom into her bedroom and stood there again, hands on hips, staring at the clothes laid out on her bed. She just couldn't make up her mind. Two dresses and a skirt and blouse: she could not for the life of her choose between them. And until she'd decided that, she couldn't decide on her colour of tights or stockings, which meant she couldn't yet choose her shoes, never mind her accessories.

She was used to dressing to suit the occasion. Perhaps that was the very problem: she wasn't sure just what the occasion tonight actually *was*. She wasn't sure of Dominic's intentions, of how he felt. Was her confusion his fault or her own? She was nervous as a cornered rat, and afraid of coming to wrong conclusions. If she dressed one way, perhaps *he* would come to some wrong conclusion, too.

It was so easy usually. For the office, she dressed hard and efficient, because that was what the office required. For a dinner party, she would be elegant and intelligent. Receiving friends at home, she was just slovenly enough so that they felt comfortable in her house.

And for an intimate dinner with a man . . . ? That depended on what she thought the man felt about her, and what she felt – if anything – in return. There was her long ice-blue dress, covering most of her body like a shield. Then there was the jersey dress, which came to her knees and showed a lot of her arms and shoulders too. Or there was the skirt and blouse. The blouse could be worn open-necked, or else clamped shut and tied at the neck with a bow.

Decisions, decisions. She turned and went back into the bathroom. If she left the choice of outfit until the last minute, she'd *have* to make a snap judgement. So be it. God, he'd laugh to see her getting in such a state. The unflappable Joyce. She'd flapped all right, the first time she'd met him. They'd become lovers only several years later, and then for a matter of weeks. He'd still been married then – though only just. It didn't work. It could never have worked. But that hadn't stopped it being good at the time.

She cleaned her teeth, rinsed, spat. Turned off the tap and stared at herself in the mirror, her hands on the rim of the washbasin.

Silverfish had aged Dominic, but she wasn't looking so young herself. She patted her hair self-consciously. She still wasn't sure whether bringing Dominic to London had been such a good idea. He certainly seemed full of energy and ideas, his mind sharp. He'd covered good ground in Folkestone, Cliftonville, Brighton. He got results from people, mainly because he looked like he was there to be obeyed and impressed. Even the Special Branch pair worked well with him. Not *under* him, but *with* him. That was another thing about Dominic, he consciously underplayed his role. He didn't need to brandish his authority in anyone's face. Yet all the time he was manipulating them.

Maybe there were still a few things she could learn from him, a few of his strengths that she'd forgotten all about. But she knew his weaknesses of old, too. The way he bottled things up, always thinking more than he said, not sharing. And now Witch had threatened him: what must the shock of finding that note have done to him? She'd find out tonight, she'd sit at the table and ask him outright, and she'd go on asking until he told her.

She'd considered putting a guard on him. After all, he was the one real and actual person so far threatened by Witch. But Dominic wouldn't have agreed to a body-guard. Besides, he was working most of the time alongside two bodyguards of a sort – Doyle and Green-leaf. But she'd phoned Trilling anyway, and had asked him to have a quiet word with his men, telling them to keep an eye open for Elder's safety. Trilling had been sympathetic, and had given her a progress report.

Too many fish, all of them possible red herrings. They were heading towards confusion rather than clarity. It wasn't Joyce Parry's way. The phone rang in the bedroom. Maybe Barclay and another of his too-vague reports. Maybe Dominic to say there was a fresh lead and he was cancelling dinner. She sat on the edge of the bed and picked up the receiver.

'Joyce Parry speaking.'

She listened for a moment, frowned, shifted a little on the bed. She pulled the corner of the duvet over her lap, as though her nakedness suddenly embarrassed her.

'What?' she said. She listened to more. 'I see,' she said. 'Yes, I quite understand. Thank you.' But the conversation lasted for several more minutes before she hung up.

Half an hour later, Dominic Elder rang the doorbell. She was dressed for travel, and knew she looked flustered and angry. Still, she opened the door to him. He was beaming. She swallowed before speaking.

'Dominic, I tried ringing you but you'd already left. Sorry, I've got to call off tonight.'

'What?' She stood at the door, holding the door itself by its edge. There was to be no invitation in.

'I know, I know. Somewhere I've got to be, cropped up less than half an hour ago. I really am sorry.'

He looked pitiable. His shoulders had collapsed forwards. He stared at the doorbell as though trying to make sense of the conversation. 'But . . . where? What's so important it can't—'

She raised her free hand. 'I know, believe me. But this can't wait. A car's picking me up in ten minutes and I haven't finished packing.'

'*Packing?*'

'Just overnight.' A pause. 'It's Barclay.'

'What's happened to him?'

'Nothing, he's just . . .' Her eyes narrowed. 'Tell me this is nothing to do with you.' He stood there, saying nothing. 'Well, thanks for the vote of confidence.' She pulled the door open wide. 'Get in here and tell me. Tell me *everything*.'

The schnapps before bed was probably not necessary. Barclay would have slept on a street of broken glass, never mind between the clean white sheets provided by the Gasthof Hirschen. It had been a hell of a drive. Dominique was of the let's-press-on school of travel, so that stops were few and far between, and what stops they made were perfunctory. Then a tyre went on the 2CV and the spare turned out to be in a distressed condition. And when a new tyre had been found and fitted, at what seemed to both of them major expense (whether converted into francs or sterling), a small red light had come on on the dashboard, and wouldn't go off, despite Dominique's attempts at tapping it into submission with her finger.

'What is it?'

'Just a warning light,' said Dominique.

'What's it warning us *of*?'

'I don't know. The owner's manual is under your seat.'

Barclay flicked through it, but his French wasn't up to the task. So Dominique pulled over and snatched the book from him.

'You're welcome,' Barclay muttered, but she ignored the jibe. He was dying for a cup of tea, and for the simple pleasures of Saturday in London: shopping for clothes and new classical CDs, reading a book or the newspaper with the CD playing on the hi-fi, preparing for a dinner party or drinks . . .

'Oil,' Dominique said.

'Let's take a look then,' said Barclay, getting out of the car. But the bonnet was almost impossible to open and he had to wait for Dominique, who was in no hurry to assist, to come and unhook the thing for him. There was less to the motor than he'd imagined.

'Do you have a rag or something?'

She shook her head.

'Fine.' He tugged a handkerchief from his pocket, pulled out the dipstick, wiped it, pushed it back into place again, and lifted it out again. Dominique consulted the owner's manual.

'Yes,' she said. 'The oil level is low.'

'Practically non-existent.' Barclay's voice was furiously calm. 'And do we have a can of oil with us?'

She looked at him as if he were mad even to ask.

'Fine,' he said again.

They were parked by the side of the autobahn. The road itself looked, to Barclay, like some old airstrip, short, pitted concrete sections with joins every few yards. The sound of the 2CV rumbling over each join had become monotonous and infuriating, but even that was preferable to this.

Then it started to rain.

They sat together in the front of the car, not even bothering with the windscreen-wipers. Drops of rain thudded down on the vinyl roof, trickling in at a few places where the vinyl had either perished or been breached. Inside the damp car, not a word was exchanged for several minutes.

'Well?' Barclay said at last. 'Maybe we could make it to the next petrol station.'

'The last sign was a couple of kilometres back. The next station is sixty kilometres away. We wouldn't make it, the engine would seize.'

Barclay did not want the engine to seize. 'So what do you suggest?'

Dominique did not reply. A car was slowing to a stop behind them. A man hurried out and started urinating on to the verge. Dominique watched in her wing-mirror and, when he was finished, dashed out and ran towards him, asking in German whether the man by chance had any spare oil.

'*Ja, natürlich,*' Barclay heard the man reply. He opened the boot of his car and brought out a large can and a plastic funnel. And even though this man was their saviour, Barclay saw why it was that some people disliked the Germans. Their efficiency in the face of one's

293

own shortcomings merely intensified those shortcomings. And nobody liked to be shown up like that. Nobody.

'What a nice man,' said Dominique, cheered by the encounter. She turned the ignition. The red light came on but then went off again. She signalled out into the autobahn and drove off, sounding her horn at the man still parked by the side of the road. She was chatty after that, and eventually succeeded in talking Barclay out of his sullenness. The rain stopped, the clouds cracked open, and there was the sun, where it had been hiding all the time. They rolled back the vinyl roof and, only thirty or forty kilometres further on, stopped in a town for a good hour, grabbing a bite at a café and then simply walking around.

The men stared at Dominique. During the drive, she had become ugly to him, but now Barclay saw her again, petite and full of life, the sort of woman who got noticed even when there were taller, more elegant or more glamorous women around: not that there were many of those in the town. Refreshed, the rest of the drive was a bit easier on the nerves if not on the body. The Gasthof Hirschen, when they'd stumbled upon it, looked just the place to Barclay, more than adequate for an overnight stop. Dominique wasn't so sure. She'd thought maybe they could press on a little further . . . But Barclay had insisted. They were only fifty kilometres, if that, from Burgwede. Fifty kilometres from Wolf Bandorff. It was close enough for Barclay. The manager had asked if they would want just the one room. No, they wanted two. And dinner? Oh yes, they definitely wanted dinner.

But first Barclay had taken a bath, lying in it until Dominique had come thumping at his door, trying the doorhandle.

'I'm starving!' she called. So Barclay got dressed and met her in the restaurant. After half a bottle of wine, his eyes had started to feel heavy. Then he'd decided to take a schnapps to his room. He'd telephoned Dominic Elder's London hotel, knowing Elder expected to be back there sometime today. But he wasn't around, so Barclay left a message and his telephone number. Then he'd fallen asleep . . .

The first thing he was aware of was a weight on him. The sheets were tight around him, constricting him. He tried to tug them free, but weight was holding them down. What? Someone sitting on the edge of the bed, halfway down. He tried to sit up, but the weight held him fast. He struggled for the lamp, switched it on. It was Dominique. She was wearing only a long pink T-shirt. It fell, seated as she was, to just above her knees.

'What is it?' he said. He was thinking. That door was locked. She's brought her lockpick's tools with her. Then he looked at his watch. It was one-fifteen.

'I couldn't sleep,' she said. She rose from the bed, padded barefoot to the room's only chair, and sat down quite primly, knees together and the T-shirt clamped between them. 'I thought maybe we could talk about Bandorff.'

'We've talked about him.' Barclay sat up, wedging a pillow between him and the headboard.

'I know, but I'm . . .'

'Nervous? So am I.'

'Really?'

He laughed. 'Yes, really.'

She smiled for a moment, staring at the carpet. 'I don't know whether that makes me feel better or not.'

'Dominique, don't worry. Like you say, either we find out something or we don't. Is it me? Are you worried about my superiors finding out? *I'm* not worried,' he lied, 'so it's stupid for *you* to be.'

'Stupid?'

'Well, no, not stupid. I mean, it's very . . . I'm *glad* you worry about me. It's nice of you to worry, but you shouldn't.'

She came over to the side of the bed and knelt down in front of it. Barclay shifted uneasily beneath the sheets. She stared hard at him.

'Michael,' she said, 'there's something I want to tell you.' She paused. The spell seemed to break, and she shifted her gaze to the headboard. 'Tomorrow,' she said. 'Tomorrow will be time enough.' She got back to her feet. 'I'm sorry I woke you up.' She smiled again and bent down to kiss his forehead. 'Try to sleep.' After the view he'd just had down the front of her T-shirt, he doubted he would.

Then she padded to the door and was gone. Just like that. Barclay didn't move for a couple of minutes, and then when he did move it was merely to sit up a little higher against the headboard. He drew his knees up in front of him and rested his arms on them. He stared at the bedroom door, willing Dominique to walk back through it. She didn't. Eventually, he slid back down beneath the sheets and turned off the bedside lamp. Etched on the insides of his eyelids were supple shadowy bodies, hanging breasts, shapes concave and convex. His forehead tingled where she'd kissed him. The birds were starting to sing as he eventually drifted off to sleep.

# Sunday 14 June

There was a big meeting at the Queen Elizabeth II Conference Centre. Central London was deserted except for the tourists, the security people, and some of the 2,500 media representatives who would cover the summit. Before the meeting, there was a photo session. Most of the security people, for obvious reasons, didn't want to become involved in the photo shoot, which seemed to suit the Home Secretary just fine. Jonathan Barker had been Home Secretary for just under a year, his political career having been steady rather than meteoric. There had been a rough few months at the beginning, with calls for his resignation after several prison escapes, a mainland terrorist attack, and a police scandal. But for the moment he could do little wrong, his second wife, Marion, having died two months back. She had been a tireless worker for charity, especially children's charities, as all the obituaries had pointed out. And it was as if some of her polish had rubbed off on her handsome widower.

Watching the photo opportunity take its course, Elder smiled. Only one of the obituaries had mentioned Marion Barker's crankier side, her belief in spiritualism. And no one had mentioned how she'd been Barker's secretary while he'd still been married to his first wife. There had been gossip about that at the time. Then the first wife had died, and slowly, without unseemly haste, Marion and Jonathan had begun to appear together in public.

It wasn't even close to a scandal. Nothing of the sort.

Yet Elder wondered how significantly it had slowed Barker's political progress. He wondered as he watched the Home Secretary smiling again, this time shaking hands with yet another dignitary. They all stood in a line off-camera, all the people who still had to have their photo taken. They preened, straightened ties, flicked a stray hair back behind an ear. They were all men. An underling gave them instructions, sending them on their way when each photo was taken. It was a real production line. And all for half a dozen photographers. The media wasn't really interested, not yet. The real scrum would begin when the summit got underway. This was a day of dress rehearsals and final checks. That was why the Home Secretary was on the scene, to give a very public thumbs-up to the security arrangements.

'Thank you, gentlemen,' the underling said at last to the photographers, who had already turned away and were winding back rolls of film, chatting in huddles. Elder stood in another huddle, a huddle of security chiefs. Trilling was there, and was in whispered conversation with an American. There were two Germans, a tall and dapper Frenchman, a Canadian, and many more . . . a real United Nations of secret agents and policemen. Elder had been introduced to them all, but they were names to him, little more. They were simply in his way.

But then he, of course, shouldn't be here at all. Joyce had only sent him because there was no one else available at such short notice. Her fury the previous evening had been tempered only by the arrival of her chauffeur. She'd still managed to make known her views. Elder was not to speak to Barclay 'under any circumstances'. In fact, he wasn't to do anything at all. But then she'd remembered this meeting . . .

The Home Secretary, sweeping back his hair as he walked, was approaching. His underling was telling him something, to which Jonathan Barker did not appear to be listening. He stuck out a hand towards Trilling.

'Commander, nice to see you.' They shook hands. Barker smiled and half-nodded towards Elder, as if to say 'I know you', when in fact he couldn't even be sure of Elder's nationality.

'Mr Elder,' explained the underling, 'is here as Mrs Parry's representative.'

'Ah,' said Barker, nodding and frowning at the same time. 'Thought I didn't see her.' His tone, to Elder's ears, was slightly ominous.

'Mrs Parry sends her apologies,' said Elder. 'Something came up last night, very last-minute, very important.'

Barker looked as though he might have something to say about this, but he was already being introduced to the Canadian, to the Germans . . . Elder had to give the underling his due: the guy knew all the names and faces. Trilling's voice was a peppermint murmur beside him.

'What's Joyce up to?'

'I don't know.'

'Barker didn't sound too pleased.'

Elder nodded slowly. Not too pleased at all . . . Well, he wasn't in such a good mood himself. If Barker wanted to pick a fight, that was fine by Elder. He'd spent a sleepless night in his room, a piece of paper by his telephone. On the paper was a note of Barclay's phone number in Germany. Joyce had warned him not to speak to Barclay. And hadn't Barclay let himself in for it? Elder had requested that no calls be put through to his room.

But this morning he'd cracked. He'd placed a call to the Gasthof Hirschen, only to be informed that Herr Barclay had already checked out. Well, that was that.

'If you'll come this way, gentlemen,' said the Home Secretary, taking charge. Introductions over, they were on their way into the Conference Centre proper.

'First stop,' said the Home Secretary, 'screening unit.' They had stopped in front of a doorway the edges of which were thick metal, painted bright orange. Two guards stood this side of the doorway, two the other. This was the start of the tour which, conducted by the Home Secretary, was supposed to reassure everyone that the security precautions were, well, more than adequate. Elder believed it; he knew they were more than adequate. He still wasn't impressed.

'Anyone entering has to pass through this metal detector. It's a special design, extremely accurate, not yet, I believe, in place in any airports due to the costs involved. Cost has not been a factor at this summit. But before even this, a body search takes place. Nothing too distracting or disruptive, and of course the heads of state will not be subject to this particular search.' A smile. 'We think we can trust them.' There were a few laughs, Trilling's amongst them. 'Any baggage is checked by hand and by a hand-held detector, before being passed through this X-ray machine.' Barker patted the machine itself. 'Again, it's British-designed and British-built and it's more sophisticated than similar devices found in airports. An inbuilt computer, for example, points out anomalies to the operator. Now, can I ask you all to submit to a search then walk, one at a time, through the doorway?'

'What happens if two people pass through at the same time?' questioned an American voice.

'They're sent back,' answered the underling quickly. 'The scanner won't accept two people. They *both* go back, just in case one has passed something to the other. Then they walk back through the detector individually.'

The Home Secretary beamed. 'Any more questions?' There were none. 'Then I suggest we proceed.'

The tour was brisk, but Elder noticed that the

underling had to field more questions than was comfortable. The Home Secretary, it seemed, had not been properly briefed; or if he had, he'd not remembered it. Well, this was only PR after all. It wasn't important.

They saw the hall where the nine-nation summit itself would take place; the interpreters' boxes; the rest-rooms; the smaller, more intimate conference rooms; the 'suites' which had been set aside for the individual delegations – all with computer terminals, photocopying machines, fax machines; the toilets; the press facilities; the monitoring room. There was even a small gymnasium. They passed technicians who were busy checking for listening devices. A policeman dressed clumsily in a suit wandered past them reining in a sniffer-dog on a leash. Cleaners seemed to be re-cleaning every spotless surface in the place, and behind them came more technicians checking for more unwanted devices.

'Tremendously impressive, I'm sure you'll agree,' said the Home Secretary. There were nods, mumbled agreement. The Home Secretary, it seemed to Elder, like most politicians equated effort with success. The more you did to secure a place, the more secure it became. Elder didn't agree. Elder didn't agree at all. The more sophisticated the security, the more loopholes it contained; the more people were involved, the greater the possible access for a stranger; and the more you relied on technology . . . Well, the word 'relied' gave it away, didn't it? You shouldn't have to rely on *anything*. They only needed to take such huge precautions in the first place because central London had been chosen as the location for the summit. And the reason London had been chosen had little to do with security and everything to do with prestige.

Elder would have chosen an isolated castle, or the top of Ben Nevis, or an underground bunker. But that would never do. These were statesmen. They didn't hide away, not at summits. Summits were events; media events, the pictures beamed around the world, photo opportunities and sound-bites of the grandest kind. No statesman wanted to hide from all that good publicity. Summits would soon be run by ad agencies.

The tour was winding up. It had taken a little over an hour and a half. Drinks and canapés were being provided in another part of the building, outside the 'secure zone'.

'I'm sorry I can't stay,' said Barker. 'I hope you'll understand that my schedule is busier even than usual.' He managed by tone and intonation to turn this into a joke of sorts, so that no one minded that they were being shuffled off to a hot little room somewhere. Not Trilling and Elder, though: they were tagged by the underling and told to come with the Home Secretary. Another underling escorted the larger group away from the scene. There were backwards glances from a few of the men. They looked like they would prefer to stay with Barker, Trilling and Elder.

'This way, please,' said the underling.

They followed the route they'd just come until they reached one of the small conference rooms. It contained a round table, eight chairs, and a water-cooler, which looked newly installed. The Home Secretary drank two beakerfuls of spring water before sitting down. Three men were already seated at the table: a senior armed forces commander whom Elder recognised straight away, a representative from the SAS, and an Intelligence officer. The Home Secretary shook hands with them, then motioned for Trilling and Elder to be seated. The underling remained standing till last.

'Right,' said Jonathan Barker, looking towards Trilling, 'now what's all this about a Dutchman?'

'Mr Elder found the connection.'

'Then Mr Elder can tell me.'

So Elder explained about the intelligence which had come from the Netherlands, while the Home Secretary nodded, his eyes making a tour of the other men round the table, as though ensuring that they were paying attention. They were certainly paying attention. The underling, whom Elder had expected to take notes with a fountain pen, unfolded a small case, turning it into a laptop computer. He tapped away at the keys while Elder spoke, like the stenographer in some courtroom drama.

Barker was staring at Elder. 'And Witch?'

'A female assassin, sir. Known to be in this country. The summit would seem a likely target of her attentions.'

'How does she operate as a rule?'

'At close range.' The question, which had surprised Elder, was a fair one and also astute.

'Then we've no problems,' said the Home Secretary. 'She's not going to get within spitting distance of anyone attending the summit.'

'We can't know that for sure, sir,' countered Elder. 'And besides, while the available evidence points to close range, there are plenty of possible hits she's made at longer range: bombs, shootings . . .'

'Well then, Mr Elder, perhaps you can suggest possible ways of tightening up security?'

All eyes were on him. A couple of hours ago he would have taken up the gauntlet. He would have revelled in pointing out all the mistakes. But they were basic mistakes – such as choice of location, for example – and couldn't be changed at this late stage. So he shrugged. The gauntlet remained on the ground.

'I've been over the security arrangements with some of Commander Trilling's men. We haven't made any recommendations.'

'Yes,' said Barker, 'but that's rather an ambiguous

answer, Mr Elder, isn't it? You may not have made any recommendations, but did you see any flaws?'

Elder swallowed. 'No, sir,' he said.

Barker seemed satisfied. 'Thank you, Mr Elder. Mrs Parry sees flaws.'

Elder's heart sank. He'd walked straight into a trap. The underling was handing the Home Secretary a sheet of paper.

'She thinks,' Barker went on acidly, '*in retrospect* that London was a poor choice of location for the summit. She *feels* security is difficult to maintain in a city of ten million inhabitants.' He placed the sheet of paper on the table. Elder saw that it was a letter of sorts, a memo. He'd guess, by Barker's pique, that it had been sent to the Prime Minister direct, bypassing Barker himself.

'I have to agree with Mrs Parry,' Trilling said quietly, 'that London is far from ideal from a purely security point of view.'

'Well, it's a bit bloody late to tell us now, isn't it?' said the Home Secretary coldly. 'It looks to me, from where I'm sitting, as though MI5 and Special Branch are attempting to cover their arses in the event that an assassination attempt *does* take place, and maybe even, God forbid, succeeds. That smacks to me of panic and impotence. Panic and impotence, Commander.' His eyes found Elder's. 'Panic and impotence, Mr Elder.'

'I'm sure Mrs Parry is only pointing out—'

'Why isn't she here today?' The Home Secretary's voice had risen enough for his underling to glance up. 'I'll tell you why, Mr Elder, because she didn't have the guts to face me on this. So she sent *you* instead. And who are you, Mr Elder?' The finger pointing at him was long and thick with a gleaming, manicured nail. 'You're in retirement. You're in London on a consultancy basis. What the hell is going on in Joyce Parry's department, that's what I'd like to know? And believe me, I intend asking her.'

'What Mrs Parry means,' said Elder, 'is that you can't cordon off central London. The IRA learned that a long time ago. You can't be secure in London.'

'This assassin, though, she's not IRA, is she?'

'She doesn't belong to a group.'

'People hire her?'

'Sometimes, not always. Look, people like Witch don't want peace. They're not the types to sit in hotel rooms and around conference tables. Look at Hamas in Palestine – the PLO were getting too much like the establishment. Witch is a one-woman splinter group.'

'Then what is her ideal?'

Elder smiled. 'People keep asking me that. Why does she have to have one?' He paused, aware that Trilling's foot was touching his beneath the table. It was a warning. It was telling him not to explode.

Barker sat for a few moments in silence, his face implacable. His voice when he spoke again was cool, not quite objective.

'We're going to go through the security arrangements again. Step by step. Don't bother looking at your watches because we'll be in this room as long as it takes.' He slipped out of his jacket and hung it over the back of his chair. He began to roll up his shirtsleeves. 'Sandwiches will be brought in, as will tea and soft drinks. There's water available whenever required. You may know that the Foreign Secretary has urgent business in the Middle East, so I'm going to be attending more of his bloody summit than was the intention. This being the case, I don't want any fuck-ups.' He paused, glancing from man to man to man. 'So, gentlemen . . . perhaps we'd better begin?'

Elder looked down at the table. He knew that several

pairs of accusing eyes were on him. The Army, the SAS, Intelligence. Stuck in here because of his department, because of a letter sent by *his* boss. Elder knew why Joyce had written the letter. She'd written it because, having checked security at the Conference Centre and beyond, having read Greenleaf's impressive report on the security arrangements, Elder had warned her to. He just hadn't expected she would take his advice.

'Let's cover ourselves,' had been his exact words. 'Let's cover ourselves from criticism.'

Yet now he felt naked as the day he'd been born.

Herr Grunner of the Burgwede Maximum Security Prison was far too polite a man to tell the two young people in front of him that their request for an interview with Wolfgang Bandorff had upset his whole weekend. His wife and he had been due to visit their son in Geneva. The son was a physicist and worked at the huge CERN project beneath the Swiss-French border. Herr Grunner knew that the letters CERN stood for Conseil Européen pour la Recherche Nucleaire. He also knew that 'nucleaire' in this case had nothing to do with nuclear bombs or anything military. The people on the project were scientists, and they were trying to probe the secrets of particle physics – hence 'nucleaire', the nucleus.

The proud parents had been taken before on a tour of the CERN complex, their heads dizzied by the size and complexity of the underground machines. But, though Herr Grunner had listened closely to Fritz's explanations, he hadn't really understood much of anything. So this trip was to be pleasure only: a trip to the mountains, a few meals, a chance to meet Fritz's Swiss ladyfriend Cristel.

And now he'd had to make telephone calls, to explain matters to his wife. The trip was put back until the following weekend. Herr Grunner's wife was not at all amused. Which was perhaps why he had brooded on the visit to his prison by a member of the French internal security agency, accompanied by a member of British internal security. It was curious after all, wasn't it? Curious that those two countries' very adequate external intelligence agencies shouldn't be involved. Curious enough certainly to merit a call to his country's own internal security agency, the BfV.

Still, when Mademoiselle Herault and Mr Barclay arrived, Herr Grunner was polite, obliging, deferential. They had to take tea in his office while he told them something of the prison's history. Not that he wanted to keep them from their appointment, you understand; this was a matter of courtesy alone, and the young couple seemed to acknowledge this.

All the same, Mr Barclay had questions for Herr Grunner.

'Has Bandorff had any visitors lately?'

'Visitors are kept to a minimum.'

'Lately though?'

Herr Grunner looked as though he might become difficult, then relented. He pressed two digits on his telephone and repeated Barclay's question in German, then waited. After a moment he began to scribble on a notepad, then gave a grunt of acknowledgement and put down the receiver.

'His mother and his sister.'

'On the same day?'

'No, on different days.'

'When did the sister visit?'

'March the twentieth,' Herr Grunner looked up from the notepad, 'at ten o'clock.'

'I take it you check the identities of visitors?'

'Of course.' Herr Grunner looked at his watch. 'Now, if we are ready . . . ?'

They were ready.

Bandorff's cell was large, more like a hospital room than part of a prison. Bandorff was allowed, as Herr Grunner had explained, a lot of his own things: books, tapes, a cassette-player, his own clothes even. There was a typewriter and plenty of writing paper, and even a portable colour TV. The walls had been painted sunflower gold, and then decorated with maps and posters, including a smiling photograph of the Pope.

Two warders entered the cell first, and would remain there throughout. Wolf Bandorff was watching television. He lay on his bed, hands behind his head, legs stretched out, feet crossed at the ankles. He seemed to be watching a quiz show. Herr Grunner bowed towards Bandorff – who nodded his head slightly in response – then left for his office. Two chairs had been placed on the same side of a small desk, both the chairs facing Bandorff. It did not look as though the terrorist was about to shift either his body or his gaze.

But as Dominique sat down, she saw Bandorff's eyes move to just below the level of the desk. He was staring at her legs. Instinctively, she tugged her skirt down a little further. He looked up at her, light glinting from his round wire-framed spectacles, saw that her wriggling was his doing, and grinned. He was in his early fifties, his hair long and silvered and swept back. Had it been thicker, it might have been described as a 'mane', but it was thin and unwashed. He was thinner than the photos – those old photos in the Witch file – had intimated. He no doubt kept in shape in the prison gymnasium. He was a good-looking man who had not gone to seed.

'You're beautiful,' he told Dominique in German.

'Thank you,' she said crisply in English.

'You're French?' he asked her in French.

'Yes,' she said, still in English.

'But you want to conduct this interview in English,' he said, nodding. He turned his attention to Barclay. 'Therefore I take it you, my friend, are either American or British?'

'I'm English,' said Barclay.

'And I,' said Bandorff, 'am German.' He began watching the quiz show again. 'And this,' he said, waving a hand towards the TV, 'is as good a theory of terrorism as I've ever seen.' His hand curled into a fist, index finger extended like a pistol barrel. The hand bucked, an imaginary bullet finding the all-too-real target.

'You miss guns, Herr Bandorff?'

Bandorff didn't reply. Barclay looked at Dominique. He was trying hard to phrase another question, but his mind was not cooperating; all it could think of was the bombshell Dominique had dropped as they were leaving Herr Grunner's office.

'Michael,' she'd said to him in an undertone, 'you know there was something I wanted to tell you last night? Well, it's this. None of this is sanctioned by my superiors.'

He'd almost passed out. 'What?'

'I'm not authorised to be here. I telephoned a colleague and got him to give me the prison details and phone number. I didn't tell my superiors I was coming.'

His walk had slowed. If he moved any faster, he felt his legs would buckle under him. 'Why not?'

'They wouldn't have let me. This is a big job. And I'm not that big. Remember, I told you back in Calais: you weren't important enough to merit someone more senior. My superiors don't know anything about any-thing . . . not yet. They think I've been following you

309

these past days while *you* made your investigations. I haven't told them anything more.'

'Jesus Christ!'

'I'm sorry.'

'Why tell me now?'

She shrugged. 'Maybe because now you can't back down and leave me all by myself . . .'

'You seem engrossed.'

Barclay snapped out of it. Bandorff was talking to him. He became aware that he'd been staring at the TV screen. He took a deep breath. 'My name is Michael Barclay, Herr Bandorff. This is Mademoiselle Herault. We'd like to ask you a few questions.'

'Do I win any prizes?'

Barclay just smiled. He took a photograph from his pocket, got up and walked over to Bandorff. The warders looked bored. Barclay stopped a foot or so from Bandorff's bed and held the photograph towards him.

'She's beautiful too, Herr Bandorff.'

Bandorff peered short-sightedly at the photo. 'I can't . . . my eyes aren't what they were.'

One of the warders said something in German.

'He says Herr Bandorff can see fine,' translated Dominique.

Barclay held his ground. The hand holding the photo was remarkably steady. Well, after all, what had he to lose? He was here because Dominique had played a trick on him. They'd run fast and loose, ignoring all the laws of the game. Rugby had been invented that way, but careers had come to a speedy end that way too. What had he got to lose?

'The photo was taken some time ago. It shows you and a young woman. For want of her real name, we in the security service call her Witch.'

'Witch?'

310

'*Die Hexe*,' translated Dominique. Bandorff glanced towards her.

'Thank you,' he said crisply, 'I do *know* what the word means.' He paused, watching for her reaction, then chuckled. 'Witch. I like the name.'

'The photo,' Barclay went on, 'shows you with a young woman, Herr Bandorff. You're in a crowd in the city of Edinburgh. You're watching the Pope.'

'Are we?'

'We're interested in the woman.'

'Why?' Bandorff was still staring at the photo.

'She's become a very proficient terrorist over the years. I believe she gained her earliest training at your hands?'

'Oh no, not her earliest training.'

A breakthrough! He'd acknowledged he knew her. Barclay had to press on. 'Do you know much about her early life?'

'Nothing at all, my friend. She came, she stayed, she left. I knew less about her when she left than I did when she arrived. While she, on the other hand, knew quite a lot about me.' He took a deep breath, sighed. Barclay could smell pork sausage, garlic, caries. 'Ah, the good old days. I'd like to know what happened to her. Can you tell me?'

'I thought maybe you could tell me. She visited you quite recently, didn't she?'

'Did she?'

'Posing as your sister. Witch is good at disguise, it wouldn't have been difficult. What did you talk about?'

Wolf Bandorff stared into Barclay's eyes and laughed. 'So young and yet so wise.' Then he turned back to the TV. Barclay stood his ground. From this close, he could see the musculature beneath Bandorff's grey T-shirt, the veins and tendons in his arms.

'She needed help, didn't she? You must have been surprised to see her after all this time.'

Bandorff spoke quietly, his words evenly spaced. 'Do you know how long they intend keeping me here?' Barclay waited for him to answer his own question. 'Another sixteen years, my friend. Another sixteen years of books, music, magazines.' He nodded towards the TV. 'When I am released, I shall make my fortune by appearing on general knowledge quiz programmes, always supposing my memory holds up.' He paused, his eyes fixed on the photograph.

'I must thank you for showing me this,' he said. 'It has reinforced one of my memories.' He looked past Barclay to Dominique. 'She *is* beautiful, isn't she?'

Barclay didn't think he meant Dominique. 'She was,' he said.

'She still is, believe me. You never forget those eyes.'

'What did she want?'

Bandorff shrugged and returned to the TV.

'She needed help,' Barclay replied, 'and you gave it. You were able to introduce her to two people in Paris who could help her.'

Bandorff looked back to Barclay and smiled. He smiled back. 'I'm fed up calling her Witch,' he said. 'What did you call her?'

Now Bandorff was chuckling. Barclay went back to his chair and sat down. He caught Dominique's eye. She seemed to be urging him on.

'Can you leave me that photograph?' Bandorff asked casually.

'Maybe,' said Barclay. But he slipped the photo back into his pocket.

'Shall I tell you something, my friend?' Barclay waited. 'I may be the only man alive who has ploughed his way through Balzac's *Comédie humaine*. Yes, all ninety-one

312

volumes. Here's my advice: don't bother.' He smiled to himself, then lowered his head so that he could scratch his nose just beneath his glasses. 'I shouldn't think Herr Grunner is happy about your visit,' he said at last, straightening. 'He enjoys his Sundays at home. Sunday . . . strange choice of day to pay your respects.'

'We're not going to get anything here,' Dominique said to Barclay, just loud enough for Bandorff to hear.

'Tell me, Herr Witchfinder,' said Bandorff, 'what are you doing here really?'

'Her most recent assassination was in the United Kingdom.'

Bandorff nodded. 'The banker, Khan?' He smiled at the surprise on Dominique's face. 'The newspapers here printed the story. I am not clairvoyant, I only read words. Clairvoyants, though, read faces, don't you think? I knew of Khan. His bank was said to sponsor terrorist groups . . . but never mine. We had to find our backers elsewhere. That photograph . . . how do you know it is Witch?'

Barclay shrugged. 'Personally I don't.'

'Personally? Personally I? But someone else, eh? Someone who has seen her since, and then saw the photograph, and who made the connection. He would be the Witchfinder General, eh?'

Barclay tried to think of Dominic Elder in such a role. It fitted all too easily.

'One thing I learned about the woman you call Witch . . .'

'Yes?'

'She changes allegiances.'

'That's hardly news, Herr Bandorff. She's been involved with several terrorist groups.'

'Still, it was one of the things I learned about her. She might also appreciate being given a sort of codename . . .

this "Witch" that you call her. She was fascinated by word games and crosswords.' He tilted his head to one side, remembering. 'She would lie in bed puzzling over them ... Ah, then there was the third thing.'

'Yes?'

'Sex, Herr Barclay. She didn't like sex. No sex for *Die Hexe*.' A smile.

'That must have disappointed you,' said Dominique coolly.

'Oh yes,' said Bandorff reflectively. 'A grave disappointment. But it went further. I felt she didn't like *men*.'

'She was a lesbian?' Dominique sounded disbelieving. Bandorff laughed.

'No, no, all I mean is that she hated men. Now tell me, you're a woman, why might that be?'

'I can think of a few reasons,' said Dominique.

'Me, too,' said Bandorff. 'I wonder if they're the same? Perhaps psychoanalysis could explain it.'

'And you've no idea where she came from?' asked Barclay.

'Oh, well, she was passed along the line. One activist passed her to another ... and so on. Each time a little more radical, a little more committed. But all those people are gone now. You won't trace her history that way. All I knew was that she wanted to change the world. That was good enough for me back then, and good enough for her. When she left, she left without warning. She'd brought no baggage, and she took none, except for her tarot pack and her teddy bear.' He was reminiscing. It sickened Barclay. 'She's become a myth, hasn't she? Who am I to tamper with myths?'

He returned to his television. A new quiz show was about to replace the old one. 'Ah, now this one is my favourite. It contains a nice element of chance.'

Barclay stood up, followed by Dominique. Was this it?

314

Was this what they'd come so far for? Barclay tried to think of other things to say. He turned to Dominique, who nodded merely. It was time to leave. But Barclay paused, reaching into his pocket again for the photograph. He placed it silently on the desk.

'Thank you, Herr Witchfinder,' said Bandorff.

Barclay and Dominique walked back the way they'd come. 'You were brilliant, Michael,' she told him. 'Have you forgiven me yet?'

'For what?'

'For lying to you ... and then for telling you the truth?'

He smiled. 'It was a shock, that's all.'

'Yes, and look what it did to you.'

Which was true. Something had galvanised him. He'd actually interviewed Wolf Bandorff and had come away with information on Witch – useless information in itself, but something to be added to the file.

'So what now?' he asked.

'Back to Paris, I suppose. Then back to London for you.'

He nodded. There was nothing keeping him on the Continent any more. Time to head back and confess that he'd come away from France with not a great deal. They were passing Herr Grunner's office.

'Should we look in and say goodbye?' asked Barclay.

'He's probably already gone home,' said Dominique. But the office door opened and Herr Grunner stood there, gesturing to them.

'Would you be so kind ... ?' He held the door open and motioned for them to enter. Past him, a man was standing in front of Herr Grunner's desk, his raincoat still on, arms folded. Dominique gasped.

'Who is it?' asked Barclay.

'Not my boss,' she said. 'But *his* boss!'

315

They were at the door now, crossing the threshold, the door closing with a quiet click after them. A figure stood staring from Herr Grunner's rain-dappled window. It turned around and spoke in a voice which chilled Barclay all the way down to his feet.

'Good afternoon, Mr Barclay,' said Joyce Parry.

The trip back to London was the least comfortable of Barclay's life. Despite the chauffeured car, the airplane waiting on the tarmac, coffee and biscuits on board.

'My car's still in Calais,' he said. 'And I've some clothes in Paris.'

'They'll be picked up,' Parry said coolly. She had her glasses on and was browsing through the big fat Witch file, Dominic Elder's file. She didn't seem to be in much of a mood for talking, which worried Barclay all the more. Not much had been said in Herr Grunner's office. Dominique had been given a few curt words of French and then had followed her superior's superior out of the room, without so much as a backward glance at Barclay. Barclay had steeled himself for similar treatment from Parry.

It hadn't come. She'd thanked Herr Grunner – in fluent German – and they'd left. He saw Dominique being driven away in a large black Citroën, while an official-looking person got into her 2CV, started it, and rolled out of the prison car park.

'Come on,' said Parry. She led him to a white Rover 2000 where a driver was waiting. He had an embassy look about him which Barclay translated into MI6. 'Straight to the airport,' Parry informed the driver.

'Yes, ma'am,' he said. Barclay heard humour in his tone, the joke being that Barclay was in for it and he, the driver, was not.

'How did you know?' Barclay asked Joyce Parry. He

316

was thinking of Dominic Elder. He had tried phoning the hotel again first thing, but they said they couldn't put through his call. He hadn't understood at the time. He thought maybe he did now. Parry turned her head towards him.

'Don't be stupid. How could we *not* know? I've heard of cavalier, but this little stunt . . .' She exhaled noisily. ' "How did you know?" ' she echoed, mockingly. She shook her head slowly. By the time they'd reached the airport, she'd decided to explain it to him anyway. 'Herr Grunner contacted the BfV, who contacted the DGSE and SIS. What do you think SIS did?'

'Contacted you?' hazarded Barclay.

'You can imagine my surprise, being told that one of my agents, who had told me he was in Paris, was actually in Germany. Perhaps you can also imagine my humiliation at having to be told your true whereabouts by bloody SIS!'

Yes, thought Barclay, there was little love lost between MI5 and SIS – the Secret Intelligence Service, also known as MI6. The French DGSE was the equivalent of the SIS, an external intelligence service. They'd no doubt contacted the DST. Dominique was no doubt receiving a similar lashing. Dominique . . .

'You're as bad as Dominic bloody Elder,' said Parry. 'This is just the sort of stupid trick *he'd* have played.' She paused. 'I know he's been in touch with you throughout. Tell me, did he tell you to come here?'

Barclay stayed silent. No point defending himself. It was best just to let her get on with it; let all the anger roll out of her. But in fact she said nothing more until the airport, where they boarded their plane. As she was fastening her seatbelt, she looked up at him.

'Why did you lie?'

He'd been preparing for this very question. 'Would you have let me go?'

'Certainly not.'

He shrugged. 'That's your answer then. You saw Dom . . . Ms Herault. *She* was going. If I'd called you for permission and you'd turned me down flat, how would that have made me look?'

'It would have made you look like a junior agent who's still got to be kept on a tight leash. Which is the truth. But I suppose that wouldn't have done, would it? It would hardly have . . . impressed Ms Herault.'

'It would have made me look like a fool.'

'So you lied to me instead.'

'I'm sorry, I know I shouldn't have.'

'No, you shouldn't. Believe me, Mr Barclay, you shouldn't. As for conspiring with Dominic Elder behind my back, it's intolerable!'

'I did what I did because I thought it was in our best interests.' He paused. 'Ma'am.'

'And you think that's an excuse?'

There was no more dialogue between them until after take-off. Barclay felt a sudden crushing fatigue, despite the sour airplane coffee. It was days since he'd had an unbroken night's sleep. Adrenaline had kept him going, but now the adventure had come to an abrupt end and his body just wanted sleep. Only fear of his boss's reaction should he doze off kept his eyes open.

Joyce Parry kept tapping the Witch file which lay across her lap. 'For your information,' she said at last, 'I learned of your little escapade *yesterday*. I arrived in Germany late last night.'

'What? Then why did—'

'I had some trouble persuading Monsieur Roche that we should let you and Ms Herault go ahead with the interview.'

318

'You let it go ahead? But why?' He was wide awake now.

She shrugged. 'Why not? What did we have to lose? Tell me, why were you there?'

'It's a long story.'

'And this is a long flight. I expect a report from you, and I mean a *full* report. If you leave anything out . . .'

'I understand.'

'I'll want it by tomorrow morning, first thing, on my desk. Meantime I want to hear it from your own mouth. Did you learn anything from Bandorff?'

Barclay shrugged. 'Tidbits.'

'But something?'

'Maybe, yes.'

'Well, at least there's *something* to show for all your bungling.'

'It's not much. He told me she hated men. He wondered what could have caused that. He said maybe psychoanalysis would provide an answer. What do you think he meant?'

'Families?' Parry answered.

'So it goes back to her parents? He also mentioned two things she carried with her: a teddy bear and a pack of tarot cards.'

Parry considered this. 'Maybe Profiling can make something of it.'

'They're both signs of insecurity, aren't they? A teddy bear brings past security, a tarot is supposed to reassure for the future.'

She stared at him, eyebrows raised a fraction. 'Maybe you've been in the wrong department all along.'

Barclay gave her just a hint of his winning smile. 'He also mentioned clairvoyance at one point, just in passing. Maybe it was a reference to the tarot.'

'Elder visited a fairground in Brighton,' Parry stated.

'Really? Coincidence?'

She shrugged. 'We'll see.'

Barclay had trouble forming his next question. 'She left a message for Mr Elder, and Bandorff hints that she hates her father.'

'What are you saying?'

'It's just, when I was at Mr Elder's, there was a photograph there of his daughter.'

Joyce Parry went very still. 'Did he talk about her?'

'He just said she was dead. "Deceased" was his word.'

Joyce Parry nodded. 'She is.'

'What happened?'

'Her name was Susanne, and she was on a school trip to Paris. There was an explosion in a shopping arcade. No group ever claimed responsibility. Three children were among the dead.'

Barclay recalled how Dominique's father had died. 'He thinks Witch did it?'

Joyce Parry was staring from her window. 'He doesn't know. He *can't* know.' She turned to him. Barclay supplied her thoughts.

'Unless he asks her himself?'

She nodded. 'That's his obsession, Michael. He's got a question he needs to ask her, a question only she can answer.'

He thought of Dominique who had lost a father, of Elder's lost daughter. It would mean nothing to people like Bandorff and Witch. He saw now why Dominique, who had been so full of action before, had said almost nothing in Bandorff's cell. She had been facing a ghost, a terror with her since childhood.

'Get some sleep,' Joyce Parry was saying. 'You look exhausted.'

She was right, he was exhausted. Yet he doubted he would sleep.

# Enterprise & Initiative

# Monday 15 June

They were arriving. Or had already arrived. Mostly, they touched down in their national jets at an RAF base outside London. A few chose to helicopter into the city itself, the rest travelled by way of a huge police escort. These were the heads of state, heading for the summit.

They came with full and impressive entourages, almost as if one-upmanship were the game. Several brought with them personal hair-stylists. All of them brought 'gofers': anonymous individuals whose job it was to find and fetch whatever was needed during the stay in London. The gofers tended to be ex-diplomats who had spent time in England and built up a network of contacts in London itself. There were some who said the gofers were the most important people of all. It was they who kept the heads of state happy.

The real show of one-upmanship, as it turned out, was to bring your own chef with you. And the chef brought with him his *équipe*, his pots and pans and utensils. Ingredients from the various homelands were brought, too, all slipping quietly through as diplomatic baggage so that no customs people need declare them illegal. Arms were brought too, of course. More diplomatic baggage, arriving in well-packed crates. High-tech equipment was packed in separate cases: scramblers, decoders, debuggers, communications systems . . .

Watching it all arrive, there were those who were glad the summit was only lasting a week. Vans were provided at the base, to be loaded and driven by members of each entourage. Some of the vans made for the Queen Elizabeth II Conference Centre, others for the embassies of the countries concerned, where the delegations were staying for the week. There was fun to be had from sorting out the secret servicemen from the rest of each delegation. Sometimes they made it easy, donning the near-mandatory dark glasses even though the day was overcast and showery. Perfect summer weather, and due to last for the whole week. The hot spell had been just that – a spell. Now someone had cast another spell, and storms were rumbling inland from the west.

So far the movement of the eight delegations into London had been accomplished without a hitch. There were several small demonstrations to contend with outside certain embassies, but these passed off with a minimum of bother. And they gave the secret servicemen a chance to try out their discreet photographic equipment. The Metropolitan Police had drafted several hundred extra officers into the capital for the week. The mood in the ranks was buoyant: there'd be plenty of overtime, plenty of holiday money made over the next seven days.

But the mood elsewhere was verging on panic. There had been a catastrophe at a large nursery garden in Cornwall: an invasion of cows. As a result, several thousand fresh flowers, just ready to be picked, had been crushed or beheaded. The flowers had been ordered to decorate the Conference Centre itself. A 'floral decorist' had been hired, and Monday afternoon was when he and his own *équipe* had intended to start their work, finishing late on Monday night. But now there were no flowers for them to work with.

A senior civil servant spent several panicky hours making various telephone calls, until at last four new and willing suppliers were located. Between them, they had just about enough spare flowers to save the day: two hundred carnations short of the original plan, but so be it. However, this in turn led to problems with security, since the new firms needed clearance before delivering the flowers. Once more, the civil servant picked up her telephone.

In a sticky, overworked office on the second floor of a building in Victoria Street, the telephone rang. Judy Clarke picked it up. Judy was in a panic too. Her boss hadn't come in yet, and it was already quarter past ten. She hadn't heard of any train disputes or hitches on the underground. Mind you, you only heard of hold-ups on the underground *after* they'd happened. Still, it wasn't like her boss. And there was so much to do! She was breathless as she picked up the receiver.

'Hello?' she said.

'Oh, hello,' said the female voice at the other end. 'My name's Tessa. I share a house with Chris . . . Christine Jones.'

'Oh, yes?' Judy's heart sank. She knew what a call like this meant. Then she brightened. 'Tessa, yes, hello. Remember me? Judy Clarke. We met at Christine's birthday party.'

'Judy . . . ? Oh yes, hello again, how are you?'

'Not so bad. Is Christine ill?'

'Not exactly. But she's had a bit of bad news, a bereavement.'

'Oh dear.'

'Family, an aunt. I think they were very close.'

'An aunt? Oh dear, I am sorry.'

'Well, these things . . .'

'So Christine's not coming in today?'

'Well, that's the thing. She's gone off. The funeral's not till Wednesday.'

'Wednesday! God, I need to speak to her. There are things that need—'

'She said she thought you could cope.'

'Yes, well, maybe we can but it's still ...'

'If I hear from her, shall I tell her to call you?'

'Could you get in touch with her? Is she at her mum's in Doncaster? Maybe if you gave me the phone number ...?'

'She didn't leave one.'

'That's not like—'

'She was a bit distraught. She's not in Doncaster anyway. The aunt lived somewhere in Liverpool.'

'Yes, I see.' Liverpool? Christine hadn't mentioned an aunt in Liverpool.

'Shall I get her to call you?'

'Yes, please, Tessa. I really need to know about Dobson's and about the MTD meeting.'

'Hold on, I'll write that down. Dobson's ...'

'And the MTD meeting. Management Training Directive. Just tell her MTD, she'll know what it is.'

'Okay.'

'And if you do hear from her, please tell her I'm sorry.'

'Yes, thank you, I will.'

'Oh, and Tessa?'

'Yes?'

'Have you got a cold or something? Your voice sounds hoarse.'

'Must be the anabolic steroids. 'Bye, Judy.'

''Bye, Tessa,' said Judy, putting down the phone. She sighed. Oh, hell. No Christine till Thursday. No one to steer the ship for the next three days. Three days off for a bereavement. She wondered how Mrs Pyle in personnel would react to that. She didn't like you taking off three consecutive days for major surgery, never mind a funeral. Liverpool? An aunt in Liverpool? Oh well, it came to us all, didn't it? Maybe she'd phone Christine's house tonight . . . talk to Tessa again, see if Christine had been in touch.

Then again, maybe she wouldn't. Derek was supposed to be taking her out to the pictures. That was typical of him, choosing Monday night. He knew the cinemas were half-price on a Monday . . .

'There goes another one,' said her colleague Martin, coming into the room.

'What?'

'A motorcade.' He walked to the window. She joined him, peering down. Four growling motorbikes preceded the slow-moving convoy of long black cars.

'Wonder who it is this time?' she said.

'I can't see. Usually there's a flag on the front of the chief's car. Can you see one?'

She craned her neck. 'No,' she said.

'Me neither.'

'I feel we should be throwing down confetti or something.'

He laughed. 'You mean tickertape. Except these days, we'd have to use the leftovers from the paper-shredder instead.'

She laughed at this, at the idea of tipping a binful of shredded documents out of the window. Martin could be really funny at times. If he took off his glasses, he wasn't bad-looking either. Nice bum, too. He seemed to sense what she was thinking and turned towards her, taking off his glasses to wipe them with his hankie. There were red marks either side of his nose where the frames pinched.

'So,' he said, 'what are you doing tonight, Judy?'

She thought for a moment, swallowed, and said: 'Nothing.'

Witch put down the receiver. Shit, *merde, scheisse*. Trust her to end up speaking to someone who *knew* Tessa. A girl called Judy ... who sounded concerned about Christine Jones. Concerned enough to pick up the phone and make some enquiries? Concerned enough to telephone the *real* Tessa this evening? Witch bit her bottom lip. Dispose of the girl Judy? No, it would be too suspicious. Two people disappearing from the same office ... a laughable idea. No, this would have to be one of those rare occasions where she was forced to trust to luck. That's all there was to it. Maybe she should read her tarot again, see what it had planned for her. Maybe she shouldn't. What good would it do if the news were bad? She'd still have to go through with it. Too late to back out now.

She had time to kill. Her meeting with the Dutchman wasn't till lunchtime. She took her hand-mirror out of her shoulder-bag and looked at herself. She'd cut and dyed her hair, plucked her eyebrows, dusted her cheeks. She felt she resembled the photo of Christine Jones on her security pass almost *more* than Christine Jones herself did. After all, the photo had been taken some time ago. Christine's hair had grown out since it was taken. But Witch's was just the right length. And Christine had let her eyebrows grow out, too. Sensible woman. It was an unnecessary and painful chore. All to attract the male ...

She placed the mirror back in her shoulder-bag. She was also carrying Christine's office-issue satchel, containing a few of her files but also some bits and pieces which were specifically, unquestionably Witch's own. She came out of the phone-booth and, in less than ten steps, was back on Victoria Street. Just in time to see the tail-end of the convoy. A policeman, who had been holding back traffic at the intersection, now told pedestrians they could cross the road.

'Just a bloody nuisance, this conference,' muttered one elderly lady, wheeling her shopping-trolley off the pavement and on to the road, making it rattle noisily as she pushed it.

A driver, stuck in line and awaiting permission to move, opened his car door and leaned out.

'How much longer, guv?' he called to the policeman.

'Couple more minutes,' the policeman called back. He shook his head at Witch. 'Some people got no patience.'

'Patience is a virtue,' she agreed. For some reason, he laughed at this. Witch walked on. She wasn't headed for 1–19 Victoria Street. She was making for another DTI building closer to Victoria Station. It was a very short walk. Not enough time for her to become nervous. She went to push open the glass door to the building, but a man, just leaving, held it open for her.

'Thank you,' she said with a smile. She strode through the lobby, her security pass held out in her hand as she passed the guard-desk. The man on duty looked at her dully, blinked, and returned to his reading. She waited for the lift to descend, and at the same time checked out the ground floor, especially the stairs. Entrances and exits were important. The stairs actually kept on going down. She wondered what was downstairs. In the lift, there was a button marked B for Basement. So she pressed it and headed downwards. The doors shuddered open, and she found herself staring at another entrance lobby – the back entrance to the building – and another guard, who was staring at her. She smiled at him.

'Pressed the wrong button,' she called, before pushing the button for level 2. It took a moment longer for the doors to close. She saw two grey-liveried drivers coming into the lobby. Their cars were parked just outside the doors. Now she remembered. She'd walked around the back of this building before. There was a slope down from street-level to the back entrance, and on this slope the chauffeurs left their cars while they waited for their ministers or other 'important people' to finish their meetings. So: back entrance, front entrance, two lifts and one set of stairs. She nodded to herself.

At the ground floor, the doors opened and two men in pinstripe suits got in, giving her a moment's glance, deciding they didn't know her, and continuing their conversation.

'Spurrier's doing a good job,' said one of them. 'That office was a shambles . . .'

Witch got out at the second floor while the men continued upwards. She was standing in a small entrance area from which led, to left and right, narrow green-carpeted halls. She chose to go right, and passed several offices. Green seemed the predominant colour: she saw lime green chairs in some of the offices, and olive green curtains. In some of the offices stood a single desk and chair. Other rooms were larger, with a staff of secretaries working away on word processors, or clerical-looking people rushing around with sheaves of paper or large manila envelopes under their arms. Telephones did not ring; rather, they buzzed, quite annoyingly. In the corridor ahead, two shirt-sleeved men were having an intense discussion. One stood with arms folded, resting most of his weight on his forward foot. The other had his hands in his pockets. Both wore pale shirts and dark ties. They looked senior. The one with arms folded turned and watched Witch approach.

'Can I help you?' he said.

Damn! She was supposed to look as though she belonged here. She swallowed.

'I'm looking for Mr Spurrier,' she said.

He grinned. '*Mrs* Spurrier, you mean.'

'Oh yes, Mrs Spurrier.'

'Next floor up,' said the man. 'You're new, aren't you?' He was almost purring. His colleague was staring fixedly, nervously, at the tips of his shoes.

She managed a coy smile. 'No, I work at Number One.'

'Ah.' Folded-arms nodded as though this explained everything. 'Back along here, lift to the next floor, corridor on the left.'

'Thank you,' she said, turning away. Another close call. What if he'd said, 'I'm Spurrier, how can I help you?' It was bad enough that Spurrier had turned out to be a woman. She was beginning to take risks. The game was becoming difficult. Difficult, but not dangerous. It would turn dangerous if she were *forced* to take risks . . . She took the stairs, not the lift. Just to experience them. At the top of the stairwell, two girls were giggling together.

'What's the joke?' said Witch, conversationally.

They looked around before confiding in her. 'The hunky policemen,' one said.

'We're wondering which one we'll get outside our window,' explained the other.

'Ah,' said Witch, nodding. Yes, she'd been wondering about that. Police marksmen on the roofs along Victoria Street: it was bound to happen. There would be times when all the heads of state would be driving along Victoria Street towards Buckingham Palace. Police marksmen on the roofs . . . and in the buildings? There were ledges outside the windows of this building. Witch had spent a long time in her several disguises checking the look of the DTI buildings on Victoria Street. Staring up at them . . . sometimes taking a photograph. Just a tourist, eating her burger lunch or killing time.

The marksmen would be sited on the ledges. But did they . . . ?

'Do you ever get the chance to talk to them?' she asked. The girls giggled again.

'Not enough,' said one.

'Not *nearly* enough,' said the other.

'God, there was one . . . when was it? Back in April.'

'March,' her friend corrected.

'March was it? Yes, when that whassisname was in town. He visited just along the road. They had policemen on the ledges then. The one outside our office . . .'

'God, what a hunk!'

Witch laughed with them, asked them to describe the man. They did, then they all laughed again. The two girls hugged their files to their chests.

'I hope we get him again.'

'I'll keep my fingers crossed for you,' said Witch. 'How do they get out on to the ledges?'

'Oh, some of the windows open. You know, like in the minister's office. You can get out that way.'

'I've never been in the minister's office,' Witch admitted.

'No? We're in there all the time, aren't we, Shelley?'

'All the time,' she agreed. 'He's got his own telly and everything in there.'

'Drinks cabinet, *all* the papers, and paintings on the wall, supposed to be really valuable.'

'Yes?' said Witch.

'Oh yes,' said Shelley. 'And if he doesn't like them, they fetch him some more.'

'I don't know about paintings. Give me a big poster of that police hunk any day!'

Witch left them to their giggles and walked along the third-floor corridor. She was keeping an eye out for Folded-arms. Maybe he'd follow her, try another chat-up line. She did *not* want him directing her personally to Mrs Spurrier's office.

She came to a solid wooden door with a plate reading Conference Room. Pinned to the door was a sheet of typed paper with dates, times and names on it. Presumably bookings for use of the room. There was no booking for just now. She turned the doorhandle. The door, though it had a lock, was open. She slipped inside and closed the door again. The room had a stuffy, unused smell. There was a plain oval table, five lime green chairs, a single uninspired painting on one wall. Two glass ashtrays sat on the table, and on the floor by the window sat an empty metal wastebasket.

Utilitarian; Witch quite liked it. She went to the window and stared out, resting her hands on the inner sill. The window was not the opening kind. It was swathed in yards of off-white gauze curtaining, the kind popular in public offices because, the popular wisdom went, the curtains would catch shards of glass exploding inwards after a blast. Witch's blurred view was of the traffic and the pedestrians below in Victoria Street. The hold-up for the VIP convoy had led to frayed tempers and congestion. She thought for a moment of the drive she was going to take tomorrow or Wednesday. She had to get her routes right. She had to find a car tonight and make a test-run. She had to find *two* cars tonight. There was so much still to do. The ledge, she noted with pleasure, was hardly wide enough to accommodate a man. The ledges on the next floor down, she knew, *were* wide enough. What was more, the ledge outside her window had crumbled a little, rendering it unsafe. Good. Very good. She examined the face of the building across the road, then spent a little time looking down on to the road itself, her lips pursed thoughtfully.

Back at the door, she examined the keyhole. An

uncomplicated affair, as easy to lock as it would be to unlock. Better and better. She opened the door again and stepped out into the corridor, closed it behind her and checked the list on the door. There were no scheduled meetings tomorrow at all, and only two on Wednesday, one at 10 and the other at 4.15. A nice gap between. Excellent. Witch was in no doubt. At last, she'd found her bolt-hole, her assassin's perch. Sometimes it happened like that, you just wandered into a place or up to a place and you saw it straight away, the perfect position. Other times, you had to search and scour and scratch your head and maybe even make other plans, look at other sites. She'd lost weeks of her life changing initial plans, executing – apt word – new ones. But today it had come easy. Perhaps her luck was changing. She turned around and saw, coming towards her, Folded-arms. Only his arms weren't folded any more. They were spread out, palms towards her.

'You see,' he said, 'you see? I just knew if I left you alone you'd get lost again.'

'I'm not lost,' replied Witch crisply. 'I was checking the time of Wednesday's meeting.' Then she bit her lip. Risk, risk, risk.

Folded-arms looked both delighted and amazed. 'What? The four-fifteen? But *I'm* going to that. Are you going to be there, too?'

She shook her head. 'The ten o'clock.'

'Pity,' he said. 'Still, we must have coffee afterwards. What do you say?'

'Great.'

'My name's Jack by the way. Jack Blishen.'

'Christine,' she said. She shook the proffered hand. Afterwards, he held on to her hand just a little too long, his eyes wolfing her. She managed a smile throughout.

'Room two-twenty-six,' he said.

'Two-twenty-six,' she repeated, nodding.

'Have you time for a drink just now? Canteen's—'

'No, really. I've got to get back. There are some papers I forgot to bring.'

'Dear, oh dear, not very bright today, are we?'

'Monday morning,' she explained.

'You don't need to tell me, love,' he said, grinning with wolf's teeth. Witch had an image of herself ramming the heel of her hand into his nose, thrusting upwards, of bone and cartilage piercing the brain. It took no more than a second. She blinked the image away. Or slice his fat gut open. She blinked again.

'You haven't seen Madam yet then?' he was saying.

'Madam?'

'Spurrier.'

'No, not yet.'

'I shouldn't bother if I were you. Not unless you're bringing her *good* news. She's brutal, Christine, believe me. Have you met her before?'

'No.'

He sucked in his breath. 'Careful how you go then. She'll tear your throat out. I've seen her do it.'

'Look, sorry, Jack, but I really must . . .'

'Sure, don't mind me. Spurrier's not so bad really. I was exaggerating. Didn't mean to . . . here, I'll walk you back to the lift.'

'Thank you,' she said. Then he put his hand on her shoulder, and she felt a fresh wave of revulsion. Fight it, she thought to herself. Fight it. She had to be strong for her meeting with the Dutchman. She had to *look* strong, more than strong – invincible. She had to keep him fooled. By Wednesday at the latest, nothing would matter any more. She clung to that thought, pulled it to her, embraced it the way the secretaries had embraced their cardboard files. Two more days at most. She would last. She would.

She had to.

There were times when the Dutchman subscribed to the notion that 'public was private'. In London, he certainly subscribed to it. What was suspicious about two people having a lunchtime drink in a Covent Garden pub, crammed with other people doing exactly the same thing? Answer: nothing. What was suspicious about two people meeting clandestinely in some locked room or on some tract of wasteland? Answer: everything.

So it was that he had arranged the meeting in Covent Garden, just outside the tube station entrance in James Street. So it was that he took her into the heart of Covent Garden itself, past the piazza with its jugglers and musicians, past the racks and the stalls with their glittering clothes and jewellery, and down some stairs to a wine-bar. Witch eventually baulked when he suggested they sit at a table outside. People on the level above could lean on the guard-rails and watch them, as they were watching the other people at the tables.

'I'd feel like an animal in a zoo,' she spat.

'And which animal would you be?' the Dutchman asked wryly.

She considered this, thinking of Jack Blishen, but did not answer. The Dutchman patted her back as he ushered her through the doors of the bar and into cool gloom. They found a table in a quiet corner.

'What would you like to drink?' he asked, expecting her to say orange juice or mineral water or . . .

'Chablis or Meursault, very cold.'

'Sure,' he said. 'Just the glass, or a whole bottle?'

'Are you having some?'

'It sounds good.'

'Better make it a bottle then.'

The Dutchman went off to the bar. 'Yes, sir?' asked the barman.

'A bottle of Chablis, please. Chilled.'

'Of course, sir.' The barman stared at him as though he had taken 'chilled' as a snub of sorts. The Dutchman took a twenty-pound note from his wallet. He was in a mood of nervous excitement. He knew the feeling well, and loved it. The feeling got even better afterwards, after a successful operation. So far this was a successful operation, but it was all out of his hands now, or nearly so. The initial planning, the various and copious briefings, all but one of them by mail, the heaping up of necessary and unnecessary detail, the contact with Crane ... Ah, the contact with Crane. That had been sublime, almost as though fate were in charge. He'd seen the advert in a newspaper, advertising the boat *Cassandra Christa* for sale. He'd made enquiries of the boat's owner. He'd found in Crane the perfect fool. These were *his* successes. These were what he was being paid for. Not even *he* knew who was actually doing the paying. Anonymity all round. What did the British say? No names, no pack drill.

'Here you are, sir.'

'Thank you.' He handed over the note, then, when the barman's back was turned, touched the side of the bottle with his palm. It was cold. He ran a finger down the condensation.

'Your change, sir. And how many glasses?'

The Dutchman accepted the change. 'Two glasses,' he said. At that moment the waiter who was managing the outside tables came into the bar. He leaned his elbows on the bartop, as though wilting with exhaustion.

'With you in a second, Terry,' said the barman,

reaching into the rack above him for two long-stemmed glasses.

'Hectic?' the Dutchman asked the waiter.

'As usual,' he replied.

'There you go, sir, two glasses.'

'Many thanks.'

The Dutchman headed off with his bottle and his glasses. When he'd rounded the corner of a stone wall, the barman and waiter stopped staring at him and looked at one another instead.

'Looks like him,' said the barman.

The waiter nodded. 'Foreign, too, just like Charlie said.'

The barman lifted a telephone from beneath the bar, picked up the receiver, took a scrap of paper from his back trousers pocket, and started to dial, reading the number from the note.

'Can't you do that after?' complained the waiter. 'I've a big order here. Look like good tippers.'

'Don't worry, Terry. I'll give you a tip personally if this comes good.' The barman listened to the dialling tone. 'Nobody at home,' he muttered. 'Trust Char— Hello? Who's that? What? Christ! Hello, Chris. Where you working? Yeah, I know it, up Charing Cross Road. Used to be a good pub.' He listened, laughed. 'All right, all right, *still* is a good pub, especially now you're there. Listen, is Charlie Giltrap there?' His face darkened. 'Oh, that's a pity. He wanted me to look out for— Oh, great, can I have a word?' The barman put his hand over the mouthpiece. 'He's just walked in,' he told the waiter. 'Talk about luck.'

'Yeah, and my customers'll be walking *out* at this rate.'

The barman held up his hand for silence. The waiter turned as three new customers came in through the

338

front door. 'Hello, Charlie? Andy here. Fine, listen, got to make this quick. You know I was to keep a lookout for a likely lad? Got one here.' He stared towards the corner around which the Dutchman had disappeared. 'Yeah, fits the bill, Charlie. He's here just now. Right, cheers.' He put down the receiver and tucked the phone back beneath the bar. 'Now then, Terry, what's the order?'

'Two bottles of Chablis.'

The barman shook his head. 'Try me with something else, son. I just sold the last one.'

Back in their little corner, Witch and the Dutchman were talking. Witch had chosen a spot close to one of the wall-speakers. The bar's music was not loud, but it would mask their conversation should anyone happen to be listening.

She paused to savour the wine. 'Nice,' she said. 'So, is my little package safe?'

'The one my men picked up from the house? Oh yes, it's safe all right. Safe and well. I've stored it in a garage.'

'I don't want to know. I just want to know it's safe.'

'Rest assured.'

Witch nodded. She remembered the iron, hot in Christine Jones's hand. The first mistake.

'Do you need anything else?' asked the Dutchman.

Witch shook her head. 'I'm ready.'

'Really?'

'Really.'

'So when will you . . . ?' He raised a hand, apologising. 'Sorry, I don't need to know that, do I?'

'No, you don't.'

'And you're clear in your mind? I can't be of any more assistance?'

'No.'

'Well, I'll be at my telephone number until ... well, until the job's done.'

She nodded, drank more wine. Her glass was nearly empty. The Dutchman filled it again. Then he lifted his own glass.

'Here's to the free world,' he said.

She smiled. 'Here's to love.' And she took a sip of her wine.

'I'll drink to that,' said the Dutchman. He couldn't keep his eyes off her. She was incredible. The first time they'd met – the only other time they'd met – had been in Paris. The initial briefing. He'd suggested working closely, but she'd turned him down. She preferred working alone. When he learned a little more about her – most of it hearsay, but accurate – he knew this for the truth. She was a loner, a mystery. She almost didn't exist at all, but then, once a year or so, would come some atrocity, some murder or bombing, a disappearance or a jailbreak, and 'she' would be mentioned. That was all anyone called her: *she*. 'She's been active again.' 'Who did it?' 'We think probably *she* did.' Stories were whispered, the myth grew.

And now here he was with her for their second and final meeting. And she'd changed so much since Paris. He hadn't recognised her at the tube station. She'd been standing against a wall, fretting, checking her watch. He hadn't seen through her disguise, until, after five minutes, he too checked his watch. Then saw her grinning in his direction. He looked to left and right, but she was grinning at *him*. And walking towards him. Christ, even her walk was different; every single thing about her was different. And yet it was her. It was her. He shivered at the thought.

'What about your exit?' he asked her now, trying to show that he cared.

'It'll happen.'

'I can help if you need any—'

'You've done your work.' She paused. 'And done it well. Now it's my turn. Okay?'

'Yes, yes, fine.'

'Tell me, why did we need to meet?'

'What?'

'Today, why did you need to see me?'

He was flustered. 'Well . . . for the . . . for your final briefing.'

She smiled. 'Unnecessary.'

'And to wish you luck,' he blurted out.

'Also unnecessary.'

'And because . . . well, I'm *interested*.'

'Don't be.' She finished her second glass of Chablis and rose to her feet, picking up her shoulder-bag and satchel. 'Enjoy the rest of the bottle,' she said. 'Stay here at least five minutes after I've gone. Goodbye.'

'See you,' he said, knowing even as he said it that it wasn't true. He would almost certainly never see her again. He looked at the bottle, then at his glass. Well, if his work really *was* over, why not? He poured a generous measure, and toasted the wall in front of him.

Witch walked on. The Dutchman was like all the others: weak. All the men she'd met in her life, all the ones she'd worked with. The left-wing terrorists who agreed with radical feminism then got drunk or stoned and tried to sleep with her. The leaders of the various groups who used too many words, filling a huge void with them, but had no conception of anything beyond the 'word' and the 'idea'. The anarchists: political shoplifters. She'd seen them all, spent time with them. In the early days, maybe she'd even believed in them for a time. It was easy to believe when you were sitting in a

341

stinking garret passing round a joint of middling-quality Moroccan.

Why had she drunk that wine? The Dutchman would worry about her now. He'd think maybe she wasn't as coldly perfect as people said. Was that why she'd done it? No, she'd done it because she felt like it. She felt like a drink. Chablis and Meursault were her father's favourite wines. It said so in the book she'd read about him . . .

She felt queasy suddenly. There were too many people around her. She ducked into an alley and felt better. The air was cooler in the alley. She began to walk along it. It was a narrow street, the backs of tall brick buildings backing on to it. Emergency exits, steel-barred and openable only from within. There was litter in the gutter. Dirty city. Cramped, crammed city. She despised it. She despised them all.

Shuffling footsteps behind her. She half-turned. Two youths, shambling along. One black, one white. The black massive for his age, bare arms taut and bulging. The white youth pale and wiry. They wore ludicrously large training-shoes, and metal medallions jangled round their necks. They weren't talking. And they were looking at her. The wine dissipated through her; she was ready for them. They still didn't say anything as they snatched her shoulder-bag. She held it beneath her elbow and struck out. Her right hand went for the black youth first. He represented the real physical danger. She chopped at his windpipe, and jerked a knee up into his groin. The white youth half-turned to look at his friend, and she caught him with the side of her forehead on his nose. Blood burst across his face. One hand went to cover his nose, the other scrabbled for the pocket of his denims. No, she couldn't allow that, no knives. She caught the hand and twisted it, all the way around and up his back, breaking the wrist for good measure.

The black youth, who had fallen on all fours, caught an ankle in his vice-like grip and tugged, trying to pull her down. She kicked him in the ribs, then in the temple. The white youth was howling now, and running for the end of the street. She looked past him, at the busy thoroughfare, but no one was paying any attention. That was the city for you. She could be mugged, assaulted, and no one would dare help. She looked down on the black youth. She had backed four feet from him, and he was pushing himself to his feet. She allowed him to stand up. He presented no threat any more.

'Go find your friend,' she said.

But he had other ideas. There was a loud k-schick as the blade sprung open. She raised her eyebrows. Couldn't he *see*? Where was the intelligence? Where was the basic survival instinct? She hadn't broken sweat yet. She hadn't even warmed up. There was a shout from the far end of the street.

'Oi! What's going on?' The youth turned. Two police constables stood in the mouth of the alley. He looked at Witch, brandishing the knife.

'Next time, bitch.' Then he ran in the same direction as the white youth, while the policemen came jogging from the opposite direction. Witch composed herself. She took several deep breaths, let her shoulders slump, and forced a few tears up into her eyes. She raised her fingers to her hair, rubbing it slowly, tousling it.

'You all right, miss?' asked the first policeman.

She nodded, but said nothing.

The second policeman ran to the end of the alleyway and looked around, then started back, shrugging.

'Never catch them now,' he said. 'These roads are like a bloody warren. How you feeling, love?'

'I'm all right,' she said faintly, nodding. 'Yes, I'm fine, really.'

343

'Course you are. Did they get anything?'

She looked at her left arm, with the shoulder-bag tucked beneath it, her left hand still clutching her satchel. 'No,' she said.

'Looked to me like you was holding your own,' said the first policeman.

'I went to some self-defence classes.'

'Very wise. Not so wise coming down a street like this.'

'It's the middle of the day,' she complained.

'They don't bother about that, not these days. Morning, noon and night. Mugging's a full-time occupation now.'

She smiled a little.

'That's better, love. Come on, let's get you down the station.'

'The station?'

'It's only two minutes' walk. Or we could radio for a car?'

'No, I can walk.'

'We'll get you a cup of tea, and let the doc have a look.'

'But I'm fine.'

'Could be in shock though, see. And then after that, we'll get a description from you, eh? See if we can catch those bastards before they pick on someone else . . . some woman who's *not* done self-defence. Okay?'

Witch nodded slowly. 'Okay,' she said, searching in her shoulder-bag for a tissue with which to wipe her eyes.

Down at the station, they really were very kind, very sympathetic. They asked her if there was anyone she'd like them to phone. A friend? Or her work maybe, to say she'd be back late from lunch? No, there was no need, she explained, thanking them. A WPC brought her some sweet tea, and a doctor took a look at her and said she'd had a fright but she was all right now. The constables looked like they were glad of an excuse to be back in their station. They sat with their helmets off, drinking tea and chatting. She gave a description – a detailed and accurate description. After all, they had a point: why shouldn't she help catch the two thugs? The thought of them attacking someone else infuriated her. If she'd thought of it at the time, she would have disabled them more thoroughly.

'And the white one,' she said, 'he sort of stumbled and I think he hurt his wrist. He said something about it cracking.'

'Broken wrist, eh? That would be handy. We could check with the local hospital casualties.'

The other constable was laughing. 'Broken wrist . . . handy,' he explained.

There was excitement elsewhere in the station. One of the constables disappeared to find out what was going on. He returned and shrugged.

'Just brought in some Dutch geezer, according to the Sarge. The Yard are on their way to fetch him, Anti-Terrorist Branch or something.'

'Yeah?' His colleague seemed to lose interest in Witch. Now this was action. But the blood had drained from Witch's face.

'Excuse me,' she said, 'is there a toilet I could use?'

They directed her along the corridor. She wandered along it, glancing into offices. Some men pushed open a set of swing-doors and marched a dishevelled man into an office. The door closed after them. Oh Christ, it *was* the Dutchman. How the . . . ? Who . . . ? Elder? Dominic Elder? Was he clever enough . . . ? She knew she needn't fear the Dutchman. He might not hold out forever, but he would certainly say nothing until after the operation was complete. If he wanted to save his skin, that was, and she thought probably he would want to save his skin. He'd rather face interrogation and a prison sentence than the thought that his ex-employers might put a contract out on *him*. And that's just what they'd do if he said anything. No, he'd keep his mouth shut. Tightly shut.

But all the same, it was another setback. The swing-doors were pushed open again. A man came through them carrying two large polythene bags. Behind him, another man brought a single bag. They held them carefully, as though they contained eggs, and both men disappeared into the office, the office which held the Dutchman.

She knew what those plastic bags contained. Not eggs: two wine glasses and a bottle. So they'd have her fingerprints now. Not that it mattered. Her prints had been altered before, they could be altered again. Painful and expensive, but an option. She wondered if she should . . . if she *dare* creep closer to the door so she could listen.

There was a call from behind her. 'You've gone past it, love. It's that door behind you.'

She turned. One of the constables was standing in the doorway, pointing behind her. She smiled in apology: sorry, still a bit shocked. He nodded back. Then she pushed open the door to the ladies' toilets. She sat in a cubicle for a few minutes, working things out. Only one thing really stood out: the Yard were on their way here. Which meant, in all probability, that Dominic Elder was on his way here. Would he recognise her after all this time? If anyone could, *he* could. It was too risky. She had to get out of this police station.

She flushed the toilet, looked at herself in the soap-splashed mirror over the wash-basin, and composed her victim's face again. She'd given them Christine Jones's

346

name and Christine's address, but had stressed that she was leaving London later today and would be out of town till tomorrow night. They hadn't bothered asking for her out-of-town address. As she walked back down the corridor, she knew, too, that she could not afford to wait. The hit must take place tomorrow, Tuesday. It would not wait till Wednesday.

Tomorrow.

'Feel better, love?' asked the constable.

'Yes, thank you. I'd like to go now.'

'No problem there. If you do think of anything else, anything you could add to your description of the two assailants . . .'

'I'll let you know.'

He scribbled his surname and the station's telephone number on to a pad of paper, tore off the page, and handed it to her.

'Normally,' he said, 'it'd be a CID matter. Maybe it will be, but they've got their hands full at the moment.'

'Yes, you said . . . something about a Dutchman?'

'That's right. Don't ask me what though. I only work here.'

She smiled. 'If I do think of anything, I'll let you know.'

'Appreciate it. Now, can we get you a cab?'

'That's all right, I'll walk I think. Some fresh air.'

'Fresh air? Round here? Some hope.'

She shook hands with both constables (they seemed embarrassed by the gesture), and even said a polite goodbye to the desk sergeant. She was about to pull open the main door when it was pushed from outside with sudden force. She took a couple of steps back.

'Sorry,' said the man, coming in. He didn't sound sorry. She shook her head, saying nothing. He paused, taking her silence as reproof, and held the door open for her.

'Thanks,' she said, brushing past him.

Outside, she felt giddy. She crossed the street quickly and melted into a queue at a bus shelter. She watched the entrance of the police station, but he didn't come out again. He hadn't recognised her.

He'd grown old. Not weak, but certainly old. Older than his years. She smiled, knowing the cause. Ah, but it was him all right, recognisably him. Dominic Elder. She wondered if he'd got her note, the one she'd left at that pub in Cliftonville. She was sure he had. He might even have gone after the fairground, talked to the boss, Ted. A dead end. Nobody there would tell him anything. And now he'd be busy with the Dutchman, interrogating him, tracking his history through Interpol. Yes, Elder would be busy, which suited her. It left her free to get on with her work. She'd best get busy. She had to steal a vehicle . . . *two* vehicles . . . and she had to drive some routes. She only had until tomorrow. Tomorrow, some time around noon, the cavalcade of world leaders would drive slowly along Victoria Street, heading for lunch at Buckingham Palace. Right past her nose.

A bus arrived and she took it, for no other reason than that she had some thinking still to do, and time to kill before evening. She climbed to the top deck and found a seat to herself near the front. Two things bothered her, both out of her hands now. One was that she had given the police Christine Jones's name and address. It had seemed prudent at the time. They only had to look in her handbag or at the label on her satchel to know who she was supposed to be. But now they had the Dutchman, and if they connected him to the assault in the alley, they would have a name and an address.

The second thing, well, the second thing wasn't nearly

so important. Even so, she couldn't help wondering, with the Dutchman in custody, would anyone be feeding and watering Christine Jones?

Elder was nursing a mug of tea and chatting to CID when Greenleaf arrived.

'Hello, John.'

'Sorry I'm late,' said Greenleaf. 'Couldn't track down Doyle.'

'Then we'll just have to do without him, won't we? Let's call it, using our own initiative. Now, using your initiative, John, did you manage to get in touch with Mr McKillip?'

Greenleaf nodded. 'I said we'd send a car to fetch him, but he'd rather make it up here under his own steam. His train gets into Victoria Station.'

'Handy for the Yard then.'

'Which is why I said I'd meet him there.'

'What time does he get in?'

'Five-ish.'

'So, by six we'll have a witness that our Dutch friend met with George Crane in Folkestone.'

'Hopefully. Speaking of the Dutchman ...'

'He's in a holding cell. They'll bring him to an interview room when we're ready.' Elder looked at Greenleaf above the rim of his mug. 'Can I take it we're ready?'

Greenleaf nodded. 'Good and ready.'

So the Dutchman was brought up to one of the interview rooms. He was complaining all the time: he was a tourist, was this how they treated visitors to their country? He demanded to contact his consulate, his embassy, anyone. He was just a tourist ... they'd no right.

'No right at all, treating me like a criminal.'

Elder and Greenleaf, seated impassively at the small metal-framed table, let him have his say. From the way his eyes refused to meet theirs, they knew *he* knew they were trouble. They both liked that. For a few moments more, they thrived on his discomfort.

'Look,' he said, 'look!' And he raised a shoe in the air, the tongue of leather flapping loose where the shoelaces had been removed. 'They take away my shoelaces, my trouser-belt, my necktie. In case I *injure* myself, they say. Why in God's name should I injure myself? I am a tourist. I don't . . .'

Elder reached into a large manila envelope which he'd brought with him. He drew out a black and white photograph and threw it on to the desk, so that it faced the Dutchman who glanced at it, then looked away again, addressing his words to the police officers behind him, all four of them, standing massively between him and the door.

'I am treated like a common criminal . . . British justice, law and order, a farce, I tell you! A farce! We in the Netherlands have more respect for the . . .'

Another photograph landed on the desk, then another. They were the photographs supplied to Commander Trilling by SIS, the ones which had accompanied the slides. The Dutchman saw himself again and again, in different places, different situations, in conversation with different people, and all during different operations.

Then Elder spoke.

'We want to know what she's planning, and we want to know where she is. We want to know quickly.'

The Dutchman met Elder's eyes for a dull second.

'What are you talking about?' he said. 'I'm a tourist.'

'No, you're not. We both know what you are. The authorities in several countries would like to speak with you. Most of them are less law-abiding than we are. They wouldn't hesitate to use ... well, whatever means they see fit, to prise information from you.' Elder paused to let this sink in. 'If you don't tell us where she is and what she's intending to do, I'll see to it that you're handed over to the least ... the least *hesitant* country possible. Speak to us now, and you'll be kept here in the UK. Do you understand?'

'I demand my rights. I demand a lawyer, I demand to see someone from the Dutch Embassy. This is illegal.'

'Under the Prevention of Terrorism Act, very little is illegal. But then, I'd have thought you'd have read up on that particular document.'

Elder rose to his feet, had a word with the guards, and left the room. Greenleaf followed him in silence. The guards stayed.

'Will anyone give me a cigarette, please?' asked the Dutchman.

'We don't smoke,' said one policeman.

Outside, Elder was talking in an undertone. 'We'll have him transferred to Paddington Green. The security here isn't good enough.'

'You think they may try to spring him?'

Elder shook his head. 'Not spring him, no. He's a gofer, a go-between. It's late on in the operation now. He's probably expendable. But they may try to kill him.'

'What?'

Elder nodded. 'He won't know much in any case, but these people, whoever it is who's hired Witch, I shouldn't think they like loose ends. And *that's* what we need to play on.'

'Get him scared?'

'Right, not scared of us, scared of his bosses – present and past. So that *we* become his only protection.'

Greenleaf was impressed. 'You sound like you've done this sort of thing before.'

Elder smiled. 'That's because I have, John. We sweat him, then, if he hasn't told us anything, we tell him we're going to put out an announcement that he's singing like a bird. Singing in return for his freedom. We tell him the announcement's gone out, then we say we're—'

'Letting him go.'

Elder nodded. 'Funny, they never want to go, given the chance. They'd rather stay. But the price of staying, the price of protection, is that they tell us everything anyway.'

'Nice.'

Elder shrugged. 'He's been around. He may not fall for it. We may actually *have* to issue the announcement. And it all takes time.'

'Time we may not have.'

'Exactly. So let's get him over to Paddy Green straight away, before Witch learns we've got him.'

'One thing, Dominic.' Greenleaf only called him Dominic when Doyle wasn't around. 'What did he have on him in the wine-bar?'

'Good point. Let's take a look.'

The Dutchman's possessions were in an envelope in the desk sergeant's locked drawer. The desk sergeant himself tipped the contents on to the surface of his desk.

'Not much,' he said.

No, not much. Cash . . . just under a hundred pounds in notes, plus some small change. The notes were crisp and clean.

'Better check they're not forgeries,' said Greenleaf.

Passport in the name of Hans Breuckner, occupation: schoolteacher. No visas.

'We'll check that, too,' said Greenleaf. 'See what the Dutch think of it.'

'I can tell you now what they'll think of it, John. It'll be a forgery. Either that or stolen, but a forgery's my bet.'

'Do we know where he was living?' asked Greenleaf.

'He hasn't said.'

'Maybe this will tell us.' Greenleaf was pointing to a small key.

'It's not a room-key or house-key though, is it?' said Elder. 'Looks more like the sort you use to lock a petrol-cap.'

'Bit too big for that,' said Greenleaf. 'Not a car-key though. My guess would be a lock-up.'

'A lock-up?'

'You know, a garage. I used to live in a block of flats, we all had a garage down near the road. And we all opened our garages with a key like this.'

Elder examined it more closely. 'It's British, by the look of it. You think he's got a flat then?'

'No, or he'd have a key for it, too. I think he's rented a garage. Maybe he's been holing up in it, maybe he's just using it for storage while he lives elsewhere.'

'Storage ... now what would he be storing in a garage?' Elder looked up. 'I'm glad you came, John.'

Greenleaf shrugged. 'Doyle would've told you the same thing.'

'But he didn't. *You* did.'

There wasn't much else of interest: a one-day travel-card, a tube-map, and two pages pulled from an *A–Z*, showing the centre of London from Bloomsbury to Victoria to the Elephant and Castle to Farringdon.

'Can't see any markings,' said Greenleaf. 'Can you?'

'No,' said Elder. 'But maybe there are pressure points where a pencil or something's been pressed against the page. Better get it into a poly bag and let forensics take a look. You know we got some glasses?'

'Glasses?'

'And a bottle. Our Dutch friend was nabbed in a wine-bar.'

'That much I knew.'

'He'd been drinking with a young woman. The barman's given us a description.'

'Witch's latest incarnation?'

'Maybe. Anyway, there were two glasses on the table. We've got them.'

'So maybe we'll end up with Witch's prints?'

'If nothing else, yes. Not that we've got anything to match them against.' Elder turned to the desk sergeant. 'Can we have a poly bag for this map?'

'Right away, sir.'

Elder turned back to Greenleaf. 'Give me an educated guess,' he said. 'How long to check every lock-up in the London area?'

'An educated guess?' Greenleaf did some calculations. 'About four and a half months.' Elder smiled. 'That's always supposing,' Greenleaf went on, 'we were given the manpower, which is doubtful anyway. All the time I'm on Operation Broomstick, the caseload's just growing higher and higher on my desk. It's not going to go away.'

'It'll soon be over,' Elder said quietly. 'One way or the other, it'll soon be finished.'

The desk sergeant, returning with a clear plastic bag, was chuckling and shaking his head.

'What's the joke?' asked Greenleaf, taking the bag from the desk sergeant. He held it open so Elder could drop the map inside.

'Oh, nothing really. Just some of the lads. Two would-be muggers, big bastards by the sound of them, they picked on this slip of a girl near Covent Garden. Only, she'd been to self-defence classes. Gave them a terrible pasting the way the lads are telling it.' He chuckled again, not noticing the fixed way in which Elder and Greenleaf were staring at one another.

'Did you happen to speak with her?' Elder asked, calmly.

'Speak to her? She was here in the station till half an hour ago.' He saw the look on Dominic Elder's face. 'What's the matter? You look like you've seen a ghost.'

Barclay sat that afternoon at his old desk in his old office. It seemed like an eternity since he'd last been there. He found it hard to believe that in the past he'd been satisfied with just his information base and his computer console. He was itching to be elsewhere, to be in the thick of things. But he knew Joyce Parry wouldn't let him out of her sight. So he'd spent the morning trying to be professional, trying not to let it worry him or niggle at him or scoop away at his insides. He'd tried. At least he could say he'd tried.

He'd handed his report to Joyce Parry first thing. Not that there was anything in it she hadn't heard on the trip back last night. He hadn't left anything out: bugging Separt's apartment, Dominique disguising herself and going to see the Australian, wearing a wire which Barclay had made for her. And then the journey to Germany, and Dominique's revelation that nothing they'd done had been sanctioned.

He felt like a shit as he typed it all in, felt he was somehow letting Dominique down. But she was probably doing exactly the same thing, thinking much the same thoughts. Neither of them wanted to lose a good job. Besides, doubtless Joyce Parry would cross-check Barclay's testimony against that given by Dominique. If he left anything out, anything she'd admitted to . . . well, that would only count against him.

Joyce Parry had listened to him in silence mostly, with only the occasional shake of the head or disbelieving gasp. And she accepted the report from him with a slight nod of the head and no words. So now he had to wait. He had to sit at his desk and wait to see if his resignation would be asked for, or a demotion agreed, or whatever. Maybe he'd end up sweeping the corridors. He hadn't felt as nervous as this since he'd been a schoolboy, caught playing truant and left waiting outside the headmaster's door. What he'd dreaded then was a letter home to his parents. The guilt and shame of having been caught. But now, uneasy as he was, he was pleased too. He'd had a few days of real adventure, and if he could go back, he'd do the same again. He allowed himself a private smile. Maybe Mrs Parry was right, maybe Dominic Elder was the kind of person who used those around him then tossed them away. It didn't bother Barclay.

He'd tried phoning Dominique three times this morning, with no reply. The international operator couldn't help. He wondered if the phone was off the hook, and if so why. He'd also forwarded a copy of his report to Profiling, as Joyce Parry had told him to do. See what the mind doctors could make of it. Something was niggling him, something he knew he'd been going either to tell Joyce Parry or to ask her. It had been at the back of his mind for several days – before Germany, maybe even before Paris. As a result, it had now slipped from his mind altogether. Something he'd been going to say. But what?

He shook it away. If he left well alone, it would come back to him. He stared at the wall above his desk: the venomous Valentine, the Fire Drill, and the quotation he'd pinned there on a piece of memo paper – this fluke called life.

He plunged a hand into his full in-tray. Reports to be read, classified, passed on. His daily bread. He'd been given a sod of a job, collating 'trigger words'. It was a little known fact that the technology existed not only to monitor telephone calls but to zero in on calls containing certain words – trigger words. It was a miracle of computer technology, but also highly fallible. The word 'assassination' for example was unlikely to crop up in a conversation between two terrorists, whereas it might in a chat between two gossipy neighbours. And the word 'summit' posed problems too, being a homonym shared with the abbreviated form of 'something'. Yes, highly fallible but potentially invaluable.

Currently, specifically, there was another problem, in that 'Witch' sounded like 'which' . . . and people on the telephone said 'which' an awful lot of times. Dominic Elder had requested that Witch become a trigger word, clutching at yet another straw.

Barclay's task was to deal with the information handed on to him by the trigger system, which meant checking the details of callers who had used a trigger word. It was a lot of work, but he was not alone. Others, too, were feeding telephone numbers into computers, seeing whether any of the callers were known terrorist sympathisers or suspect aliens, or even just suspect. A lot of work and a lot of futile effort. Somehow, from what he knew of her, Barclay couldn't imagine Witch picking up a receiver and saying, 'Hello, Witch here. It's about that assassination I'm carrying out at the summit . . .' He started to tap the first set of details into his computer.

'Barclay.'

It was Parry's voice. By the time he turned, she'd already retreated back into her office. Ah well, this was it then. He took a deep breath and got to his feet, surprised to find his legs so steady beneath him. He walked to her office doorway and knocked once on the door. She motioned him in. She was reading something on her desk, one of many reports that would pass through her hands that day, as every day. She took off her glasses before speaking.

'Mr Elder wants you down at the Conference Centre,' she said casually.

'What? Why?'

'His argument runs that you know as much about Witch as anyone, so why waste your – talents – here when you could be helping him.' She made the word 'talents' sound like it was something rotten on her tongue. 'Let me make one thing clear.' She looked up at last. 'You're not off the hook. *Neither* of you is off the hook. This is strictly a short-term reprieve, and it can be terminated at a moment's notice.'

'Understood, ma'am.'

She nodded, slipped her glasses back on, and returned to her report. 'What are you waiting for then?'

'Yes, ma'am.'

Joyce Parry waited a full sixty seconds after he'd gone before she allowed herself a smile.

Elder was waiting for him in the Conference Centre foyer. 'Come on,' he said, moving away as Barclay approached. 'Let's get you some official ID.'

Elder moved briskly. He seemed very different to the person Barclay had met in a Welsh cottage garden. He looked like a man who'd discovered his purpose in life . . . or, perhaps, rediscovered it. He was a little disappointed though. He'd been expecting more of a welcome. Hadn't they worked together throughout the French adventure? And hadn't they both received dressings down for it?

358

They went to a small room where forms had to be filled in. A glowering woman then asked a few questions before transferring the details from the forms on to a card, typing the details quickly but meticulously. Then Barclay had to sign the card before moving to a booth where his photograph was taken.

'It's just like matriculation,' he said to Elder. But Elder, leaning against a desk, said nothing in reply. At last, the camera disgorged a small plastic-coated card containing the typed details, Barclay's signature, and a tiny photograph of him. Elder handed him a red and blue striped ribbon attached to a clip at one end and a safety-pin at the other.

'Clip it on to your lapel,' he ordered.

Barclay did so. 'Why the ribbon?'

'Red and blue means security. There are different ones for media, general staff, delegates . . .'

'You've seen my report?'

At last Elder gave a grim smile. 'Joyce gave me the highlights over the phone.'

Barclay swallowed. 'And?'

'And what?'

Barclay waited. 'Nothing,' he said.

Elder looked at him. 'Look, number one, I wouldn't have got caught. Number two . . .'

'Yes?'

'Never mind. Come on.'

Elder led the young man back through the corridors. He'd 'sprung' Barclay to keep him out of Joyce Parry's way. She was angry, and with good reason. But then Elder had done her a favour, taking the force of Jonathan Barker's heat and spending a long Sunday in a fuggy room talking about defending the indefensible. So she was letting Elder have Barclay. He knew he was in a strong position anyway; *he* could always shuffle back to

Wales. But he was also in a very weak position, because he wanted very much to stay put. Joyce was allowing him a lot of rope, more even than he'd expected.

After all, if the shit really did hit the fan, Joyce would be closest.

He saw that Barclay was bursting to talk to him. That was why it wasn't a good time for them to talk. He'd wait till the young man calmed a little. He knew that Barclay's career was hanging by a thread, but that had been Barclay's decision, not his. All the same . . . It was true that Elder would have done exactly the same as Barclay all along the line. He'd done as much before. And as for never getting caught . . . well, that wasn't entirely accurate. Several times he'd come close to disaster; closer than he liked to admit . . .

A message on the already-overworked Tannoy system. 'Call for Mr Elder. Call for Mr Dominic Elder.'

They made for reception. The place was chaotic. Flowers were being delivered, and nobody seemed to know where they were to go. One-day security passes were being made up for half a dozen sweating florists. The switchboard was jammed with incoming calls, and someone had arrived to fix the malfunctioning baggage X-ray machine. Tomorrow, the summit would begin, and on the surface all would be placid. But underneath they'd be kicking like hell.

'I'm Dominic Elder,' he said to a receptionist.

'What?' she said, cocking a hand to her ear.

'Dominic Elder,' he said, more loudly. 'There's a call for me.'

'Yes, hold on.' She picked up a receiver and handed it across the desk to him, then flipped a switch. 'You're through.'

Elder listened for a moment. 'Can't hear a thing,' he

said into the mouthpiece. 'It's pandemonium here. Can you speak up?'

He listened again. Barclay, standing behind him, looked around the foyer. Some people were just entering the building. Instinctively, he knew they were French: their clothes, their gestures, the way they moved. There were two women, one a tall redhead and the other shorter, wearing a red beret and round sunglasses. As she entered the dim interior, she slipped off the sunglasses.

Barclay nearly collapsed. It was Dominique. She saw him, pointed, and laughed. Then she bounced over and kissed him right cheek, left cheek, right and left again.

'Hello, Michael. What are you doing here?'

'Never mind me, what are *you* doing here?'

Elder turned around. 'Keep the noise down!'

Barclay took Dominique's arm and led her away from the reception desk. He was trembling and couldn't control it.

'I'm here with the French delegation,' said Dominique.

'I was expecting you to be in chains in the Bastille.'

She laughed again. 'There is no Bastille, not for a long time.'

'Well, you know what I—'

'Yes, but your superior, the woman . . .'

'Joyce Parry?'

'Parry, yes. She told Monsieur Roche all about the threat posed by Witch. Our own President could be her target. So now Monsieur Roche is worried. And guess who is the French expert on Witch?'

Barclay nodded, understanding.

'There may be a punishment for me when I go back to Paris, but for now . . .' She opened her arms wide. 'Here I am!'

One of her crowd called to her.

'*Oui*,' she called back, '*j'arrive!*' She turned back to Barclay. 'I must go with them.'

'Yes, but where are you staying? When can I see you? What about tonight?'

'No, tonight I have to work. But you are attending the summit, so we will meet.'

'Yes, but—'

There was a sudden tug at his arm. It was Dominic Elder.

'Come on,' Elder said, 'things to do.'

'Yes, just a—' But Dominique was waving a farewell as she headed back to the French group.

'That was Doyle on the phone,' insisted Elder, still tugging a reluctant Barclay towards the exit. 'They've located Breuckner's hotel. Let's go take a look.'

'What?' Barclay twisted his neck for a final glimpse of Dominique. She was in conversation with a tall, long-faced man. The man was looking towards Barclay. Dominique was not. 'Who's Doyle?' he said. 'Who's Breuckner?'

'Christ, you *are* out of touch, aren't you? Hasn't Joyce told you anything?'

'No.' They were out of the building now.

'Then I'll bring you up to date on the way. By the way, was that . . . ?'

'Yes, that was her.'

'Pretty girl,' Elder said, pulling Barclay further and further away from her. She reminded him a little of the woman he'd opened the police station door for, the woman he was sure had been Witch. He kept hold of Barclay's arm. 'By the way, you've got lipstick on both cheeks.'

The hotel in Bloomsbury was every bit as upmarket as Elder had been expecting, this being the age of expense-account terrorism, of *legitimised* terrorism. You could bomb a place of worship, strafe a busful of women, then a few months later be sitting down to peace talks with a posse of well-known politicians and negotiators, your photo snapped for front-page posterity and the six o'clock news.

'Very strict about his privacy,' said the manageress, leading them upstairs. She had her hair swept into a beehive, revealing large ears and a bulbous forehead. 'Only wanted his room cleaned once a week.'

'How long has he been a guest, Mrs Hawkins?'

'Almost a month now. Prompt with payment, beginning of each week.'

'He paid cash?'

'Yes, cash. Along here.' She led them to the room, and produced a key from the folds of her skirt. 'Very quiet man, but secretive. Well, I always try to mind my business ...'

'Yes, Mrs Hawkins, thank you. A policeman will be along shortly to take your statement.'

She nodded with sharp jolts of her head. 'Always happy to help the authorities.'

'Thank you, Mrs Hawkins. Leave the key, and we'll lock up afterwards.'

'Right you are.'

'And remember, nobody else is to enter before the forensics team gets here.'

'Forensics ...' She jabbed her head again, then giggled, the tremor running all the way through her large frame. 'It's just like on the television, isn't it?'

Elder smiled. 'Just so, Mrs Hawkins, just so.'

He pushed Barclay into the room then followed him, closing the door softly but determinedly on the hotelier. Then he swivelled Barclay round to face him.

'You'll see her tomorrow,' he said. 'Now snap out of it.

You're no good to me like this. I'd be as well sending you back to the bloody office.'

That did it. Barclay straightened up, and his eyes seemed to come into focus.

'Sorry,' he said.

'Okay, now let's see what we've got here. Remember, don't touch if you don't need to. We might find some prints when forensics get here – *if* they ever bother to turn up.'

'Whose prints?'

'Witch's maybe. Or – outside chance – whoever's paying her. But that really *is* an outside chance.' He paused. 'You did a good job in that cartoonist's apartment, let's see you do it again now.'

Breuckner wasn't messy. The bedclothes had been pulled back and straightened, his clothes were hanging neatly in the wardrobe, and on the bedside table sat a copy of the previous day's evening paper, a travel alarm, and a used ticket to Madame Tussaud's.

'Travels light, doesn't he?' said Elder. 'To say he's been here a month.'

'For a holidaymaker, he certainly hasn't collected many souvenirs.' Barclay reached down and lifted a shoe. 'Shall I check the heel for a radio transmitter?'

Elder smiled. 'Radio transmitters are more *your* line.'

'You know I left a couple of bugs at the cartoonist's?'

'Don't worry, someone'll take care of them.'

'Really?' The relief in Barclay's voice was all too evident.

'But don't tell Joyce I told you. She'll want you to sweat for a bit.'

'Understood.'

The search continued, throwing up nothing out of the ordinary except the sheer lack of the usual traveller's detritus: no used travel tickets, used carrier bags, stamps, foreign change, no guide books or souvenirs.

Barclay squatted down and angled his head to peer beneath the bed. 'Something under here.' He looked around him, then got up and went into the small bathroom adjoining the room. He came back with, of all things, a loo-brush, which he used to manoeuvre out from under the bed whatever was there.

'No fingers, you said,' he informed Elder, who stood over him smiling.

'I just hope that brush was clean,' said Elder.

Magazines. Glossy magazines. Dutch writing on their covers. There were three of them. Still using the loo-brush, Barclay awkwardly turned some of the pages.

'Yes, I get the gist,' said Elder.

'S and M,' said Barclay, closing the magazines. 'Heavy duty stuff.'

'Really? You have some expertise in this area?'

'I know what's legal, and this stuff isn't.'

Elder clapped his hands together. 'Bloody good point, Michael. If we nab friend Breuckner for nothing else, we can have him under the Obscene Publications Act. Importation of material likely to offend. Anything else under there?'

Barclay had another look. 'Over the other side,' he said. 'Looks like a paperback.' He walked round the bed, crouched again, and swept from beneath the bed an A–Z book of London streets.

'I'll bet the pages for the city centre are missing,' said Elder. 'He had them in his pocket.'

'There's a piece of card.' Barclay pointed to where a cardboard edge protruded from the book. Elder took a pen from his pocket and eased it between the pages marked by the card. Then slowly he used the pen to open the book. The piece of card was a one-day travelcard, nearly a month old. The pages opened were those showing Hackney, Leyton and Clapton.

'Interesting,' said Elder. His first thought was of the address given to the police by the woman calling herself Christine Jones. It had been around this area. But no, not quite . . . her address was just off this particular map, one page back in the book in fact. So, rule that out.

'What do you think, sir?' asked Barclay. They were both crouching now, with the book between them on the floor.

'There was a key in the Dutchman's pocket.'

'Yes, so you said.'

'Greenleaf—'

'Doyle's partner?'

Elder nodded. 'Greenleaf reckoned it might be the key to a lock-up.'

'Plenty of lock-ups round there,' Barclay said, nodding towards the map.

'Really?'

'Yes. Lots of tower blocks. Well, at least there used to be in Hackney. I had a friend lived on the top floor of one.'

'Well, it's worth a try. At least it gives us a starting-point. I'd better get on to Special Branch and tell Greenleaf. What time is it?' He checked his watch. 'No, he'll still be out at Christine Jones's address. Not that *that'll* take long. My guess is, nobody at that address will even have heard of anyone called Christine Jones. The lock-up idea is more interesting though.'

'Maybe we should get some copies made, help speed up the search.'

Elder nodded. 'Copies are being made.' He looked around the room. 'Nothing else for us here, is there?'

'We haven't checked the bathroom or under the carpets or . . .'

'Not really our department. The police'll do all that. I just wanted a quick look at the place before they started. Hold on though.' He walked up to the bedside cabinet and looked at the evening paper. 'Open at the crossword, but he's hardly even started it.' Elder stared at the clues and the answers entered in the grid. 'Mmm, no, nothing there.'

'You thought maybe a code?'

'It's a handy way of leaving a message for someone if you're in a hurry. Stick the message in a crossword grid, no one gives it a second look.'

'Unless they like crosswords.' The thought struck Barclay . . . what was it Wolf Bandorff had said? *'She was fascinated by word games and crosswords.'* Word games and crosswords.

'Did I ever tell you what Dominique and I found at the Australian's?'

'Pamphlets about Wolf Bandorff?'

'Yes, but there was a crossword too, from the *Times*. Strange paper for an Australian anarchist to be reading in Paris.'

'Go on.'

'Well, the crossword had been done. The Australian said *he* liked crosswords.'

'But we know from Bandorff that Witch likes word puzzles. You think the crossword belonged to Witch? It's possible she spent time at the flat before taking away the cartoonist's car. Still, it's a bit late in the day to be any help.'

'No, hold on, something else. There was a page torn out of the paper. The Australian said something about it saving on toilet paper. But why only the one page? And why wasn't the newspaper in the toilet if that was its function?'

Elder smiled. 'You're learning,' he said. 'So what you're wondering is, what was on the torn-out page?'

Barclay nodded. 'Maybe it was something to do with the summit, or with her particular target. We don't *know* who her target is yet. There could have been some clue in that newspaper.'

'Well, which day was it? Which edition?'

Barclay shook his head. 'I don't know.'

'But Dominique might.'

'And she's at the Conference Centre.'

'Come on then,' said Elder. 'Let's go find her.'

There was a knock at the door. It was the fingerprint team. 'All yours, gentlemen,' said Elder. He was now as anxious to be back at the Conference Centre as he had been to leave it in the first place.

But when they got to the foyer and asked at the desk, they were told that the new additions to the French security retinue had already left the building, and no one knew where they were headed.


Greenleaf and Doyle returned to the house in the evening, just after seven. They'd tried in the late-afternoon, but no one had been home. So then they'd hared off back to Victoria Station to meet McKillip off his train and deposited him at Paddington Green, where he was delivered into the hands of other Special Branch men. And now they were back in Stoke Newington again.

'Wild goose chase,' muttered Doyle, pressing the doorbell. 'Have you noticed how Elder's started giving orders? I mean, who the fuck is he to give orders?'

'He's all right,' said Greenleaf.

Doyle turned to him. 'Oh, yes? You *would* think that, wouldn't you? Very pally, the two of you.'

'We're *all* together on this. It doesn't help if personalities become the issue.' Greenleaf pressed the bell.

Doyle feigned amazement. 'When did your Chair come through?'

'What?'

'Your Chair in Psychology, when did it come through?'

'Don't talk daft.'

As Doyle was reaching yet again for the bell, the door flew open. A frazzled-looking young woman stood there. Behind her, along the entrance hall, lay a trail of dirty clothes issuing from a rucksack.

'Yes?' she said.

'Good evening, miss,' said Doyle, showing his ID. 'We're police officers. We're looking for Christine Jones. Does she live here by any chance?'

'Yes, Chris lives here.' The woman frowned. 'I'm Tessa Briggs. Has anything happened to Chris?'

'Not that we know of, miss. Could we come in for a minute?'

'Yes, of course.' She left the door open for them, and started back down the hall. 'Come into the living-room. Sorry everything's such a state. We just got back from a short holiday. It was supposed to be a weekend away, but we couldn't drag ourselves back.'

'I can appreciate that,' said Doyle.

There was a yell from upstairs. 'Tess, have you started that wash yet? I can't hear the machine. Who was that at the door?'

'Two policemen,' Tessa yelled back. 'Asking about Chris. Come downstairs!'

In stepping over the threshold, Doyle and Greenleaf had to step over some mail still lying on the carpet where it had dropped through the letterbox. Greenleaf stooped to pick it up. Two letters for C. Jones, one for T. Briggs, and a postcard. There was a small table in the hall, and he dropped the mail on to it before following Doyle into the living-room.

Doyle, already seated on the sofa, was asking Tessa Briggs about her weekend.

'It was great,' she said. 'We went canoeing. First time I've been. Scared the life out of me, but I'd do it again.'

'We being . . . ?'

'Oh, Rachel and me and our two boyfriends.'

'Not Miss Jones then?'

'No, Chris stayed here. Only she's not here just now, she's gone off for a couple of days . . . she left a note on my computer.'

The two policemen looked at one another. This seemed to tally with the story given to the constables by the person calling herself Christine Jones. Doyle raised an eyebrow. The meaning to Greenleaf was clear: wild goose chase. There was a framed photo on the mantelpiece: three young women, arms around shoulders, grinning towards the camera. Greenleaf picked it up.

'Which one's Miss Jones?'

'In the middle,' said Tessa Briggs.

Yes, he'd have known that: her photo pretty well matched the description of her given by the two constables and by Elder, who apparently had seen her leave the police station. Greenleaf handed the photo to Doyle, who looked at Christine Jones and nodded, handing it back. Even to Greenleaf, it was beginning to look like a dead end.

'When did Miss Jones leave?'

'No idea.'

'You didn't contact her over the weekend?'

Tessa Briggs shrugged, as though the thought had never crossed her mind. Now another woman came into the room. She looked red-faced from exertion.

'It's all right,' she said with a big smile, 'I've hidden the crack beneath the arms cache.'

Greenleaf managed a wan smile; Doyle just stared at her.

'Only joking,' she said. 'I'm Rachel Maguire. What's up?'

Greenleaf noticed how Doyle reacted to the name – Maguire. An Irish name, as Irish a name as Doyle. And suddenly it came to Greenleaf: terrorists had Irish names, *that's* why Doyle was so defensive about his own name.

'Yes,' Tessa was saying. 'What *is* up? You haven't said.'

'It's Miss Jones,' said Doyle, recovering. 'She was mugged this morning.'

'Mugged?' The two women spoke in horrified unison. 'Is she all right?'

'She's fine,' Greenleaf said, calming them. 'Not a scratch on her. The attackers ran off. They didn't get a thing.'

'God, that's horrible. Where did it happen?'

'Near Covent Garden,' said Doyle.

'In broad daylight?'

'It's when most crimes occur, miss.'

'Where does Miss Jones work?' asked Greenleaf.

'She's a civil servant,' said Tessa.

'DTI,' said Rachel. 'On Victoria Street somewhere.'

'Right at the start of Victoria Street,' Tessa added.

'Number 1–16 or 1–18, something like that.'

Again, Greenleaf and Doyle exchanged a glance. Victoria Street . . . that was a bit close to the Conference Centre.

'How has she seemed lately?' asked Greenleaf. 'I mean, has she been worried about anything?'

The women shrugged. 'What's that got to do with her being mugged?' asked Tessa.

'Nothing,' said Greenleaf. 'I was just wondering, that's all.'

'Look,' said Rachel, 'if she was mugged but she's all right ... just what *exactly* are you doing here?'

There was no answer to that, so Greenleaf supplied one.

'Just routine, like I say, miss, in cases like this. We like to check afterwards to see whether the victim's remembered anything else.'

'Oh, like a description?'

'That's it, yes.'

Doyle rose to his feet. 'Anyway, we *would* like to talk to Miss Jones when she gets back.' He took a card from his wallet. 'Maybe she could give us a call. Or if she gets in touch with you ...'

'Yes, we'll let you know,' said Tessa, accepting the card.

'We'd appreciate it,' said Doyle. 'Goodbye, Miss Maguire. We'll leave you to get on with your laundry and your crack dealing.'

Rachel Maguire managed a weak smile.

''Bye, miss,' said Greenleaf. Tessa accompanied the two policemen to the door. 'Oh,' said Greenleaf, 'I put your mail on the table there.'

'Thanks, bills probably.'

'Probably,' agreed Greenleaf. 'And a postcard, too.'

'Oh?' She glanced towards the table.

'Goodbye, Miss Briggs.'

'Yes, goodnight,' said Tessa Briggs. 'Sorry we couldn't be' – the door closed – 'more help.'

Doyle put both hands to his eyes and rubbed. 'And so,' he said, 'another long day comes to an end. Time for you to buy me a drink.' He started off towards the front gate.

'I told Elder I'd phone him,' said Greenleaf.

'Why?'

'To let him know if we found anything.'

'It can wait till tomorrow.'

'The summit *starts* tomorrow.'

'Really? Somehow that'd slipped my mind.'

Greenleaf closed the gate after them. 'She works on Victoria Street.'

'I know.'

'It's a bit of a coincidence.'

'Look, a woman called Christine Jones gets mugged near Covent Garden. Elder's so paranoid he sees Witch round every corner. We've checked, and as far as we can tell, her story's straight.' Doyle unlocked the passenger door, then went round to the driver's side, unlocked it, and got in.

'She beat off the attackers,' added Greenleaf. 'We should've asked her housemates if she had any training. Maybe I'll just—'

'You go back there and you're walking home.' Doyle waited until Greenleaf had settled in the passenger seat and closed his door. 'I'll say one thing for Elder,' he murmured, 'he really did get the car cleaned.' Not that this impressed Doyle: he liked his car to smell like a car, which in his mind meant cigarette smoke, fumes, and old bits of discarded chewing gum. Now, the interior smelt of air-freshener and polish. He lit a cigarette. Greenleaf wound down his window.

'Come on,' complained Doyle, 'we'll freeze.'

'Shirley complains when I go home smelling like an ashtray.'

'Jesus,' said Doyle. He took two long drags on the cigarette, then opened his own window long enough to flick it out. 'Satisfied?' he said. 'Now wind your window back up.'

Greenleaf did so, and Doyle started the car. 'There's a pub in Islington, you won't *believe* the beer.'

'We should call into Paddy Green, see if they've put together a line-up for McKillip.'

'After we've had a drink,' Doyle insisted. He sounded irritated; maybe it was the phrase Paddy Green . . . The car pulled away from the kerb.

'What's that?' said Greenleaf.

'What's what?'

Greenleaf had caught sight of something in the wing mirror. There was a noise, like a yell. He turned around and looked out of the rear windscreen. Tessa Briggs was leaning over the gate, calling something, waving something.

'Stop the car,' he said.

'What's up?'

'It's Tessa Briggs.' Greenleaf wound his window back down and Tessa, having opened the gate, ran to the car.

'God, I thought you weren't going to stop!'

'What is it, Miss Briggs?'

'This.' She handed a postcard through the window. 'It's supposed to be from Chris. Postmarked Saturday.'

'Supposed?' said Greenleaf.

'That's nothing like her writing,' said Tessa. 'Now tell me, please, what the hell is going on?'

Greenleaf read the card and handed it to Doyle, who read the greeting out aloud.

'"Hard work but fun. See you soon. C."' He turned the card over, then back again. 'And it's printed.'

Tessa was shaking her head. 'Nothing like Chris's writing,' she said. 'And she wouldn't *print* a message anyway.'

'Wild goose chase?' Greenleaf asked. '"Greetings from Auchterarder". She's got some nerve.'

Doyle studied the card yet again, then looked up at his partner.

'Better phone Elder,' he said.

'Where are you phoning from?' asked Dominic Elder into the mouthpiece.

'From home, Doyle just dropped me off.'

Elder was lying on his bed in his hotel room, an arm over his eyes. There were no lights on in the room, but the orange glare of the street-lighting penetrated the curtains, exacerbating his migraine. He was tired, dog-tired. He knew he needed rest. For the first time, he felt real homesickness for his little cottage, its cosy den, his slumber-chair.

'So what do you think?' asked Greenleaf. He'd already told Elder about the postcard.

'It's such a giveaway, obviously we weren't supposed to find it until the end of the mission. Meaning the mission must be soon.'

'Think she knows we're on to her?'

'That depends on whether she needs to get in touch with our friend the Dutchman. Someone's monitoring the hotel switchboard. The two constables who brought her in say they didn't mention anything about a Dutchman being arrested, but then they could be lying.'

'You're suggesting my colleagues might be covering themselves rather than telling the truth?'

'If they didn't say anything, chances are she doesn't know. She wasn't anywhere near CID, which is where our Dutchman was. All the same, if she was so close to him, I can't help feeling she'll know.'

'Then she'll know how close we are to her?'

'And how close is that, John?'

'We know who she's pretending to be. Key to a lock-up, missing civil servant. We'll find Christine Jones in a garage somewhere.'

'Somewhere around Hackney.'

'If your hunch about the A–Z is right, yes.'

'Don't forget, Barclay found the A–Z.'

'I won't forget. But whose snitch was it found the Dutchman in the first place?'

Yes, Charlie Giltrap. Elder owed Charlie rather a large drink for that.

Greenleaf was still talking. 'Is Barclay your . . . is he some kind of protégé?'

'Not exactly. Meantime, the key is being copied tonight. Inspector Whitlock is going to coordinate the search.'

'Whitlock?'

'Stationed in Hackney. I'm told he's a good man for this sort of job.'

'So the Dutchman grabbed Christine Jones . . .'

'And now Witch has assumed her identity. I hear McKillip was able to identify our Dutch friend.'

'Pointed straight to him.'

'Good, we can hold him a bit longer then. Bit late all the same. His part in the operation has almost certainly finished.'

'You think she'll try a hit from this building in Victoria Street?'

'Yes, 1–19 Victoria Street.' Elder paused. 'Or maybe one of the other DTI buildings along the route.'

'There are details already assigned to every one of them.'

'Yes, and she'll no doubt realise that.'

'But you still think she'll try? It's suicide.'

'I know, I can't really understand what she's playing at.'

'How do you mean?'

Elder sighed. 'Oh, nothing probably. It just seems . . . she's just making too many mistakes, John.'

'Maybe she's getting old, eh?'

Elder smiled in the darkness. 'Maybe.' There were sounds at the other end of the line. A clinking of china. A muffled 'Thanks, love, won't be long', presumably from Greenleaf to his wife. Elder felt cold and empty, he felt a longing for something he daren't quite put into words.

'We'll place guards on the doors,' Greenleaf was saying.

'And inside the buildings,' suggested Elder.

'I don't know, Dominic, we're stretched as it is.'

'Just a suggestion,' said Elder, hoping Greenleaf would take his meaning: It may be just a suggestion, but I've made it and so that puts it in your hands. If you *don't* put men inside the buildings and she *does* succeed in killing someone my conscience is clear . . . how about yours? It was just like his warning to Joyce Parry, the one she in turn had passed on to the PM, bypassing the Home Secretary.

'I'll see what Commander Trilling says,' Greenleaf said after a long pause. Yes, he'd taken Elder's meaning, and he would pass the buck along.

'Every security man on that route,' Elder went on, screwing up his eyes with effort, 'must have a recent description of Witch and a photograph of Christine Jones. All passes must be checked. It's obvious that Witch now looks like Miss Jones; it's just as obvious she'll use Miss Jones's pass to get past DTI's own security.'

'Even though she knows we know?' Greenleaf persisted.

'It sounds crazy, but I've got a feeling she'll try. We'll have to be ready for her, which means we'd all better get some rest tonight.'

'I could do with it. You sound like you could, too.'

'Me?' said Elder. 'I'm just about to go for my evening run. A quick sprint around Hyde Park.'

Greenleaf laughed tiredly. 'Give me five minutes and I'll join you there. See you in the morning, Dominic.'

'Goodnight, John.'

With eyes still closed, Elder managed to place the receiver back in its cradle. It rang again almost immediately. He groaned and groped for the still-warm receiver.

'Elder here.'

'Mr Elder, it's Barclay.' The young man sounded frantic, or maybe just frustrated. 'I've hunted all over . . . restaurants, bars, clubs . . . no sign of her. All anyone at the embassy said was she's out on the town with the other new arrivals. But at last they've come up with the name of her hotel. Do you think I should—'

'Michael,' said Elder gently, 'I think you should go home and get some sleep. Tomorrow morning will be time enough.'

'Yes, but if I find her tonight I could take her to *The Times* offices and—'

'Michael, answer me one question.'

Barclay's breathing was fast and ragged. From the background noise – drunken yells, music blaring, teeming life, car horns – he was calling from a phone-booth somewhere in the West End. 'Sure,' he said, 'go ahead.'

'Why do you want to find Dominique so urgently? Is it maybe because you feel left out of her life all of a sudden?'

There was a long silence. 'That's two questions,' Barclay said at last.

'Rhetorical questions, too, I think. Go home, get some rest, and be at the Conference Centre early. We know Dominique will be there.'

'Yes.' Barclay sounded as if all the air had been let out of him. 'Yes, okay.'

'Goodnight then.'

Elder hung up the phone. It rang again. 'Oh, for Christ's sake.' He picked it up. 'Elder,' he snapped.

'Dominic?' It was Joyce Parry. 'Are you all right?'

He softened his voice. 'Oh, hello, Joyce. Yes, yes, I'm fine. Sorry about that.'

'Been a long day, huh?'

'Yes,' he agreed, 'it's been a long day.'

'And a successful day too, by all accounts. Congratulations.'

'Premature, I'd say. You know we actually had Witch *inside* a police station?'

'And she got away, yes. Hardly your fault, Dominic. And we *do* have the Dutchman. People on the Continent are very pleased about that.'

'Good for them.'

Joyce Parry laughed. 'It helps us with SIS. After Barclay's German escapade, we need it.'

'But will it help mend the rift between you and the Home Secretary?'

'Who knows. He can be a spiteful little sod.' She paused. 'How about a nightcap? I thought we could have a drink at the—'

'That's sweet of you, Joyce, and any other time, I'd be . . .'

'But tonight you're whacked? Fair enough. How did Barclay bear up today?'

'More than adequately.'

'Really? You're not just covering for him?'

'He's just called me. He's still busy working.'

'I *am* impressed. He's always been first out of the office here, soon as five-thirty comes.'

'Maybe he's changed.'

'Maybe. Just so long as you haven't taught him too many of your tricks.'

He smiled. 'Joyce, about that drink. Might room service be available?'

She considered her answer. 'It might.'

'On one condition.'

'What's that?'

'Bring some paracetamol as well. Either that or massage oil.'

'Alcohol, drugs and baby oil . . . sounds just like the old days.'

Elder laughed. 'I think the relevant word there is "old", Joyce. Definitely old.'

He put the receiver down again and counted to ten. No more calls came. He knew he should get up, tidy the room a bit, and tidy himself too. But still he lay, the arm across his eyes, thinking of an encounter he knew must come, and come soon. Just like Operation Silverfish. He wriggled on the bed, rubbing the itch in his back. Silverfish. *You should have been a priest.* Maybe she had a point. Finally, he got up and turned on the bedside lamp, squinting into the light as he opened the wardrobe and took out his case. There was a shirt in the bottom, rolled up. It was torn and tattered, and stained a dull brown, almost the colour of rust. It was the shirt he had worn . . . And wrapped up inside it was a gun, a Browning nine-millimetre pistol. He lifted out the gun and put the shirt back in the case. The pistol felt icy and unnatural in his hand, but the longer he held it the warmer it became and the more natural it felt, until he was hardly aware of it there at all.

'This time,' he whispered to himself, running his eye along the sight. 'This time, Witch. That's a promise.'

# The Shooting Gallery

# Tuesday 16 June

Barclay was at the Queen Elizabeth II Conference Centre almost before it had opened for the day. But the foyer was already buzzing with security and the media. Everyone was handed a sheet detailing the day's itinerary. Supposedly, this had been held back until the day itself for 'security reasons'. But in fact most of the delegations, in pre-summit chats with the press, had given away the details anyway. A large section of the Conference Centre had been set aside for representatives of the media, and they wouldn't be allowed to linger in the foyer. A restless young woman was already weaving through the bodies, seeking out media-coloured ribbons. She looked at Barclay, seemed to think he *must* be a reporter, and was about to tell him that breakfast was available in the ... But then she saw that he was wearing a security-coloured red-and-blue ribbon, so she veered away at the last moment.

Some German security personnel were sharing a German joke. One of them, seeing the colour of Barclay's ribbon, nodded a greeting towards him. Barclay nodded back. His cheeks were tingling: he wondered if the joke was the one about the British secret agent and the German terrorist. A couple of the Germans kept placing a hand against their chest and running it down the front of their buttoned suit-jacket. It was clear to Barclay that they were armed. In fact, as more security personnel appeared, he began to wonder if he alone was unarmed. Still there was no sign of Dominique. He read through the itinerary again, already knowing it by heart. The first session was to be short, a sort of official welcome. A couple of speeches, then a photo-shoot. The real business would begin in the afternoon, after an 'informal' lunch at Buckingham Palace. He wondered how informal 'informal' was. Not very, he thought.

'Morning, Michael.'

It was Elder. He had heavy bags under his eyes, which were red at their corners. Having spoken, he stifled a yawn.

'Good morning, sir.' Barclay examined Elder's suit for bulges, and found none. Well, at least someone else around here wasn't toting a gun.

'Bright and early, eh?'

'Well, early anyway.'

Elder nodded, stifling another yawn. 'I could do with some coffee,' he said at last. A room had been set aside for the British security contingent, and in it sat a steaming coffee-machine. Elder made straight for a large polythene bag full of beakers, tipped some 'creamer' into one, then poured himself coffee. Barclay refused. 'Creamer,' muttered Elder. 'What in God's name's that?'

'Something with no milk products in it,' guessed Barclay. Elder shuddered, but drank the drink anyway, screwing shut his eyes for the first couple of gulps.

He exhaled noisily. 'Hit the spot,' he said. 'Now listen, we've had some more news.'

'Oh?'

'A civil servant called Christine Jones. She's missing. We think Witch has abducted her and is using her identity.'

Barclay whistled. 'Where does she work?'

'1–19 Victoria Street.'

Barclay nodded. 'Makes sense.'

'So today, and every day if it comes to it, Victoria Street's our priority.'

'When did you find all this out?'

'Last night.'

'Why didn't you tell me when I phoned?'

'Michael, you were overheated as it was. I didn't want you to explode. Besides, we know a lot, but we still don't know who Witch's target is.'

'So you don't think my idea about *The Times* is a lost cause?'

'Absolutely not.' Elder, having finished the coffee, poured himself another cup, not bothering to add creamer this time. 'Absolutely not,' he repeated. 'I want you and Dominique to follow it up.'

'Speaking of which . . . I should be in the lobby in case she arrives.'

'Fine, I'll come with you. I'm going to take another wander along Victoria Street.' He finished the second cup.

'Feel better for that, sir?'

Elder nodded, stifling yet another yawn.

'You obviously didn't get much sleep last night,' said Barclay, solicitously.

'No,' said Elder with a smile. 'Not much.'

Barclay saw that the smile was in memory of something. It didn't take him long to work out what that memory might be.

Dominique, entering the foyer unaccompanied, was yawning too. She looked like she'd had a heavy night of it. Barclay, who'd just been thinking about Elder and Joyce Parry, didn't want to consider what Dominique had been doing.

'Dominique,' he said, approaching.

She raised a hand to her forehead. 'Michael, please, I

am dying. English beer . . . how do you manage to drink it?'

Barclay smiled. 'Dominique, this is your near-name-sake Dominic Elder.'

She tried to brighten a little. She looked very pale, and hadn't bothered with the morning chore of make-up. But her eyes sparkled as she smiled. 'Monsieur Elder, I am pleased to meet you.' She put out a small red-gloved hand for Elder to take. 'The famous author of the Witch file.'

Elder swallowed another yawn and made a non-committal sound.

'Listen, Dominique,' said Barclay, 'something's come up. It might be a clue to Witch's intended victim.'

'Oh yes?' She just failed to sound interested.

'Remember the Australian anarchist? His flat?'

She rolled her eyes. 'Monsieur Wrightson and his apartment. Ugh, how could I forget?'

'There was a copy of *The Times* there.'

'Yes.' She seemed puzzled now, but her interest was growing.

'With the crossword done.'

'Yes.'

'And remember what Bandorff said . . . Witch liked to do crosswords.'

She nodded slowly. 'So you add one to the other,' she said, 'and you assume the crossword was done by Witch and not by Mr Wrightson?'

Barclay shrugged. 'It's a theory.'

She considered this, acknowledged with a shrug of her own that it was possible. 'So what?' she said.

'The thing is,' Elder broke in, 'there was a page torn out of that newspaper, according to Mr Barclay here.'

Another shrug. 'A page, maybe several pages. Used for toilet paper, according to—'

'Perhaps *Witch* tore the page out,' continued Elder.

'You see,' said Barclay, warming to the subject, 'it could be some clue to her chosen victim, a profile of them or something.'

'Oh, yes, I see.'

'So can you remember which day's *Times* it was?'

She laughed. 'I cannot even remember which *month* it was.' She saw that they looked crestfallen. 'I'm sorry,' she said.

'Don't be,' said Elder. But Barclay's dejection moved her to remember.

'There was a photograph,' she said. 'A large black and white picture on one of the inside pages. I recall it because it attracted me. A photograph of New York from the air, and lots of *ballons*.'

'Balloons?' said Elder.

'Yes, the big ones with baskets beneath them.'

'Hot-air balloons?'

'Yes, lots of those, rising over New York.'

'The Picture Editor's *got* to know when that one appeared,' said Barclay, brightening again.

Elder was nodding. 'Off you go,' he said. 'And be lucky.'

Barclay looked to Dominique. 'Coming?'

She looked undecided. 'I should . . . my colleagues . . . I am supposed to be the expert, you know.' Then she made up her mind. 'Oh God, yes, of course I am coming.'

A broad smile spread across Barclay's face. 'Good,' he said.

Elder watched them leave. A nice young couple, but he wouldn't want to have to depend on them. He patted his chest, and let his hand slide down the front of his suit. Then he walked outside. The morning was overcast, threatening rain. The forecast for the rest of the week was even worse. Wet weather seemed to exacerbate his

387

back problem. God knows, after last night he felt achy enough as it was.

'You look rough,' said a voice to his left. It was Doyle, accompanied by Greenleaf.

'Maybe fragile is a better word,' Elder admitted.

Doyle laughed, and patted his jacket ostentatiously. 'Well, don't worry about a thing, Mr Elder, we'll look after you.' His voice fell to a dramatic whisper. 'Tooled up.'

Elder stared at the bulging jacket. 'I'd never have guessed.'

'It makes me nervous,' said Greenleaf. He looked nervous, wriggling at the unaccustomed weight strapped to his side, beneath his left arm. Neither Special Branch man wore a suit really fitted for carrying a gun. Not like Elder's suit, which was unfashionably roomy to start with. Elder many years before had given the suit to a tailor in Shoreditch who had eased it out a little to the left-hand side. The result was that he could have worn a .44 Magnum without any hint of a bulge, never mind his favoured pistol.

'I picked up itineraries for you,' said Elder. He took from his pocket two folded sheets of A4-sized paper, and gave one to each of them. Doyle glanced down the list.

'Not much here we didn't know already. When d'you think she'll make the hit? Lunchtime?'

Elder nodded. 'That would be my guess. After this morning's handshakes and champagne. The cars are supposed to leave for Buck House at noon, but I suppose it depends on how long the photo opportunity takes.'

'They won't keep Her Maj' waiting,' said Doyle knowledgeably.

'You're probably right,' said Elder.

'Speaking of photo opportunities . . .' Greenleaf reached into the plastic carrier bag he was holding and came out with a xeroxed sheet. 'We've had these distributed to everyone.' On the sheet was a picture of Christine Jones and a description. The picture wasn't terribly good.

'I got it last night,' Doyle said proudly. 'Went back to the house. There weren't many snaps to choose from. We had to crop that one as it was.' He reached into his jacket pocket. 'Here's the original.'

Elder studied the photo. It showed Christine Jones and a female friend posing on a beach. Christine was wearing a one-piece swimsuit, her friend a very brief bikini.

'Mmm,' said Elder. He looked up at Doyle, who was looking at the photo, then he glanced towards Greenleaf, who smiled. Yes, they both had their ideas as to why Doyle had chosen this particular photograph.

'And,' added Greenleaf meaningfully, 'there are extra men on guard inside 1–19.'

'Not inside the other buildings?'

'We couldn't stretch to it.'

'No way,' said Doyle, retrieving the picture. 'We're like india-rubber men as it is.'

Greenleaf was rummaging in the bag again. 'We thought these might come in handy.' He lifted a walkie-talkie out of the bag and handed it to Elder. It was heavier than it looked. 'They've not got much range, but . . .' Another walkie-talkie was handed to Doyle. When Greenleaf lifted out the third, the bag was empty. He crumpled it and stuffed it into his pocket.

'Not exactly unobtrusive,' commented Elder.

'True,' said Doyle. 'Carry one of these and every bugger knows what your game is.'

Greenleaf said nothing but looked slighted. Elder guessed the walkie-talkies had been his idea. 'I'm sure they'll be invaluable,' Elder said.

'Here they come,' said Doyle. Which was, in a sense,

true. Cordons had been hastily erected, traffic stopped. Uniformed policemen were suddenly in greater evidence than ever. Motorbikes arrived with their indicators flashing, the drivers had a word with someone, then they turned and headed back the way they'd come.

'Yes,' said Doyle, 'here they come.'

The three men stood well out of the way as they watched the delegations arrive. Doyle was not impressed. 'Why do they need all these cars and all this razzmatazz? Be a lot cheaper if they just flew the big cheeses in – first class, natch – and had them all sit round a table. Look at all these bloody hangers-on.'

'I believe,' said Elder, smiling, 'the term is aides.'

'Hangers-on,' Doyle insisted.

One car deposited the Home Secretary and his private secretary. Jonathan Barker fastened a button on his suit jacket as he emerged, smiling for the cameras. A gust caught the parting in his hair, and he swept the stray locks back into place. He glanced towards where Elder and the others stood, and frowned slightly, bowing his head so the newsmen wouldn't catch the look.

'"Shagger" Barker we call him,' said Doyle from the side of his mouth. Elder laughed, quite loudly, further discomfiting the Home Secretary. The private secretary scowled openly at the trio as he followed his minister into the building.

'Why "Shagger"?'

Doyle shrugged. 'He just looks the type, doesn't he?'

'He was happily married until a couple of months ago.'

'Yeah, to his secretary. Says a lot about him, doesn't it?'

'Does it?'

When the last delegation had entered the Conference Centre, Greenleaf expelled a long whistle of air between his teeth.

'The collective sigh of relief,' said Elder. The police and other security people all looked a bit easier now that everyone was safely inside.

'To think,' said Greenleaf, 'we're going to be doing this at least twice a day for the rest of the week.'

'Well, let's hope we are,' said Elder. 'I'd rather breathe a sigh of relief than a gasp of panic.'

Doyle chuckled. 'I wish I could say clever things like that.'

'I take that as a compliment, Doyle, coming from the man who invented "Shagger" Barker.'

Doyle made a little bow. 'Now what?' he asked.

'Victoria Street,' said Elder. 'Fun's over here. Let's see how security's shaping up.'

Witch had been in the Victoria area since daybreak. Just after midnight, she'd stolen a car. It was her second car theft of the night, her first being a four-year-old Peugeot 305. For the second, she wanted something similar – fast but unshowy – and finally settled on a three-year-old Alfa Romeo. She'd gone outside London to accomplish this. A car stolen in London and then driven around London could be spotted by police. A car stolen in East Croydon and driven around central London might not. She had brought the first car, the Peugeot, back into the city and parked it on the corner of her chosen cul-de-sac off the King's Road. Then she'd returned to East Croydon by the late train, a train full of drunk commuters and even drunker youths, and found the Alfa Romeo. Back in London, she had driven one particular route three times, with slight detours and amendments, memorising the final, chosen route until she felt she could drive it blindfolded.

Then she'd slept for an hour or two in an all-night car park, slouched in the front seat of the Alfa, awaking to a tingling feeling in her gut, a feeling that told her it was time. Time to put theory into practice. Time for the final day.

She'd watched the various entourages arrive at the Conference Centre, headphones clamped to her head. Her personal hi-fi's radio news told her that the morning session would be short. Yes, because they were going to lunch at Buckingham Palace; she'd read that in one of the briefs prepared by the Dutchman.

The Dutchman was another unreliable factor, now that Elder had his hands on him. That was why she was here early, just to check what extra security precautions they'd taken.

As the sleek black cars had arrived, while she was listening to her radio, she'd been watching Dominic Elder. No chance of his spotting her of course. She was just one of a crowd who had stopped on their way to work to watch, from behind the metal barriers, the famous people arriving. She'd tucked herself in between two large men. And she watched Elder, watched him talking to two other men – they looked like police to her, probably Special Branch, MI5's dogsbodies. One of them made a big show of the fact that he was armed. The other was quiet, almost sleepy in comparison. Elder looked tired and alert at the same time. Like her, he wouldn't have been getting much sleep recently. Like her, he'd been waiting for this day. Beneath the shabby suit he would be carrying his own gun, the Browning. It was typical of him to buy British. Typical of him to keep faith with something which had failed him before . . .

She'd watched for a few moments, and she'd looked up occasionally to spot the marksmen, armed only with binoculars thus far, as they examined the scene from their lofty heights. Then she drifted away. Her car was parked outside a mansion block in a street behind

Westminster Cathedral, tickets on the windshield showing she'd paid for three hours' parking. Three hours was
the limit. She'd toyed with the idea of breaking into
another car and taking a resident's parking permit to
stick on the Alfa's windscreen. But any traffic warden
worth the name would pause to compare licence plate
details.

She was playing a cassette on her personal hi-fi: an
Ohm mantra repeated over the sound of a human
heartbeat. It calmed her as she walked back to the car,
got into it, and rummaged beneath the passenger seat for
her civil service satchel and a green Harrods carrier bag.
She glanced around her before opening the satchel and
peering inside, seeming happy with what she found
there. Her own choice of pistol was an Italian-made
Beretta nine-millimetre 92F, a link to her days in
Bologna as a member of Croix Jaune. She'd first handled
a Beretta during the Gibson kidnapping. Christ, she'd
been the only one of them who knew how to handle a
gun. She'd practically had to teach them. Still, despite
the clumsy trap laid for them, they'd all managed to
escape with the ransom money. It had come in useful,
that money . . .

She slipped the gun out of her satchel and into her
jacket. She'd stitched a special pocket into it, hanging
loose from the jacket by two straps. It was funny how
often the authorities would want to search your baggage, but not your clothes. She had a feeling this might
be one of those days at the DTI.

She closed the satchel again and got out of the car,
this time taking satchel and carrier bag with her. She
had a little time to kill. She noticed as she passed that
there were men hanging around outside some of the
buildings on Victoria Street itself, and especially outside
the DTI Headquarters. It was only to be expected. She

walked to a small supermarket and bought two large fresh chickens, two packs of fresh sandwiches, and a catering-sized tin of cheap instant coffee, then retreated to Victoria Station and locked herself in a toilet cubicle, where she did what she had to do. An attendant knocked eventually and asked if everything was all right.

'Everything's fine,' Witch called back. 'Bad curry last night, that's all.'

The attendant chuckled and moved away. Witch flushed the toilet and came out. The attendant, a small brown-skinned woman, was waiting.

'Sorry,' the woman said, 'it's just that you've got to be careful. We get all kinds coming in ... injecting themselves, that sort of thing.'

'I understand,' said Witch, washing her hands. 'Like you say, you've got to be careful.'

She walked around the back of Victoria Street, to where her car was, and from there to the back entrance of 45 Victoria Street. There was a guard with a dog outside the door. The dog barked as she approached, rearing up on hind legs, causing the guard to rein it in on its leash.

'It's all right,' he told her.

'I've some chickens here,' she said.

'That'll be it then, not that he doesn't get fed enough.'

She walked past him. She wasn't concerned, there was nothing for her to be concerned about. She was a government employee, she made this trip every day. Nothing to worry about. She entered the building and showed her security pass to the guard who stood in front of his desk. He looked at it a bit more carefully than usual, and thanked her.

'I don't often forget a pretty face,' he said.

'I usually come in the front way,' she explained, 'but it's pandemonium out there.'

'I'll bet.'

Witch slipped the pass back into her handbag. She had altered the name on Christine Jones's card to Caroline James, knowing they would be on the lookout for poor starving Christine. She made to move past him.

'Sorry, miss, I need to check all bags today.'

'Yes, of course.'

'It's pandemonium in here too.' He looked through her handbag first, then her official bag. 'I'm on my own. They've sent my partner up the road to Number One.'

'Really?' She allowed herself a small smile.

He was looking at her shopping.

'Chicken's on special offer at Safeway,' she said.

'Really? I like a bit of leg myself.' And he gave her a wink, to which she responded with her most winning smile. He glanced towards the other items: it was obviously her turn to provide the office coffee, and lunch today consisted of nothing more than a sandwich.

In her Harrods bag were some clothes, a pair of shoes.

'Partying tonight, eh?'

'That's the plan,' said Witch.

'Thank you, miss,' the guard said.

'You're welcome.'

She walked to the lifts, pressed the button and waited.

The lift arrived. She got in and pressed the button for the third floor. On the way up, she did not blink. She just stared ahead, even when the lift stopped at the ground floor and some people got in. There were guards pacing the space outside the lifts. They did not look at her. She looked through them. Then the lift was ascending again. She got out at the third floor and made for the Conference Room. God, wouldn't it just be her luck to bump into that slimeball from yesterday, Blishen, Mr Folded-arms? But she didn't. She looked up and down the corridor, saw that no one was paying her any attention, and opened the door of the Conference Room.

Inside, she worked quickly. She took out both chickens and reached inside them, where the plastic bags of giblets had been until she'd flushed them down the toilet in Victoria Station. Now the hollow chickens housed small soft packages wrapped in grey polythene and black tape. She dumped the chickens in the wastepaper bin, and reopened the packs of sandwiches, which she had closed herself using tiny strips of clear tape. Inside were thin coils of copper wire and small connectors, plus a tiny screw-driver. She joined the two packages by runs of wire, working quickly and calmly. She held one foot wedged up against the door, preventing anyone from opening it while she worked.

At last she was satisfied. Time for a break, she thought. She lifted out the large tin of coffee and prised off its lid. The toilet at Victoria had taken a lot of punishment: giblets, sandwich fillings, and an awful lot of instant granules. The blonde wig inside the tin still smelled of bitter coffee. She shook it free of brown specks, then dumped the tin in the basket beside the chickens.

She lifted the clothes and shoes from her bag, stripped and changed. With lipstick and the aid of a hand-mirror she turned her lips vermilion. Make-up is the beginning of disguise. She'd learnt that early in life at the fairground: she could be virgin or whore to order, twelve or sixteen, above or below the age of consent. She could smile and be unhappy; or weep while she was overjoyed. She'd been playing a game of dressing-up with her life until the Irishman had come . . .

She looked at herself now and blinked. A question had framed itself in her mind. Who am I? She shook it away as she brushed out her wig. She knew who she was. She knew what she was. And she knew why she was here.

Wasn't that more than most people knew?

When she turned the Harrods bag inside out, it was just a plain white cloth bag with green handles. She placed her cassette recorder on the floor near the door, unplugging the headphones. The recorder came with its own built-in speaker, and, more unusually, included automatic rewind and repeat functions. Witch swapped her Ohm and Heartbeat cassette for another tape and switched the machine on.

In the lower ground floor of the building, the guard was tuning his radio to something musical when there were steps on the stairwell. A man appeared. The guard knew him. He was from the police. The police were all over the place, on window-ledges and in corridors, patrolling the foyer and the main entrance. He half-expected to see one of them hiding beneath his desk. The policeman was waving something, a notice or leaflet.

'Here, George,' the policeman said, 'has anyone given you one of these?'

The guard slipped his spectacles back on. 'What is it? No, nobody's given me nothing.'

'Typical,' said the policeman. 'If you want a job doing, do it yourself. Well, you can keep that one anyway.'

A bell sounded once as the lift doors opened. A couple got out, a man in a pinstripe suit and a tall, big-boned woman.

'Back in ten minutes,' the man said.

'Right you are, sir,' said the guard. The policeman watched the couple leave.

'Dirty sods couldn't wait till knocking-off time, eh?'

The guard was laughing as he turned his attention to the sheet of paper. He recognised the name, he'd been told to look out for it. But now there was a photo, too.

'I don't know,' he said.

'What's up, George?'

The guard tapped the photo with a finger yellow from cigarettes smoked to the nub. 'I think I've seen her this morning, about twenty minutes ago.'

'You sure?'

'Christine Jones, that wasn't the name on her pass. I've been on the lookout for Christine Jones.'

The policeman was already slipping a radio out of his pocket. 'This is Traynor,' he said into the mouthpiece. 'I'm in number 45. Suspect is inside the building. I repeat, suspect is inside the building.'

There was silence, then crackle and a disembodied voice. 'It's Doyle here, Traynor. Secure all exits, and I mean *all* exits. Start searching the floors. We're on our way.'

Traynor made for the stairs then paused. 'You heard him, George. No one in or out of here, okay? Anyone wants out, send them to the ground floor.' He turned, then stopped again, turned back. 'George, what was she wearing?'

'Mmm . . . blue jacket, dark blue . . . white blouse, dark skirt.'

'Right.' This time Traynor started climbing the stairs. George switched his radio back on and began fiddling with the dial again. He looked out of the window, but the pinstripe man and lipstick woman had gone. Ah, Radio Two, he'd found it at last. Manuel and his Music of the Mountains, lovely. George settled back in his chair.

Doyle and Greenleaf put together reinforcements and brought them into the building. They were both a little breathless, but ready for anything. The news had been circulated, more men would be on their way.

'Any sign?' Doyle asked Traynor.

'Not yet. She's dressed in a dark-coloured two-piece

and white blouse, but then so are half the women in the place.'

'Which floor was she headed for?'

Traynor shook his head.

'We've just got to be methodical,' said Greenleaf.

Doyle looked at him. 'Methodical, right. How long have we got before the bigwigs go to lunch?'

Greenleaf checked his watch. 'Quarter of an hour.'

'Right then,' said Doyle, 'we can afford to be methodical for about five minutes. After that, we start screaming and kicking down doors.'

'Progress report, gentlemen.' This was said in brisk, clipped tones by Commander Trilling, almost at marching-pace as he entered the foyer and joined them.

'She's in here somewhere, sir,' said Doyle.

'But we don't know where,' admitted Greenleaf.

'Well, I'll tell you one place she's not – she's not standing here with us!' Trilling tossed a mint into his mouth. 'Let's start from the roof down. Snipers like height, don't they?'

'Yes, sir.' Doyle turned to Traynor. 'What are you waiting for? Roof and the top floor down!'

'Yes, sir.' Traynor started giving orders to his unit.

'You start at the top, Doyle,' said Greenleaf, 'I'll start at the bottom. Keep in touch by walkie-talkie and we'll meet halfway.'

'Right,' said Doyle.

'Where's Elder?' asked Trilling. Greenleaf shrugged.

'I think he was headed for the lower ground floor.'

'Let's try to keep him there, eh? He'll only get in the way.'

Doyle grinned at this, so Greenleaf swallowed back a defence.

'Right, sir,' he said instead, heading for the stairs. The

last thing he heard Doyle saying was: 'And check the lift-shaft, too. Remember that film with the cannibal . . .'

Doyle stood outside the third-floor conference room. Traynor was with him. So was a civil servant who worked on the third floor.

'It's usually open,' she said. 'I can't think why it would be locked.' She was young and blonde and chewing gum.

Doyle nodded, then put a finger to his lips and tried the doorhandle quietly, trying to turn it one way and then the other. It was definitely locked. He put his ear to the door and listened. Silence. Then a shuffling sound. He thought about knocking, then thought better of it. He motioned for them to follow him further down the corridor.

'I'm lost,' he whispered. 'Is this the front of the building or the back?'

'The front, sir,' Traynor whispered back.

'Can we get someone on the ledge to take a peek inside?'

'I'll go check.' And off Traynor tiptoed.

'Back to your office,' Doyle whispered to the girl. 'It's too dangerous here.'

He thought she was going to swallow her gum. He gave her hand a reassuring squeeze in his and nodded along the corridor. Off she walked, on silent tiptoe. Doyle went back to the door and listened again. Silence. He put his eye to the keyhole, but it was the wrong type. He couldn't see into the room. There was a gap between the bottom of the door and the floor. He lay down, but again could not see into the room. Traynor was coming back.

'No can do,' he said when they'd moved away from the door. 'The ledge isn't wide enough or something.'

'What about across the road? Can anyone see any-thing from across there?'

'I'll radio and check.'

'And get some more men up here. We may have to storm the place.'

'Don't we have the SAS to do that sort of thing?'

'Don't be stupid, Traynor. It's only a hardwood door, not the Iranian bloody Embassy.'

Greenleaf appeared. A distance behind him, Doyle could see Trilling.

'Is she in there?' Greenleaf hissed.

Doyle shrugged and nodded towards the Commander. 'Do me a favour,' he whispered to Greenleaf, 'keep the old man away from here. He'll only be in the bloody way, and you know he can't keep his voice down.'

Greenleaf nodded, moved back along the corridor, and stopped in front of Commander Trilling, talking to him softly.


Elder was questioning the guard called George. He was beginning to get a sour feeling in his stomach about all of this, the whole set-up.

'I'm not even sure it was her,' George was saying now. 'I mean, it's hard to tell with some women, isn't it?'

'Well, has there been anyone else, anyone new to you?'

The guard shook his head. From Elder's walkie-talkie came information that the procession of cars was leaving the Conference Centre, moving in slow convoy past the building he was standing in. He felt like screaming.

'Look,' said the guard, 'I've got to get back to work.' He walked over to the outside door, where a police officer was stopping a man in a pinstriped suit from entering the building.

'He's all right,' said the guard to the policeman. 'It's Mr Connaught from the third floor.'

'I only went out to get these,' Mr Connaught was

explaining, waving some documents. 'I'd left them in my boot.'

The policeman looked to Elder, who nodded assent. The officer moved aside, letting Connaught into the building.

'What's going on?'

'Security,' the guard explained. 'Some woman they're after.' This reminded him of something. 'Who was that blonde lady you were with?'

Connaught shook his head. 'Met her at the lift. Don't know who she was exactly.'

'Oh, Christ!' said Elder, making for the stairs.

There was that shuffling sound again, like someone who was seated moving their feet on the floor. Doyle took a deep breath and knocked, keeping his back hard against the wall to the side of the door, rapping with his fist and then removing it from any line of fire. Silence.

He knocked again, a little harder. 'Anyone in there? We've got a meeting starting in five minutes. Hello, anyone there?'

Silence. From their distance, Greenleaf and Trilling were watching him. When Greenleaf spoke, he spoke in an undertone which Doyle couldn't catch. Trilling's idea of an undertone, however, would not have gone unheard in a football stadium.

'I see . . . Yes, of course . . . As you see fit . . .' Then a message came over Greenleaf's radio (Doyle had switched his off: it sat on the ground beside him). Greenleaf listened and mumbled something into the radio.

Doyle licked his lips. No use pretending any longer; no time left in which to pretend. Traynor was returning, pushing past Greenleaf and Trilling. He had four men with him.

402

'Net curtains are in the way,' Traynor whispered. 'Nobody across the street can see anything. No movement at all.'

Doyle nodded. 'I can hear somebody though.' Patches of sweat were spreading from beneath his arms. And now Greenleaf was creeping forwards.

'They're passing the building right this second.'

'Can't hang around any longer then,' said Doyle. He withdrew his pistol, raising it high above him, gripped in both hands and pointed ceilingwards. He closed his eyes for a moment. 'Right,' he said to the men around him. 'We're going in.' They were all withdrawing their weapons now, a series of quiet snicks as safety catches were slipped off. Doyle looked at Traynor. 'You keen to kick down that door?' Traynor nodded. 'Okay, two of you behind me, two of you other side of the door. Soon as the door opens, we're in. My side low, other side aiming over our heads. Take the diagonals. Got that?'

They nodded, assumed their positions. Doyle, back to the wall, crouched low. Traynor stood in front of the door, took a moment to size it up. Greenleaf, who had gone back along the corridor to let Trilling know the score, had withdrawn his own weapon and was now advancing again, walkie-talkie gripped in his free hand, watched by Trilling. Doyle gave Traynor the nod. Traynor took a step back, both hands around the butt of his gun, aiming it straight at whatever was behind the door. He raised his right knee, so that the sole of his shoe faced the door, just below the handle. And took a deep breath.

Dominic Elder ran up the stairs, across the reception area, and out of the glass doors on to Victoria Street. He ran into a crush of people, waving, some of them cheering, held back by metal-grilled barriers from the road. There was a dull slow roar from the motorcycle escorts. And then there was glitter in the sky, and a net-curtain, blown out from its window and wafting in the breeze.

And then there was the explosion.

A dull boom. Not a large explosion by any means, but enough to panic the crowds. The motorbikes suddenly speeded up, as did the cars. Front fenders dented back fenders as the cars behind put their foot down. They were speeding away from the scene, and the security men on the street had guns in their hands and were trying to see what had happened. But it was raining glass. That was what was happening. Large and small shards and splinters, landing at velocity. And the screams were no longer solely of fear.

'What happened?' he yelled into his walkie-talkie. 'John, what the hell happened?' He was jostled by people fleeing the scene. Doors were kicked open as people attempted to find shelter. Anywhere but on the street. Barriers clattered to the ground as people scrambled over them.

The walkie-talkie crackled. He struggled to hear it. 'Bomb inside the door. Hair-trigger.'

'Anybody hurt?'

'Traynor, leg blown off. Doyle . . .'

'What about Doyle?'

'Concussion.'

'The room, John . . . is there anyone in the room?'

A pause. 'Negative, Dominic. The room's empty. Repeat, the room is empty.' Then: 'Jesus Christ.'

'What is it?'

'Chickens, two supermarket chickens.'

They'd walked straight into a bloody trap! If Witch had left nothing else, she'd left yet another warped calling card. Which meant what? That the real attempt would take place elsewhere? Up ahead maybe? The motorcade was moving off in disarray. Christ, a trap . . . he couldn't believe . . . couldn't take it in. Why? What was the point? Suddenly, a hand gripped his arm. He reached inside his jacket, turning towards the— But it was only Barclay.

'Jesus, you gave me a fright.' His grip on the pistol relaxed. Barclay saw what had been about to happen.

'Sorry,' he said. 'What's going on?'

Elder nodded upwards, where the curtain still fluttered like a flag. It didn't look like a flag though; it looked like a shroud. 'Bomb,' he said. 'Witch led us into a trap.'

Sirens were nearing, ambulances. Uniformed police officers were attempting to comfort the prone and wounded bodies. A helicopter surveyed the pandemonium from on high. The convoy had disappeared from view. Barclay was yelling something above the noise.

'What?' Elder yelled back.

'I said we know who she's—'

The ambulances were drawing to a squealing halt in front of them. Barclay put his hand out towards Dominique, palm upwards, only to find that she wasn't there. She was ten feet away, tending to a woman's cuts. He walked over, opened the flap of her shoulder-bag, and took something from it, then came back to Elder, handing him a folded page from *The Times*. Elder looked at it. A full-page advert for British Aerospace.

'Other side,' yelled Barclay. Elder turned the page over. The obituaries column. There were four, a couple of churchmen, head of an Oxford college, and . . . Marion Barker, the Home Secretary's wife.

Elder's face creased into a huge frown. He looked at Barclay, who was nodding. Dominique, looking paler than ever, was coming back to join them. An ambulanceman had taken over from her. She watched as he worked on the woman. The woman caught Dominique's eye and smiled at her, mouthing 'thank you'.

'You think her target's the—'

'The Home Secretary,' said Barclay. He shrugged. 'Unless you think it's the Oxford don's widow.'

A police sergeant was approaching, his arms stretched out like a barrier. 'Clear the area, please. Please clear the area.'

'Yes, sergeant, we're just going,' said Dominic Elder quietly, not really aware of what he was saying. Then his eyes came back into focus. 'Come on then,' he said. 'Back to the Centre.'

They joined the evacuation of Victoria Street. More ambulances and fire engines were blocked in a traffic jam, the traffic having been halted to allow the motorcade sole access to Victoria Street in the first place. Sirens blared, blue lights circled, but the drivers in front complained that there was nothing they could do till the barriers were moved. One ambulance mounted the pavement, only to find itself firmly wedged between the vehicle in front and a concrete lamppost.

At the Conference Centre, a crowd of people stood on the steps, wondering what had happened. Elder pushed past them and into the foyer. He walked quickly to the reception desk. 'The Home Secretary,' he said, 'I need to know ... did he go to Buckingham Palace with the rest of them?'

'I'll just check.' The receptionist made an internal call. 'Jan, what was Mr Barker doing this lunchtime?' She listened. 'Thank you,' she said, cutting the connection. 'He went home,' she said. 'Car collected him ten minutes ago.'

'Thank you,' said Elder. Barclay and Dominique were waiting just inside the door. 'He's gone home,' Elder told them. 'I know his address.' He was outside again, the young couple following him. He started to descend the steps, looking about him. 'What we need now is a car.'

Dominique continued past him and perused the line of cars parked outside the building. 'How about this one?' she said. It was a marked Metropolitan Police Rover 2000. 'It's even got the keys in.' She was already opening the driver's door. 'You can direct me, come on.'

Elder got into the back, Barclay into the passenger seat. Dominique had started the ignition, but was now looking at the controls around her.

'What's the problem?' said Barclay.

'My first time in a right-hand-drive car.' She pulled the big car out of its parking space. 'See if you can find the siren, Michael.' After a few false attempts, he did so. People looked at them as they pulled out into the main road. 'Which way?' she called back to Elder.

'Keep going along here,' he said. 'I'll tell you when to turn.'

Dominique nodded, shifted up a gear, then thought better of it, shifted down again, and slammed her foot on the accelerator. Barclay was thrown against the back of his seat. He looked around, but Elder didn't seem at all fazed. He was yelling into his walkie-talkie.

'John? John?'

'Dominic, where are you? I can hardly—' The signal broke up.

'I'm heading towards Jonathan Barker's home. We think he's Witch's target. Over.'

He listened to a lot of crackle and static. Then: 'Sorry, Dom . . . signal's break . . . didn't catch a . . . please rep—'

'We're out of range,' said Barclay.

'Yes,' said Elder, throwing the walkie-talkie on to the seat beside him. It bounced off the seat and on to the floor, where it erupted into static before dying. Elder looked out of the window. 'Right here!' Dominique slammed on the brakes and sent the car whipping around the corner. Barclay was desperately trying to fasten his seatbelt.

'You don't trust me, Michael?' she called. 'I am a Parisian driver. *C'est facile!'*

Elder reached between them for the police radio.

Jonathan Barker, Home Secretary, had a town house in Belgravia's Holbein Place. It was one of his three UK residences, the others being a converted vicarage in Dorset and an old hunting-lodge on Speyside. His address in London wasn't quite public knowledge, but neither was he a low-key minister – he'd given several early-morning doorstep interviews to the media during his short time in office. The parking space in front of the house was kept free, courtesy of two bright red traffic-cones which sat in the road whenever Barker's chauffeured car was elsewhere. It was an arrangement which worked, mostly. The most frequent transgressors were workmen and tourists, who would shift the cones on to the pavement so as to have room to park their vans or BMWs.

Today, it was an Alfa Romeo.

The chauffeur swore under his breath and stopped the minister's car in the road, a little way behind the Alfa, giving the driver room to move it. Always supposing the driver was anywhere around. The chauffeur sounded the car-horn, just in case the driver was in one of the houses near the minister's.

The minister's bodyguard spotted something from his passenger seat. 'There's somebody still in the car,' he said. And so there was, a woman. She appeared to be consulting a map. The driver sounded his horn again.

'Come on, you dozy bint.'

'She must be deaf.'

'Come on.'

Throughout this exchange, Jonathan Barker sat in the back of the car with his private secretary. They were discussing an afternoon meeting, with the aid of an agenda on which the minister was scratching with a slim gold fountain-pen. Suddenly, the minister seemed to realise it was lunchtime. He handed the agenda to his private secretary and slipped the pen into his breast pocket.

'Sort it out, will you?' he said to the men in the front of the car. 'I'm going inside.'

And with that, he got out of his car. So did the private secretary. And so, with a muttered, 'I'll sort it out all right,' did the bodyguard.

And so did the woman. The chauffeur couldn't believe it. He rested his hand on the horn again and called out: 'Come on, darling, you can't park there!' But she appeared not to have heard him. The bodyguard was just behind her as she bent down, looking as though she was locking her car door. The minister and his private secretary were mounting the pavement behind the Alfa Romeo.

'Excuse me, miss, that's a private parking bay, I'm afraid.' The guard didn't think she'd heard him. Bloody foreigner. He touched her shoulder.

Witch, crouching, slammed her elbow back into the bodyguard's groin, then clasped the hand on her shoulder and twisted her whole body, taking the man's arm with it, turning it all the way round and up his back. He sank to his knees in pain. The butt of the Beretta smashed against the back of his neck. He slumped unconscious to the ground.

Now her gun was on the minister.

'Into the car!'

He hesitated.

'You,' she said to the blanching secretary, 'back into the minister's car. You,' to Jonathan Barker again, 'into *this* car.'

'Now look here . . .'

But the private secretary was already shuffling back to the Rover where the driver sat motionless, trying to decide whether to try ramming her or merely blocking her escape or even reversing to a safe distance. She settled his mind for him by swivelling and expertly shooting one front and one rear tyre. The driver yelped and ducked beneath the level of the windscreen. The private secretary had fallen to his knees and was crawling on all fours. Witch turned her eyes on Jonathan Barker.

'You're dead.'

People were looking out of their windows now. A few pedestrians had stopped and were watching from a safe distance. Jonathan Barker decided he'd stalled long enough. She walked around the car towards him. He opened the passenger door.

'No, the back,' she said. Her aim with the pistol looked steady as he opened the car's rear door and leaned down to get in.

'I think you must be making a—' The sentence went unfinished as Witch flipped the pistol and smashed the butt down on Jonathan Barker's skull. He fell into the car and she pushed his legs in after him, closing the door and running to the driver's side. Then she started the car and sent it hurtling out of the parking space. It would be a short drive. Her other car was parked and waiting.

As she drove off, the private secretary opened the Rover's passenger door.

'A lot of help you were,' he squealed at the chauffeur. 'I didn't notice you exactly *leaping* into action.'

'No, but at least I got the licence plate. Here, hand me that phone. We'll have the cunt in five minutes.'

But in five minutes, all they had was a general alert and the arrival of a single police car ... which didn't even contain police.

'Who are you?' asked the private secretary. Neighbours had come out of their houses and were milling around. The bodyguard sat on the edge of the pavement, holding his head. A woman was trying to give him an aspirin and some water.

Elder took it all in with a single sweep: the flat cartyres, the empty parking space, the sickly looks on the faces of the three men.

'What happened?' he asked, ignoring the private secretary's question.

'Where are the bloody police?' asked the private secretary, ignoring Elder's. 'I called them.'

'They're a bit busy at Victoria Street. I suppose all available units have rushed down there.'

The man's interest was deflected for a moment. 'What happened?'

'A bomb. Nothing serious. It was just a ...' A what? A flanker? Yes, that's what it was. A tactic to shift attention solidly and completely on to Victoria Street, so that *this* could happen. She'd bought herself valuable time. Five minutes already, and still no police had arrived. Too late to go chasing her now, though Elder could see Dominique was keen. She was still sitting in the police car's driving-seat, ready for the off. Barclay was getting the story from one of the neighbours who'd seen everything.

'It's a mess,' Elder said, more to himself than anyone else. 'A shambles. She led us all the way up the garden path and in through the front door. Only we were in the wrong house, the wrong garden, the wrong bloody street!'

What he still couldn't work out was the one simple question: why Jonathan Barker? Why go second division when the premier league were there for the taking?

Why?

The question bothered him, and others, for the rest of the afternoon. He talked it through with Barclay and Dominique. He talked it through with Joyce Parry, and with Trilling and Greenleaf. Doyle was in hospital, though unwillingly. They were keeping him in overnight, if such were possible. Trilling, shaken by the bomb, had developed a stammer, but Greenleaf seemed fine. Certainly, he was up to the task of re-interviewing the Dutchman and informing him of Witch's devastating double-cross. Would the Dutchman's employers believe that he *didn't* know anything about it? Or would they suspect he must have been in on it with Witch?

Always supposing it *was* a double-cross. It was. The Dutchman was evidence of that.

The Dutchman was scared. They allowed him to watch the news reports on TV, just so he would know this was no bluff. He did not blink as he watched. And afterwards, with the tape recorders turning, he talked. But he had little enough to say. He told Greenleaf about Crane, told him where to find Christine Jones (they were close to finding her anyway, thirsty and frightened but otherwise unharmed). He wouldn't say anything about the men who'd employed him in the first place, the men who'd paid him to liaise with Witch. But he did admit to meeting her in Paris, at the Australian's apartment.

He did not, however, know the answer to the question: why Barker? He kept shaking his head disbelievingly. 'They paid her a million,' he kept saying, 'a million to kill the US President . . . and she pulls a stunt like this.' He looked up at Greenleaf. 'She must be crazy.'

Greenleaf tended to agree.

The media, of course, had their own ideas. First reaction was that the double-blow was the work of the IRA, of at least *two* active service units, one attacking the motorcade while the other abducted the Home Secretary. This made sense to the reporters: who else but the IRA would go to so much trouble to kidnap the Home Secretary? Then the speculation started, all about IRA 'cells' in London and how there might be more of them, about safe houses where the gang (numbering at least a dozen) could be hiding. There was a blackout on the real story, of course. None of Jonathan Barker's neighbours had been allowed to speak to the media, and those who had had been disbelieved. One woman? No news editor was going to believe that. So the idea of the gang stuck, and Londoners were asked to keep their eyes open for anything suspicious.

London, thought Elder: that's the last place she'll be. He was sitting in Joyce Parry's office. Outside, Barclay was showing Dominique around. It looked as though MI5 had adopted her, which didn't bother Elder: a friend in the DST camp would no doubt be welcome at the department, and especially one who might rise through the ranks . . . There had been a potential spot of bother earlier on, when some furious policemen had tried to arrest her for taking their car, but Elder had calmed them.

He was calm himself now; well, calmer. Again, they'd come so close and yet were back to square one. For a couple of naive, undisciplined cavaliers, Barclay and Dominique hadn't done so badly. He took *The Times* obituary column from his pocket and read it again. Had this started the whole thing rolling in Witch's mind? Had this somehow persuaded her that instead of fulfilling her objective she should run away with the Home Secretary? It still didn't make sense. Marion Barker, *née* Rose. Secretary to Jonathan Barker . . . then his first wife died and later on he married Marion. Nothing so unusual about that. Tireless worker for various charities and so on. Lifelong interest in spiritualism . . . What else did he know about her? What did he know about Jonathan Barker? Not much.

'Dominic, sorry I've been so long.' Joyce Parry came into the room, went to her desk, and began lifting files out of her briefcase.

'How did it go?'

'PM's furious, of course. He doesn't know what's worse, the scratches on the delegates' limos or someone buggering off with Jonathan Barker.' She looked down at him. 'You got close.'

'Not close enough. If I'd let Barclay go on digging last night instead of sending him off to bed . . .'

'Don't blame yourself. I don't know anyone who's done more on this.'

'Barclay has. So has Miss Herault.'

'And whose idea was it to involve Barclay in the first place?'

He smiled. 'As you know, my motives at the time were not exactly . . .'

'Honourable?'

He nodded.

'Well, honourable or not, we came bloody close.'

'Is that what you told the PM?'

'Of course. No doubt Commander Trilling will tell him something else entirely, but we'll see.' She sat down at last, leaning back in her chair, arms falling down over its sides. A brief smile passed between them, a shared memory of the previous night. Then it was back to business. 'So what now?'

Elder sat forwards. 'Joyce, I need to see the file on Barker. I mean the *real* file, warts and all.'

She formed her lips into an O. 'Absolutely not.'

'Joyce . . .'

'Do you know how restricted that is? *I* hardly get access to those files.'

'Joyce, you've got to understand. His wife's obituary set Witch off. The answer's got to lie somewhere in Barker's past, or somewhere in his wife's. Jonathan Barker's life is at stake here. I think *he'd* want me to see that file.'

She was shaking her head. She was still shaking it as she sighed and said, 'I'll see what I can do.'

'Now, Joyce, it's got to be now.'

'Dominic, it's not that simple.'

'Yes it is. Get the file, Joyce. Please.'

She looked at him, considering. 'You always have to take shortcuts, don't you?'

'Always.'

'You want her badly.'

'Very badly,' he agreed.

Joyce Parry sat for a moment, her eyes on her desk. 'I'll get the file,' she said at last.

Sitting in Joyce Parry's office a little later, Michael Barclay looked decidedly grumpy. And not without cause. Everything he'd shown Dominique, from his computer to his wastepaper-bin, had been received with a shrug and five short words: 'We have better in France.' She'd been impressed by none of it. She sat beside him now, one leg crossed over the other, her foot waggling in the air, and looked around the room. Inwardly, she was still crackling. Her drive through the London streets had been exhilarating. They'd come so close to confronting the assassin. And yet in the end, it was reduced to this: sitting around in an office waiting for something to happen. She felt she would *explode* with the energy inside her. Why didn't someone *do* something?

Dominic Elder knew what she was thinking. It was the sort of thing he'd have been thinking twenty-five years ago. Who needs patience? Let's get out there and *hunt*. Only just over two years ago, that same instinct had led him straight to retirement and a scar that would never disappear.

'The gang's all here,' said Joyce Parry, walking through the ever-open door. She paused inside the room, turned, and closed the door behind her. Then she went to her desk and sat down. She did not have a file with her.

'Nobody told me there was going to be a party,' she said to Elder, having first smiled a greeting towards Dominique.

'I thought, after what they've been through, Mr Barclay and Miss Herault deserved not to be left out of anything at this late stage.'

It smacked of a prepared speech. Parry didn't reply to it. Instead she said, 'I've changed my mind.'

'Yes, so I see.'

'I've read the file, Dominic. There's a lot in there that isn't relevant to this case.'

'How can you be sure?'

'I can't. So instead of reading the file, you can question me. I'll answer anything. That way, whatever isn't touched upon isn't touched upon. It stays secret. Agreed?'

Elder shrugged. 'It seems a long-winded way of—'

'Agreed?'

'Agreed,' he said. Barclay and Dominique were paying

attention now, their own problems forgotten. Dominique burst in with the first question.

'Is the Home Secretary suspected of being a double agent?'

Joyce Parry smiled. 'No,' she said.

'I think you're on the wrong track,' Elder told Dominique gently. 'What we have here is something altogether more ... personal.' He turned to Parry. The idea, growing in his mind these past hours, was monstrous, almost unthinkable. Yet it had to be tested. 'Did Jonathan Barker have an affair with his secretary?'

'Which secretary?'

'Marion Rose.'

Joyce Parry nodded. 'That's my understanding.'

'This was before his first wife died?'

'Yes.'

'Long before she died?'

'Probably, yes. A number of years.'

Elder nodded thoughtfully. Doyle had known something about it, had heard some rumour. Hence his nickname for Barker. 'Did his wife know?'

'I shouldn't think so. She wasn't the type to keep that sort of knowledge to herself.'

Now Barclay interrupted. 'There's no suspicion surrounding her death?'

'No, the post mortem was meticulous. She died from natural causes.'

'To wit?'

'Lung cancer. She was a heavy smoker.'

'Yes,' said Elder, 'so I seem to remember. What about Barker during this time?'

'What time?'

'The time he was having an affair with Marion Rose. How was his career shaping up?'

'Pretty well. He wasn't quite in politics then, of course.

417

But he was in the running for a candidacy. He got it, won the seat, and that was him into parliament.'

'At quite a young age.'

'Twenty-nine.'

'Yes, twenty-nine. No children by the first marriage?'

'No.'

'Did the first marriage have its problems then?'

'Not that we know of. Apart from the glaring fact that Barker was having at least one affair.'

'This was his second marriage – Marion's first?'

'That's right.'

'A quiet woman?'

'Yes, until recently. I mean, her profile increased.'

'Mmm, the image-men got their hands on her. Charitable good works and so on, but unassuming with it . . . the model MP's wife.'

'I suppose you could say that.'

'He didn't get into parliament at the first attempt, did he?'

'No.'

'Why not?'

'Because he lost.'

'Yes, but *why* did he lose?'

A shrug. 'Swing to the—'

'But *why*, Joyce?'

She paused, swallowed. 'There was a rumour he was a bit of a ladies' man. A localised rumour, but it put enough voters off.'

'But by the second by-election?'

'He was cleaner than clean.'

'And has been since?'

'Yes.'

'And he's risen and risen.'

'Not exactly meteoric though.'

'No, slow, meticulous, I agree with you there. And there've been no scandals?'

'Not in parliament, no.'

'But outside parliament?'

'Just the one you referred to, and that was never public.'

'What? His fling with Marion? Mm, wouldn't have gone down well though, would it? Wouldn't go down well even now, even as ancient history – MP sleeping with secretary while wife's dying of cancer. Bit of a black mark. He was a millionaire?'

'By the time he was twenty-one.'

'Father's money?'

'Mostly, yes, but he put it to good use.'

'A wise investor.'

'A chain of record shops, actually, just in time to clean up on the Beatles and the Stones.'

'Like I say, a wise investor.' Elder rubbed at his forehead. 'To get back to his affair with Marion, what do we know about it?'

'You tell me.'

'All right,' said Elder, 'I will. What happened to the child?'

'Child?'

'There *was* a child, wasn't there?'

Joyce Parry looked down at the desk. 'We don't know for sure.'

'No? But there were "localised rumours", yes?'

'Yes.'

'Dear me, a pregnant secretary, a wife dying of cancer, and he's put himself forward as a constituency candidate. Maybe for the second and potentially the last time. I mean, the last time if he didn't win.' Elder tutted and turned to Barclay. 'What would *you* do, Michael?'

Barclay started at the mention of his name, then

thought for a second. 'If I was a millionaire . . . pay off the secretary. She could go and look after the kid in secret, a monthly allowance or something.'

'Mmm . . . what about you, Miss Herault?'

'Me?' Dominique looked startled. 'Oh, I don't know. I suppose I would perhaps persuade my lover to abort.'

Elder nodded. 'Yes, that's probably what I'd do. What about you, Joyce?'

'An abortion, yes, if she'd agree to it.'

'Ah . . .' Elder raised his index finger. 'If she'd agree to it. What if she wouldn't?'

'Tell her it's finished between us?' suggested Barclay.

'That would break her heart, Michael,' said Elder. 'She *loves* you. She'd do anything but leave you. It would turn her against you if you spurned her. She might go to anybody with her story, the papers, the TV, anybody.'

'Then we're back to square one,' said Joyce Parry.

'If she loves this man,' said Dominique, 'surely she will agree eventually to the termination, no?'

'Yes,' said Elder. 'Yes, she'd agree all right. The question is: would she go through with it?'

Dominique gave a big shrug. 'We cannot ask her, she is dead . . . isn't she?'

'Oh yes, she's dead all right.'

'Then who can we ask? I do not understand.'

'It's not as though we've got a crystal ball,' said Barclay.

'Michael,' said Elder, turning to him and slapping a hand down onto his knee, 'but that's precisely what we *have* got. And that's exactly what we'll use . . .'

With Trilling's blessing, Greenleaf took a breather long enough for him to visit Doyle in hospital. Doyle's head had been bandaged, and his face was bruised. He was awake, but kept his eyes tightly shut for most of the short visit and complained of a thumping headache. A nurse had warned Greenleaf of this, and he had been told not to spend too long 'with your friend'.

Walking towards the bed, Greenleaf wondered about that word 'friend'. *Were* Doyle and he friends? Certainly they were closer than they had been a scant fortnight before. They worked well enough together, but that was only because they were so utterly different in outlook and temperament. The shortcomings of each were made up by the other.

The hospital was hectic. Victoria Street victims, being treated for cuts and shock. In some operating theatre, they were working on what remained of Traynor's leg. But Doyle's ward was quiet enough. He was lying with his head propped on a single white pillow. They'd changed him out of his suit and into regulation pyjamas, thick cotton with vertical stripes the colour of uncooked liver. The nurse had asked Greenleaf what they should do with Mr Doyle's handgun. Greenleaf carried it with him now, inside a rolled-up white carrier. Doyle's shoulder-holster was in there too.

Greenleaf still hadn't handed in his own gun. Somehow he was getting used to it, nestling beneath his jacket there.

'Hello, Doyle.' He dragged a chair over to the bedside. The cabinet was empty save for a jug of water and a plastic beaker. Greenleaf placed the carrier beside the water-jug. Doyle opened his eyes long enough to watch this happening.

'Is that my gun in there?'

'Yes.'

'Thank God for that. Thought maybe I'd lost the bloody thing. Bet they'd have taken it out of my wages.'

'There's these too.' Greenleaf produced a packet of mints. 'From Commander Trilling.'

'It's the thought that counts, so they say.'

Greenleaf smiled. 'How are you feeling?'

'Chipper. Can you get me out of here?'

'They're holding you overnight.'

Doyle groaned. 'I was seeing my bird tonight.'

'Give me her number and I'll send your apologies.'

Doyle grinned, showing stained teeth. 'I'll bet you would, John-boy. No, it's all right, let her sweat. She'll be all the keener tomorrow. Have we caught that bitch yet?'

'Not yet.'

'Leading us a merry dance, isn't she?'

'Have you heard about Barker?'

'Yeah, couldn't happen to a nicer bloke. What does she want with him?'

Greenleaf shrugged. 'Nobody seems to know.'

'We were set up, weren't we?'

'It looks like she set *everybody* up, Doyle.'

'Yeah, everybody. What does Elder say?'

'I don't know.'

'You don't know much, do you, pal? Where is he?'

'Back in his office, I suppose.'

Doyle tried to sit up, though the effort cost him dear. He gritted his teeth and levered himself on to his elbows. Greenleaf rose from his chair to help, but Doyle growled the offer aside. 'Listen,' he said, 'stick close to Elder, John. He knows something we don't, believe me. If anyone catches her, it's going to be him. Stick close, and *we'll* get a pop at her too. Savvy?'

Greenleaf nodded, then saw that Doyle's eyes were closed again. 'I savvy,' he said. Doyle nodded back at him, and let his head fall back on to the pillow.

Greenleaf was remembering . . . remembering the note Witch had left for Elder. What special bond was there between them? Maybe Doyle had a point.

'Last time I had a head like this,' Doyle said, 'was the

morning after that party in the boxing club. Remember it?'

'I remember it.'

Doyle smiled faintly. 'Good night that, wasn't it? Knew back then that you were a good man, John. Knew it even back then.' Doyle's voice grew slurred and faint. 'I've still got that French booze. When I get out we'll have a bit of a party. Good man . . .'

Greenleaf waited till he was asleep, the breathing regular, then he got up, moved the chair away, and lifted the carrier bag from the bedside cabinet. He touched Doyle's shoulder lightly, smiling down on the sleeping figure.

'You're not so bad yourself,' he said quietly, almost too quietly to be heard.

Barclay's car had been brought back from Calais, so they drove south in that. Barclay did the driving, while Dominique sat beside him thumping his leg and demanding that he go faster.

'Either that or we swap places. And turn off that noise.'

'Noise?' Barclay bristled. 'That's Verdi.'

Elder sat alone in the back seat. He wasn't in a mood for conversation, so he stared from the window and kept his responses brief whenever a question was asked of him, until both Barclay and Dominique seemed to take the hint.

He had seen it suddenly, crystal clear. Barker's second wife, so recently deceased, had been a spiritualist. When Elder had visited the fairground, the palm-reader had been too direct in her denial of having seen Witch. It had jarred at the time, but there'd seemed no real connection until now. His back was burning, and he had to sit forward in his seat so as not to graze it against the car's rough fabric. Have patience, Susanne, he thought to himself. Have patience. He knew he was addressing not his daughter but himself.

This time when they reached Brighton he knew exactly where to go. A few of the bigger rides had already been packed away and transported elsewhere. He still had Ted's list in his diary, all the other fairs taking place in the region.

As they headed for The Level, he sat right forward, his head between Dominique's and Barclay's. 'Now listen,' he said, 'hopefully I'm going to have a word with a ball-gazer. If she's still around, that is. I want you two to take a look around . . . a *good* look around.'

'You think Witch may be here?'

'It's possible.'

'Shouldn't we have some back-up?'

'Does she know what you look like?'

'No.'

'Then why do we need back-up? Anyway, there'll be back-up. Turn left here.'

Barclay turned left. It was early evening and the fair was doing some business, but not much. A late-afternoon downpour had drenched the spirits of the holiday-makers. Elder knew where Gypsy Rose's caravan was. It was near the ghost train. Only the ghost train had gone, and in its place was a stall of some kind. But the palmist's caravan was still there, hooked up to an estate-car. He could see it from the road. 'Drop me here,' Elder ordered. The car slowed to a stop, and he got out. 'Park at the end of the road and walk back. Remember, you're on holiday. You're just having a look. Don't go behaving like snoopers or coppers or anything else. Just behave . . . naturally.' The door closed, and Elder watched the car move off. Dominique seemed to put her hand to Barclay's hair, ruffling it. He watched a moment longer before walking across the grass towards Gypsy Rose Pellengro's caravan.

'Mr Elder?'

The man who confronted him was heavy-built, balding. He had his hands deep in the pockets of a windcheater beneath which he wore a white T-shirt. He looked like a manual worker, maybe a carpenter or builder, but respectable. He was one of Special Branch's best.

Elder nodded, looking around. 'Anything?'

'Quiet as the grave. I don't know how she affords that Volvo of hers.'

'Her kid has money.'

Late on Sunday night, Joyce Parry had reported to Elder Bandorff's mentions of tarots, clairvoyance and psychoanalysis. First thing Monday morning, Elder had briefed the man supplied by Special Branch. Not that he thought Witch would creep back to the fair, but there was always the chance.

Even so, he'd still not been sure of the connection between a gypsy palm reader and a female assassin. Marion Rose, he now knew, was the connection.

'Don't wander off,' he warned the undercover officer. Then he paused before the caravan door and knocked twice.

'It's open.'

Elder turned the rickety handle and let himself in.

It took her a moment to recognise him. 'I thought you'd be back.'

'Second sight?'

'No, I just got a feeling from you . . . a bad feeling.'

'You know why I'm here?'

She was seated on a bench at a table, and motioned for him to sit opposite her. A tarot deck lay on the table. She gathered the oversized cards up.

'No,' she said, 'I've no idea.'

'I don't know what you call her ... what you christened her ... but *we* call her Witch.'

'Witch?' She frowned, shuffling the cards slowly. 'Funny name. Nothing to do with your daughter then?'

'You know it's not.'

'Yes, I know.'

'You knew that day too. Do you know what she's done?'

'What?'

He looked around the caravan. There was a small portable TV on the floor in one corner, and a radio on the edge of the sink. 'You really don't know?' he asked.

She shrugged. 'Why should I?'

'Surely someone at the fair has said *something*?'

'What has she done?' she asked, rather too quickly.

'She's abducted her father.'

Rose Pellengro flinched. A few of the cards fell from her hands to the table. Elder picked up one of them. It was the High Priestess. He picked up another. It was Strength.

'Linking the Abyss to the Centre,' Rose Pellengro murmured, looking at the two cards. She paused. 'Abducted? I don't know what you're talking about.'

'I thought I was talking to someone with *vision*,' said Elder disappointedly. 'Very well, I'll make it a bit clearer. She has kidnapped Jonathan Barker.'

The cards fell to the table in a heap. The woman's cheeks reddened.

'Was Marion Rose one of your ... clients?' Elder asked softly.

Rose Pellengro seemed deep in thought. Then she nodded. 'Oh yes, she was a regular. We seemed to have an affinity. She'd travel miles to come and see me.'

Elder nodded. 'This affinity, she felt it, too, didn't she? So much so that she confided in you.'

Pellengro smiled. 'This was in the days *after* priests but before psychiatrists. Yes, she told me all about her ... her problems.'

'One particular problem, I think.'

'Ah yes, one problem. A large one.'

'She was pregnant by Jonathan Barker, and he wanted her to get rid of the child.'

Rose Pellengro eyed him shrewdly. 'You know a lot.'

'But not all of it.'

She nodded slowly, thoughtfully. 'Yes,' she said. 'His career had to come first. He twisted her round.'

'What happened?'

'Marion didn't want to lose the child. She was very religious in her own way. She was a *believer*. I decided to help her.'

'You took the child, fostered it?'

'As far as Barker was concerned, Marion had gone to a clinic. Actually, she stayed here with me. When the baby was born, I kept it.'

Elder released a long-held breath. This was what he had suspected, the truth of Witch's identity. 'Did she ... did the mother keep in touch?'

'Oh yes.' Pellengro sifted through the cards. 'At first she kept in touch all the time. I thought maybe Barker would become suspicious, but not him.' She tapped her head. 'He was too stupid, his mind only on himself.'

'Then what?'

'Then?' A shrug. 'Marion started visiting less and less. By that time, Barker's wife had died. They were to be married. More children arrived ... born in wedlock. *Proper* children. She stopped coming altogether. She never came again.'

'And the child? The girl?'

A faint smile. 'You call her Witch, but to me she's Brigid Anastasia. Brigid, the Celtic goddess of fire, Anastasia, resurrection. Brigid Anastasia ... A real mouthful, isn't it? I always used to call her Biddy. I brought her up, mister. I educated her as best I could. She was always wild. Wild like fire.' Her eyes were glistening. 'She once stabbed a boy who was bothering her. Then at fourteen she ran off with an Irishman. He'd been hanging around the fair for weeks. We were in Liverpool. When she went, I thought he'd killed her or something. But she sent me a letter from Ireland. She sent a lot of letters in the early days. Then she didn't send any at all. Instead, she'd just turn up at my door. I never even recognised her half the time.'

'But this time ... this trip ... it was different?'

'Different, yes. Because she'd found out who her mother was.'

'How?'

The woman shrugged again. 'She had vague memories of a lady visiting her when she was a toddler, picking her up and hugging her and crying and making her cry, too.' A tear slid down Rose Pellengro's left cheek. 'And when she was a bit older, I told her a little. Not much, but enough.' She sniffed. 'Enough so that when she read the death notice ... One of the papers had a photo of Marion. Biddy wasn't daft. She remembered all right. And she knew now who her father was and what he'd done.'

She reached into the cuff of her cardigan and tugged out a small lace handkerchief with which to wipe her eyes and blow her nose.

'Did she tell you what she was going to do?'

Pellengro shook her head. 'Oh no, nothing like that. She just said she wanted to hear the story. Well, she's old enough, isn't she? So I told her the whole thing. I

428

thought maybe she'd . . . well, I didn't think she'd . . . Oh God, what does she want him for?'

'What do you think?'

'*I* don't know.'

'Tell me, what do you think she's been doing all these years?'

'She's never said.'

'And you've no idea?'

'I thought maybe a prostitute?'

Elder shook his head.

'What then?'

'Never mind. Where will she take him?'

'God in heaven, how would I know that?'

'We've got to find her, you know that, don't you? If we're too late, she may be charged with murder.'

'Oh, she wouldn't kill him, would she? Little Biddy? I know she's been a bit wild in her time, but she's a woman now.'

He gripped her hands in his own. 'Rosa, tell me what you told her. Tell me *everything* you told her.'

She stared at him wide-eyed. 'Who are you? What are you? Are you the police?'

'I'm a father,' he said.

She blew her nose again, staring at him. Then she began to gather up the tarot, and as she did so, she started to speak.

Almost half an hour later, he made his way out into the evening air. His legs were stiff, and he rubbed them. He gestured to the Special Branch man, who came over to him.

'Stick around,' Elder ordered. 'She might come back.'

There was no sign of Barclay and Dominique. He had choices now, several choices, and he was keen to get away from this place. He passed Barnaby's Gun Stall.

'Here, guv, have a go?' cried the young man. He didn't recognise Elder. The wooden cut-out was still there, the target destroyed with such accuracy. *A young lady ...* The whole fair was Witch's cover, because she was part of it and always had been.

Where were they? Then he heard a shriek, and he saw them. Dominique was on the dodgems, Barclay watching from the sidelines and smiling. She shrieked again and tried to avoid a collision, but too late. Elder could not help but be affected by the scene. He stood, leaning against a rail, and watched. Barclay saw him at last and joined him.

'Sorry, sir,' he said.

'No need to apologise, Michael. Let's call it necessary R and R. Listen, there's something I want to get from the car. Just point me in the general direction and give me the keys.'

Barclay dug the keys out of his pocket. 'The car's parked on Islingword Road. Top of Richmond Terrace and turn right.'

Elder nodded. 'Thanks,' he said, turning away.

'You're coming back, aren't you, sir?'

Elder nodded again. He wanted to say, It's not your fight, it's not worth the risk. Instead, he glanced towards Dominique. She made up his mind for him.

He wondered what they would do. Maybe a train back to London. Or stay the night in Brighton. Elder had never seen himself as a matchmaker. He didn't see himself as one now. All he knew was that he had to do this alone. The young couple represented too much baggage, too much of a responsibility. And besides, there was a score he had to settle. Silverfish.

Wolf Bandorff had said Witch hated men. In fact, she hated only the one man. Aged thirteen, she had asked

430

Rose Pellengro about her parents. Rose had told her some of the story, enough to fuel hatred but not enough to identify the people involved. Witch had pressed, but Rose Pellengro would say no more. But the obituary of Marion Barker had struck a chord, and this time, confronted with the name, Rose had admitted the truth. The man who had forced Witch's mother into discarding her was Jonathan Barker. Suddenly, there was someone for her to focus her vague, long-held hatred on. The Home Secretary.

The young Brigid Anastasia had run away with an Irishman. It was a short sea-crossing from Liverpool to Ireland. Maybe the man himself was a terrorist, or maybe she had drifted into the company of terrorists afterwards. Female and a teenager she would have proved useful to the IRA, running cross-border errands. Perhaps they had even sent her as far as Germany to liaise with Wolfgang Bandorff and his group. From Germany, she'd drifted south to Italy. In a sense, she'd been drifting ever since. She had no cause, no real set of ideals. All she'd had was anger, an anger she could do little to assuage. Until now.

Elder didn't doubt that she had taken on the London job before discovering her father's identity. But when she did discover his identity from the newspaper in the Australian's apartment, she had come to a decision. Instead of going ahead with the assassination, she would carry out a stunning double-bluff, fooling both her employers *and* the security forces. It was no mistake that she'd made such a noisy and messy entry into the country. She'd wanted them to know she was there. And while security had been tightened around the summit, while all that effort and manpower had been focused on the gathering of world leaders, Witch's real target had gone unnoticed and underprotected. She'd taken her employers' money, doubtless with thoughts of retirement and disappearance after this last task: dealing with her father.

The Alfa Romeo had been found abandoned off the King's Road. No doubt she'd switched cars. The Alfa had been stolen the previous night in Croydon. There was no way of knowing from where the second car had been stolen, or what make it was. Police were now on the lookout for any one of forty-six reported stolen vehicles from in and around the London area. Elder had the list with him. Roadblocks had been set up, but only on major roads, a stupid and wasteful procedure only set in motion because it would mean the police were doing *something* to stop her getting away with it.

Well, Elder was doing something too. From his talk with Rose Pellengro, he had noted six possible locations, six places where Witch might take her father before . . . before what? Killing him? Would that be enough for her? Whatever, Elder knew she would not linger over her task, so he dare not linger over his.

Joyce Parry was in a meeting in her office when the telephone buzzed. She picked it up.

'Hello?'

'Mrs Parry? Barclay here.'

'Michael, are you still in Brighton?'

'Well . . . yes, actually.'

She knew from his tone that something was wrong. She sat forward in her seat. 'What is it?'

'It's Mr Elder. He's gone off in my car.'

'Gone off where?'

'We don't know. He said he had to go and fetch something . . .'

Joyce Parry rose to her feet, taking the telephone

apparatus with her, holding the body of the telephone in one hand, the receiver in the other.

'Has he talked to the palm reader?'

'Yes.'

'What did he find out?'

'He didn't say.'

Parry let out a sharp hiss of breath.

'Sorry,' said Barclay, sounding despondent.

'Michael, go talk to the palm reader, find out what she told him.' She looked at her visitor, as though only now remembering that he was there. 'Hold on a second,' she said into the receiver, before muffling the mouthpiece against her shoulder. 'Elder,' she said. 'He's gone haring off in Barclay's car.'

Greenleaf got up from his chair. 'We need a description of the car.' He came to the desk and took a notebook and pen from his pocket.

'Michael?' Parry said into the mouthpiece. 'What kind of car is it?' She listened. 'White Ford Fiesta, okay. And registration number?' Barclay gave it to her, and she repeated it for Greenleaf. 'Right,' she said. 'Go talk to Madame Whatever-her-name, and call me straight back.'

'Will do,' said Barclay's voice. 'Just the one thing. There's something I've been meaning to ask. It's just come back to me. What was Operation Silver—'

But Joyce Parry was already severing the connection. Greenleaf took the receiver from her and pressed some numbers home, pausing for his call to be answered.

'Inspector Greenleaf here,' he said. 'I've got a car needs tracing. Notify every force in the country. As soon as anyone sees it, I want to be the first to know. Understood?'

Joyce Parry slumped back down on to her chair and

rubbed her face with her hand. Dominic, Dominic. Where the hell are you? *And why don't you ever learn?*

He drove first to Salisbury, where, according to Marion Rose, Jonathan Barker had first held her hand, first planted a kiss on her cheek. He had done so as they came out of the cathedral after attending a choral concert. Elder drove up to the cathedral, got out, walked around, got back into the car, cruised around the town for twenty minutes, then headed off. Second stop: a hotel in Henley-on-Thames. Pellengro told him this was where Marion and Barker had first made love. The fortune teller even recalled the hotel's name.

'In my business, a good memory helps. You sometimes get a client coming back after two or three years. Helps if you can remember what you said to them last time.'

He parked in the hotel car park, and checked the other parked cars for any on the stolen list. None. The hotel itself was busy, but there was no sign of Witch. Tired, he stopped at a burger drive-in and bought coffee, then bought more later when he filled the car with petrol. He was headed north, doing this because, as with the roadblocks, there was nothing else to do. He had no leads, no real ideas. He didn't have anything.

And no one would thank him for any of this anyway. Running off on his own, just like in the old days. Barclay would tell Joyce, and Joyce would not be pleased. She would not be pleased at all. Last night, she had massaged his back.

'It hasn't healed,' she said. 'I thought by now it would have.'

'Sometimes it clears up, then it starts again.'

She had traced the outline with her finger. 'Is it sore?'

'More itchy than sore, but then if I scratch it . . . yes,

it's sore. And I know what you're thinking: serves me right. Which is true. I learned my lesson.'

'Did you, Dominic? I wonder. I wonder if Silverfish taught you anything.'

Silverfish, stupid name for a stupid operation. A terrorist cell in London. Kept under surveillance. The mention of a meeting to take place in the city between senior members of four European terrorist organisations. But the whole thing had been botched, the terrorists escaping. Including a woman, a woman Elder thought he knew. There was an immediate clampdown: checks on airports, ferry terminals, fishing ports. One of the terrorists, a Spaniard, was arrested at Glasgow Airport. Then came Charlie Giltrap's phone call.

'Might be something or nothing, Mr Elder. Just that there's this woman been sleeping rough on a bit of waste ground near all that building work in Docklands. She don't talk, and she don't look right, if you know what I mean. I mean, she don't fit in.'

Which had been enough to send Elder down to Docklands, to an area of scrapyards, building-sites and derelict wastes. It was late evening, and he hadn't told anyone he was going. He'd just do a recce, and if back-up was needed he'd phone for it.

Besides, he had his Browning in his pocket.

After half an hour's hunting, he saw a crouched figure beside what remained of a warehouse wall. It was eating sliced white bread from a bag, but scurried off mouse-like at his approach. So he followed.

'I only want a word,' he called. 'I'm not going to move you on or anything. I just want to talk.'

He cornered her in the shell of another building. It had no roof left, just four walls, a gaping doorway, and windows without glass. She was crouched again, and her eyes were fearful, cowed. But her clothes weren't quite ragged enough, were they? He came closer.

'I just want to talk.'

And then he was close enough to stare into her eyes, and he knew. He knew it was all pretence. She wasn't fearful or cowed or anything like that. She was Witch. And she saw that he knew.

And she was fast. The kick hit his kneecap, almost shattering it. He stumbled, and the flat edge of her fist chopped into his throat. He was gagging, but managed somehow to get the gun out of his pocket.

'I know you,' she said, kicking the gun cleanly out of his hand. 'You're called Elder. You've got a nice thick file on me, haven't you?' Her next kick connected her heel to his temple. Fresh pain flared through him. 'You call me Witch.' Her voice was calm, almost ethereal. A kick to the ribs. Christ, what kind of shoes was she wearing? They were like weapons. 'You're called Dominic Elder. Even *we* have our sources, Mr Elder.' Then she chuckled, crouching in front of him, lifting his head. It was dark, he couldn't make out ... 'Dominic Elder. A priest's name. You should have been a priest.'

Then she rose and he heard her footsteps crunch over gravel and glass. She stopped, picked up his pistol. He heard her emptying the bullets from it. 'Browning,' she mused. 'Not great.' Then the gun hit the ground again. And now she was coming back towards him. 'Will you put this in your file, Mr Elder? Or will you be too ashamed? How long have you been tracking me?'

She was lifting his arms behind him, slipping off his jacket.

'Years,' he mumbled. He needed a few moments. A few moments to recover. If she'd give him a few more moments, then he'd ...

'Years? You must be my biggest fan.' She chuckled

again, and tore his shirt with a single tug, tore it all the way up his back. He felt his sweat begin to chill. Christ, what was . . . ? Then her hand came to within an inch of his face and lifted a piece of broken glass. She stood up, and he thought she was moving away again. He swallowed and began to speak.

'I want to ask you something. It's important to me.'

Too late, he felt her foot swinging towards him. The blow connected with his jaw, sending him spinning out of pain and into darkness.

'No interviews,' she was saying. 'But I'd better give my biggest fan an autograph, hadn't I?'

And then, with Elder unconscious, she had carved a huge letter W into his back, and had left him bleeding to death. But Charlie Giltrap had decided Elder might need help. It was a rough area down there; a man like Mr Elder . . . well, he might need a translator if nothing else. Charlie had found him. Charlie had called for the ambulance. Charlie had saved Elder's life.

One hundred and eighty-five stitches they gave him. And he lay on his front in a hospital bed feeling each and every one of them tightly knitting his skin. His hearing had been affected by one of her kicks – affected temporarily, but it gave him little to do but think. Think about how fast she'd been, how slow he'd been in response. Think of the mistake he'd made going there in the first place. Think maybe it was time for an easier life.

But, really, life hadn't been easier since. In some ways it had been harder. This time he'd shoot first. Then maybe his back would heal, maybe the huge scar wouldn't itch any more.

His next stop was another hotel, this time near Kenilworth Castle, the probable site of Witch's conception. Barker, usually so cautious, had one night drunk too many whiskies, and wouldn't let his secretary say no later on, after closing time, up in their shared room. The hotel was locked and silent for the night. There were only two cars in the car park and neither was on the stolen list. Three more to go: York, Lancaster and Berwick. If he pushed on, he could have them all checked by late-morning. If he pushed on.

Dominique booked them into the hotel, pretending that Barclay also was French and could speak no English. The receptionist looked disapproving.

'Any luggage?' she sniffed.

'No luggage,' said Dominique, barely suppressing a giggle. The woman stared at her from over the top of her half-moon glasses. Dominique looked back over her shoulder to where Barclay stood just inside the hotel door. She motioned for him to join her, but he shook his head, causing her to giggle again before calling to him: 'I need some money!'

So at last, reluctantly, he came towards the desk. He was worried about Dominic Elder. He'd argued that they should go back to London, but Dominique, pragmatic as ever, had asked what good that would do? So instead they'd had a few drinks and eaten fish and chips out of paper. And they'd played some of the machines in the pier's amusement arcade.

'This is a family hotel,' warned the receptionist.

They both nodded towards her, assuring her of their agreement. So she gave them a key and took their money and had them sign their names in the register. When Barclay signed himself Jean-Claude Separt, Dominique nearly collapsed. But upstairs, suddenly alone together in the small room with its smells of air-freshener and old carpet, they were shy. They calmed. They grew sober together, lying dressed on the top of the bed, kissing, hugging.

'I wonder where Elder is,' Barclay said at last.

'Me, too,' murmured Dominique drowsily.

He continued to stroke her hair as she slept, and he turned his head towards the large window, through which seeped the light and the noises of night-time. He thought of Susanne Elder, and of Dominique's father. He hoped Dominic Elder would get an answer to his question. Later still, he closed his own eyes and prayed for restful dreams . . .

It wasn't quite dawn when Elder reached York. The streets were deserted. This was where Marion had told Barker she was pregnant, and where he'd insisted she have an abortion. Poor Marion, she'd chosen the time and the place to tell him. She'd chosen them carefully and, no doubt to her mind, well. A weekend in York, a sunny Sunday morning. A stroll along the city walls. Radiant, bursting to tell him her news. Poor Marion. What had she thought? Had she thought he'd be pleased? She'd been disappointed. But where on the city wall had she told him? Pellengro hadn't known, so neither would Witch. Elder, many years ago, had walked the circuit of York's protective city wall. He knew it could take him an hour or more. He parked near Goodramgate, a large stone archway. There was a flight of steps to the side of the 'gate' itself leading up on to the ramparts. A small locked gate stood in his way, but he climbed over it. It struck him that Witch would have trouble dragging a prone body over such a gate. But on second thoughts, he couldn't imagine the Home Secretary would have much trouble climbing over it with a gun pointing at his back.

Parts of the wall were floodlit, and the street-lighting was adequate for his needs. The sky was clear and the night cold. He could see his breath in the air in front of him as he walked. He could only walk so far in this direction before the wall ended. It started again, he knew, a little further on. He retraced his steps and crossed Goodramgate, this time walking along the wall in the direction of York Minster itself. He hadn't gone ten yards when he saw the body. It was propped against the wall, legs straight out in front of it. He bent down and saw that it was Jonathan Barker. He'd been shot once through the temple. Elder touched Barker's skin. It was cool, slightly damp. The limbs were still mobile however. He hadn't been dead long. Elder stood up and looked around him. Nobody, obviously, had heard the shot. There were houses in the vicinity, and pubs and hotels. It surprised him that no one had heard anything. A single shot to the temple: execution-style. Well, at least it had been quick.

There was a sudden noise of impact near him, and dust flew from the wall.

A bullet!

He flattened himself on the wall, his legs lying across Barker's. He took his pistol from its shoulder-holster and slipped off the safety. Where had the shot come from? He looked around. He was vulnerable up here, like a duck on a fairground shooting-range. He had to get back to the steps. She was using a silencer. That's why nobody had heard anything. A silencer would limit her gun's range and accuracy, so probably she wasn't *that* close. If she'd been close, she wouldn't have missed. She was somewhere below, in the streets. He decided to run for it, moving in an awkward crouch, pistol aimed at the space in front of him, in case she should appear. She did not. He scrambled back down the steps and over the gate. The city was silent. Outside the walls, a single car rumbled past. He knew he'd never reach it in time. His own car was less than fifty yards away in any case. But he'd no intention of returning to it. He had come this far. He wasn't going to run.

A sound of heels on cobblestones. Where? In front of him, and fading. He headed into the narrow streets of the old city, following the sound. The streets were like a maze. He'd been lost in them before, unable to believe afterwards that there were so few of them ... just as those lost in a maze cannot believe it's not bigger than it is.

He couldn't hear the footsteps any more. He stood for a moment, turning his head, listening intently. Then he moved on. The streets grew, if anything, narrower, then widened again. A square. Then more streets. Christ, it was dark. Back-up. He needed back-up. Was there a police station anywhere nearby? Noise, voices ... coming into the square. Three teenagers, two girls and one boy. They looked drunk, happy, heading home slowly. He hid his gun in its holster and ran up to them.

'Have you seen a woman?'

'Don't need to, I've got two here.' The boy gave the two girls a squeeze.

Elder attempted a sane man's smile. 'Is there a police station?'

'No idea.'

'Are you in trouble?' asked one of the girls. Elder shook his head.

'Just looking for my ... my wife. She's tall, younger than me. We managed to get separated, and ...'

'On holiday are you? Thought so.'

'Here, we did see that woman ... where was she? Stonebow?'

There were shrugs.

'Down that way,' said the girl, pointing.

'Thanks,' said Elder. As he moved off, he heard the boy say 'Silly sod' quite loudly. The girls giggled.

Down this way. Hold on though . . . He stopped again. What was he doing? Witch had already taken a shot at him. She knew he was here. So why not let *her* find *him*? Was she behind him, following, watching patiently as he ran himself ragged? That would be typical of her, biding her time until he was exhausted, then catching him off-guard. Yes, he could run this maze for hours and never find her. Not unless she wanted to be found. He walked back the way he'd come, glancing behind him. What he needed was a dead end, and he found one: an alleyway leading from The Shambles. He staggered into it, tipping over a litter-bin, and leaned against the wall, breathing hoarsely, coughing. One hand was against the wall, supporting him, the other was inside his jacket, as though holding his ribs or rubbing away a stitch. Whenever he paused in his loud breathing, there was silence around him, almost oppressively heavy. And inside him, a pounding of blood.

'Hey, priest.' Her voice was quiet. He had not heard her approach. He turned his head slowly towards the mouth of the alley. It was dark in the alley itself, but the street was illuminated. He knew he could see her better than she could see him. But she knew it too. Perhaps that's why she was standing to one side of the alley's mouth, partly hidden by the corner of the wall. She was aiming a pistol at him.

She looked different. Not just physically different – that was to be expected – but somehow calmer, at peace.

'Are you satisfied now?' he asked between intakes of breath. 'Now that your father's dead?'

'Ooh, Mr Elder, and there I was thinking age had slowed you down. Yes, I'm satisfied.' She paused. 'Just about.' The gun was steady in her hand. She had made no attempt to enter the alley itself. Why should she? It was a dead end. He was not going to escape.

'What now? Retirement?' he asked. 'Your Dutch friend tells us you were paid a million dollars for the assassination.'

'A million, yes. Enough to buy a lot of retirement. What about you, Mr Elder? I thought *you* were retired, too.'

'I was, but how could I turn down the chance of finding you?'

He saw her smile. 'Finding me *again*,' she corrected. 'Tell me, Mr Elder, how's your back?'

'Good as new.'

'Really?' She was still smiling. 'You must be ready for another autograph then. Something a bit more permanent.'

'Do you remember,' he said, 'in Docklands, just before you gave me that final kick . . . ?'

'You started to ask me a question.'

'That's right. I want to ask it now. It's important to me.' He paused. 'It's the reason I've been hunting you so long.'

'Go ahead and ask.'

He swallowed drily, licked his lips. His mouth felt coated with bad coffee.

'Paris, eight years ago, in June. A bomb went off in a shopping arcade. Was it you?'

She was silent for a tantalising moment. 'You'll have to be more specific.'

'No, it was either you or it wasn't.'

'No interviews allowed.' Her finger began to squeeze the trigger.

Elder called out: 'Biddy, no!'

The use of her real name froze her for a second. A second was all Elder needed. The hand inside his jacket was already gripped around the Browning's butt. He swung and fired, diving further back into the darkness as he did so. He fired off three shots, stumbling backwards all the time, seeking safety in the shadows and the dustbins and the stacks of empty boxes. Three shots. None of them returned. He waited, listening. Some dogs had been startled awake and were barking in the distance. A window opened somewhere nearby.

'What the hell was that?' he heard a voice say. 'Sounded like guns. Call the police, love.'

Yes, call the police. Slowly, Elder got to his feet and walked to the mouth of the alley, keeping close to the wall, his gun-hand hanging at his side. Then he stuck his head out into the street.

And the cold metal mouth of a pistol touched his forehead.

Witch was standing there, smiling unsteadily. Her grip on the gun wasn't steady either. She was wounded. He daren't take his eyes off hers, but he could see a dark stain spreading across her right side. She placed the palm of her hand against it, then lifted the hand away, her fingers rubbing slickly against each other. Elder could smell the blood.

'Biddy,' he said, 'you don't hate me.' His whole head felt numb from the touch of the pistol against his brow. He felt dizzy, giddy. Witch's smile grew wider.

'Hate you? Of course I don't hate you. It's just that I don't want to . . .' she swallowed '. . . to disappoint you.' She fell against the shopfront, her gun-arm dropping to her side. Elder took hold of her and eased her down so that she was sitting on the ground, legs in front of her, back resting against the shopfront, the same rag-doll posture in which she'd left her father. Only then did he remove the pistol from her hand. From the lack of resistance in her fingers he knew she was dying, if not already dead. He heard feet running, several pairs of feet, and calls.

'Down this way?'

'No, down here.'

'The car's parked at Goodramgate.'

'Try The Shambles.'

'Take that street there . . .'

And then someone was standing in front of him.

'Found him!' the voice called. It belonged to a uniformed constable. The constable looked young, still in his teens. He stared in horror at the bloody bundle nestling against Dominic Elder.

'Is she . . . ?'

And now more footsteps. 'Dominic! Are you all right?' Joyce crouched down in front of him, her eyes finding a level with his. He nodded.

'I'm fine, Joyce. Really.' He looked up. Greenleaf was standing there too now, pistol in his hand, not looking at Elder but at Witch.

'Here she is, John,' said Elder, still holding the unmoving body. 'Here's what all the fuss was about. A kid who didn't like her dad.'

'Her dad?'

'Jonathan Barker. He's on the wall between Goodramgate and the Minster.'

'Not alive, I presume?'

'Not alive, no.' Elder looked down at Witch again. She looked like Christine Jones. Now, she would always look like Christine Jones in his mind, just as for two years she'd looked like a down-and-out. He wondered what she looked like really. He wondered if even she knew.

Greenleaf holstered his gun. 'We call them "domestics" on the force,' he said. 'Family fallings-out . . .'

'That's what this was then,' said Elder, letting the body go and rising slowly to his feet. 'A domestic.'

Joyce Parry slipped her arm around his waist. Her

fingers spread out across his back. His back had no feeling at all.

# Departure

Doyle kept his head bandaged for a few days, even though the doctors had told him he needn't bother. But he said he liked the way it made him look, and so did his girlfriend.

'She says I look like a war hero.'

'Or a lobotomy patient,' added Greenleaf.

Elder laughed. They were standing in the East End boxing club, which again had been hired for one of Doyle's by now notorious parties. The French lager was piled high in cardboard boxes of forty-eight bottles per box. The punch-bags were in use, as were the parallel bars.

'He's sharp, isn't he, Dom?' said Doyle, nodding towards Greenleaf.

Elder nodded. 'But how do you feel really, Doyle?'

'Oh, I'm fine. Just a spot of amnesia.'

'Oh?'

'I seem to have forgotten all my character defects. Ay-ay, here comes lover boy.'

They turned towards the door. Barclay was walking tall, having just arranged by phone with Dominique that he'd be spending next weekend in Paris with her.

'Mama's idea,' she'd said, but he hadn't believed it.

Doyle had turned away from Barclay and towards the table. When he turned round again, he was holding a bottle of beer.

'There you go, Mikey. You don't need a bottle-opener, just twist the top.'

'Right, cheers,' said Barclay. Greenleaf knew what was

coming. As Barclay twisted the bottle-top, a welt of foam burst from the bottle and sprayed his shirt.

Doyle tutted. 'Still a bit lively from the trip.'

Later, while discussion raged as to which curry house should receive the party's late-night custom, the one they'd used last time having said never again, Elder slipped away. He was going to hunt down a black taxi, but saw in the distance a seedily-lit cab office, so started walking towards it.

'Stealing my car again?'

He turned and saw Barclay following him. And when he looked, he was indeed standing next to the white Ford Fiesta. Barclay unlocked the passenger door.

'Hop in, I'll give you a lift.'

'You don't know where I'm headed.'

'I'll give you a lift there anyway.'

The trip took the best part of half an hour. At the end of it, Joyce would be waiting for him. Like last night and the night before. Tonight was their final night together: Tommy Bridges was going off on holiday and Elder's garden needed him. But Joyce had some holiday-time owing, too, and she was making plans to visit before the month was out. They'd see how it went. Now that Witch was behind him, maybe Dominic could relax a little. Maybe.

'A penny for them,' said Barclay.

'I'm wondering whether to envy you or not.'

'Why's that?'

'It's hard to put into words without an overload of clichés.'

'Try anyway.'

'You're just beginning, Michael.' Elder stopped abruptly. He couldn't say it. Barclay nodded anyway.

'I get the message,' he said.

Elder smiled. 'I hope so.'

'By the way, how's the patient?'

How indeed. Earlier today Elder had travelled to the hospital in Leeds. Witch was on a life-support system, her brain activity still sluggish. Without the machines ... The doctor had shrugged. He couldn't see the point of keeping a killer alive.

Elder could ... well, sometimes he could. He sat by her bed for half an hour, alternately staring at her face, at the tubes running from nose and mouth, and at the machinery itself with its constant bleep and the slow hiss of pumped air.

'You never did answer me,' he said quietly. He turned from her, the better to examine the workings of the machines around them. He followed the snaking line the cables took to the electrical sockets at the bottom of the cream-painted wall. He glanced now and then at the plugs, at the machinery's several on/off switches, so clearly marked.

So, so clearly marked.

And finally, he rose to his feet, quietly, softly, so as not to disturb. There was a flutter from her eyelashes, movement behind the eyelids themselves: REM, they called it, Rapid Eye Movement. She was dreaming. He wondered what she was dreaming of. He touched her bare arm, feeling its delicate warmth. Her face was ghostly pale, her lips almost colourless. Elder leant down over her and planted a kiss on her forehead. The machine gave a sudden double-blip, as though somewhere inside her the kiss had registered. Elder smiled and stepped away from the bed, placing the chair back against the wall, and finally standing in front of the machines themselves, his fingertips just touching the cool painted metal.

☐ **Beggars Banquet** £6.99
IAN RANKIN
0-7528-7714-3

☐ **Black & Blue** £6.99
IAN RANKIN
0-7528-7715-1

☐ **The Black Book** £6.99
IAN RANKIN
0-7528-7724-0

☐ **Bleeding Hearts** £6.99
IAN RANKIN (writing as
Jack Harvey)
0-7528-7728-3

☐ **Blood Hunt** £6.99
IAN RANKIN (writing as
Jack Harvey)
0-7528-7729-1

☐ **Dead Souls** £6.99
IAN RANKIN
0-7528-7716-X

☐ **The Falls** £6.99
IAN RANKIN
0-7528-7725-9

☐ **Fleshmarket Close** £6.99
IAN RANKIN
0-7528-6563-3

☐ **The Flood** £6.99
IAN RANKIN
0-7528-8094-2

☐ **A Good Hanging & Other
Stories** £6.99
IAN RANKIN
0-7528-7712-7

☐ **The Hanging Garden** £6.99
IAN RANKIN
0-7528-7726-7

☐ **Hide & Seek** £6.99
IAN RANKIN
0-7528-7717-8

☐ **Knots & Crosses** £6.99
IAN RANKIN
0-7528-7718-6

☐ **Let It Bleed** £6.99
IAN RANKIN
0-7528-7719-4

☐ **Mortal Causes** £6.99
IAN RANKIN
0-7528-7720-8

☐ **A Question of Blood** £6.99
IAN RANKIN
0-7528-7713-5

☐ **Rebus's Scotland** £7.99
IAN RANKIN
0-7528-7771-2

☐ **Resurrection Men** £6.99
IAN RANKIN
0-7528-7721-6

☐ **Set in Darkness** £6.99
IAN RANKIN
0-7528-7722-4

☐ **Strip Jack** £6.99
IAN RANKIN
0-7528-7723-2

☐ **Tooth & Nail** £6.99
IAN RANKIN
0-7528-7727-5

☐ **Watchman** £6.99
IAN RANKIN
0-7528-7730-5

☐ **Witch Hunt** £6.99
IAN RANKIN
0-7528-7731-3

All Orion/Phoenix titles are available at your local bookshop or from the following address:

Mail Order Department
Littlehampton Book Services
FREEPOST BR535
Worthing, West Sussex, BN13 3BR
*telephone* 01903 828503, *facsimile* 01903 828802
*e-mail* MailOrders@lbsltd.co.uk
(Please ensure that you include full postal address details)

Payment can be made either by credit/debit card (Visa, Mastercard, Access and Switch accepted) or by sending a £ Sterling cheque or postal order made payable to *Littlehampton Book Services*.
DO NOT SEND CASH OR CURRENCY

**Please add the following to cover postage and packing**

*UK and BFPO:*
£1.50 for the first book, and 50p for each additional book to a maximum of £3.50

*Overseas and Eire:*
£2.50 for the first book plus £1.00 for the second book and 50p for each additional book ordered

---

BLOCK CAPITALS PLEASE

*name of cardholder* .................................... *delivery address*
.................................... *(if different from cardholder)*
*address of cardholder* ....................................
.......................................... ..........................................
.......................................... ..........................................
.......................................... ..........................................
*postcode* .................... *postcode* ....................

☐ I enclose my remittance for £ ....................................

☐ please debit my Mastercard/Visa/Access/Switch (delete as appropriate)

card number ☐☐☐☐☐☐☐☐☐☐☐☐☐☐☐☐☐

expiry date ☐☐☐☐      Switch issue no. ☐☐

signature ....................................................................

*prices and availability are subject to change without notice*